The
DIVIDED HEART

KATHLEEN BENTLEY

I moved with my husband Max from Kalgoorlie, Western Australia to Ulverstone, Tasmania in 2012 on our retirement. I volunteered for community work, had a couple of paid positions too, but then I completed workshop painting with soft pastels and pastel pencils and fell in love with painting with this method of art. Today I am fortunate enough to sell some of my works. During the COVID lockdown I lost interest in painting for a while as I had these voices in my head wanting me to tell their story, so I did. The result is this book, followed by two others. All relate the adventures of Caroline.

Through her experiences Caroline has to evaluate her previous preconceived ideas, beliefs and biases; with cultural differences as well and to realise that difference is just that - not wrong nor right- just different. Caroline also has to commit to two men in her life and juggles her guilt and her joy, and questions how she can love two people at the same time.

She discovers her warts as well as her strengths, and collects respect from all she comes in contact with. She falls in love with Japan, its landscapes, seascapes, traditions and its people. There are skirmishes she becomes involves in, one where her life is threatened, but finds that love - though a rocky road to traverse - conquers all.

The story evolved after I returned from a South Asian cruise with a girl-friend. I wrote the three books in 18 months. Yes, I was overwhelmed too, as I had never written a book previously.

I have enjoyed the journey of both writing and publishing the book and look forward to presenting the other two books in the coming year.

I live and enjoy my life in Ulverstone with Max, my husband. We are surrounded by beautiful scenery and community members are warm and friendly, so who wouldn't be happy?

This book is published by Kathleen Bentley,
40 Amherst Street, West Ulverstone, Tasmania, 7315

First printed by Ingram Spark in 2023

Copyright Kathleen Bentley 2023

The cover format and design for this book was by okomota, graphic designer (laurieokomota@gmail.com) and are protected as per above.

Title: The Divided Heart / Kathleen Bentley

ISBN 978-0-6456198-0-5

ACKNOWLEDGEMENTS

There are several people I wish to thank for helping me with my novel.

First, Allan Jamieson, President of the Fellowship of Australian Writers North West Branch, of which I am a member. I appreciate Allan's advice, guidance, patience and availability when I needed one or all of these. He was very supportive and I value his assistance.

Second, I am very grateful to my dear friend Eileen Naylor who patiently proof-read copies of my book, correcting typos and syntax.

Third, last but not least, I am indebted to my husband Max for his contribution of support and encouragement during the process of writing the book, of proof reading as the story evolved and for his advice throughout.

I don't believe I could have completed *The Divided Heart* without all three wonderful people - so many thanks to you.

BUT, I must not forget you, dear reader, for purchasing this book, which is part of a trilogy. There are two more books waiting to be published which continue the story of Caroline: *Divided No More* and *Eternally Yours.* I hope you enjoy *The Divided Heart* and will want to hear her continuing story of love, lies, secrets, heartaches and adventures in these subsequent books.

Kathleen

CONTENTS

FOREWORD

Let's get this straight from the start: This story is not about me nor about my life, rather it is a true story about a woman who frequents the library and with whom I have developed a strong friendship, initially within the confines of the library. First, I'd better start by saying that I live on the beautiful North West Coast of Tasmania and I am the current librarian in the small town of Ulverstone, which lies between the ocean and rolling hillsides of lush farmland.

Ulverstone was settled by those who thought they were blessed for finding a wonderful place to live in which to bring up their children. When the town developed a port to transport the trees felled for construction and joinery, the town grew and prospered however, in the 1950's and 60's many young people moved away due to lack of employment. A trend that began around the 1930's when the port was moved to Burnie west along the coast, due to ships getting larger and needing a deeper draft.

Well, back to me. I joined the library in Ulverstone when I finished my studies and was employed as Assistant Librarian taking over as Head Librarian when Audrey Maitland, the librarian at this time, retired some 10 years or so ago. Oh, sorry I should introduce myself – my name is Constance Donnelly, although everyone calls me Connie, and I love my work and the community in which I live.

Now let me tell you about my friend. I have obviously changed everyone's names to protect their privacy and I tell this story only now because it is such an incredible story of love, commitment and, I suppose, the strength and tenacity of the human spirit. My friend, Caroline Fischer, was a woman in her late 60's. I first met her and her husband when they retired to Ulverstone from Western Australia several years ago. She had picked out a couple of travel books and that got us talking about various places we had each visited, both within Australia and overseas. It then became a bit of a habit to continue to discuss these when she returned the books and I was able to suggest others which covered countries on her wish list to visit. I was sorry to hear that her husband Philip was not well and was not able to travel, but she accepted this and appeared to enjoy a good life with him. They did a lot of things together: gardening, cooking, walking, craftwork – she was a pastel artist and Phil was a leather worker, while also making jewellery out of cow and sheep bones and deer antlers. Both were able to sell the products of their labour which they found satisfying. Caroline held exhibitions throughout the year all along the coast and Phil often joined her exhibitions with his craftwork, so both appeared quite content. Sometimes Phil joined his wife at the library but his choice of books were action packed in the genre of John Grisham, Chris Ryan and Lee Childs however, he was knowledgeable about other countries and cultures so we enjoyed our discussions.

They had both made places for themselves in our small communities up and along the coast and had, initially, made friends by joining a local Rotary Club. They also joined several art groups in the local and surrounding communities which, of course, saw them volunteering to man respective galleries when exhibitions demanded volunteers to do this. Caroline was also a regular at the local church and enjoyed the friendships which had developed there. Phil was not able to attend so he cooked a roast lunch each Sunday as his contribution, which Caroline always appreciated. They appeared content with their life and happy with each other.

At first, while our friendship did not progress beyond the library and its store of travel books, we shared some memories of growing up and found we had similar stories to tell of school times and growing up in the 1950's, as we were of similar age, so we had a few laughs.

Quite an attractive woman, belying her age, Caroline suffered injuries sustained in a fall she had some 40 years previous and for which she suffered constant back pain. Phil who suffered heart problems with corresponding shortness of breath so was unable to exert himself, even walking was a difficult exercise. Most of the household chores fell on Caroline's shoulders which she apparently willingly and happily coped with. Only the vegetable garden suffered, but she had laughingly told me that she was mowing lawns after over 40 years of abstinence and enjoying the exercise.

One day Caroline came in to change her books. She appeared excited and disclosed that she was soon to embark on a cruise to South East Asia with her friend, Esther Conway. Now I also knew Esther who was an avid reader of real-life adventure and travel stories. Esther was in her late 70's with a mind as sharp as a tack. She would often regale me with funny episodes of her life. I digress.

Caroline and I discussed some of the problems she might experience on her travels especially the diseases relevant to the countries she would be visiting. I suggested she visit her GP to obtain information about the various precautions she needed to take to avoid these. I wished her well when she left the library armed with books on Malaysia, Thailand and the Maldives.

Several weeks passed then, towards the end of March, Caroline came into the library and disclosed the great time she'd had on the cruise. She had loved the countries she had visited, their cultures and their people. She related her shore trips to Malacca, Penang, Langkawi and Kuala Lumpur in Malaysia then Phuket in Thailand, together with Trincomalee and Colombo in Sri Lanka and Male and Uligamu in the

Maldives. She spoke of the woman employed in the making of Tunamite paste, on a very small island in the Maldives, which was very popular as an Asian substitute for Vegemite! The stories Caroline related were wonderful and I certainly was bitten by the travel bug. Caroline also discussed various aspects of the cruise ship, including the ship's crew, their service and the food and other amenities on the ship, and how she had enjoyed the days at sea which enabled relaxing times between trips ashore. She spoke of being pampered in the health spa, having massages, manicures and pedicures then bathing in the ships' swimming pool and lazing in the sun on 'at sea' days. Also, of the various restaurants and the great food they served, especially on the gala nights when she had eaten a five-course dinner complete with appropriate wines. She shared jokes about the camaraderie she had shared with other cruise members and appeared to have had a lot of fun and, much needed relaxation.

We laughed about her beguilement over a gold and diamond pendant. She laughingly related how she had texted Phil thanking him for purchasing this for her at a mere $3,000 American dollars – reduced from $7,000 American dollars – but added that he hadn't answered this text. Caroline spoke fondly of the tour of Singapore prior to boarding the ship. She described her enjoyment of exploring old China Town, the beautiful Orchid Garden and the Garden by the Bay and how much she had appreciated the kindness of everyone she had met, especially the Tour guide, a Singaporean who explained the history of his native land as they explored the city. Then suddenly Caroline leaned forward and whispered, "And - I had a shipboard romance with a lovely Japanese businessman. We remain in touch and he says he is coming to Tassie in a couple of months." To say I was surprised would be an understatement.

Caroline chattered on while I stamped her books. She gathered these up then leaned forward again saying, urgently this time, "Oh, you won't mention my small indiscretion to anyone will you because this is a big secret, we were very discreet, and even Esther has no knowledge of it." I reassured Caroline that this wasn't something I would do, so her secret was safe with me however, I asked whether she had had unprotected sex to which she replied "Yes". I then asked whether she should have some tests to ensure that she hadn't caught any communicative diseases. Caroline was horrified and declined my suggestion. She emphatically stated that her lover wasn't 'that sort of guy'.

He apparently had been rather shy and was unaware of some aspects of sexual conduct, so she assumed that he hadn't been overtly sexually active. I suggested that if she changed her mind she should see her doctor. I queried the health of Phillip and Caroline confirmed that he was very sick so unable to do anything even mildly strenuous. She whispered confidentially,

"Well, we have been sleeping separately for some years now due to his restlessness at night and he hasn't been able to do anything for a long time. Well, you know what I mean, due to his health problems and medications." Caroline paused and gave a light smile.

"My Japanese friend, Kao, has filled this gap in my life. It has been wonderful to feel like a woman again. Although I am happy being Phil's carer and companion, I miss the intimacy we once had and sadly, Kao is able to give me this. I say sadly because I love Phil so very much and I would give anything for everything to revert back to how it was before he became sick, but this is just not going to happen."

She whispered confidentially that Kao had advised her that every 6 months or so he visits all the offices of his company which included Sydney as well as Hong Kong,

Singapore, Soul, Manila and New York. He apparently was due in Australia again in May and he had told her that he would like to visit her in Tasmania. I felt both happiness and sadness for Caroline. Happiness because she had found Kao who appeared a suitable suiter, and sadness due to the demise of her intimacy with Phil. I hoped that everything would work out, but I wondered what the future held in store for her.

CHAPTER 1

CAROLINE'S STORY

I was listening to Esther at morning tea after church on a Sunday during November while she spoke about a cruise she was due to go on in February. Esther was saying how she was going on the cruise alone as none of her friends were able to join her due to various reasons: not being well enough to travel, not having the time or not having the available funds for such a trip. She revealed that she would be flying to Singapore and joining a small cruise ship that could visit the islands of Malaysia, Thailand, Sri Lanka and the Maldives. It sounded wonderful and wasn't overly expensive – and I had always wanted to visit the Maldives – so I offered to join her on the cruise if she was happy for me to do so. Well, Esther was certainly happy to have my company and advised me that we would be part of a tour group of 23 on a ship that only catered for 1,200 passengers so it could access ports that larger cruise ships couldn't, due to their size. I now had to clear this with Phil, but I knew he would be supportive, and he was. He said I had earned a break and that he expected me to return refreshed and as brown as a berry, so in mid–February Esther and I flew to Singapore and joined the tour group. Everyone appeared friendly and welcoming especially the Tour Director, a woman in her 40's called Gail. We were all booked into the Orchard Hotel in Orchard Road for the night and would join the ship the following day.

Next morning after breakfast we boarded the bus which would provide us with a tour of Singapore, visiting places of interest as we waited to board the ship. Our Tour Guide for the day was a Singapore resident who gave us heaps of information about the formation and development of Singapore and we visited various temples, markets and saw the wonderful twin towers. We also visited the buildings that had been occupied by the British government apartments and saw the incredible new building developments. It was interesting to learn that any foreign company wanting to move to Singapore and erect a corporate structure could do so if they agreed to faithfully restore one of Singapore's ancient buildings and, maintain this building for 25 years. Finally, in late afternoon we were driven to the docks, embarked and settled into our cabin. It was small but serviceable. The size wasn't important as we only needed it for sleep and the two beds were ample also there was enough room for the two of us to get changed, so we were happy. The best thing about the cabin was that the window was almost level with the sea so we both had a wonderful view of the waves as the ship moved along.

Several days later I was enjoying the cruise. The ship was great, the cabin was great, the crew were great, so far the trip ashore had been great. We had visited Malacca and found the people we met both friendly and helpful – and colourful. Of course, Esther was a great companion, we did things together and some things separately due to our individual interests, so we were never in each other's pockets. I was having a great time! At 8 00 am on our first full day at sea, after a very tiring trip ashore the previous day, I was having a leisurely breakfast in the buffet restaurant. There was hardly a spare seat to be had and, as I was to learn through experience, that this was fairly normal for breakfast. Yesterday, at breakfast I had asked if I could join an American couple of around my age and enjoyed a lively discussion of the Trump era of American politics! So I wasn't particularly surprised when a voice asked me if I was waiting for someone – I was sitting on a table set for 4 people. I looked up to see a young Asian man smiling nervously down at me. I said no, and that the seats were vacant. He asked whether he and his father could join me and, of course, I said yes. The young man returned with an elderly man in tow who bowed slightly and said he hoped they were not disturbing me and apologised for the imposition. They sat down opposite me and we made small talk about the boat, the weather, how we came to be on the cruise, our countries of origin then, when this fizzled out, I returned to the news broadsheet the ship provided each day for various nationalities on board. Mine was the Australia version. When I had finished breakfast, I arose and was surprised that the two gentlemen opposite me also arose and bowed their goodbyes, the elderly gentleman saying that they had appreciated my company, had enjoyed our dialogue and perhaps we could catch up again. I don't quite remember what I said but it was probably, "That would be nice." I left the dining room and joined Esther at the pool where we spent the morning sun-bathing, swimming and reading.

It was several days before my path again crossed those of the two Japanese gentlemen. I was entering the dining room for breakfast around 9.00 am as they were leaving. We exchanged pleasantries and I went on my way however, the next day a trip ashore was organised so I was having breakfast earlier, around 7.30 am, when a familiar voice asked if he could join me. It was the elderly Japanese gentleman. He introduced himself as John Shegata, apologising for not doing this before and I reciprocated stating my name. We talked and I found him quite amusing. His sense of humour was very similar to mine and I couldn't help thinking that no matter where we lived, we humans were all pretty much the same. John discussed Japan, its economy, its politics which made my head whirl, but it was very interesting. He wanted to understand Australian politics and why we changed Prime Ministers so many times!! I tried to enlighten him! Eventually I had to leave and meet the other members of my group, so we were all together and ready to go ashore. As we parted John smiled, we shook hands and he said that he had appreciated my company and that he would like to join me for breakfast another time. I said something like, 'Yes, I would enjoy that' and went to meet my friends.

I was just finishing breakfast a few days later when my new Japanese friends joined me. The son, Hugh, made his excuses but John sat down opposite me. We talked of the previous trip ashore and I was surprised that he hadn't gone ashore but had continued working for most of the day in his stateroom. Apparently this was very much a working holiday for both of them. John said he would like to see me the next day at breakfast. We were due to sail about 10pm tonight and it would be a sea day tomorrow. I cannot remember what I said but it was probable a casual and flippant, "If I can get out of bed early enough" thinking I would probably be tired after a shore day.

About 9 am the following morning I had just emerged from the shower when I heard a knock at the cabin door. I shouted, "I won't be a minute."

Thinking it was the steward I brushed a towel over me and rubbed my hair then I threw on my robe and opened the door. I could have died a thousand deaths. There John stood looking immaculate in cream linen slacks and a pale yellow polo shirt. He smelt divine. I felt, and I am sure I looked, like a drowned rat. I wished the ground would open up and swallow me - then I thought that I would only be in someone else's cabin below mine! John looked me over, and I died again thinking how terrible I must look, before he said,

"I am sorry Caroline for this intrusion but I thought you may be ill as I didn't see you at breakfast today." I reassured him that I was in good health and had not thought that we had made breakfast a certainty but apologised for my tardiness. I was SO aware that I was devoid of makeup, of my blue satin robe printed with tiny gold stars clinging to my damp skin, and my wet tousled hair. I imagined that I looked an absolute mess.

John kept staring at me then breathed, "Caroline you are a lovely lady." Suddenly I was in John's arms and he was kissing me passionately. Somehow or other we ended up on my bunk. Afterwards I thought *"Wow"* but John was beside himself with apologies and admitted that he felt ashamed because he wasn't prone to acts of spontaneity and he had done nothing like 'this' before. He thought he had hurt me, but I assured him he had not and that I had actually enjoyed the experience. This appeared to both surprise and please him. John then suggested lunch to redeem himself for his actions but I assured him this wasn't necessary and anyway I wasn't free for lunch. We agreed to meet for a coffee later that afternoon.

I walked into the ship's coffee shop at 2.30pm and John arose to meet me. He shook my hand, thanked me for attending, stating that he had thought I probably wouldn't. He again apologised for his behaviour earlier that morning stating he was not a spontaneous man. I reassured him there was no harm done and we sat, sipping our coffee and discussing his life in Japan and my life in Tasmania. As I rose to leave John caught my right hand, he kissed its palm and thanked me for meeting him. He then looked me in the eye – I noticed that his eyes were the colour of dark chocolate – and he said softly,

"Caroline, it is my dearest wish that at some time, in the near future, you will allow me to be spontaneous again."
We looked at each other, laughed and I said something like,
"That would be nice."
And so our relationship began.

CHAPTER 2

THE LOVE AFFAIR

John and I were discreet but saw each other as often as possible, usually in John's stateroom. I found him quite ignorant of sexual enjoyment. Sex with John was over very quickly and sometimes I didn't even have time to climax. John told me that his Japanese name was Sahashi Kazuyoshi and stated that traditionally in Japan their family name came first rather than, as in Western society, where the given name was used first. I confessed that I wouldn't be able to remember or even pronounce his given name and asked if I could shorten it to Kao. Kao laughed and agreed. After the third encounter I felt I needed to say something about our sexual habits, especially my needs which were not really being met. Kao made love like a man running for a bus - it was over mostly before I had begun! Kao apologised and said he was ignorant of such things but would be pleased to be guided by me. He explained that coupling, as he called it, in Japan when he was first married was for procreation only and not for pleasure, so all of this between the two of us was entirely new for him. Well, I must say he learnt well and our lovemaking developed into something that we both enjoyed and loved experimenting with.

Kao would often read Japanese poetry to me. I particularly loved the poems in one book and Kao surprised me by revealing that he was the author of this and several other poetry books. Further, as well as having a keen following in Japan Kao had a strong following in France and, when attending Paris for a book launch, he would be treated like a rock star! I was impressed. On board ship, in his stateroom, Kao would often prepare a Japanese meal for lunch and we would discuss politics, religions and Shintoism. It was weird but I seemed to have similar beliefs to the Shinto code, a code which Kao had followed all his life. He told me some of his family history that his great, great, great, great grandfather had been a stone mason who had supplied statutes to Shinto shrines and temples in and around the Kyoto region. This was the beginning of the family construction business which was further developed by his great, great grandfather. Kao was very proud of his family's tradition and related the story of how his grandfather had developed the company further by buying into banking and other businesses, even to investing finance in Australia in the late 19th century. I was surprised to learn of the significance of this investment which was apparently in the millions of dollars. Kao also alluded to his father's political career and his role in advising the Emperor during the signing of the surrender documents after World War II. Gradually, we were able to peel the layers off each other so that we began to understand what made us tick, according to our relevant culture. Of course we made love and it just was incredible every time. It was all mind blowing.

When we docked at Colombo I decided to explore this city on my own as I had no desire to join the rest of my group on the planned tour, which could take up to 10 hours – far too long for me as I tired easily. When Kao found I would be on my own he offered to show me around Colombo and before I knew it I was in a chauffeur driven car on the way to the city. The driver was a mine of information and advised us on the various temples and important buildings we passed or investigated and we sipped Bollinger champagne in the back seat of the vehicle and nibbled on Japanese delicacies. I felt quite decadent!

We explored the markets and the shopping centres, but I had to stop saying I liked this piece of jewellery or that dress because Kao wanted to buy these for me and I had to stop him. He appeared somewhat perturbed but didn't push. I did allow him to buy me a lovely sarong in colours of red and gold, very beautiful. We stopped for lunch at a small hotel and Kao reassured me that the food there was exceptional. He was correct but I didn't ask what exactly I was eating, just in case! We arrived back to the ship about 3.00 pm and went straight to Kao's stateroom. As soon as the door closed behind us Kao pulled me towards him and kissed me passionately. He kissed my forehead, he kissed the tip of my nose, his lips brushed mine as he lifted my dress over my head. Kao then kissed my cleavage and undid my bra, letting it drop to the floor, then he moved to my stomach which he caressed with his lips before slowly slipping my panties down, which I stepped out of. Kao then kissed me passionately again. This kiss cascaded through my body until it reached my feet. I was overcome by desire. Kao led me to his bed. Kao possessed me completely. Our love making was a fitting end to a wonderful day.

It was so good to be free with Kao for a whole day without looking over our shoulder to see whether or not we had been discovered by any of our shipmates. We continued to grab whatever time I could get away and be with him. Our lovemaking was so good. I wanted Kao all the time. This was terribly hard when events meant I couldn't see him. Once we even managed sitting together at the theatre when Hiroto, (Hugh) Kao's son, surreptitiously led Esther and I to where, gosh, there were only two seats left on the first row of the balcony! I sat with Kao on my right and Esther on my left. We dared not hold hands, although I was very much aware of Kao as our arms touched periodically. It was just as if I was given an electric shock every time this happened. Kao and I hadn't arranged to meet after the show but I needed Kao so much I knew I had to find a way to see him. The opportunity arose when Esther divulged that she would be going to the piano bar to meet Gail and a few others from our group and would I be coming? I declined, explaining that I needed some fresh air and would probably go for a walk before retiring. She said she would try not to wake me when she joined me later.

As I left the theatre I sighted Kao and Hiroto waiting at the lift and joined them. Kao feigned mock surprise that I was now free to join him. I chided him gently saying he was very naughty for teasing me so during the show. We laughed as we made our way to his state room. Kao closed the door behind us and pulled me close to him. His kiss was strong and demanding. Desire overcame me and Kao was soon undressing me and ushering me into his bed. Our lovemaking was urgent and fast. Afterwards he kissed me gently, caressing my body and murmuring my name. We were soon making love again, this time slow and deliberate. It was wonderful. I left Kao after 2 hours of absolute bliss and returned to my cabin. Esther had not returned. I had a quick shower and went to bed. Within minutes Esther arrived relating the funny side of her evening. She was amazing and always saw the funny side of every situation.

All too soon the cruise was over and, while waiting in port at Singapore the day before disembarkation, Kao and I said our goodbyes. We would both miss what we had had, our friendship and our lovemaking but the time had come to part – as we always had known it would. On the morning of disembarkation Esther had gone ahead to meet our group while I checked that we hadn't left anything behind. Just as I was about to leave the cabin the phone rang – it was Kao. He was at his Singapore office but revealed that he had taken a room at the Hilton Hotel, just around the corner and over the road from the Orchard Hotel, where Esther and I would be staying overnight. Kao said he was due to fly to Japan that evening and asked whether I would I have some time that afternoon to meet with him. Of course I said yes.

Esther and I spent a lovely morning looking around the shopping centres of Singapore. We went back to the Orchard for lunch then lazed by the swimming pool. At 2.30 pm I excused myself, saying I felt like a lie down prior to the planned evenings' entertainment which was to attend the *Garden in the Bay,* light and music show and I said I would join her later at the pool. I went up to our room, had a quick shower and walked the short distance to the Hilton. Kao met me at reception and walked me to a car which was waiting outside. After a short trip around retail areas of Singapore when, once again, Kao tried to buy me everything I was remotely interested in, I finally agreed to a lovely red silk night gown before we returned to the Hilton. There Kao made us both a hot chocolate (he has a sweet tooth) and poured us both a Japanese liqueur, which I called Ambrosia, because it was as nectar from the gods. That afternoon was beyond description: Suddenly I was shy but Kao seemed to understand. He put his hands on my shoulders and drew me close. It was if we were two completely different people, that we had discovered we were beyond the 'bubble' of the ship: the romance and the make-believe that seemed to be part of shipboard romances. We discovered that we were real people, in a real world and – that we possessed real feelings for each other.

We stumbled towards the bed, undressing as we went, leaving our clothes as and where they fell. With his mouth teasing mine, Kao laid me on the bed. His fingers caressed my face, followed by his lips then his tongue played over my lips filling me with desire. Mouth pressed to mouth, the scrape of teeth, the sultry meeting of tongues as I sank into the peace and pleasure Kao was offering. He was gently pushing my desire to the surface. His long penetrating kisses and gentle languid caresses increased my need as he hovered over me. Our eyes met and held. The naked love that brimmed from Kao's eyes reverberated through me as if I had been hit by lightning. "Oh, the scent of you is overwhelming and very seductive Caroline" Kao moaned as he pulled me closer. I raised my hips to meet him and almost screamed in pleasure as he entered me. Such ecstasy! We made love unlike anything before. It was tender. It was passionate. It was beautiful. We truly became one – our bodies fused together. We melted into one another. We were not separated by skin, bone or sinew. I can't describe it any other way, but it was unbelievable. We looked into each other's eyes, and we KNEW.

Kao then kissed me gently and sweetly until passion overwhelmed us once more. This time our lovemaking started gently. Kao stroked my breasts and, as he moved down, he rubbed his cheek on my belly then caressed me with his tongue. I caught my breath as he slid his tongue over the sensitive crease of my thigh. He cupped his hands under my hips and I parted my legs accepting his tongue into the most fundamental and desirable domain of sexual pleasure. Kao slid his body up mine, gently massaging with his hands until he reached my face. He nuzzled my ear and my hair, then languidly brushed his lips over mine before kissing me. My body burned as I tasted the sweat on his lips. I felt the hot need of his kiss as I am sure he felt mine. Our passion reached a crescendo when Kao suddenly plunged inside me. I gasped. He continued slow and deep. I felt tears of passion escape my eyes and roll down my cheeks as we melted into each other once again. Kao tenderly kissed the tears away as I told him that I loved him so very much. He said that his heart was full, as we reached our peak together. I believed I would never feel the same again. This would be the last moments we would have together. Then Kao opened his mouth as if to say something more but I put my fingers over his lips to silence him because it was in his eyes. I could see that Kao was going to ask me to stay with him and, oh I wanted to do this so very much but I knew it would be a big mistake. We both had responsibilities in our respective countries and, I could no more survive in his world than he could in mine.

Kao kissed my fingers and gave a small nod. Afterwards we showered, dressed and sipped our liqueurs. I don't recall either one of us saying anything, but we looked at each other knowing that this would be the last time we would see each other. Kao held my hand as we walked to the lift. He kissed me then in the lift and held me tight – I almost cried. Outside the Hilton we shook hands – in Singapore it is a fineable offence to show affection in public. Kao bowed low and, as I went to reciprocate, Kao stopped me saying, "Caroline you have honoured me enough since I met you. You have given me wise counsel, you have discussed many topics with me: religions, world politics, finance, and you have always been honest with me. You have also exhibited various views which I had not considered, so our discussions have always been robust and invigorating - and thought provoking. You have honoured me with your body. You have given me much understanding about things I had previously no knowledge of. Our togetherness has been amazing – we have become one."

Kao paused then continued, "You have given me everything you have – and more. I am indebted to you. Memories of you will be with me always because the sun will not warm my face as your smile does, the stars will not shine as bright as your beautiful blue eyes. You have captivated my heart, you have my breath, and you have invaded my soul. You need to do nothing more to honour me, my lovely lady. I am yours for eternity and beyond." I could not speak but managed to croak, "Oh Kao" while my gaze never left his face, his eyes were downcast. I felt as if a door had closed - very tightly. Kao looked at me then and said "Go now Caroline. Please. Do not look back. We must always look towards all the future may bring. I shall ask my ancestors to guide your footsteps and to keep you safe always as you journey through life." I wished Kao well and my heart ached as I joined other pedestrians crossing Orchard Road.

I didn't look back. I felt full of remorse as several days earlier Kao had asked for my e-mail address and I had written it down for him but I had changed the end from .com to .au. I don't know why I did this. Perhaps I thought that what happens on the ship should stay on the ship!? I felt ashamed and I wished I hadn't done this. I truly regretted this selfish act and believed that I would never hear from Kao again. I thought my heart would break. I walked to the corner of Orchard Road, turned it and climbed the steps into the Orchard Hotel. I had resisted temptation and had not looked back.

After I had changed into my swimsuit I joined Esther at the pool enjoying just over an hour with her. I tried not to think of Kao. Returning to our room to get ready for dinner, Esther had the first shower and it was then I noticed the phone had a light flicking indicating a message. The message was from the Concierge advising that a small package had been left for Mrs. Fischer. Puzzled I slipped down to the desk while Esther was still in the bathroom. I sat in reception and opened the package. It contained a beautiful diamond and silver eternity ring in a velvet box - from Kao. His message read thus:

"Caroline my lovely lady, please do not be cross with me, but I wanted to give you something so very much, something that would remind you of me and our time together. This ring is a modest token to remind you of what I indicated earlier that you will eternally be a part of me – and I believe that this ring speaks of eternal commitment in Western culture. I hope it fits and that you will wear it to remind you of me.
Eternally Yours, Kazuyoshi".

I put the ring on the little finger of my right hand - the only finger that it would fit. *Japanese women are very tiny, I* thought. It was just right - a beautiful ring from a beautiful man, remembering beautiful times spent together and, it would seem, someone who declares his love forever. My heart ached for Kao.

Esther and I enjoyed our evening at the *Garden in the Bay*. The music and light show was really great – in fact breathtaking. Afterwards we made our way back to the Orchard Hotel and ordered drinks and snacks, discussing the evening and the event we had just witnessed. The show was magnificent and an absolute must see for every tourist to Singapore. We had also met a great group of people and we discussed the amusing events emanating from these.

CHAPTER 3

HOME AGAIN

I don't remember much after that – the trip to the airport, the plane home - it was all a blur, but it was great to see Phil waiting at the airport. Our reunion was emotional. Esther and I chatted about the cruise during the drive home and Phil laughed with us as we related some of our amusing experiences. After a couple of days at home I gradually picked up the threads I had left behind: I frequented the weekly Senior's meeting, returned to my painting as I had exhibition organised during the impending months, and reconnected with the church choir. But most of all it was good to see Phil again as I had really missed him – yes really – and although there appeared to be a hole in my heart, I was able to put 'things' into perspective and immerse myself in my life once more. About 10 days after I had returned home I was REALLY surprised to receive an e-mail from Kao. I remember thinking what a resourceful and tenacious man he was.

The email was formal and respectful partly, I suspect, because he didn't know whether Phil would also read it. In a nutshell Kao wrote how they 'both' had enjoyed meeting me and they were due to be in Sydney in May and would like to catch up when they came to Tasmania later that same month. He stated that they would be honoured if we (Phil and I) could join them for lunch and, if this was possible, they would leave the booking to us. Tasmanian arrival details would follow. As the e-mail was written for anyone to read, I mentioned it to Phil who thought the invitation was delightful and urged me to e-mail back our pleasure and to accept their invitation. This I did, and the tone of my e-mail was such that Kao was left in no doubt that only I would be reading all other emails from him.

In April my friends, George and Sonya, asked if I would become a live-in carer for their cat Tomtom for a few weeks. They live in the small farming community of Paradise about 5 kilometres inland from Sheffield, tucked under Mount Roland - a beautiful part of North Western Tasmania. The previous year I had cat sat with Tomtom and I was very pleased to do this again. He was definitely a cat with personality. George and Sonya would be overseas for about a month as they intended touring Canada. I took down the dates and I arranged a visit beforehand to establish my contact with Tomtom prior to their leaving. Tomtom recognised me immediately even though it would have been about 6 months since I last had contact. Sonya gave me instructions as to the welfare requirements of Tomtom and George showed me the marvels of technology relating to their sound system and television. We arranged when I should arrive and when I should return home. I left with the front door key and advised that I would indeed be at their home at the appointed time on the appointed day.

In subsequent texts and e-mails to Kao I included an offer to accommodate him during his stay in Tasmania should he have the time as I would be cat sitting at Paradise during the period he would be in Tassie. Kao's reply came swiftly and began,

"My heart filled with joy to receive your e-mail with your kind invitation to reside with you when I visit Tasmania, which I accept with the utmost of pleasure."

Further, Kao stated that he had three cats at home in Kyoto so would enjoy the company of Tomtom. Kao indicated that he would be in Tassie in May 'sometime' but would e-mail me when his plans were finalised. With this in mind I continued with my lifestyle, and Phil and I enjoyed life together. We shared the household and garden chores gardening together.

Phil would vacuum and wash the floors while I did the washing and the dusting. We shared the cooking and enjoyed the meals the other would cook. As for gardening, I mowed the lawns and weeded the garden while Phil pruned the bushes and trees and took responsibility for the vegetable garden. This was a bit of hit and miss, depending on Phil's health and his ability to work in the garden, but he gained satisfaction in what he achieved. We enjoyed helping each other and we were affectionate. We shared a sense of humour, so every day we were able to laugh regardless of the pain we each suffered. I was active in several art groups and, when required, I would volunteer to man various arts and crafts exhibitions both in Ulverstone and surrounding communities.

I saw Esther regularly and we laughed over moments on our cruise and reminisced about the various places we had visited and the wonderful people we had met. I hadn't confided in her regarding my relationship with Kao. I was sure she wouldn't approve as she knew and liked Phil and I believed that she would be upset and feel that I had betrayed him. I also kept in touch with my friend Connie at the library and I am not sure whether she was interested or not but I kept her updated with information about Kao's trip to Tassie. I think she was concerned for my welfare as she urged caution. I was already thinking about the separation Kao and I had had over the last few months and whether this would have some influence on our relationship. I guess I was concerned that my feelings for Kao may have changed or that his feeling for me may have changed - but only time would confirm or reject my concerns. Kao was due to arrive in Tasmania in two weeks. I wondered whether we would capture that old magic we had enjoyed on board ship, then I remembered the afternoon we had spent together in Singapore, which I still dreamed of. Part of me ached for every moment with him to replicate those feelings while another part of me hoped there would be no magic so we could both return to our individual lives without thoughts of each other.

May came around and in due course my friends went on holiday to Canada, so I was now looking after Tomtom, the cat, in Paradise. Tomtom and I had a good relationship. We enjoyed each other's company. He loved me to chase him around the house every morning after breakfast, meaning that we both were able to have a bit of exercise! As well as looking after Tomtom, I enjoyed going for walks in the surrounding countryside and painting the scenery. I was a passionate pastel artist and I had brought an unfinished painting with me to Paradise to complete.

I had only been in Paradise for a couple of days when I received a text from Kao advising that he was arriving earlier than first thought due to a change of his business plans. The text advised that he would be arriving early the following morning, as he had to return to Japan in the middle of May and hoped that this was not an inconvenience for me. It certainly wasn't an inconvenience as I would be cat sitting until the middle of June. It just meant I had to bring my plans forward, do the shopping and make sure the house was tidy, which it was anyway so no big deal for Kao to arrive earlier than initially planned. Notwithstanding, my heart rate increased several degrees as I envisaged Kao being with me by lunchtime the following day. It would take him several hours of driving to cover the distance from our capital city Hobart, where his plane would land, to Sheffield a regional town which was the shopping centre closest to Paradise. I texted back that I would meet him in a coffee shop in Sheffield, as the house may be difficult to find, and he could follow me back to the house at Paradise. I further suggested to Kao that he ring me just prior to his leaving Hobart so I was waiting for him when he arrived. I envisioned that Kao would arrive in Sheffield around 11.30 am which would give me plenty of time to get organised.

I wrote a list of everything I needed for tomorrow's lunch and dinner. I had to visit Sheffield's butcher, bakery and supermarket and soon had a list with a few extra ingredients for additional meals later in the week. I was going to enjoy cooking for Kao. I then drove into Sheffield, did the rounds of the shops, bought the required goods and drove back home. Tomtom was intrigued with the crackle of the bags and paper which had held the food so I rolled a large piece of paper into a ball and threw it on the floor whereby the cat jumped on it and chased it across the room. That left me some peace to get everything categorised. I had bought a lamb roast, together with lots of vegetables, as I knew this was Kao favourite Western food. I also intended to make a Pear Tart with Frangipani Cream as I knew that Kao had a very sweet tooth! Later in the week I planned to make a Malaysian Laksa with prawns as he was also a seafood fan so I hoped he would like this dish which was a favourite of mine, but immediately I intended to make a fruit cake. That done and cake in the oven, I set aside the scone ingredients as I wanted to make these in the morning. Everything put away in either the refrigerator or pantry. I poured myself a glass of Sauvignon Blanc, cut slices of cheese and grabbed a box of savoury biscuits. I was too excited to eat a full meal. Tomorrow couldn't come soon enough.

By 10.30 the following morning the scones had been baked, the lamb prepared, vegetables cut and in a baking dish. This morning I had also prepared the green beans I had bought yesterday. They were now waiting to be cooked on the stove. By 11.00 am I had slid the meat and vegies into the oven to slow cook. I had previously made the dessert which was cooling but it could be quickly reheated when the roast and vegs came out of the oven. I checked the table which I had set last night for three people. I knew that Hiroto would be driving but I wasn't sure whether he would be staying for lunch. I hoped so, for I believe there is nothing worse than the smell of a good meal cooking when your alternative is to leave and eat take-away food! I cast my eye over the table and everything looked fine.

As it was a cold, clear, although sunny, day, I took the wine out of refrigerator and placed it on the benchtop close to the table. I devoted a little time to giving the wine glasses another polish, and the house a quick vacuum then moved into the bathroom to apply makeup and brush my hair. I changed my clothes quickly and made myself a mug of coffee, sitting down on the couch. Immediately Tomtom jumped up on my knee, examined me reproachfully then settled down. Kao had telephoned earlier stating he was leaving Hobart. I had checked the time and he was a little later than I had envisaged – 9.30 am – so I was expecting him to arrive in Sheffield around noon. I checked my watch, 11.35 so I had plenty of time to get to *Clarissa's*, the café where I was meeting Kao and Hiroto. I grabbed my jacket, struggling into it as I picked up my purse and keys and I left the house. I was feeling nervous as I drove into town. I wondered how our reunion would go and thought that the worst case scenario could see Kao staying at the motor hotel where I knew Hiroto was staying. However, if all went well then Kao would be staying with me for as long as his time allowed.

CHAPTER 4

PARADISE

I was lucky to find a parking spot almost outside of *Clarissa's* which was also close to the motor hotel where Hiroto was going to stay. I parked the car and entered the café. A quick look around the shop told me that they had not yet arrived so I ordered a flat white coffee and sat close to the open fire. As I watched the flames leap and listened to the hiss and crackle of the fire, I crossed my fingers and hoped 'it' would all work out – whichever way it went, it was meant to be. My eyes stayed on the door and I was duly rewarded with the arrival of Kao and Hiroto a few minutes later. Kao looked anxiously around the cafe until his eyes met mine. We smiled at the same time and he looked relieved. They came over and both Kao and Hiroto gave me a hug before sitting down. The waitress came over with my coffee and took their orders. I thought how wonderful Kao looked. I couldn't keep my eyes off him. Had he always been this handsome? I thought, and I wondered what on earth attracted him to me as he could have any woman he wanted. Kao's clothes spoke of affluence and I remembered on the cruise that it had been obvious that money was certainly not a concern of Kao's as he wanted to buy me everything I liked! I was so lost in thought that I had to apologise and ask Kao to repeat himself. The waitress returned with Kao and Hiroto's coffee and Kao reached out and held my hand rubbing the back of my hand with his thumb. He spoke softly as he told me he 'was so very pleased' to be with me again and that he had missed me every day we had been apart.

Kao spoke of their trip from Sydney and their time in Hobart, giving a brief overview of the business that brought them to Tasmania, before discussing their road trip to Sheffield. Kao described the scenery as some of the best he had witnessed in the world, and Hiroto expressed his surprise at the quality of the roads, as he had thought Tasmania was not as up to date as mainland Australia. We all laughed and agreed that we were often mistaken in our assumptions of places and people. I asked Kao what he and Hiroto had planned for their trip to my part of the world and Kao answered that he and Hiroto had reserved rooms at the motor hotel. This disappointed me but I didn't say anything. Kao then explained that as he understood the house and cat I was looking after were out of town he thought a room in town may be opportune if he and I had dinner in town and didn't want to drive back home. While I accepted Kao's explanation, I still thought he had given himself somewhere to stay should our relationship falter. I rationalised that he may be just as concerned as I of possible changes to our feelings for each other during the months spent apart. We had finished our coffee so as I stood I asked Kao what he wanted to do next

Kao frowned and caught my hand, "Is your invitation still open?" he asked softly. Our eyes met and I nodded. He smiled and asked whether I would mind waiting while they checked into their rooms then he would accompany me home. I queried whether Hiroto would also be staying (with me) but Kao shook his head, explaining that Hiroto would have work to do during the day and would prefer to work undisturbed on his own. We left the café together and I found that Kao and Hiroto's car was parked directly behind me, which made us all laugh. We drove in our respective cars the 200 metres to the motor hotel. I advised Kao that I was happy to wait in the car, but then invited Hiroto to have lunch with us. He was hesitant but I insisted saying that it would be my pleasure and he looked at his father who gave him a nod. The two men did not keep me waiting long. Kao approached my car opening the door and asking if he could travel with me, I said yes of course and we set off towards Paradise with Hiroto following. Once at the house, I showed Kao the way to the bedroom and Hiroto unloaded Kao's suitcase and brief case from the car which he placed on the bed. I checked the roast and vegetables which were almost cooked. I lit the stove under the beans and made the gravy. At that moment Kao and Hiroto returned to the sitting room so I introduced Tomtom who had being prowling around mewing. Kao made a great hit with Tomtom who rubbed against his leg before rolling on his back waiting for a stomach rub. The cat happy and settled, I poured Kao, Hiroto and myself a glass of Sauvignon Blanc each and Kao outlined the plans he had made for this trip.

From Kao's talk it was pleasing to hear that we would have eight days together, but he alluded to a political situation which necessitated his return. I didn't ask for details as I felt this was Kao's business and if he wanted me to know more he would tell me so at a later date. I turned my attention to dinner. It was 1.00 pm when I asked Kao and Hiroto to please sit at the table. I then served lunch and Kao was overjoyed that I had remembered his love of roast lamb with all the vegetables. They both ate with gusto and Hiroto revealed that they had eaten a small breakfast on the aeroplane before landing so both were very hungry. Kao expressed his delight with the dessert, which saw him ask for a second helping! I cleared the dishes and placed them in the dishwasher, Kao then asked if he could contribute something. When I said yes, as I made the coffee, Kao went into the bedroom returning with a bottle. He said he hoped I would remember this. 'This' I discovered was a bottle of Japanese liquor, the same liquor we had shared on the cruise. I was delighted and poured everyone a sherry glass of the golden liquid. It was a fitting finish to a great meal – good food, good wine and good friends, what more could you ask? Hiroto then made a move to leave. I checked the time and was surprized to find that it was 3.30pm. Hiroto thanked me graciously and said he would no doubt see me during the ensuing days. I helped him on with his overcoat and Hiroto left with a wave of his hand.

Kao and I were now alone, and I must confess I was a little nervous. Kao had moved to the couch so I quickly tidied the table and joined Kao. He looked at me for a moment, then took my hand, "You have no idea how I have waited for this moment when I would be with you again", he uttered slowly and softly. He raised my hand and kissed it gently, closing his eyes as he did so. "When I walked into that café and I caught the smell of your perfume I knew I was home." he paused, "It was SO good to see you again I thought I might cry", he laughed then and said, "Your hospitality knows no bounds my lovely lady. The meal, the wine ... and you – all delightful", he added, "and you may compliment your cook, for the lamb was the best I have tasted". I smiled and thanked him saying I was pleased he liked the meal.

Kao stated that I was just as lovely as when he saw me last, but a lot happier and asked why that would be? I countered by saying he shouldn't fish for compliments and that he should wait for these to come naturally. We both laughed and I loved the way his eyes crinkled at the corner when he did so. I admitted to Kao that I too had missed him although I did manage to pick up the threads of my life as it was before him. He admitted that he had also done so with his life, then revealed that he had become embroiled in a political situation, which involved the American President's visit to Japan and this was the reason he had to return. Kao added that he had planned to have two weeks with me but unfortunately that didn't seem possible now. I expressed regret that his visit was cut short but emphasised that we could still enjoy the time that we did have together, and Kao agreed. With that Kao stood announcing I hadn't welcomed him appropriately which had disappointed him.

"I understand however," he said "that your welcome should only be between the two of us". With that Kao, still holding my hand, pulled me to my feet and into his arms. He felt warm and his arms felt strong as they engulfed me. We smiled then kissed. It was oh such a sweet kiss and I felt Kao's warmth flooding through my body. He held me close as we kissed again. He felt sooo good.

Kao sat down and, disappointed, I followed suit. Suddenly Kao became serious, "Caroline, I need to discuss something with you". I sat back into the couch as he continued, "I have anticipated our reunion often. I envisaged that I would pick you up, throw you on the bed and we would couple immediately we were alone, then I remembered our first coupling and was embarrassed", he smiled sheepishly. I also smiled at the memory. "I then thought that we had both waited this long we could both wait a few hours more. Do you agree?" Kao asked. I nodded and he continued, "Well, I would like you to consider this: Could we take our reunion slowly? Anticipation, I think would lead to more pleasure when we do become one later this evening. I say this because I feel as if I have not romanced you since we first met and would like to do so today. Can you understand what I desire?" I smiled and squeezed Kao's hand. "Kao you have romanced me at every opportunity, but I do understand what you are saying and thank you for your consideration. I am happy to follow your lead. If you will gain pleasure from this then so shall I," I replied.

Kao put his arm around me and as I nestled into his shoulder he said, "I must be honest with you and say that I had some concerns about today. I wondered if you still felt the same way about me. I wondered whether I would feel the same way about you. I wondered whether I was in a fool's bubble which would explode when I saw you again, but then I remembered Singapore. I felt the emotion we shared was too strong to ignore or for it to just dissolve over time. As I entered the coffee shop my heart beat fast and I asked my ancestors to tell you that you were very special to me. At first I couldn't see you and was so afraid that you would not come, then I saw you smiling at me, and I smelt a faint waft of your perfume. I know this sounds silly coming from an old man but my heart sang and I very nearly cried with pure joy to see you again." I thought what a wonderful, loving man he was.

Kao hugged me and kissed the top of my head then he spoke of his plans for his time with me. He explained that he had a set routine while away from Japan in order to keep fit and to keep his business affairs in order. He advised that he usually arose at 7 am and spent an hour in the gym, then showered and dressed for the day and was ready for breakfast at 8.30. He would work from 9 am to 11 am answering text and email messages and talking to Hiroto but often he would have to contact his Kyoto office. Kao stated that after 11 am I would be all his, then he asked if I had a problem with any of this. Well I didn't as this allowed me time to wake up, shower while he was at the gym then I would be able to get breakfast ready. While he was working I could get Tomtom organised and clean up after breakfast. Kao also stated that he wanted to see as much of the surrounding countryside as possible. He would like to take me out for dinner at least once, or lunch if I preferred, and he wanted me to organise dinner for Phil and I together with he and Hiroto. I was happy to go along with Kao's suggestions but I thought lunch would be more realistic due to Phil having to stay overnight with me if we had dinner in Sheffield, or I would have to stay overnight with Phil if we dined at Ulverstone. Kao agreed that lunch sounded a much better arrangement.

That settled, I advised Kao that I would arrange lunch for this Wednesday when I returned to Ulverstone for my weekly art workshop. I also said that I was happy with his schedule, especially the bit about I would have him to myself from 11 am onwards! For the rest of the afternoon and early evening Kao explained some of the workings of his company and the more he revealed the more concerned I became. Concerned because it was obvious he was a very rich and powerful man in this huge organisation, which stretched across the world. Again, I wondered what on earth he saw in me as he could have any woman he wanted. It was almost the end of the day and as the light faded I left Kao on the couch and switched on the light, asking if he was hungry and would like something to eat. It was 6.30 pm and I thought Kao might be getting hungry but to my query he advised that he was still enjoying the delicious lunch I had served him. Again, he expressed his appreciation for my 'cook's' efforts. I smiled and thanked him. I suggested a snack in about an hour of the Orange and Carrot soup I had made yesterday followed by scones with jam and cream and, of course, the obligatory coffee and Japanese liqueur. Kao said that he couldn't refuse such a meal and we both laughed.

Kao continued telling me about his Company and the offices he had around the world and explaining his regular visits to all of these, the CEO's of which were all family members. I eventually served the soup, floating a teaspoon of cream in the middle of the soup. Kao was most appreciative and loved the soup. He also loved the scones and actually had three. I was glad I had made a dozen! Over coffee I indicated to Kao where the gym and office was. Both were at the rear of the house and were suitably equipped so Kao would have no trouble operating the gym and office equipment. We finished our coffee and liqueurs and returned to the couch. Just before we sat down Kao pulled me towards him and we kissed for a long time. I hoped that Kao's time for bed would soon be upon us as it was obvious to me that Kao wanted me as much as I wanted him.

We discussed several places we could visit in the morning and both agreed that a drive to the various communities around Paradise would give Kao an overall idea of the general countryside. He was very interested in the type of farming within the district and he discussed the farming interests his company held and said he had enjoyed the drive through the various farming land during his journey from Hobart. I placed the mugs and liqueur glasses on the draining board next to the sink and felt Kao hands on my shoulders and his lips caressing the nape of my neck. I felt a tremor go through me. I turned and we kissed. Gently at first then, as desire grew, we kissed hard and passionately. Kao started to undo the buttons on my dress, but I took his hand, switched off the lights and led him into the bedroom. There he completed the task of undressing me and he quickly removed the rest of his clothes, as I had started undressing him. We lay here for a while as he caressed me, kissing me gently all over my face before moving his lips and hands down my body. I did likewise until neither of us could wait any longer and, as Kao would say, we became one. I had really missed him and he had obviously missed me too because our lovemaking was unimaginable and breathtaking. I cannot describe what I felt. I do not know how long we were together but it seemed like an eternity. I thought that it was lovemaking for the gods, not for humble old folk like me and Kao. When we stopped we were both exhausted. Kao hugged me saying he would never ever leave me again but, sadly, I knew that he would have to, but not for a few days. I went to sleep with his arms wrapped around me.

CHAPTER 5

UNDERSTANDING CULTURAL DIFFERENCES

I awoke some hours later and found the bedside light still on. As I got out of bed I heard Kao ask if I was going to 'my' bed to which I replied that I was just going to the bathroom. I returned to bed some minutes later to find Kao sitting up in bed. He then queried where he would be sleeping. Puzzled I replied, "Why here of course Kao". He looked puzzled and asked for clarification. I thought that I had been perfectly clear but reiterated, "Well Kao you are sleeping here with me. Is this a problem?" I hoped it wasn't a problem but thought maybe he didn't want to sleep with me.

He continued to look puzzled then asked, "You mean sleep here with you all night, until morning?" and when I answered in the affirmative his next statement was a REAL surprise. "Well, Caroline I haven't slept with anyone before". I was amazed and thought, at first, that he must be joking but just one look at this face convinced me that he wasn't. "But don't you sleep with your wife?" I asked. Kao just shook his head. "Surely when you were trying for children you would sleep with your wife" I suggested. Again, Kao shook his head and explained. "No, the Shinto priest gave us 3 days in the month in which to try for a child. If nothing happened then we would try again the next month for 3 days, but I didn't stay with my wife, I didn't sleep with my wife, I returned to my apartment". I was appalled.

"Well Kao", I said "In Western culture we stay and sleep with our partners – every night". Kao looked surprised. He shook his head and asked how we slept. I told him that we slept very well indeed and it was very nice to snuggle up to someone on a cold night. He stated that he was worried that he might be restless or somehow keep me awake. I laughed and advised that a steam train couldn't keep me awake. I told him not to worry and he should, hopefully, enjoy the experience. Kao looked far from convinced but lay back in bed as I turned off the light.

A few days later Kao and I found ourselves at a function organised by the Sheffield Council in relation to the annual festival held in November each year. All invitees were either sponsors of this event or participants. I had previously donated two paintings, one of Mount Roland and the other of Sheffield's railway station to the Council. These had been hung on the walls of the public gallery where the community undertook their business with council's various departments, and this was where the function was held. These two events were celebrated on this night. First the festivals' committee would be announced and thanked then recognition of the paintings donated would follow. Kao was keen to meet community members to learn more about the area and the farming techniques used and I was looking forward to catching up with those individuals I had met during last years' festival. I was apprehensive as some of those present might recognise me as being the wife of Phil, but I was reasonably confident that I could pass Kao off as a family friend.

The evening was progressing well, we were both mingling with the guests which had separated us, but Kao appeared to be enjoying himself as much as I was. I caught Kao's eye from across the room and he indicated that I should join him. As I covered the short distance between us I heard him say to his companions, "I don't think you have met my wife", smiling he turned to me then said, "Caroline this is Robert and Julie from Hathaway's Pharmacy". I knew neither so shook hands with both and remarked at the amount of guests at the function. Julie then asked me what I did and I explained that I was a pastel artist and had donated the two paintings on show, I also added that Kao was a long-time friend of the family and he often joked that I was his wife due to his quirky sense of humour. We both laughed then Julie described her days at the pharmacy. A few moments later we were interrupted by people who commanded our separate attentions. Following final speeches the function drew to a close.

Kao caught my eye again and indicated he was ready to go home. As we walked to the car I commented on the evening but Kao was silent. When we reached the car Kao opened the passenger door for me and, as I prepared to get in, Kao said harshly, "Why did you laugh at me, don't you feel that you are my wife? Must you make me lose face in front of everyone?" I was stunned, to say the least, and sat in the car. Kao closed my door and sat in the driver's seat. I told him that I didn't consider myself as his wife as I was married to Phil, moreover, that both Phil and I were known in this community. I said I was sorry as I had not sought to embarrass him. Kao did not answer and we drove back to the house in silence. Immediately we entered the house I switched on the electric kettle and prepared to make hot chocolate for the two of us. Kao poured out the liqueur then said, "Please sit Caroline we have to talk". I put the mugs of chocolate on the table in front of the couch and sat. "I have to say what is in my heart so please do not interrupt me while I speak". I took a sip of the liqueur and remained silent. Kao sat beside me. I noticed his face was white, and his eyes looked dark, almost black. He looked – I don't know – angry, disappointed, hurt?

Kao began by saying, "I can only conclude from your behaviour tonight that you are ashamed of me". I drew a breath and opened my mouth but Kao's look kept me silent. He continued, "When we are here or out on our own – just the two of us - you are wonderful. You appear happy in my company – as I am in yours - but when we are out like this evening you disown me. You show me no affection, you tear my words apart. I am embarrassed I lose face so I feel I am an embarrassment to you. I do not understand why. Is it because of the war? I wasn't in the war. My father was not involved in any fighting due to his capacity to build and repair roads, bridges and reconnect communication outlets which the Americans had bombed. My father was a pacifist at heart. We lost relatives in Nagasaki – but do I condemn people from other nations? No, I do not!" Kao stopped, sipping his hot chocolate and then liqueur. I attempted to take his hand but Kao pulled it away and said, "If you are ashamed of me why did you invite me tonight? I shall go now and not bother you again because you cannot possibly care for me. Better not see you again than to be with someone who only loves part of you". As Kao took another sip of his liqueur I tentatively asked, "May I speak now?" Kao nodded but didn't look at me.

I stated that I wasn't ashamed of him or of our love for each other, but he had to try and understand Western culture and my standpoint, as I have tried to understand his. Further, I explained again, that both Phil and I were reasonably well known amongst the Sheffield and surrounding communities, so introducing me as his wife would cause some gossip amongst the invited guests we had met at the function that evening. I chose my words carefully so Kao would fully understand the damage he might have done to both Phil's character as well as mine.

"This would bring my character into disrepute, causing me to lose face within the community and affecting loss of face for Phil also". I accused Kao of only seeing his own point of view, of only seeing his own hurt and that he was blind to the damage he was doing to both my reputation and that of Phil's – who was innocent of any wrong doing. I explained that introducing me as his wife was tantamount to admitting that he and I were lovers and that Phil was a fool because he was unaware or ignoring this, the latter being worse. I stated that it was clear Kao did not fully understand the culture he found himself in which, I said, I found amazing as he had been visiting Western countries for many years. I emphasised that this was not Japan where it appeared to be OK to take on another woman to warm your bed at night and to which the wife fully subscribed. I explained that most people of our culture believed in love and fidelity. We married for life but, unfortunately, marriages didn't always work out the way we had hoped.

We talked long into the night but I saw no change in Kao's thinking. In the end I told Kao I was tired and going to bed. I finished with "You must try to see that our cultures are different and, while you are in my culture, you should try to understand it and be guided by its rules – just as I would in your country. If, however, you find this untenable, then I shall understand if you leave tonight. I shall miss you but I shall understand. There will be no regrets, no recriminations. I am sorry tonight ended as it did but I want you to remember this - I do love you." I stood saying I understood that he was hurt but this was of his own doing and I asked him to think about it. I took the mugs and liqueur glasses and placed them near the sink then walked back across the room. As I passed the couch where Kao remained sitting I added, "I am going to bed now, if you want to stay with me you will be most welcome, but if you leave, I wish you all the best for the future". As I turned towards the bedroom Kao caught my hand and stood. He pulled me to him and held me close for a moment.

He then spoke, "Caroline, once again you have given me much to think about, but I want you to know this: you have been like a wife to me, more than my wife in Japan. You have truly cared for me while I have been here. You have denied me nothing and I appreciate this. I am amazed that you do everything, the cooking, cleaning, washing, ironing, looking after Tomtom – just about everything. And your cooking is superb. You care for me so well and I shall never forget everything you have done for me". Kao kissed me on the forehead saying he would like to stay if I was OK with that. I said I was and went to the bathroom where I removed my makeup. Kao was already in bed when I reached the bedroom. I quickly undressed and got into bed. Kao had his arm across the bed to which I nestled into. He hugged me and, kissing me on the forehead, he bade me goodnight. I fell asleep almost immediately.

Next morning I awoke to find myself alone in bed, except for Tomtom who objected to being woken. I immediately thought Kao had left but a quick look around the room revealed this was not the case as his clothes from the previous night were tossed across the bedroom chair, so I surmised that he was in the gym. Kao suddenly appeared at the bedroom door carrying a tray comprising of food and hot drinks. He had prepared a Japanese breakfast for us to share. He sat on the bed next to me and described the various dishes on the tray. I hesitantly picked up a piece of jellied eel followed by a piece of smoked fish which I placed in a vacant bowl. Kao urged me to try the salad and the noodles which I placed on top of the seafood. I also chose a slice of hard-boiled egg and added that to my dish. Kao watched me as I carefully mixed the ingredients of my bowl then I took a piece of the eel with my chopsticks. It tasted good so I smiled and told him so.

Kao was pleased and started to eat his own breakfast. He was far more adept with chopsticks than I nevertheless I enjoyed my first Japanese breakfast and thought how sweet it was of Kao to prepare this for me. I took a sip of the green tea, which I love and usually had with my Western style breakfast. Kao finished his meal and sipped green tea while waiting for me to finish. As I placed my cup back on to the tray Kao cleared his throat then said, "Caroline, I was thinking that you may like to accompany me to visit several farms as my Company is interested in buying a farm within this vicinity".

He stopped, looked at me and cocked an eyebrow before continuing, "Would this be of any interest to you", he enquired. I answered in the affirmative and asked when he would like to leave. He answered that as soon as I was ready. That said Kao picked up the tray and, as I went into the bathroom, I heard him washing the dishes. I had to smile as I knew that Kao was far from being domesticated so I appreciated the effort he was making.

Showered and dressed we left the house just after 9 am. As we settled into the car Kao turned to me saying, "Caroline, I must apologise for last evening. You slept so soundly but, alas, I did not. I ruminated on our discussion and I am ashamed to say you were quite correct. I was seeing things from my point of view and made presumptions which I had no right to do. I should have been considering you and, yes, I need to consider the cultural differences of your world and mine. We shall speak more of this when we return home but I just wished to clear the air before we left for the day. I know we care for each other, and I don't want anything to spoil what we have. If I have to evaluate my position and my thoughts and feelings within your culture then I will do so. Please say you forgive my thoughtlessness". I drew Kao close and kissed him saying that of course I forgave him. Kao sighed a sigh of relief and returned my kiss then informed me that we were to drive into Ulverstone where he had made an appointment to see a real estate agent who had several suitable farms to show us. He asked me to help him by giving a woman's point of view on each of the properties and I agreed with pleasure. We arrived at the real estate office with a few minutes to spare.

Tony Bosneer introduced himself and showed us the portfolio he had prepared. He offered us coffee which we were happy to accept as we read through the portfolio. There were nine farms he had chosen to check out during the next few days but, as we leafed through the information provided, it was obvious that several did not fit Kao's criteria. He required a farm within 20 minutes of Ulverstone, it had to have two dwellings on the one property, or room to build a second dwelling, and the land had to be suitable for beef farming with plenty of permanent water. This left four properties for us to examine. After finishing our coffee, Tony drove with Kao in the passenger seat and discussed the details of the first property. We arrived within 10 minutes of leaving Ulverstone, which appeared to be a good omen. This 1970's house had been built on top of a hill fairly close to a major road, leaving the original home standing down the slope of the hill near a stream, a tributary of a major river. A cursory inspection revealed this newer dwelling appeared quite modern, had 5 bedrooms, a large kitchen/dining room, and a modern bathroom comprising of a shower and separate bath. We moved on to the older home.

From the outside the weather board and iron house, built around the turn of the century, looked in fairly good condition. Although the weatherboards needed a good coat of paint to keep them well preserved. I was also pleased to see the house had been reroofed in recent years which meant no leaks (?). Having the house used as a holiday home for relatives of the owner was a bonus as this had kept the place reasonably well maintained. All that was required was an inspection of the inside so we could assess what repairs, renovations or modifications were required to bring it up to Kao's high standard. These two properties appeared to suit Kao as he planned to employ a farm manager who, with his family, would occupy the newer dwelling with the older house updated as a holiday home to suit the managers within Kao's Company. We walked across a short veranda and entered the house through the front door. The hall stretched from front to back leading into a large kitchen. A wooden kitchen table surrounded by 8 wooden chairs filled the centre of the room. A

Welsh dresser stood to the right and on the same wall to the left of the dresser a pantry stood which would suffice for provisions. Outside the kitchen door fully enclosed a back veranda leading outside to the back garden. We walked back through the house and found that there was a good sized laundry, a reasonably modern bathroom, 3 good sized bedrooms, with a master bedroom opposite the lounge room at the front of the house. Kao and I had a quick private conversation as we walked through the house together, discussing what was required and which rooms required the most attention. Kao seemed satisfied as I added that the newest home would amply serve the needs of a family as the owners and his family of his wife and three children already lived there. We thanked the owner and his wife before joining Tony at the car.

As we drove to our next destination Kao was hunched over reading through the details of the property. We arrived a few minutes later and saw a brick and iron house built around the mid-1950's. While it was the only house on the property there was plenty of land on which to build another home. There were several dams on the property so water for the animals was not a problem. This house, similar to the first property we had viewed, would satisfy the needs of a medium sized family with a few modernizations. However, there was a long drive from the major road to the dwelling, which might deter some families if they expected children to walk to catch the school bus and then walk back home again after school.

After thanking the owners, we moved onto our next property which, I assessed, would be about a 20-minute drive from Ulverstone. The occupied house, built in 1953, was suitable for a family. The layout was very similar to the previous houses and would need a modest amount of money to modernise.

The fourth property was a bit of surprise. Both Kao and I had almost rejected it as it was a smaller property than Kao had envisaged, however, the layout of the land and the position of the house was exceedingly pleasant and it was less than 20 minutes from Ulverstone. The house was just peeping over the crest of a hill so was quite private from the road. Down the hill behind the house a creek ran so the outlook from the rear of the house was quite pretty with willows bordering the creek. We inspected the homestead which was very modern brick and tile residence which required no renovations at all. There was no second residence but a good sized paddock, further down the hill and closer to the creek, would accommodate a two or three-bedroomed house. This would reduce the overall land available for the beef cattle to just under the minimal amount of 1,000 acres. The farm road was only a few metres from where the school bus picked up and later deposited the children, so not a long walk for them. We thanked the owners and retired to the car for the ride home.

We thanked Tony and said that we would discuss the merits or otherwise of each property and would contact him the next day. We had much to cogitate over lunch. We both agreed that a decision on which property was most suitable and therefore buyable was not necessary unless the property really 'jumped out' at us. Separately we assessed each property out of a top of 10 points in relation to criteria cited then compared notes and discussed each one as we each saw it. All properties had good and bad points. The cost of refurbishments seemed no problem according to Kao. Moreover, it was the property as a whole that seemed to be the best incentive for purchase. We decided to sleep on it and renew discussions in the morning. That said, we enjoyed a very good lunch of steak, chips and salad washed down with a decent red wine at the local pub then drove home. We both had much to think about.

CHAPTER 6

THE FARM

I was grateful that I had chosen a pair of good walking shoes that morning as some of the tracks had been a bit rough in parts, but Kao had helped me over the worst terrain so I was well looked after however, I was not feeling so good. Walking around each property often on uneven ground had its toll on my back. I was exhausted from this exercise and from the associated pain in my back and legs. I felt I might have to admit to Kao to not being as well as I had tried to make out all was OK, but wasn't sure how to go about this. Kao came to the rescue, of course. He is very perceptive and very direct so as we arrived home he enquired how I was feeling. I replied that I was just tired. He helped me off with my jacket and sat me down at the table.

He took both my hands in his saying, "Now Caroline, please do not make me act like that great detective", (I am a great fan of Agatha Christie's Poirot). "I ask you again because I can see you are not comfortable, and please be honest with me. Where are you hurting?" I squeezed his hands - he was so insightful. I explained about my back injury and that there were times when I suffered much pain, this being one of those times. I said I needed a bit of rest and a couple of pills and I would be OK. Kao's face showed his concern as he declared that I should lay down at once and he would get me the pills I required. Also, he added, he would see to dinner later when we became hungry. He laughed then and when I said I didn't think my disclosure was anything to laugh about he agreed but said what a couple of idiots we were. This amazed me as Kao was always careful not to say anything which might be construed as negative about one another. Kao saw the look on my face so he explained saying that he also took pills as he had a heart murmur, but reassured me that there was no cause for alarm. We both laughed and agreed that we really should be honest with one another.

Kao kissed me gently leading me into the bedroom where he helped me undress and get into bed, having first shaken the two pillows which I now leant against. He brought me the prescription medication I had asked for together with a glass of water and watched me as I chose a couple of tablets and swallowed them. I asked Kao about the heart murmur but he dismissed my concerns by revealing his constant contact with a cardiologist. He tucked in the blankets and asked if I was warm enough. I was. I said I would like read for a while so he passed me the book I had been reading, from the bedside table, he picked up the book he was reading and settled down next to me. It was a pleasant way to end an enjoyable, if painful, day. I had just opened my book when Kao put his book down and looked over at me. I knew he wanted to say something, probably of a serious nature, but knew him enough to know that he would get around to it in his own time but I didn't have long to wait.

"Excuse me Caroline", he said. "I did not have the time I thought I would have today to digest everything you said to me last evening but what happened is too important to leave things unsaid and I have plenty I want to say, so please allow me to finish before you make any comments". I nodded in agreement.

"Caroline you are a very stubborn woman, well I find you so. This is not necessarily a bad thing for your stubbornness forces me to reassess my point of view or position in whatever is under discussion, and I find myself turning corners I had not deemed possible – even changing courses in mid-stream. My colloquialisms are correct?" he asked. "You look puzzled but I shall press on and I am sure I shall make myself clearer as I go". He stopped and cleared his throat.

"All my life I have been told that I am right in what I believe in and what I do and that I am never to compromise my ideals – and I still believe this to be true, BUT" Kao emphasised, "this remains true only in my own culture which I am now only realising. I wasn't thinking of the implications that my introducing you as my wife would have on you or on Phil. In Japan you would be honoured as my wife as I honour you and in my heart you will always remain my wife. Business is a different world and I can work within most cultures - it comes naturally after a time – so why can't I adjust to being with you in your culture and accepting that? I don't know, but I know I have to change, and I believe I am already starting on the path of understanding where you are coming from, as well as understanding the great disservice I have done you, and your husband. Since I met you I have gained many insights and knowledge that I was ignorant of, and I am grateful for this. I feel you can educate me about more and more about the world in which you live. Sometimes I have been overwhelmed with the knowledge you just casually pass on to me. Sometimes you bring forth subjects which have been in my mind, at other times we have spoken together of the same topics, and we have laughed. That's another aspect of your company that I love – you make me laugh. I have never before laughed so much as I have with you, so I have much to be thankful for." He paused.

"Sometimes I don't recognise myself and the way I am thinking. Sometimes I feel a stranger to myself and, at times, this is hard to come to terms with. I feel like a chrysalis ready to burst forth as a butterfly, while hoping I won't be a moth". Kao laughed and I smiled. I hadn't realised that the changes he had to make would affect him so profoundly.

"So my lovely lady, if I may still call you that, I humbly ask you to take to heart what I have just said. Also, to find it in your heart to forgive my selfishness and my ignorance for not understanding your culture enough to treat you how you should be treated, and that is with love and respect at all times, so I now throw myself on your mercy and ask to be forgiven and, believe me when I say, I shall try to do the right thing in the future at all times. I expect you will need time to digest everything I have said, so I shall return to my book and leave you to yours or to your thoughts". Kao stopped then, our eyes briefly made contact then he picked up his book and opened it. I opened my book but the words jumped all over the page so I pretended to read while being aware of Kao's subtle movements. I decided that while Kao's long speech had been sincere, there was a touch of pathos emphasised to gain some sympathy, so leaving Kao to ruminate over what I may or may not do or say would not hurt. I was aware that Kao glanced my way several times during the two or so hours we read our respective books in silence.

At last Kao asked if I was hungry. I replied that I was peckish rather than hungry. After asking what 'peckish' meant, he admitted he was also peckish and asked me what I wanted to eat. I suggested that he warm up what was left of the Orange and Carrot soup and to cut some of the crusty bread to go with this. I also suggested that he may like to bring in the two small bowls of individual Fruit Trifle which were in the refrigerator. Kao smiled and said he would delighted, as I knew he would be, I was conscious of his love of sweet food! A few minutes later I could hear Kao's movements in the kitchen so I settled down and continued reading. In no time at all Kao returned with tray containing lunch. We talked about Tomtom's latest adventure as Kao had thrown a rolled piece of paper for the cat to chase which he did with much gusto. When we had finished, Kao cleared the dishes and I heard him loading the dish washer. He returned and took up his position on the bed, picked up his book and returned to reading.

I watched him for a while then Kao looked up asking if there was anything wrong. I smiled and said no. I then thanked him for the meal and that I would like to say something, and would he please not interrupt me until I had finished. Kao nodded and closed his book. I informed him that I had listened intently to what he had to say earlier, which I had digested.

"Kao I am pleased that you will now consider the culture in which you find yourself before you make judgements, which have previously been based on your own culture." I began. "I accept the cultural differences have been a bit of a stumbling block in our relationship but, for the most part, we have both adjusted to the ideals of both our cultures and, so far, we have enjoyed a relatively cohesive relationship. I understand it is challenging to consider other ways of thinking and behaving when all your life you have been taught to use specific values which are basic to the very way you live your life. I believe that we are, step by step, learning to understand one another as I am also gaining an appreciation of your culture and you with mine. Most importantly Kao, this is much bigger than the two of us, for it encompasses the cultures of two very different cultures. These experiences can be passed on to others – our family, friends, and other relationships within our respective communities in which we exist." I paused and caught my breath before resuming.

"Only by being aware of why certain politicians in different countries operate as they do, and a general cognizance of the disparities between countries, I believe remains the most essential of elements to avoid disputes which may possibly lead to war between nations. While you and I are only at the tip of the iceberg Kao, just think of the people we may be able to influence to better understand how and why people in your country operate differently to those in mine, and vice versa. Change has to start somewhere – and Kao – your favourite parable can be translated to reflect this: *Yearning cannot change destiny, only patience and a pure heart may realise dreams.* If only nations throughout the world could appreciate that 'difference' doesn't mean 'wrong' and could try and understand each other more. It appears there is a lot of conceit, misused pride and arrogance within countries when coalitions could realise the dreams of a world without disharmony and war - and that 'difference' is just that". I paused before adding, "That's all I wanted to say - except I love you and of course I forgive you. I realise that it is difficult to adjust to another set of values, some of which may be in violation of your own home-grown standards, so I appreciate your efforts to understand and react to my culture as I have tried to consider yours before acting or speaking. At the end of the day we are travelling in the right direction". I stopped then as Kao was kissing me.

"You are a wonderful and wise woman who would be a great addition to your government", he declared. "I thank you for your forgiveness and I swear I shall try to remember the differences of our two cultures. I really don't want anything to come between us so please correct me when necessary". He hugged me and I crossed my fingers and hoped that we had passed a milestone in our relationship.

We then discussed each of the properties we had visited during the day. He asked me which one I had liked and it appeared that we both thought the last property had the most potential even though we would have to build another dwelling to house visiting members of staff from Kao's company. We both agreed that this dwelling could be built to Kao's requirements, thus he gets just what he wants and it is a new house so no intrinsic problems. Kao said he would contact Tony in the morning and would arrange a further meeting with the owners. He was hoping that the owners would remain to manage the farm.

We returned to reading our respective books when Kao suddenly turned to me.

"Caroline may I ask you something that has been concerning me as I am not sure what you mean?" I said of course I would help if I could. Kao then stated that he was perplexed when I had told him that I loved him as he wasn't sure what I meant. He knew it was something wonderful for when I had said that my eyes were full and bright so he knew it was important and he had felt a fool for not fully understanding the word 'love' even though he was aware that people in the Western world put a lot of store in it. I gathered my thoughts before beginning my narration. I explained as best I could, suggesting a correlation between my declaration and his relating to his heart 'being full'. I asked him what he thought his heart was full of. He admitted that he didn't know but sometimes when he looked at me he thought that his heart would explode due to the intense feeling he had. I put my right hand over my heart.

"This is full too, of my love for you Kao" then I took his hand and placed it over my heart. "My heart is full of love for you. I too feel pain with the intensity of my feelings". I then placed Kao's hand over his heart with my hand covering his and said gently, "Your heart is full like mine. What do you think your heart is full of, maybe it is full of some feeling like mine?" I queried. Kao looked puzzled and thought for a moment.

"So Caroline, is this 'fullness' called 'love' then?" he asked. I smiled and asked him what he thought. Kao put his hand on my heart and my hand on his heart before stating that in the Japan he grew up in there were no words to describe 'love' more succinctly for those feelings we have for each other.

"I would say for instance that your face pleases me. In a relationship such as betrothal or marriage we give each other gifts or do things for family, such as work hard, to prove our respect and affection" he explained.

I caught my breath as now I understood why Kao tried to give the items that I had admired in Colombo, Singapore and since he arrived here – and I had refused most of these. Had he thought that I didn't care for him at these times? I wondered, so I said.

"Kao thank you for pointing out the cultural differences because I now understand why you wished to give me gifts all the time". Kao smiled sadly.

"I wondered why you refused most of the things I wanted to buy for you as I could not understand why you denied me the right to show you the deep regard I have for you". I laughed and Kao looked quizzically at me. "I am not laughing at you Kao, but at myself. As I said at those times, and the reason I refused has not changed, I was and am satisfied with having you and you alone. I did not appreciate the importance of your gift giving then. I had no knowledge of your cultural rituals involved in relationships however, I do now so please accept my long overdue apologies. Kao what you feel for me is what I feel for you." Kao's face broke into a large grin.

"Oh I think I can see a clash of cultures here" he said and we laughed together. "So Caroline", Kao said gently taking my face in his hands, "I say this to you – my heart is truly, truly full – I love you more than life itself", He kissed me then, such a sweet kiss. I looked into his beautiful brown eyes, just like melted dark chocolate which I wanted to drown in. Kao kissed me again as I melted into his arms then he wished me a good night, undressed and climbed into bed. He kissed me again, we both switched off our bedside lights and I snuggled up close to him. I was asleep in seconds.

CHAPTER 7

DINING IN - DINING OUT

Wednesday dawned bright and sunny with a slight breeze. There had been a frost overnight and the back lawn, still to see the sun, twinkled with a million diamonds. The frost had already melted on the front lawn as this received the early sun. Kao was still in the gym so I had a shower and dressed before preparing breakfast. Kao came in the kitchen door then and he kissed the nape of my neck as I was bent over pouring green tea for us. Today was my day at Ulverstone gallery where I had a group learning the art of pastel painting from 10.00 am until 12.00 pm, after which I would be meeting Phil at our home prior to our lunch with Kao and Hiroto. Phil and I had invited both Kao and Hiroto to our home for pre-lunch drinks and, at Kao's request, to examine my art studio where unsold paintings were exhibited. We would then have lunch at the *Jack Spratt* sea food restaurant, which overlooked the River Leven.

I was feeling a little nervous and hoped that neither Kao nor I would, unknowingly, display any sign of our affection for one another in front of Phil. I had no desire to hurt Phil and I relayed my concerns to Kao when he joined me for breakfast. Kao also expressed this sentiment and promised to act appropriately - as only a casual acquaintance from the cruise ship. He thought that we should keep to discussing cruise ship memories of the countries we visited together with our lives since we both returned to our particular homes. I agreed that this appeared to be the safest, however, I still had misgivings as I hated to deceive Phil in this way. I had never done so in the past, and I hoped all would go well. While Kao was in the office answering e-mails, texts and telephone calls, I readied myself for my trip to Ulverstone. I had agreed to drop Kao off at the motel in Sheffield where Hiroto was staying before travelling the one hour trip to Ulverstone, so I needed to leave by 9 am. I packed the car with my travelling art supplies and the painting-in-progress. I had just put on my coat and was checking my handbag when Kao left the office shrugging on his coat. He grabbed his scarf and we left the house. Kao and I kissed as I dropped him off at the motel and I drove on towards Ulverstone.

The pastel workshop went well. I had six artists who were in various stages of proficiency. I enjoyed guiding and encouraging those who were interested in learning the various techniques relevant to this art form. I shared their enthusiasm and sense of achievement when they overcame their individual frustrations. They were each producing good paintings and they were learning quickly from the tips and procedures I shared with them. In any case I loved painting and I hoped I was also passing on the enthusiasm I felt for pastel painting, so I would have been just as happy if no one had turned up for tutelage! Time flew, as it usually did in these workshops, and it was soon time to pack up. While doing this, and saying goodbye to my students, my thoughts turned to the approaching lunch and I began to feel nervous. I hoped everything would go well, and regretted listening to Kao when he advocated for this meeting with Phil, but it was too late to change anything now so I took a deep breath, packed everything into the car and headed home.

Phil was pleased to see me of course and gave me a wonderful hug and a big kiss. It was good being with him again. This may sound strange but I loved both Phil and Kao but for different reasons. I had never believed this was possible prior to just this happening to me! I was able to compartmentalise each relationship in that when I was with Phil I rarely thought of Kao and when I was with Kao I rarely thought of Phil. I guess this was easier as Kao lived so far away and I was not able to see much of him. This visit was magic because I was cat sitting I was free to spend an extended time with him. It would be difficult, if not impossible, to spend whole days and nights with him otherwise. Kao would just have to realise that I wasn't free to be that available. I sighed as I renewed my makeup and changed my clothes. Phil looked good wearing his suit and he complimented me on my attire. He had drinks arranged and ready to offer Kao and Hiroto, although he expected Chieko, Kao's wife to attend. I supposed Kao had an excuse why she hadn't accompanied him on his trip to Australia, but that was the least of my concerns. I asked Phil to pour me a gin, lime and lemon which I sipped while Phil enjoyed a beer.

I kept a watch for Kao to arrive and hoped he was driving and did not have a chauffeur driven car. A car drove up our driveway, a small sedan from which both Kao and Hiroto alighted and rang the doorbell. I greeted them both. We were polite and formal, with both men bowing before shaking hands. I introduced both by their Western names of John and Hugh respectively, and prayed I could maintain this for the duration of the afternoon. I queried Chieko's absence and Kao replied that she had not been well and thought the trip to Australia would be too tiring for her, so Hiroto had joined him on the pre-paid holiday. This seemed a reasonable explanation, so the conversation turned to their trip from Japan and how much of Australia they had visited. After the first drink Kao asked if he could see my paintings. Phil poured everyone another drink which we took with us as we crossed the lawn to the studio.

Most paintings were hung, although there were about 10 propped against the walls as lack of wall space prohibited their hanging. Kao and Hiroto studied each one. I related the story behind each one: the actual place in Tasmania I had painted, or where the animal had been found etc. Both men showed interest in my art and I wondered whether this was an act or they were genuinely impressed with my work. They also appeared fascinated by Phil's leatherwork which was displayed on a couple of shelves in my studio. Phil was happy to describe his techniques to them, which apparently intrigued both. We walked back to the house and Kao expressed his admiration for both Phil's craft skills and my artwork with Hiroto nodding his agreement. We finished our drinks and Phil helped me on with my jacket. We had decided to take both cars to the restaurant as Kao had informed us that he had another engagement later in the afternoon, so they would need to leave directly after lunch.

The lunch went well. We talked and we laughed. Kao was keen to find out more about the Australian political situation and pressed Phil to explain the frequent changes to our Prime Minister. Phil did a better job than I when I tried to enlighten Kao on board ship. Phil had good insight and knowledge of the various politicians and their egos. Kao then discussed Japan's political situation and the problems they had with the American President. He shared some experiences with us and had us laughing out loud; he was very funny. Time flew and it was time for us to break up the party. As we were struggling into our jackets and coats, Kao gave me a sheet of paper and revealed that both he and Hiroto were interesting in buying several of my paintings.

"I have written the titles of the paintings we would like to take with us. Would you be able to pack them for us to collect on our way back to the airport next Tuesday?" he asked. Then, assured that this would be no problem, Kao and Hiroto took leave of us. Their car turned left and Phil and I turned right at the crossroads, arriving home shortly thereafter. I was amazed when I read Kao's note as he had listed four paintings that had taken his fancy and wanted to purchase. I wondered whether Kao really liked the art or whether he was just being generous because I had painted them.

Phil expressed his enjoyment of the lunch and of Kao's and Hiroto's company and we laughed over some of the experiences they had related to us. Phil and I had not ordered coffee at the restaurant so Phil now made coffee for us both. I was driving back to Paradise shortly as I didn't want to leave Tomtom for too long on his own. Phil and I finished our coffee then Phil walked me to the car. He gave me a hug and a kiss as he helped me into the car. I reversed out the driveway and gave him a wave before driving off back to Paradise. It was 3.55 pm so I should arrive at the motel in Sheffield where Hiroto was staying before 5.00 pm, when I would pick Kao up for the drive back to Paradise.

Kao was waiting for me as I stopped at the Motel and we drove back to the house and Tomtom. Hiroto had declined my invitation to accompany us back for dinner, citing lots of paper work to complete but I think he was being very tactful. Immediately we reached the door Tomtom met us meowing his disapproval of having been left alone. Both Kao and I gave him lots of attention then he settled down on his favourite seat and washed himself thoroughly. Kao poured a scotch each and we sat on the couch discussing the luncheon engagement. I thanked Kao for being discreet however, I was surprized with his retort,

"Caroline, when are you going to tell Phil about us?" For a moment I couldn't speak, I was very surprised, as we hadn't discussed this previously and anyway I had no intention of telling Phil anything about my involvement with Kao. I expressed my feelings to Kao stating that telling Phil would only upset him both as my husband and also as a man because he already felt that he had lost his manhood and I was not about to confirm this by making this revelation. I related back to the differences between our two cultures by pointing out that what may be acceptable in Japanese culture was not necessarily acceptable in Western culture – and taking a lover due to the spouse being unable to perform sexually definitely wasn't acceptable in my culture. Kao pointed out that many Western men were seeing other women when they were married so he could not understand my argument. I pointed out that these affairs were clandestine - behind the wives back. After half an hour or so of discussions Kao relented and we both agreed to disagree, but I felt that this discussion was not yet over and Kao would bring it up again at some future time.

I cooked bacon and mushroom omelettes for dinner followed by ice cream for dessert. After coffee on the couch, Kao followed me into the bathroom and watched me while I took off my makeup. As I started brushing my hair Kao took the hairbrush from me and continued brushing. It felt good as this task always relaxes me. When Kao finished we both retired to the bedroom with Kao reminding me that he and Hiroto would be playing golf the following day. Hiroto would be picking him up at 9.00 am and returning him around 6.00 pm. I suggested he ask Hiroto to dine with us and Kao agreed that was a good idea.

The following day dawned bright and sunny – a great day for golf. As planned, Hiroto called for Kao and I received a hug and kiss from Kao before they drove off. I had the whole day to myself and to spoil Tomtom. He loved being chased so after he had breakfast, and I had finished the mornings chores, we played *Catch me if you can,* which he loved. After racing around the house several times we both tired of the game and retired to the couch. Tomtom settled himself on my knee and promptly fell asleep while I read my book. After a couple of hours Tomtom alighted and went for a snack. I made a sandwich and a coffee and returned to the couch, switching the television on before sitting down. The mid-day movie wasn't very interesting so I switched the TV off and listened to a CD of Chopin's Nocturnes while finishing my lunch. Tomtom settled down on his favourite chair and snoozed. I decided I may as well get dinner started so grabbed the ingredients from the refrigerator and the pantry. I had decided to cook *Beef and Chickpea Tagine* a favourite of mine. It wasn't difficult to make but it takes approximately 4 hours to cook.

I soon had this dish prepared and in the slow cooker. I chose to also cook a boiled fruit cake for dessert, served hot with custard, then cold as a cake for morning teas thereafter, but I had plenty of time to do this. It was a glorious day – warm and sunny with a warm breeze - a good day for a walk. Checking that Tomtom was well supplied with food and water, and was snoozing on his favourite chair, I silently left the house and began my walk. The air was clear and the smell of farms filled the air with all their variants of perfumes. I felt the sun on my face and arms and relished its warm glow. I walked towards Mount Rowland and marvelled how magnificent it looked. Tall and craggy timbered close to its peaks, with the sun creating shadows on its rocky outcrops. I took several photographs which would go into my computer folder for future reference. I climbed over a gate and went down a slight decline to the creek below. Chattering over stones and slopping over others, I loved to hear the running water making its own music as it went along its way. I found a sunny spot on the grass and sat, folding my legs underneath me.

I could hear the buzzing of many bees but could not distinguish in which direction they were busy, but they just added to the ambience of the moment. I saw a large herd of beasts on the lower slopes of the mountain. They looked like Black Angus from this distance. A very peaceful pastoral scene lay before me and I was so grateful to my friends for enabling me to enjoy this moment in time, while looking after their home and Tomtom. The music of the creek was quite soothing and I understood how composers could gain inspiration from listening to the movement of water, whether a creek or an ocean, or even listening to the wind moving through the trees. The whole of nature was here within my grasp and I felt that I belonged and, moreover, that I was part of the music of life. A very humbling thought! I was brought back to reality when a shattering engine interrupted my reverie. I couldn't contemplate what it was at first and then I saw a tiny red helicopter come over the faraway hills through the trees and towards me. It grew in size as it approached then suddenly it veered away as if it didn't want to spoil my reverie. I smiled to myself and waved it goodbye. Apart from some distant crows arguing, as they do, peace reigned once more. Reluctantly I stood and retraced my steps. I was feeling hungry.

Back at the house Tomtom still slept. I had enjoyed my walk and feeling revitalised I poured myself a generous glass of Sauvignon Blanc and took a sip. Tomtom stretched and said hello, wanting to know what was happening, so I played chase with him until we both tired of the game. While he checked on the rear garden from the bathroom window, I opened a bottle of Shiraz for dinner and made a camembert sandwich. I settled down with my book and it wasn't long before Tomtom gave me the pleasure of his company and joined me for a cuddle. We shared a comfortable hour then I gave the house a quick vacuum, had a shower, put makeup on and dressed in jumper and slacks. I turned the cake out onto a wire tray and I washed my glass.

CHAPTER 8

SAYING GOODBYE

I had enjoyed my day yet I was anxious to see Kao and Hiroto. I wondered who had won the golf. I knew that Kao's handicap was seven but I wasn't aware of Hiroto's handicap. Kao and Hiroto arrived about 6.30 pm and were soon settled at the table with glass of wine discussing their day on the Ulverstone golf course. They both related some of the comical encounters (or made them up!), anyway everything they said appeared very funny helped, I am sure, by the wine we were sipping. Both Kao and Hiroto had used the shower at the motor inn before coming to Paradise so there was no need for any delays. I served dinner and both Kao and Hiroto appeared to enjoy both the main and dessert courses. We then enjoyed coffees and liqueurs. Around 9.00 pm Hiroto thanked me for the dinner and bade us both a good night. I had enjoyed my day of cooking for tonight's dinner and I had enjoyed the meal with both Kao and Hiroto. I had not seen a lot of dialogue or interaction between them previously and I had observed that each had a deep regard and respect for the other. I retired to the bathroom to remove my makeup then I slipped into bed. Kao was not far behind me. It was almost 10.30 pm though not late but I felt quite weary and I had noticed that Kao had also looked tired after his 18 holes of golf and, I suspect, a glass or two of something at the Clubhouse afterwards. I cuddled up to Kao, we kissed and shortly thereafter I fell asleep.

During the night I reached for him. He felt so good and I realised how much I would miss him when he returned to Japan. I still could not believe why I attracted him so much, but I did understand that he loved me. I had tried not to lose my heart, but in spite of this I knew that I loved him. I had tried so hard to keep some of myself to myself, but he reached into my very being and encapsulated all that I was into a small package with his name on it. Sometimes I could not breathe when he was close, nor could I think or speak. The passion I felt for him was overwhelming at times and I always wanted him. I felt a whole woman when I was with Kao. I melted in his embrace as he melted into me. Yet I still had feelings for Phil and if I had to choose I know it would always be Phil. I just couldn't reconcile this. I was perplexed and I had no answers. I thought about this conundrum: both men were very dear to me – I loved each without reservation, but how could this be? There seemed to be no answers. Guess I would just have to accept. Just as I would have to accept what the future had in store for me. I reached for Kao and ran my hand over his body. His body responded and Kao rolled over towards me, murmuring my name. We kissed and made love. It was wonderful, exciting and fulfilling. In all our lovemaking this was the most incredible. I think this was because I gave him everything I had. It was similar to our time in Singapore but at a deeper level. I just emptied myself into him, and that is how I can try and describe the experience. I felt that I had passed the last bastion and that I was Kao's lover for ever. I had no power to stop what would happen in our futures. Exhausted we kissed and whispered goodnight to each other. I felt Tomtom on the bed and he settled between us. I am sure we all slept well that night.

The rest of Kao's visit passed pleasantly enough. He had finalised the purchase of the last property we had viewed and the owner had agreed to manage the farm for Kao's Company even though this meant he would move from milking cows to managing a Wagyu beef herd. Kao had also asked me to be part of the negotiations between the owner and Hiroto, who would be staying in Sydney for another month. To which I agreed, but the news I didn't like hearing was when Kao told me that he would be with me only for one day more. Pain shot through my heart, yet I had mixed feelings over this news. I didn't want him to leave but, in way, I would be relieved as I was becoming used to having him around. Getting into bed together Kao wrapped me in his arms, saying tenderly,

"My lovely lady I do so enjoy being with you. I wish I could put you in my suitcase and take you with me", we both laughed, "I just want you to know that I love everything about you. Every time I see you I take away new insights to ponder on, which I do. I feel I am learning lots to mull over in the coming months, but I want to tell you what I love the most when I am with you". He paused, kissed me and ruffled my hair, "I love the smell of your hair, the smell of your perfume, and I love the smell of your skin. I also love the taste of you. All this heightens my need for you - all I have to do is to close my eyes and I feel you close in smell and taste. And I love the feel of your skin on my skin – the most sensuous of all. These are the things I take away with me". We kissed and our lovemaking was so gentle and tender - and wonderful.

We made the most of our last day together. Kao took me out to lunch. It was very pleasant and I thoroughly enjoyed the outing, but we were both aware that this would be our last lunch together. We held hands and promised to keep in touch. We arrived home around 3.00 pm and after appeasing Tomtom we kissed and I suggested we go to bed, which we did. We managed to sleep after a while then, when I awoke, I made my way into the kitchen. Kao followed me and announced he would like to present me with a Japanese meal to which I concurred. First he poured me a glass of Shiraz then there was much activity in the kitchen. In due course Kao called for me to sit at the table and he served me the most delicious meal I have ever tasted. After the meal I complimented Kao on his culinary expertise as we sipped our liqueurs. Kao took my hand, kissing its palm he told me how much I meant to him and that he would miss me very much indeed. I said something similar and that I couldn't imagine life without him. We returned to the bedroom and I watched while Kao packed, leaving his toiletries to pack in the morning. He talked of his plans for the new property, that he would stock it with the finest breeding Wagyu beef cattle which he would export to Japan and hopefully find markets within Australia. Kao also discussed his plans when he returned to Japan. I thought how hard he worked – usually twelve hours a day, six days a week, but he appeared to enjoy what he did. From reading his Company's 2018 Financial Report, Kao had no need to work ever again and, even though he had spoken of retirement, he had no firm plans when this would be. Kao would say when I had asked, "Oh, in about two years". It was like asking him how long a piece of string was!

As Hiroto was picking him up at 6.30 the next morning, Kao suggested we had an early night. I agreed, especially as it was almost 10 00pm so it was hardly an early night. Kao closed his suitcase and placed it on the bedroom floor. We both undressed and got into bed. I cuddled up to Kao and went over the plans for the construction of the new dwelling. He had seen the architect who had promised to draw up the house plans after consulting me, and his Project Manager would oversee the build. The architect would also employ various trade people to complete the home. Kao asked me to complete the interior, advising that I should send accounts to Kao's oldest son Thomas (Takahiro) the CEO of the Sydney office for payment. When asked about the budget for the completion of this property, which also included a driveway and landscaping, Kao revealed $700,000 had been allowed. I thought this was over generous but Kao said that it was best to come under budget than having to request extra money if the budget was too 'mean'. What came next was unexpected and a bit of shock,

"Caroline, please do not get cross with me", he kissed my hand then continued, "The Company is buying this property but it is mainly for us," he went on quickly before I could say anything, "it will be convenient for us to meet there when I return to Tasmania. I don't like the idea of having to meet in such impersonal places as hotels or motels. I want us to be happy in our own special place. Somewhere we can call home and I know, before you remind me, that it will be difficult for you to stay the night with me but that doesn't mean we can't meet and enjoy our togetherness in comfort and in private".

Well, Kao has given me a lot of surprises but this took the biscuit – I was speechless. Perhaps I was a bit slow to see this but looking back it was clear that Kao had this in mind. Otherwise why would he consult me on all matters pertaining to the properties we had visited? How could I be cross with him? Kao was still looking at me anxiously, so I smiled and kissed him and told him how wonderful he was. Kao relaxed then emphasised he had absolute confidence in me to ensure the house was built to my specification and he hugged me close. I was overwhelmed and shared my fears with Kao that this was just so big, so involved that I wouldn't be able to sustain his faith in my abilities, but Kao just laughed.

"I am sure you will build us a lovely home, somewhere we shall be very proud of" he said. Kao ruffled my hair, kissed my forehead, then my nose, then his lips found mine. Our lovemaking was slow and deliberate. I melted into Kao. Every time was different. Every time was the best, as this was.

Although I slept well, I was very aware of Kao's movements. I wondered how I would sleep without him. I loved listening to his gentle breathing as he slept. I loved cuddling up to him and I loved his response when I did. Undoubtedly I would miss Kao very much – more than I cared to think and much more than I should. The alarm awakened us both at 5.30 am. Kao rolled over and we made love one last time, then he showered and dressed. He wouldn't hear of me accompanying them to the airport. Hiroto would be with us shortly and Kao urged me to return to bed. I had made him a green tea but he refused breakfast as he said he would get this on the aeroplane. Kao was packing his toiletries when Hiroto arrived at 6.30 am. Hiroto took his suitcases and placed them in the car boot. I gave Hiroto a hug and we agreed to keep in touch during the new house build. Kao held me close. We expressed our love for each other and that we would also keep in touch. We kissed for the last time then Kao got into the car. Hiroto and Kao waved goodbye as the car disappeared down the drive and on to the main road.

I stood and listened as the car traversed the road until I could hear it no more. I was aware that he would be calling in on Phil to pick up the paintings I had packed for him and hoped that all would be well and he wouldn't provide any information to Phil about us being together. I went inside the house and closed the door behind me. Tomtom blinked and meowed. Obviously it was far too early for his sleep to be disturbed. I made a coffee and sat on the couch where Tomtom joined me. I felt lost. I wondered whether Kao could visit again later in the year as he had planned. I thought of the house he wanted me to build and how he had asked me to design the interior. He had given me something concrete I could do for us both, which would keep him close to me. I thought of all the things we had done together during his two weeks at Paradise: the long walks, the picnics down by the stream, the Council's community event we had attended, the lunch with Phil and Hiroto, the other lunches and dinners we had shared, the foot and back massages he gave me, the way he would brush my hair, and my teaching Kao how to strip and remake a bed, to iron a shirt and to cook roast lamb, together with the long talks, all contributed towards getting to know each other better – and loving each other more.

I was also pleased that Kao had ceased calling his wife 'mother', as he had since she had borne their first child and was now using her given name of Chieko. She had apparently asked why after all those years he had changed his name for her. He had replied that it was at my insistence as she was not in fact his mother but his wife which entitled her to receive respect for her as an individual. Chieko had expressed her warm feelings for me and stated that Kao had given her identity back to her – she was now a person in her own right and not just the mother of their sons, or head of domestic duties undertaken by their various servants. It was a small gesture but it had an incredible effect on Chieko and, indeed, on the family as a whole. Kao had thanked me for lifting the blinkers from his eyes as he had not understood how degrading it may have been to Chieko when it was a term of affection for him. He revealed that all his family had gained from my wisdom, especially his wife who had become a woman in her own right. He was both surprised and supportive of this change. I was so very pleased for them and grateful for Kao to take on board what I had said without dismissal of this suggestion or ridicule of the sentiments behind it. Well Kao was gone and I would, hopefully, see him again in November for his birthday. I wondered how well I would fit back into my life with Phil now that I had become used to Kao being around.

CHAPTER 9

BACK TO UVERSTONE

The next few days passed quickly and my friends arrived home after their trip, so I said goodbye to them and to Tomtom and drove home. I need not have worried about fitting into my old life, because I was happy to see Phil again and he gave me a big hug and a kiss. He had prepared a lovely meal as a welcome home surprise. We chattered about the trip George and Sonya had recently undertaken, the antics of Tomtom and the walks I had taken while at Paradise. Phil brought me up to date on his happenings while I had been away, although I had previously heard most of this during our daily telephone contact. I checked the diary and we considered the trips we had to make to see doctors and specialists, together with the social outings we had been invited to, choosing the ones we wanted to attend. I set about answering these invitations with either a no or a yes. I also checked my emails and replied to those that required answering. Meanwhile when it was sunny Phil sat outside reading a book and I often joined him. He would give me a brief review of the story so far and I discussed my book, then we both returned to reading.

Over the next few weeks life passed pleasantly enough. Phil and I spent most of our days together. We always started and finished our day with a morning and goodnight kiss. During the day we were affectionate towards each other. He usually told me he loved me several times a day and would often give me a hug. Also, when one of us had to go out on our own we would say goodbye with a kiss. We also shared the household chores and the gardening. We took it in turn to cook, with Phil being a very good cook and, thankfully, he appreciated my cooking also. We both enjoyed trying out new recipes in cakes and desserts as well as lunches and dinners.

On sunny days we would often go for a picnic at various places, perhaps by the sea or maybe at a local beauty spot. We also attended the opening of several Art Exhibitions in various towns along the coast. I still ran my pastel workshop while Phil continued to teach leather work. We often swopped news of the skills our students were accumulating and their growing interest at gaining prowess in their field. Also, we both felt fortunate at the interest in our individual crafts: Phil was selling quite a bit of his jewellery and I had sold several paintings, and this gave us both the inspiration to continue with our work. We also attended live performances in and around Ulverstone: Jazz evenings, plays, musicals and dinners relative to the organisations we were involved in so life was passing pleasantly by.

I received several e-mails from Kao, to which I replied. Kao's e-mails were full of news about his life in Japan and, of course of how he was missing me. My e-mails were in a similar vein. I found Kao's e-mails disturbing as they unsettled me and it took me some time to reschedule my brain back into Ulverstone life again. In all his e-mails Kao subtly, but persistently, mentioned my discussing our relationship with Phil, which I assiduously avoided answering. After receiving word from Kao that November was definitely when he would be over next, I mentally ticked off the weeks and days to when I would see him again. I had to consider that Kao may have met someone else during this time, as he had certainly gained an awareness of love and sex with me. In the early days of our relationship I had found his knowledge of both, well, meagre especially about a woman's climax of which he had no understanding, but he had been a fast learner and had proved a very competent lover who was both attentive to my needs and enjoyed giving me much pleasure. I wished I could clone both Phil and Kao into one person – life would then be truly wonderful! But then pigs would fly! Then I received an e-mail from Kao with news that really surprized me. He said he would be arriving in Tasmania for a brief visit and hoped I would be free for lunch, giving a date for the following week. I replied that yes, I would certainly be able to see him and was looking forward to it.

At last the day arrived when Kao would be with me. It coincided with a day I usually had a meeting, so I left home without having to give an explanation to Phil. Oh it was so good to see Kao again. We met very close to home and I directed Kao to an out of the way café where we ordered lunch. Kao said that after leaving me last time he had written a poem on the plane, and he wanted me to have it. He gave me a small piece of paper with writing on it which I read – twice. I had not had a poem written for me previously – and by one of Japan's leading poets – and I read it twice because it was so beautiful:

My soul is full of fire. It is new.
It is you. You fill my heart
With passion.

You are wisdom, you are compassion,
You are truth, you are joy.
You are love.

You are a windswept valley
Full of all these elements ...and me -
You are home.

I could hardly breathe, it was so beautiful, and I was so aware of my wonderful Kao sitting with me, holding my hand and wiping away my tears with his other hand.

"So you like it?" he asked softly and I kissed his hand in reply, unable to put my feelings into words. Kao could not stay very long, unfortunately, so we refused coffee and left the café. I sat with Kao in his car where we kissed, oh for a long time then he said he had to go. He had to be back in Sydney that same afternoon and when I queried this, as I wasn't aware of any planes flying East, he just shrugged and said he had the Company plane so he would make it OK. I thanked him for the poem and we kissed one last time and then I got out of his car and into mine. I waved Kao goodbye and watched him drive away. I was overwhelmed by his visit, his poem and his casual remark about the plane, this was something new I had learnt about him and his organisation. I sat in the car park for a while before I could summon the energy to very slowly drive home. I read the poem again before I went inside the house. I folded the paper and placed it in my diary.

The days passed into weeks and the weeks into months. Overall the weather had been good to us – some wet and windy days but mostly warm and sunny. The early blooming of daffodils, jonquils and wattles heralded that spring was just around the corner. Crops were growing well and paddocks were full of new lives with the lambs and calves in abundance frolicking in the sun. With the days becoming warmer and getting longer, I think everyone was thinking 'roll on summer'. Phil and I had started to plant our vegetable garden and already the seeds were pushing through the soil while plants were spreading and growing tall. I was planning a visit to Western Australia to visit my sisters, so I checked on the internet of available flights west. I wanted to go in the middle of September and return home for my birthday in October. In an e-mail I revealed my plans for the W.A. trip to Kao. He replied quickly suggesting I return home via Japan. I was amazed with Kao's line of thought and admonished him for it, stating that this would be out of the question. Of course he asked 'Why', which was so typical of him. Kao had all the answers and he suggested I spend the last week of my holidays with him and his family in Kyoto. He offered to fund the whole trip of flights etc. in relation to Tasmania to Perth return airfares, including cab fares, plus all the expenses relative to my trip to W.A and to Japan.

In subsequent e-mails Kao continued to cajole me into agreeing to his 'master plan', as he called it. Over the following three or four days we must have sent each other a dozen or so e-mails on the subject and, in the end, he wore me down and I capitulated. Kao was over the moon and advised that his wife Chieko was organising for their home to be completed revamped. He declared that she was as excited as he was that I would be visiting, and Kao warned me that I would be honoured as royalty! I found this daunting and said that I hadn't deserved such treatment, but Kao said Chieko was grateful for the joy I had brought to the household through my love for him. I was touched and humbled by Chieko's response to my visit. I felt privileged to be part of Kao's family and honoured by his wife's preparations for my visit. I wanted so much to meet the family and thought that my lack of Japanese and Chieko's lack of English would be no barrier for us to enjoy and appreciate each other's company.

What dampened my enthusiasm was the deception I necessarily I had to use with Phil regarding the Japanese part of my trip. I was excited to be going and was bursting to share my plans with him, but of course I could not. I also felt I was deceiving Kao as I am sure he now believed that I had told Phil of my impending trip. Gosh, life was becoming very complicated, but I had only myself to blame however, what I feared most was some sort of accident that might befall me while I was travelling to, or while in, Japan. How would I be able to explain that? I guess all would inevitably be revealed should any accident befall me!

CHAPTER 10

WESTERN AUSTRALIA and BEYOND

Well, I was all packed and ready to start my trip to Western Australia to visit my sisters. Phil was taking me to the airport. It was an early plane so we didn't linger over breakfast before loading the car with my suitcase and heading off towards the airport. After I had checked in Phil and I sat in the waiting area where we both expressed disappointment that Phil was not able to accompany me due to his ill health however, he wished me an enjoyable time and, when the flight was called, he kissed me goodbye. I waved to him from the tarmac and as I settled into my seat I sighed with relief and relaxed. I was looking forward to seeing my sisters again as the last time I had seen them was just over two years ago. Like me, getting old had posed some problems for them, as neither of them could travel to Tasmania to visit Phil and I anymore so I tried to get to Western Australia every two years or so. The flight to Melbourne was short and my plane to W.A. did not leave for another two hours so I found a comfy seat, got out my book and started to read. The time passed quickly and I was soon boarding the plane for Perth and on my way to W.A.

On landing I secured a taxi to my eldest sister's home where I was warmly welcomed by Margaret. The next week was spent shopping and just generally enjoying life with my sister. At the start of the second week Margaret and I visited Joanne and Artie, my other sister and her husband. They lived in a country town approximately two hour's drive from Margaret's home. We had a lot of fun catching up on everyone's news and reminiscing about our early life. It was great seeing Joanne and Artie again and sharing their stories with Margaret. We had a few laughs but I thought how frail my sister and her husband were becoming and, I suppose, they probably thought the same about me! Margaret and I arrived home just after 7.30 pm. I prepared a snack plate of salad vegetables and cheeses and I also poured us both a glass of white wine, so we were organised for a relaxing evening. The rest of the week was just as enjoyable. We visited Joanne and Artie again, Margaret and I had a Chinese lunch at a Perth restaurant, and I bought a couple of jumpers, which were marked down. We visited a few new suburbs which contained some good book shops – Margaret and I are avid readers so enjoyed mulling through the books on display. We also enjoyed several picnics at beautiful Scarborough Beach and North Beach, close to Fremantle. We visited the city of Fremantle several times. I loved the Coffee Strip, Cicerello's for lunch, then visiting the Roundhouse and the Maritime Museum but, most of all I loved walking along the beach. I also did a bit of the cooking to give Margaret a break from domesticity. We ruminated a lot about her life and about mine, remembering amusing times of when we were growing up, so we had a few laughs.

All too soon my time in W.A. was over and I found myself at the airport again, only leaving not arriving this time. While I was looking forward to the trip to Japan I was nervous. I had no idea what to expect and I hoped that Kao would meet me as he said he would. Now I was on my way I had some misgivings and hoped that nothing would happen that would see me having to admit to Phil that I had colluded to deceive him. We were destined to land at Tokyo Airport at 8.00 pm that night and I wanted to be fresh when we did as I did not know what would happen after this. Would we travel directly to Kyoto or would we stay overnight in Tokyo? These were the thoughts in my head as I settled back and waited for sleep to overcome me on the long flight to Tokyo. I awoke to the clink of glass and realised dinner and drinks were being served. I accepted what was offered and asked for a white wine which, in due course, I received. The meal was nothing special and instantly forgettable but the wine was drinkable. After the debris of dinner was collected I enjoyed the coffee and found that the remainder of the wine was quite nice with it. I retouched my makeup and read my book. I had finished the previous book so this was a new one that I hadn't read before and I found it to be very interesting. It was a novel about a family moving from the city to the country and contained some funny episodes the children found themselves in. After a few hours I was feeling sleepy so dozed fitfully for a while. I must have fallen asleep as the movements of my neighbour awoke me with a start. She apologised for waking me but I smiled and said it was OK as I had to wake up anyway. We made small talk for a while then I picked up my book again.

The stewardesses began to prepare for landing. The butterflies returned to my stomach. I was VERY nervous. All the things that could go wrong flitted through my consciousness. I took a deep breath and checked my makeup in the powder compact mirror. The young girl I felt to be did not return my look, instead a tired old lady looked back at me from the mirror. I felt depressed. I was confused when I should be feeling happy. I feel silly now talking about my feelings but I began to think of all the stories in the papers and on television about women disappearing when they met their overseas lovers, and I prayed that this wouldn't happen to me for no one in Tasmania knew where I was. No one knew of my diversion - Western Australia to Tasmania via Japan - it seemed ridiculous. I swallowed my misgivings and concerns and joined my fellow passengers disembarking.

I had all my customs paperwork ready but found that not one of these was necessary for, as I entered the Arrival Lounge I was ushered through the crowds and into a small room where Kao was waiting. Oh, I was so pleased to see him as I had thought I was being detained by the airport authorities!

Kao gave me a huge hug and welcomed me to Japan. An airport official took my customs information and Kao explained that these would be processed in a short while and then we would be on our way. He said due to the lateness of the hour, and because he thought I may be tired after the long flight, he had booked a room in Tokyo for the night and suggested that we should catch the bullet train to Kyoto after lunch tomorrow. This would give us time to see a little of Tokyo which he thought I may find interesting. I thanked Kao for his thoughtfulness and advised him that I really didn't want to meet his family looking as if I had been in a ship wreck! Kao laughed and told me I looked 'wonderful'. The Customs official returned with my documents all processed so Kao took my suitcase and I followed him through the airport to the exit where – yes, you guessed it – the obligatory chauffeur driven car awaited. Helping me into the car, while the driver placed my suitcase and hand luggage in the boot, Kao positioned himself as close as was possible to me and held my hand. All my misgivings and concerns evaporated. I was so pleased to be with Kao and excited to be meeting his family the following day. Even so the butterflies were still active but, I believed I would have them under control by morning.

Kao had booked us into a very swish hotel and we were heralded to our room by a uniformed employee. The room was immense with thick carpet on the floor and the fluffiest towels I had ever seen. There was a wonderful bouquet of fresh flowers on the dining table with a bowl of fresh fruit and a box of chocolates keeping it company. From the window there was a fantastic view of the lights of Tokyo and I imagined the view would also be as good in the morning. Kao was smiling as I looked around and appeared pleased with my reactions. He checked to see if I was hungry and, when I answered in the affirmative, he queried if I wanted to go down for dinner or have it brought to the room. I opted for room service, so we studied the menu. I left the ordering to Kao and said I would have a quick shower. The shower was lovely and hot. I felt my weariness evaporating and when I turned the water off Kao came into the bathroom and helped dry me. Of course we kissed and I felt that I could stay with him forever. All thoughts of my life in Tasmania were erased at that moment. Kao helped me into the guest bathrobe and we sat on the couch in the lounge/dining room, where Kao had poured us both a glass of his famous Japanese liqueur. We sipped and talked while we waited for dinner to arrive. Kao was obviously very happy to see me again and 'honoured' that I would be staying at his home. I said I had tried very hard to learn the Japanese language but I had found it very difficult although I had learnt some phrases. I tried out a few phrases and Kao corrected my pronunciation.

Dinner arrived and was served from a mobile table. The waiter poured wine for us and when he was satisfied that there was nothing further he could do he bade us a good evening and left. Kao raised his glass and toasted 'to us' after which he said, "Before we eat Caroline I would like to say again how happy I am to have you here in my country. I want you to get to know my family and to understand my life here and how you fit into it. This is something perhaps you have not considered, for you never question me about my life beyond us when we are apart so you only know a small part of who I am. I hope the next few days will not inhibit you, it may well overwhelm you, but I don't want anything I say or do to upset you and cause any friction between us". I must say that had me wondering, but Kao went on, "You know how much I love you and, to say my heart is full would be an understatement, but I am aware that you must be tired after your trip so, if you do not mind, I would like my real welcome to you to wait until the morning. It is then when we awake I can be as spontaneous as you allow but better mannered than in our first encounter as lovers". I laughed and agreed that I was tired but that I longed to snuggle down with him in bed, also that I could wait until morning, but reminded him that this was just a few hours away. With that we ate and drank and talked and talked and, eventually, retired way past midnight. It was so good to feel Kao's arms around me. We kissed and caressed each other – I loved running my fingers through Kao's hair, it was as soft as silk and, previous to meeting him, I had thought that Asian gentlemen had thick, coarse hair but this was not so in Kao's case, he had beautiful soft hair. As I slipped into sleep Kao was whispering lovingly to me and I was so looking forward to what the morrow would bring.

I awoke as if from a bad dream, although I did not know what I had been dreaming. We had left the balcony door open, as the air-conditioning was quite cold, and a lazy warm breeze was blowing into our room. I gently eased myself out of bed, cloaked myself in the bathrobe and went out onto the balcony. I leaned on the rail and took in the sights and sounds of the big city. I felt cold and could not understand why I would feel so alienated and alone. The guy I loved was just a few feet away and asleep. I was happy when I went to bed but now I felt uneasy. Was I worried about tomorrow, meeting family members I did not know? Perhaps I was feeling guilty over the subterfuge I was engaged in, deceiving Phil as to where I was? I shivered. I thought about Phil then and my change of heart to tell him about Kao. I ruminated on his response to my unburdening my guilt at his feet. I guess I wanted to clear my conscience, but at what cost? I tried to see my situation from Phil's point of view. I had always thought that my admitting to a relationship with Kao would compound his guilt for not being able to make love to me, but was I correct in assuming this? I knew that Phil was a straight down the line man. He thought in black and white, no greys and, I suddenly realised with such clarity, that this would not be the way he would act. Phil would make me make a choice between him and Kao and, if I found this difficult, he would end our marriage. That would be it! Did I want this? I know that Kao would rejoice but this wouldn't mean I would automatically move in with Kao. In fact I know I wouldn't move in with him. I accepted a long time ago that I could not live in Kao's world and he could not exist in mine, so where did that lead me.

I suddenly saw how selfish I was and had been. I wanted to tell Phil about my relationship with Kao to take away the guilt I felt and, from the beginning of my relationship with Kao, I had only thought of myself. Had I wanted to control our relationship to fit my needs? Oh gosh, what a mess this was. For a moment I felt as if I was in a Hollywood movie, it was all so surreal. If my marriage was unhappy, partly broken or I was subject to domestic violence perhaps I could be forgiven for falling in love with another man, but not one of these reasons was true. I had a perfectly happy marriage to a wonderful guy and we had shared our ups and downs together and our relationship was the stronger for this. I have no excuses for behaving as I have and, potentially, I could cause two wonderful gentlemen unhappiness or even heart break. I was in a dilemma – of my own doing. I had thought that telling Phil would be for the greater good of everyone, but I was so wrong – it wouldn't be for the greater good of anyone. No one would win, so had I decided not to tell Phil? Yes, I was adamant about that but for a different reason now, but what about Kao? Do I continue to see him and let nature take its course? I believed that Kao would, ultimately in the fullness of time, find someone else closer to home because the distance between us was tiring and tiresome. Oh, he so deserved to be happy. He was a really nice guy and, even though I have strong feelings for him, I would welcome him finding someone who he could really share his life with. I felt so sad then and a thought passed that this may be the beginning of the end with Kao.

I looked down at the traffic flowing past the hotel and wondered what everyone was doing at this hour, where they were going, but then I forced myself to remain focused on the dilemma I found myself in. Kao and his family were so looking forward to my visit and had made great preparations for it, so I could not disappoint any of them. I made up my mind that I should 1 enjoy my time with them and with Kao, but I needed to seriously talk to him about my concerns, fears or whatever I am feeling at this moment in time. I owed it to be honest with him, as we both agreed we should be. I left the balcony and slipped quietly into bed, throwing my bathrobe onto the bedside chair. I thought Kao was asleep as he was lying on his back, but he put his arm around me as I settled into the bed and asked if everything was alright. I said yes and apologised for waking him.

"My dear Caroline", he said stroking my hair, "there is nothing we cannot achieve or overcome together my lovely lady". The tears just rolled down my cheeks and I hoped he wouldn't notice. To use Kao's words – my heart was full with love and I would do anything so as not to hurt him. Kao kissed my head and tightened his arm around me, I think he knew I was upset but he allowed me the space to keep it to myself, knowing that if I had to share it with him I would do so in my own time. Eventually I went back to sleep but I slept poorly, awakening several times before falling into a dead sleep just as dawn was breaking.

CHAPTER 11

JOURNEY OF ENLIGHTENMENT

I awoke to the smell of coffee and the clink of china which I deciphered was coming from the balcony. I stretched, put on the bathrobe as I got out of bed and went into the bathroom. After brushing my hair, my teeth and washing my face I joined Kao sitting outside enjoying the early morning sun. He arose as I joined him. He hugged and kissed me and asked me how I was. He looked at me intently as I said that I was fine. He said he would be there for me if I needed a friendly ear and I thanked him. We sipped our coffees and Kao suggested that I may find a familiarisation trip around Tokyo interesting before we travelled to Kyoto, and I agreed this was a good idea. He hadn't ordered breakfast but was waiting for me to decide what I wanted to do. I was happy to eat in our room and that appeared to suit Kao also as he rang room service and ordered. I wasn't very hungry so only wanted some fruit to eat and there was plenty of that in our room for me to pick out what I wanted. Kao ordered his usual of steamed rice, miso soup, grilled fish, and various side dishes which included *tsukemono* (Japanese pickles), *nori* (dried seasoned seaweed), *natto* (fermented soybeans), *kobachi* (small side dishes consisting of vegetables), and a green salad. These I added to my knowledge of the spoken Japanese – which was limited. Kao had brought out onto the balcony the bowl of fruit when he returned from ordering breakfast and I chose an apple and an orange, cutting them both up into bite sized portions

I felt a bit uncomfortable as Kao was a shrewd judge on how I was feeling, but I expected that this was an essential element of his business however, I was aware that he was watching me and that he sensed that all was not well. Kao took my hand and queried,

"You are happy to be here with me in Japan?" My eyes met his as I squeezed his hand I said that of course I was. I told him how much he meant to me, leaning over and kissing him gently. Kao raised my hand and kissed it saying how much it meant to have me here, getting to know him better, meeting his family and visiting his place of work. He said that he would do everything possible to make my visit enjoyable and that my happiness was his happiness. I felt like crying. As usual he was very sweet.

At that moment Kao's breakfast arrived so I said that I would have a shower while he ate so the bathroom was free when he wanted a shower. He just nodded. I kissed his forehead and moved into the bathroom. Once there I had a wonderful hot shower and as I turned the water off I found Kao waiting with a lovely fluffy towel. He helped to dry me then he disrobed for his shower. I never tired of looking at his body. He was very fit and, he had told me, that when at home he enjoyed walking, cycling and playing golf as well as working out in the gym. Also, he said that he tried to keep up a standard of physical fitness when away from home. Well, I could testify to that as in Paradise he worked out almost every day. In comparison I felt a bit of a blimp – well, my only exercise was walking. I tried to do this every day but I didn't always succeed! I dried my hair and was beginning to get dressed when Kao joined me after his shower. He kissed the nape of my neck and when I turned around his kiss was long and passionate. I pulled him towards the bed where we made love. Oh, I had missed him so much and it was so good to be with him again. Afterwards I lay curled up in his arms. I then knew what Kao had meant when he said in Paradise that he was home, because I felt just that – that I was home because where Kao was, well, that was home.

Kao declared that we had both wasted a lot of water as we had to shower again, and we both laughed. He graciously let me shower first. I showered quickly and he was quick to follow suit. I had already dressed and was putting on some makeup when Kao joined me. Catching my arm he sat on the edge of the bed and pulled me towards him until I was sitting on his knee.

"Caroline my lovely lady," he said, "I do not know what ails you, what I do know is that you have something on your mind. I am not asking you to reveal what that might be but only to say I wish I could help in some way. I hope you will tell me when you think the time is right. I remember what you have always told me: *A problem shared is a problem halved.* I hope you will enjoy the day I have planned for us and that you will begin to have happier thoughts". We kissed and there was no doubt about how we felt about each other. Just like the kisses of the previous evening – two people in love and enjoying each other's company – kissing was all that was required. I looked forward to the day ahead.

We left our hotel and traversed the way deeper into Tokyo city. We visited the Imperial East Garden where once Tokugawa Shogun governing during the 17th and 18th centuries and later emperor Meiji who ruled during the 19th century resided in Edo Castel. Although the main buildings no longer exist, we could make out the remains of walls, gates, moats, guardhouses and the foundation of the massive castle tower which stood on the hill. An elegant and beautiful Japanese garden has been created at the foot of the hill where the secondary circle of defence once stood. This area also includes a bamboo grove, rose garden and iris garden and the overall perfume was almost hypnotic. We enjoyed this beautiful oasis in the middle of a very large and busy city for over an hour then Kao hailed a taxi and we embarked on a revealing trip across the city taking in a sake brewery where we learnt how sake is made, the beautiful Meniji Shrine together with the Senso-ji Temple then we took a boat and enjoyed lunch sailing around Tokyo Bay. We admired the views of the Rainbow Bridge and I was enjoying a rest as well as the lovely meal and the wine. It was good to take a breather from all the walking we had done that morning however I did appreciate Kao taking the time to show me around, because I was aware of the political climate in Japan at this time and wondered if Kao actually should be elsewhere.

We were enjoying our coffee when Kao took my hand, looking at the eternity ring he had given me in Singapore and rubbing his thumb across it. I wondered what he was thinking and what he was trying to find the right words to say.

"Caroline we should move on to Kyoto soon. I hope you are as excited as I am that you will be visiting my home. I still hope that one day it will also be your home" he smiled and squeezed my hand then he raised it to his lips and kissed my palm. "I am nervous about your visit and hope you like everything I have. I am sure you will like my cats". He laughed then continued, "I think sometimes that you feel uncomfortable about how I live my life which, I know, is so very different from yours but I am sure you will keep an open mind and take into consideration our cultural differences". I nodded in agreement and reassured Kao that I too was excited as I was keen to learn more about him and his life in Japan. Kao explained that we were to embark on the journey to Kyoto by the Bullet Train or *Shinkansen*, which was not only the fastest, but it incorporated speed with comfort. It sounded a great way to travel and I was looking forward to the journey.

We alighted from the boat and made our way to the railway station. I was amazed at the number of eateries and variety of the food offered. Just walking through Tokyo Station was a culinary adventure. The train arrived a few minutes later. We boarded and I found the seats functional and comfortable. Kao disclosed that we were in a Green Car, which was apparently equivalent to Western First Class. Kao held my hand and spoke about the journey, where the train stopped and how long the journey took. I was surprised to learn that the *Nozomi* Bullet Train traversed the 515 kilometres at an average speed of 300 kilometres an hour. We covered the distance between Tokyo and Kyoto in less than 2 hours - I had never travelled at such a land speed before.

It was a beautiful sunny day without a cloud in the sky. The outside temperature was 36 degree but in the carriage it was a cool 22 degrees and very pleasant. We travelled through countryside varying between undulating pastures and belts of woodland beyond which were mountains. The land was interspersed with a smattering of farms and other buildings which I assumed were villages. The landscape was really beautiful and some parts were similar to Tasmania so I was content, enjoying the views while holding hands with Kao. He appeared happy also and I hoped that he was no longer concerned about what had been worrying me earlier. Kao had ordered drinks for us which were nonalcoholic fruit and vegetable juice - and delicious. I was feeling confident that all would go well in meeting his family. I was particularly looking forward to meeting Chieko, Kao's wife, and their youngest son, Haruki. Kao put his arm around my shoulder and kissed my cheek. He said I looked happy and I was. I think he was relieved, and I thought this must be an enormous responsibility for him as head of his home to ensure that all went well, and I would have to be very careful not to do or say anything which would make Kao lose face in front of his family or those who serve him. I promised myself that I would enjoy this time with everyone and take away lots of happy memories. I felt somehow that our relationship had moved on. I wasn't sure what that meant but I felt a subtle shift in our relationship – I was feeling emotionally closer to Kao and this was unexpected, in light of what I was thinking earlier today. I thought that as I was confusing myself, so I must be confusing

Kao. Maybe I just thought too much. It felt so good being close to Kao. I could feel him breathing as I cuddled up closer to him. I felt him squeeze my shoulder in response so I closed my eyes and enjoyed the moment. Kao whispered that he loved me and stroked my face with the back of his hand. There was nowhere else I wanted to be. All too soon the train began to slow and we prepared to alight. I queried whether we would be met and Kao said there would be a car waiting but I would have to prepare myself for the welcome I would receive this evening at his home. Kao helped me into the car and we held hands while Kao pointed out places of interest to me saying that he was looking forward to showing me Kyoto in the coming days.

At last we turned off the road and drove through ornate gates. As the car slowed Kao explained that the road eventually led to the family's Shinto shrine. "Shrines are made of natural materials, ours is made of cypress wood, and they are designed to provide a home for the particular *kami* or god to whom they are dedicated however, a shrine is not restricted to a single *kami*. Like ours, entrances to shrines are marked by wooden *Torii* gates, painted orange or black which symbolise the boundary between the secular everyday world and the infinite world of the kami. I would like to show you our shrine if you are interested Caroline", Kao smiled when I said I would love to see it.

The car weaved its way through an avenue of cherry trees, unfortunately the blossoms had finished but I could imagine how lovely this avenue would be when the trees were in full blossom. The house was incredible. I felt once more that I was on a movie set! It was an old Japanese two story wooden house, with a tiled roof that had intricately carved eaves, shutters and doors with designs of various leaves, flower petals and faces (that I thought resembled monkeys) decorating it. Red paint dominated the structure. It looked too small for a

family of five and then there were the servants to house
however, as we walked through the front door I could see the
house had depth enough to house the family and then some.
Later, I would find that the servants had their own homes
behind the main house, close enough to be on hand when
required but far enough away for privacy for both parties.

We removed our shoes in the *genkan* and put on the
slippers provided. A young girl helped me with mine before
kneeling and sliding open a paper door. Kao ushered me into a
sparsely furnished room with several cushions arranged neatly
on the floor around a small table. When I turned to face him
we were alone. I looked to Kao for help as I didn't know what
to do, but as I went to ask him what I should do, the young girl
returned with hot cloths to wipe our hands and face. Kao then
showed me around the rest of the ground floor which was very
typical of Japanese living until the 1950's, as Kao informed
me. Through a door behind the traditional rooms I discovered
were the private quarters of Chieko while Kao's apartment
took over the entire first floor. I followed Kao up the stairs and
into his apartment.

I walked into a wonderfully furnished room. No
hardship here! The left and right walls were each hung with
ornately traditional clothing decorated in red and gold patterns.
There was a king sized bed next to the wall directly in front of
where we stood. Full length windows at either end of the room
framed views of the front of the house, with its avenue of
cherry trees. The window at the opposite end of the room
overlooked the rear showing a beautiful typical Japanese
garden in Shinto style (rather than Zen Buddhist style as more
familiar Japanese gardens are designed, Kao explained). At the
bottom of this garden a wooded area containing a variety of
bamboo and elm trees stood. Kao led me across the room and
through another door which opened onto a sitting room
comfortably furnished with a three-seater couch and two large

armchairs, a bookcase which ran the length of the room. There was a writing desk against the other wall with a Japanese lute (*satsuma biwa*) hanging on the wall behind it. The floor was covered with a richly coloured carpet and the design echoed that of the window furnishings.

As I gazed around the room, I took in the wonderful pottery jars and other relics of a bye gone age which added to the richness of the room. For all this, the room had an intimate and cozy feel to it and I felt that I could easily adapt to living here! Kao was standing next to me and I realized that he was watching me closely as I took everything in.

"It's an inspiring room" I breathed with a smile, "Just wonderful". Kao face creased in a smile, he looked relieved. "You like it then?" he queried and put his arm around my shoulders. "Of course I do, it really is lovely". "Good," he said then, "I will leave you now so you can freshen up. We will have pre-dinner drinks at 6.30 pm then dinner at 7.00 pm. Is that OK?" he asked. I nodded and I asked where I would meet him. He gave me directions, to retrace my steps back down the stairs, and he would be waiting for me. Kao kissed me gently and stroked my cheek saying he would see me later, stating that he had bought me a dress which I could wear that evening if I wanted to, adding that I was under no obligation to do so. I smiled as he left me. My eyes searched the room for this dress and when I had found it I was not disappointed. It was made of really beautiful shot silk which shone a deep magenta or turquoise depending on how the material moved and how the light touched it. It was sleeveless with a deep vee neck and a very full ballerina length skirt. It had a filmy translucent jacket with three quarter sleeves which echoed the colours of the dress. On a bedside table there was a velvet box with a note, it read:

"My dear lady, my heart is so full of love for you and the honour you have brought to my home by agreeing to spend time with my family. I cannot thank you enough so I hope you will accept these small tokens of what you mean to me. You are free to wear them or not, whatever you wish. I have had great pleasure in choosing this gift for you and my wish is for you to take it home, together with my love and affection. I look forward to officially welcoming you to my home this evening, as do the rest of my family.

Eternally yours, Kao".

My eyes filled and I had to dab them with a tissue so I could see what was in the box. As usual Kao had both surprised and amazed me. The box contained a pair of beautiful diamond drop earrings together with a matching diamond necklace - I wondered how I would explain this when I returned home!

I loved Kao for his generosity and thought of the pleasure he would gain when he saw me wearing them. I walked into the bathroom, disrobing as I went, ran the shower and stood under it. Oh, the water felt so good. I could feel myself revitalized after the day walking around the sights of Tokyo and travelling in the Bullet train. I thought of the dress and the diamonds and how Kao would have taken such care to choose them especially for me and I knew that I just had to wear them tonight. I was a bit disappointed that Kao wasn't here with me but I justified his absence by thinking of all the arrangements he had to make, and was making, to ensure that I had a pleasant evening. I dried myself and rubbed a towel through my hair before putting on the bathrobe. I reached for the hairdryer and started to dry my hair and was surprised to hear a knock at the door.

Thinking that it must be Kao I called out for him to enter and was surprised to find the young girl I had seen downstairs earlier enter the bedroom. She motioned that she was here to help me and introduced herself as Akiko. She dried my hair and, when I moved into the bedroom, I found that Akiko had arranged my underwear on the bed and was ready to help me get dressed. After I had been dressed in my bra and panties I attended to my makeup and, when I was satisfied, she helped me into the dress and zipped me up. She then placed the necklace around my neck, fastened it then helped with the earrings. I was amazed at the person who looked back at me from the full length mirror. The dress was really beautiful as were the diamonds which shone brightly in the late evening light. I thanked Akiko in Japanese, *arigato,* and she bowed before leaving the room. I put on the little voile jacket making sure the diamond necklace wasn't obscured, checked that the earrings were centered and that my makeup was OK then I took a deep breath and opened the door to the landing. My watch read 6.25 pm so I hoped this was an acceptable time to make an appearance. I walked down the first six steps of the staircase and reached the landing where the stairs turned to the right before descending a further six steps to the large entrance hall.

CHAPTER 12

ACCEPTANCE

As I turned the corner I nearly fainted as there were two rows of people lined up after the last step leaving room for me to walk between. I supposed the family were on the right as I spied Kao as first in line, and I guessed the servants were on the left as two women held platters of finger food and two men held trays of drinks. All family members were beautifully dressed in traditional Japanese kimonos. Kao was dressed in a black top together with pleated pants. The family crest was embroidered in gold on each side of the jacket chest together with a large, engraved metal crest fastening his jacket (I presumed). He wore wooden shoes with white socks and a small black hat. He looked magnificent. An elderly woman was at his side, I presumed she would be Chieko. She was slightly shorter than me and a little slimmer. She was dressed immaculately. Her kimono was maroon, richly embodied with the images of white storks, a symbol of longevity, and the waistline sash (*obi*) was brocade which beautifully matched the colours of the kimono.

Kao came forward and took my hand as I descended the last two stairs saying, "Let me introduce my family Caroline. Caroline this is my wife Chieko". I smiled at the wonderful woman who was making me so welcome in her home. In Japanese I said, *"Anata ga watashi o anata no utsukushī ie de totemo kangei shite kudasaru koto o kōei ni omoimasu"*. ("I am honored that you make me so welcome in your beautiful home".) I bowed before her. She politely thanked me as she bowed. I then reached forward and gave her a big hug. She had tears in her eyes as she hugged me back. She thanked me for bringing much happiness into her home. I couldn't translate everything she said but some words didn't need translation, facial expressions spoke volumes. Kao looked surprised then stated that Hiroto, next in line, needed no introduction. I acknowledged Hiroto and we both bowed, then Kao introduced me to his youngest son Haruki whom I had not met previously. Again, we both bowed. With the introductions over, the servants offered food and drinks to everyone and Chieko made sure that I was served and had plenty to nibble on while sipping the drink that Kao had chosen for me. I was grateful he had done this as I had no wish to offend Chieko by choosing a drink only to find I disliked it.

I felt truly blessed and found that it was all so amazing - the colours, the people, the ambience – I reminded myself I had to be on my best behaviour and promised myself that I would make sure I kept my drinking to a minimum, this was not a day to get even a little tipsy! Chieko appeared happy that I had spoken a little Japanese and we managed to continue to communicate with my little Japanese, her little English and gestures. Of course both Kao's sons could speak fluent English and they helped as did Kao when either I or Chieko had difficulty understanding the other. I caught Kao's eyes which were bright and shining, his face aglow. He looked very happy and I was so pleased for him that, so far, everything was going to plan and turning out well. I smiled at him and he smiled back. I could read the message in his eyes and hoped he was able to read mine. I turned back to Hiroto who was explaining the various kimonos and the meaning of the designs, which I found fascinating

All too soon a mellow gong sounded and Kao approached and placed my hand on his arm. He went to lead me into dinner but I stood aside and gestured for Chieko to go ahead. This was important as, although I was obviously an honoured guest, this was her home and she should be deferred to. As she passed me on the arm of Hiroto I bowed and she smiled her thanks. Kao was obviously pleased with my gesture and squeezed my hand. I found I was sitting between Chieko and Kao at a rectangular table with the rest of the family accommodated around the same table. I was surprised to find settings for four additional places but these were vacant. I obviously didn't remark on this as I supposed that some dinner guests were running late. However, Chieko was to enlighten me through Kao that she had expected their eldest son, Takahiro, and his family to join them but unfortunately business had kept them in Sydney and they were not able to attend 'this very important occasion'. I was overwhelmed that she thought my visit was such and, moreover, had invited all the family to be here to welcome me. I relayed my feelings through Kao to Chieko.

The first course of dinner was already on the table and appeared to be a traditional Japanese meal consisting of small bowls containing a variety of vegetables and pickles. I wasn't sure what was expected of me or from which bowls I should select the food to eat as I was familiar with only a couple of these dishes, but dear old Kao came to my rescue and served me a small portion from four bowls. Kao chose *sabazushi*, which is pickled mackerel tightly wrapped around rice and encased in a thin sheet of *kombu* seaweed, a dish that I adore. He also chose s*enmaizuke*, a delicious Kyoto pickle made from a local white turnip root called *shogoin*. The thinly sliced turnip is seasoned with sweet vinegar, *konbu* seaweed and *togarashi* pepper. *Senmaizuke* means 'thousand layer pickle' and the thin disks of pickle are super crunchy with a sweet and sour taste. He also chose another two portions of food I was not familiar with but I trusted Kao to know what I would like so was quite happy with everything he had chosen. I gratefully thanked him. Luckily Phil and I ate Chinese food frequently so I was able to use chopsticks, while not as adept as my Japanese friends I did not disgrace myself and I believe I received a bit of respect for using these and not the knife and fork provided in my cutlery setting. I was enjoying the food and the wine but had to ask Kao not to keep filling up my glass as I was afraid I would become tipsy, but Kao assured me that the wine was non-alcoholic and that he had chosen it especially as he rarely drank alcoholic beverages. Again, I thanked him and relaxed, it really was a beautiful wine. Throughout this first course Kao explained that the type of food we were eating was known as Kyoto kaiseki, or *Kyo-kaiseki*, which uses the simple flavours of Japanese traditional Kyoto cooking. Kyoto cooking is seen as an art form, balancing taste, colour, and texture, but Kao emphasised that Kyoto kaiseki was usually a meal in itself so the dishes presented were only part of the whole experience. It was obviously Kao wanted me to learn as much about Kyoto as possible during my short stay and he was eager to share some of the history of Kyoto.

"Caroline, Kyoto is Japan in a nutshell. It is the cultural and historical heart of the country and the best place in Japan to experience traditional temples, shrines, gardens, geisha, shops, restaurants and festivals. This is because Kyoto escaped the devastation of the atomic bombs of the last war, so most of the ancient buildings and lifestyle remained untouched. Kyoto is renowned for its specialist food and for the Nishijin Textile Centre in the weaving district here in Kyoto which also has a museum, a shop selling kimono and obi, together with other textile goods. I would like to take you and show you what they produce while you are here."

I told Kao I would be very interested in seeing everything that Kyoto had to offer. Kao leant towards me and whispered that he and his family had prepared a surprise for me. I asked what this may be but he only laughed and said it would no longer be a surprise if he told me. Chieko was trying to follow our conversation, which had been in English. She leaned forward and asked Kao why we were amused. Kao was still laughing and obviously told her where she also laughed but in her napkin. She patted my hand and we smiled at each other, her eyes twinkling in merriment.

Well, I didn't have to wait long for my surprise. The used dishes and bowls were soon cleared from the table when a man servant approach Chieko and she and Kao excused themselves from the table. They went out of the room and into the front hallway. I couldn't see what was happening as they closed the door behind them. They reappeared a few minutes later followed by a tall man, a lovely lady and two delightful children. I gasped with surprise as the man was the image of Kao and could only be his eldest son fresh from Sydney. There was much joyfulness as the newcomers were introduced to me as Takahiro their eldest son, his wife Ikumi, and their two children, a daughter aged 6 called Chikata and a 4 year old son, Kimiya. Ikumi was dressed in a beautiful aqua kimono with a matching obi and looked enchanting while the children were dressed in simple robes or *yukata* (lightweight kimonos). Chikata was dressed in a pink kimono with splashes of a deeper pink with a matching obi, while Kimiya wore a white kimono patterned with various hues of blue animals and sporting a blue obi. Takahiro was dressed similarly to Kao, but I didn't think he looked as splendid! I was amazed how alike Kao and Takahiro were, there was no denying that they were father and son and I presumed this was the surprise that Kao had referred to.

Takahiro and his family took their places at the table and refused the first course as the next course was due to be brought out. Kao and Chieko were smiling in anticipation – of what I wondered. I did not have to wait long. Soon the bowls for the next course were being placed on the table and I just couldn't believe my eyes for in each of the bowls placed on the table the composites of the meal resided – roast potatoes, roast carrots, green beans, AND roast lamb! Small jugs contained mint sauce and a rich looking brown gravy. I must have looked surprised because Kao and Chieko were laughing and everyone smiled as the joke was shared. I loved the way a simple Aussie dish was presented in Japanese style. I just laughed and shook my head. I helped myself to the food displayed - no help required from Kao this time.

I felt everyone watching me as I helped myself from the bowls of meat and vegetables. When I came to the mint sauce and gravy I poured a little gravy on top of my accumulated meat and vegetables, then took a piece of meat in my chopsticks and dipped it in the mint sauce before eating it. When everyone was satisfied that all was well, they all helped themselves from the bowls in front of them and I imagine there were many different comments about the fare. Kao leaned forward and whispered that he hoped I had not minded the ruse and, more surprising, he admitted to having prepared and cooked the roast lamb. I had enjoyed the joke with everyone and I was impressed as well as fortunate to have Kao who had obviously worked hard to please me. We laughed together (I remembered to laugh into my napkin) while enjoying the meal, albeit a very different version to which I was accustomed. I noticed that most of the family had left the mint sauce uneaten in their bowls. I understood that mint sauce was a very much an acquired taste so I was not surprised, but most of the meat and vegetables had been eaten and I found that even a roast meal could be eaten with chopsticks - if it was served Japanese style.

When all the dishes had been cleared away an array of delicious desserts filled the table. Kao described them for me: coffee jelly, a simple dessert of jelly made with black coffee and topped with whipped cream and vanilla icecream; *anmitsu*, a delightful combination of different textures including firm *kanten* jelly, sweet fruits, chestnuts and a coarse sweet red bean paste called *anko*, made from red algae. The cubes of white translucent jelly was *agar*, a much more powerful gelling agent than gelatin. The small pot of black syrup, known as *mitsu*, was served on the side with green tea ice cream also decorating this dish. I asked Kao to stop there as I would not remember everything he had described. He laughed and just said to help myself as he was sure I would love everything offered. He was quite correct. I did enjoy everything I ate. The desserts were delightful. I felt extremely full - but more was to come! Served with dessert were several dessert wines and several bottles of sake which, I was informed, were all different according to the prefectures where they were produced. Kao poured me a dessert wine which I found was just beautiful, but he also poured me a Kyoto sake which was also very nice AND powerful – I felt my knees go weak almost immediately and was pleased I was seated! I refused a second glass. There was lots of talk around the table, in English as well as Japanese and the ambiance was warm and friendly. I felt truly blessed to be accepted and welcomed into such a wonderful family. Kao had a healthy glow about him which wasn't only due to the fact that I appeared happy but probably more related to the amount of sake he had drunk.

Ikumi was making her excuses as she arose from the table to take the children to bed. She brought them over to Kao and Chieko to have goodnight kisses and I was overwhelmed when they put their hands around my neck and kissed me too. I must confess I really choked up and had to swallow hard. Ikumi smiled at me and said in perfect English how pleased she was to meet me and we should see more of each other before I returned home. I agreed and Kao squeezed my hand. As she left the room Kao and I smiled at each other and Kao whispered whether I was tired, I acknowledged that I was and he smiled.

"Well Caroline, I think we should also make our excuses". I asked whether we should wait for Chieko to leave first and he raised his left eyebrow and asked, "And who is master of this house Madam?" I smiled and capitulated. He arose from the table and pulled my chair back so I could also leave. We said our goodnights to Chieko and the rest of the family when Chieko made a comment to Kao, who actually blushed. I looked at him questioningly but he just smiled and took my hand.

We left the room and mounted the stairs to Kao's apartments. When we entered, Kao closed the door and kicked off his wooden shoes, exclaiming that they were not very comfortable. I told him how wonderful he and all his family had looked all decked out in their formal gear. I wondered what Chieko had said to make him blush. He laughed and said she had alluded to what we may get up to when we went to bed. I laughed too and thought that Chieko had seemed to be a very proper Japanese lady but really she was just a woman like the rest of us. Kao pulled me close and gave me a very loving kiss. He said he was very proud of me and that I had endeared myself to everyone. He also spoke of his feelings for me and that he felt he could not love me any more than he did just at this moment. We kissed again then Kao said he had to have a shower and I said I would have one after he finished in the bathroom. Kao helped me out of my beautiful dress and he unfastened the lovely diamond pendant and I thanked him for his generosity. It took a long time for Kao to make it to the shower!

CHAPTER 13

LEARNING MORE

At last I was enjoying the heat of the running water and felt all my tension disappearing. I hadn't realised how stressed I had been throughout dinner, even though the atmosphere had been relaxing and friendly. As usual Kao was waiting with a towel and helped dry me – between kisses, of course. We eventually found ourselves in bed where Kao made love with his usual tenderness ending with such passion that we were both exhausted. I lay in his arms, neither of us spoke, words were not necessary. I guess we slept for a while and when I surfaced Kao was reading his book in the lounge room. I struggled awake, got out of bed and put on my dressing gown. Kao greeted me and asked whether I was hungry. I was still full after dinner and said so. Kao smiled and advised he had prepared two drinks for us. I asked what they were and he just replied, "Guaranteed to make you feel wonderful". I sipped my drink and it was just delicious and I told Kao so. We discussed the family reunion and I expressed my impressions of the evening. Kao was overjoyed with my reactions to his family's attire (the kimono) the meal, his family and the formality yet friendliness of the evening. He was especially pleased with my reaction to the kimono. Moreover, Kao revealed again that he was so proud of me. He said that from the moment I appeared on the stairs he was in awe of me.

When I looked puzzled he explained that coming down the stairs I looked so at home in his home.

"You were just so_beautiful Caroline - not that I don't think you are always beautiful - but this was special. You were in my home and you appeared as if you had always been there. You looked so regal, I almost gasped – the dress, the diamonds well, they just added to your natural beauty. I felt my heart stop and I could hardly breathe. Then you spoke in perfect Japanese, thanking Chieko in appropriate formal style, it was so majestic, then you finished with a hug. This was so unexpected as we Japanese are not so demonstrative. Chieko was almost overcome she hadn't expected such warmth from you. We were all moved by your simple but amazing show of respect and friendship. I don't think there were any dry eyes". His eyes were bright and full of love. I answered saying that I was just so honoured because everyone had dressed so formally and this had made me feel honoured, very special and very welcome.

Kao smiled and said that I did not realise how profound my influence had been and how he had mellowed due to my influence.

"I seem to have a new zest for life which all my family have recognised. My family will be forever in your debt for making me more human", he laughed before continuing, "Oh, Caroline, you have no idea the impact you have had on me and, by extension, all my family members. I cannot thank you enough for taking the blinkers from my eyes and allowing me to see the world as it really is. I owe you so much". He kissed my hand again but his eyes were closed. I felt Kao's emotion and I kissed the top of his head. We sipped our drinks and revelling in each other's company. Kao collected our glasses and placed them on the coffee table in front of us. We discussed the activities Kao wanted us to be involved in during the next few days. I told him that Chieko had asked me to spend the next morning with her and I had agreed to go to her apartment at 10.00 am the following day. Kao appeared pleased that we would be getting to know each other better. He said he'd had a quick discussion with his eldest son who advised that he and his wife wanted to spend the afternoon with us tomorrow and had suggested lunch in Kyoto. Chieko would be very happy to have the children as she didn't see them very often so that would leave the afternoon free for the four of us to enjoyed time together when I could get to know Takahiro and Ikumi better. Kao added that both spoke good English so I had no need to worry about communications.

He paused before asking if I would like to join him when he visited the family's Shinto shrine at 8.00 am the next day. Kao explained that the nature of a Shinto *jinja* or shrine is a sacred place where *kami,* the gods, live and which demonstrate the power and nature of the kami. Every village and town or district in Japan will have its own Shinto shrine, as will many private homes, dedicated to the local kami. Japanese see shrines as the source of their spiritual vitality and often attend the same shrine regularly throughout their lives that is why it is important to have one in the home. "Our shrine was built by my ancestor over 800 years ago, enlarged some 300 years ago and throughout history our family have regularly honoured the *kami* who have enabled us to have a good life", Kao revealed. "*Jinja* are both restful places filled with a sense of the sacred, and as such we regard them as our spiritual home"

Kao continued, "Shrines need not be buildings - rocks, trees, and mountains can all act as shrines, if they are special to kami that is why *Jinja* are often located in the landscape that emphasises their connection to the natural world, and often include sacred groves of trees, and streams, as you see here in our own garden leading to the shrine. Thus, showing the coexistence between individual man and the whole earth, celestial bodies and deities, whatever name they are given." I found this most illuminating. Kao's ability to get me to understand something that was so important to him was humbling. He said that Japanese people don't visit shrines on a particular day each week. People go to major shrines at festival times, and at other times when they feel like doing so. Japanese often visit the local shrine when they want the local *kami* to do them a favour such as good exam results, a good outcome to a surgical operation for a relative, and so on. I was impressed with what I had heard and when Kao added that he would like to ask the Priest to bless our union I did not mind. I understood how much this would mean to Kao so I indicated that I would be pleased for this blessing to take place. I could see at once that Kao was very happy with my reply. Kao said he was interested in me understanding more of the Shino way of life and wanted me to visit two *Jinja* as well the family's shrine.

The first, Fushimi Inari Taisha, was the largest in Japan and one of the oldest, having been erected in 711. It is apparently dedicated to the rice goddess Inari and, more widely, to wealth. Kao mentioned that there was a beautiful walk marked by thousands of vermillion porticos called *torii* but he thought that, although it was beautiful, I might find it rather tiring. He would also like me to see Heian-jingu, a Shinto sanctuary located north-east of Kyoto which was built in 1895. I was impressed but thought I might be Shinto-ed out by the end of my visit however, I was enraptured by Kao's enthusiasm to show me as much as possible of his life in Kyoto. Kao continued that it was his family's responsibility to maintain these shrines and to support the lifestyle of the priests involved. This, Kao added, was a traditional responsibility for his family since his ancestors had established these within the crafts of stonemason and master stone carver and had donated these to the community and, Kao explained, was still seen as an important element of the family's responsibilities. Kao also revealed that later in the week he would like to take me visit a Sumo training academy to watch a Sumo wrestling match, also to visit to Hiro Imafuji, a kendo trainer. Kao said he was very interested in this traditional sword fighting which was quite competitive in Japan. Kao informed me that it involved a long, single-edged sword used by Japanese samurai similar to *katana* (sword) training which involves a wooden bokken (bokuto) or *shinai*.

Kao said he would also like me to witness a concert of traditional musical instruments including the *biwa*, a traditional four stringed lute, *koto*, a traditional stringed musical instrument originated from the Chinese *zheng*, and *taikos* or drums. I asked whether the *biwa* was similar to the one he had hanging on the wall over the writing desk. Kao was surprised but pleased with my observation and said that his was also a *biwa*. He continued that he wanted to show me Nijo-jo, a castle located in the city centre. He explained that it was built in 1603 for Tokugawa Ieyasu and was the residence of the first shogun of the Edo period (1603 – 1867). This is quite wonderful as, apparently, it has floors known as nightingale floors that chirp when you walk on them. They are designed as a defence against ninja assassins. We both laughed at this and I said I would feel very safe exploring this building. Kao further explained that at the end of the Ieyasu reign, the castle of Nijo was converted into an imperial palace for the Shogun with a second building representing the Emperor's Palace. The Shogun's Palace was handed over to the city of Kyoto and then opened to the public as a tourist site in the 20th century and was listed as a World Heritage Site by UNESCO in 1994. I could see that my visit was going to be full on every single day.

Kao stated that all the members of his family were committed to serving the community in whatever way they could and sited many examples of community involvement from helping to build schools, medical centres and hospitals to, more closer to home, educating their servants' children throughout primary, secondary and trades schools or through to university. He said they were also involved in assisting these children to gain employment on graduation. When I queried the former assistance to build schools etc., Kao said his company would work with prefectures who would supply the materials while his company would provide the workforce and machinery necessary to complete each project. Kao said that in the past his family would help find wives and husbands for their employee's children when they became of age. I was overwhelmed by Kao's commitment to his community and expressed this to Kao.

While he appeared surprised, Kao was also obviously pleased if a little embarrassed, that I was so impressed.

"Well Caroline, our commitment is not just to this community or to Japan," he said, "our company is available to help poverty, illness and natural disasters in any country in any part of the world. For instance, through Foodbank we distributed over 25 million meals to impoverished Australians during 2017/2018 year, through Slingshot we assisted new businesses get started and, through our subsidiarity company, National Foods, we purchased the Dairy Farmer Milk Co-operative and we can now offer considerable discounts to members, supermarkets and the wider communities throughout New South Wales and South Australia as well as cutting the costs of producing high quality milk and its by-products".

My head was spinning. Although I had surmised that Kao's company was large and multi-faceted, I was only just realising that I had greatly underestimated its scope – so I said "Wow!" which made Kao laugh. He reached over and kissed me on the cheek, his eyes twinkling. I shook my head and thanked him for the thumb nail sketch of his company. He obviously had not heard of that expression before as he looked quizzically at me, so I explained. We both laughed. Kao said that was enough for one night and he would tell me more when I asked for more. Kao then announced that I deserved a hot chocolate. He stood up and walked to a door which I had thought led to a cupboard as it was very inconspicuous but I was very surprised to see that when Kao opened the door he entered into a small kitchen. Kao was humming away to himself as he made the drinks before taking them into the bedroom. "I thought you might like them in bed as it is getting late", he said as he returned to the lounge. I expressed my delight as I stood up and made my way into the bedroom. Kao followed me and helped me into bed, arranging the sheet and doona over me, making sure I was well covered. I almost disappeared from sight, the bed was so soft that I sank into its voluptuousness.

Kao returned to the lounge and I heard the clink of glasses. I smiled to myself and thought 'Here comes the liqueur' which indeed saw Kao return with two glasses of that wonderful amber liquid. He slipped off his dressing gown and climbed into bed. I admired his body as I always did. I had explored every nook and cranny many times and was waiting for the time when I could do so again. We clinked our glasses together and sipped. I don't think I shall ever find any other drink more enjoyable than Kao's liqueur. The hot chocolate was really good too - and Kao had rescued some of the dinner desserts. He placed the plate on the bedclothes on my knees, so we munched and sipped and laughed and relaxed. It was wonderful - a simple but enchanted bedtime meal. When we finished Kao took the dishes into the kitchen and closed the door behind him. He returned to bed and asked whether I was feeling tired. I smiled and said I wasn't at all and he returned my smile. Kao switched out the lights above the bed and reached for me. We kissed and took our time to make love. It was a wonderful ending to a beautiful day. As I slowly sank into sleep I knew I would sleep well tonight, and I did.

CHAPTER 14

KYOTO

While the television news told of the forthcoming tornado No: 9 destined to hit Japan on Saturday morning, there was no hint of such an event on this beautiful morning. Kao listened intently. While this tornado wasn't news to him, he liked to keep up to date with the latest developments as he had his workforce on standby to be galvanised into action for the huge clean-up in the wake of tornado. Kao's workforce would also be operational with the protection of Kyoto major buildings as well as private homes within the prefecture. Although the typhoon was not due for almost a week, work was already on the way to ensure stable barriers to windows and the old or frail buildings were in place. I had planned to return home on the Monday, but this was after the typhoon and Kao was already talking of me leaving earlier so I would miss *Hagibis*. However, I wanted to stay and leave when we had originally planned on the Monday following the storm, but Kao thought this may place me in some danger, so we agreed to talk again in a couple of days and decide then when I would leave.

Kao had informed me that prior to supper tonight I would, hopefully, enjoy a concert of tradition Japanese musical instruments. He smiled when he told me about the concert and knew Kao so well that I knew there was more to it than he was telling me, but I could be patient and would enjoy whatever he had in store for me tonight. I had lots to look forward to today: First, the visit to Kao's family Shinto shrine for a blessing at 8 o'clock, then from 10.00am with Chieko after which Kao and I would lunch with Takahiro and Ikumi then, prior to supper tonight, a concert of tradition Japanese musical instruments – a very full day!

With Kao consulting the weather bureau representatives, I showered and dressed in a casual cotton *yukata*. Yukata date back more than 1,000 years, when noble persons wore it to and from taking a bath. In the 17th to 19th centuries the custom of wearing yukata spread to ordinary people and while there also is yukata for men, it is mostly women who wear it. A standard yukata ensemble consists of a cotton undergarment (*juban*), obi, sandals (*geta*), a foldable or fixed hand fan, and a carry bag (*kinchaku*0). While yukata literally means bath(ing) clothes, although their use is not limited to after-bath wear and many Japanese wear it for outings to meals, concerts and casual outings. Traditional white *yukata* used to be worn indoors during the day to appear crisp and cool, while indigo blue *yukata* was worn for going out in the evenings because the scent of indigo, used to dye the fabric, repelled insects. My yukata was lavender in colour, patterned with tiny buds and deep violet lotus blossoms. My *obi* was deep violet and very simple. The yukata is an ideal summer garment as it is light to wear so cooler than the heavier kimono. As with kimono, the general rule is that younger people wear bright, vivid colors and bold patterns, while older people wear dark, matured colors and dull patterns.

A child may wear a multicolored print and a young woman may wear a floral print, while an older woman would confine herself to a traditional dark blue with geometric patterns. Men in general may wear solid dark colours. In addition to its comfort, yukata is loved in Japan as a garment which draws out the charm of a woman to the greatest extent. The wearer must walk with smaller steps and keep her back straight especially when sitting as this may crush the *obi*. Therefore, wearing it always makes you behave in a refined manner, it certainly made me change the way I walked and behaved!

I rang the bell in the wall next to the light switch and almost directly Akiko presented herself. I was able to communicate that I needed assistance with the yukata and *obi*, and Akiko was happy to oblige. She added some artificial orange blossom to my hair then bowed and left the room. There was a knock at the door and to my call of 'yes ', Kao walked in and from his look he was pleasantly surprised with my choice of attire. He took me by the shoulders and kissed me gently murmuring that I looked wonderful. I thanked him and kissed him back. He was wearing a male dark grey *yukata* and a simple *obi*. Again I thought he looked fantastic and I felt that the tradition dress really suited him. Kao took me by the hand as we walked downstairs, through the beautiful gardens and into the Shino shrine. Kao explained the order of the different rooms within the shrine. Routine prayers to the *kami* are made at the entrance to the hall, and a trough stands to accept offerings from worshippers. The main hall (*honden*) is used for special occasions such as ours as it seats approximately 20 people, a worship hall (*haiden*) for general prayers catering for up to four people and an offering hall (*heiden*) used for prayers and donations, although it is only used for special ceremonies. The *honden* is the *kami* sanctuary where only priests are allowed to enter because it is the place where the *kami* are thought to live.

Kao continued to enlighten me about the use and meaning of a Shinto shrine. He reflected back on the *torii*, which literally means a bird abode, and is a traditional Japanese gate commonly found at the entrance of, or within, a Shinto shrine where it symbolically marks the transition from the everyday to the sacred. A *shintai*, either a natural object or manmade, represents the existence of the *kami* and is usually placed in the shrine or is outside close to the shrine. Kao pointed out the *shintai* or *go-shintai* represents the sacred body of the *kami* and may take various forms from a mirror or a stone to a natural feature like a waterfall. Kao declared that because over the years the *shintai* is usually wrapped in more and more layers of precious cloth and stored in more and more boxes without being ever inspected, its exact identity may become forgotten. He asked me to look around when I entered the shrine to see if I could see what it was. He smiled then and introduced me to the Priest, or *Kannushi*. We all bowed.

The Kannushi spoke very good English advising that the ceremony would be in Japanese but he would translate as he went along, which I said I appreciated. He was aged I guessed in his late 30s or early 40s with a goatee beard and greying hair tied back into a pony tail with a fall of hair over his forehead. He wore a black hat and he was dressed in a white tunic (*ho*) over white baggy pants (*hibakama*). He carried a *Shako,* or wooden mace (symbol of office). He also wore black wooden clogs *(asagutsu).* The *Kannushi* began the ceremony which was simple but incredibly spiritual, taking about 20 minutes. We each had to vow commitment to each other with the Priest blessing each of us and the words we spoke. He asked Kao's ancestors to preside over us in the decisions we made, and he asked them to keep our footsteps on the true and honorable path as we travelled through life. He also called upon various Shinto gods, or *Kami*, to bless us.

I especially was moved by the *Kannushi's* appeal to *Benzaiten* (or *Benten*), who is the goddess of all things that flow including music which, I thought, was particularly relevant to both Kao and I. She is also associated with love, which made her extra special to our ceremony. She is one of the seven Lucky Gods. Another *Kami*, I recall, was *Taira no Masakado*, a samurai who challenged the Imperial court in Kyoto. He is considered a very powerful and quick to anger *Kami* who can call on floods, plagues or butterflies accordingly, depending on whether he is made angry or happy, so he must be constantly appeased. We had to promise to honour his name and make special offerings to him to appease him. The Priest's translation was such that I was able to follow the ceremony with no difficulty, after which Kao and I toasted each other with sake. We then toasted the Priest with sake. Kao gave him a small soft brown leather draw string bag containing coins and they both bowed. After we thanked the priest, Kao and I bowed exiting the shrine and walking slowly back towards the house. Reaching a wooden seat on the way back to the house Kao indicated for me to sit and he sat next to me. He put his arm around my shoulders and said how happy he was and what a wonderful experience it was having me in his home. He told me again how he saw me fitting in so well and that he would find it difficult to say goodbye when I returned to Tasmania. Kao stroked my hair as he said,

"Caroline I have never asked you this before but I know you understand what is in my heart. My dearest wish lovely lady is for you to become my official wife, here in Japan. I have enquired and find no legal reason why this cannot happen. It would not violate any Australia laws however, I know you will have reservations and I just wanted to suggest this to you so you can think on it. Please don't say anything today. You have already made me very happy by participating in the blessing and I am happy to leave it at that. I just wanted you to know what I have long thought about and you being here makes it feel so right, but it also must feel right for you too".

He kissed me then and I felt all the love he was offering me in that kiss. My eyes misted and I snuggled into his neck. I had no words to say. We sat there for a while then Kao suggested coffee so we wandered back to his apartment and enjoyed coffee on the veranda of his lounge. We didn't speak much, just enthused about the blessing ceremony and of the previous evenings gathering, but I guess he was thinking as much about what he had said in the garden as I was.

CHAPTER 15

CEMENTING TIES

I enjoyed my morning with Chieko and we were able to make ourselves understood by the other. She brought out family albums and I was delighted to see pictures of the Kao and Chieko just after their wedding ceremony. Both looked very young but extremely regal and formal. We laughed together over the photographs taken when their boys were young, and Chieko reminisced about the antics they would get up to. She expressed regret the Kao had not been around the children when they were younger but praised him for providing for the family, stating that he had always worked hard to provide for all of them. She said she had received everything she wanted or asked for. Kao had been very generous with finances if a little partisan in the early years. It was obvious that they had all led a privileged life, but Chieko appeared unaware of this and accepted that their life was normal. The family did not appear ostentatious about their wealth and lived reasonably modestly however, I wondered what would have happened if I had been born in Japan to parents not so privileged, would I be sitting here now, I don't think so - not because of any bias but because I just would not have met Kao, we would have moved in very different circles.

Chieko was very interested in my contact with Kao. While not asking directly – as this would have been most impolite – she really wanted to know about our sex life. She found it inconceivable that people would actually enjoy coupling (her word for sex) with each other, for while she had much respect for Kao, and a certain amount of affection, she did not like coupling and only bore the act to procreate. She revealed that from puberty it was drummed into all young Japanese of her day that this was the only reason for coupling, as was the fact that Westerners defiled each other regularly which was why relationships failed and there was so much trouble in the Western world. I talked of married life and relationships in my world and of the joy couples received by making love with each other, as this was the ultimate demonstration of their love of each other. We discussed this at some length and while I did not mention my intimate relationship with Kao, I believe she began to understand that there was much more to a loving relationship than sex for three days a month in order to become pregnant.

Chieko revealed that in all of their married life they were guided by the family's Shinto priest who had prophesied when they married that both 3 and 8 were very lucky numbers for the couple. This meant they would have three children with eight years between them. I calculated that this meant they would have sex - for procreation only – for 12 days only during their entire 40 plus years of marriage life! I was horrified, but for Chieko this was acceptable. I couldn't but think – no wonder she doesn't like sex. Chieko further surprised me by disclosing that when women had reached an age when child bearing was no longer possible they could release their husband to search for another mate. This was usually a much younger woman who could bear him children. She expressed her initial surprise when Kao had told her about me as she thought I was too old for children, but then Kao had revealed that this was not important to him and that he had fallen in love with me so just wanted me for myself. She said while she did not understand 'love', he had chosen well and everyone had commented on how different he was now.

Chieko wondered how life would have been for the two of them if they hadn't been led to believe that coupling was so restricted and expressed, somewhat wistfully, I thought, their life might have held more joy. I commiserated with her and when I asked whether she would like me to talk to Kao about renewing their relationship she smiled and said it was too late for them, that they were set in their ways and, when she saw us both together and how happy we were in each other's company, she was pleased and satisfied that Kao's life was full. She said her life was also full as she had the grandchildren, her friends and she enjoyed going to the theatre. She had enjoyed running the home, making sure everything was as it should be and while Kao and she had led separate lives living in their own apartments – never sleeping together – she added with a blushing smile with a look in my direction, their home had been happy seeing their children grow into fine young men.

Chieko divulged that they had chosen Ikumi for Takahiro but since my influence Kao had decided that the younger boys could choose their own wives, with a little input from them both. All their children would follow their father into the Company business. Takahiro, trained in Business Management, was already General Manager of the Company and CEO of the Sydney office and would take over in Kyoto when Kao retired. Hiroto had finished his University degree in Business Law and was employed in the Kyoto office and was soon to take up a post in the New York office working under his Uncle, while youngest son Haruki was just completing his University degree in Accountancy and would work for 2 years in the Kyoto office then take up a position in the Manila office as an accountant. The two younger boys would learn all about the business of the Company before taking up substantial positions in the firm when fully trained. Chieko was obviously very proud of their boys and I knew Kao was also. I believed the Company would continue to be in good hands for some decades to come.

Chieko's girl, Masco, served us coffee and some very enjoyable cakes and sweets. I thought that if I stayed in Kyoto much longer I would need a private jet to take me home for I wouldn't be able to fit into a commercial flight. Just aside - I was a bit uncomfortable with the hovering of servants everywhere you went. It wasn't the hovering so much as the fact that they were THERE. I guess this is what a privileged life is all about, but I just felt uncomfortable however, I just didn't see how Chieko and the rest of the family could exist without these helpers and I suppose it gave them all employment - and benefits to their families that they would not have otherwise. It was hard not to judge when things were different from one's own culture. I took my leave of Chieko and thanked her very much for her time and for the confidences. She hugged me and said she had enjoyed my company and wished that I would live permanently in Kyoto. She said there was plenty of room in the family home, or if I wished, Kao would be happy for us both to live in another home on the property. I said that, currently, I couldn't move over but that I would keep her invitation in mind. I also expressed my appreciation of her friendship and how warmly she had welcomed me into her home and into her life. As I walked back to Kao's apartment I was overwhelmed with emotion that Chieko would share with me stories of her early intimate life with Kao, her thoughts and feeling of sex, her relinquishing of Kao and her acceptance that I was now in his life.

Lunch with Takahiro and Ikumi was equally enjoyable but for different reasons. They chose to take Kao and I to the Kyoto *Kitcho Arashiyama* in Ukyo Ward, where it was renowned for its *kaiseki*. I was reminded that *kaiseki* was not a single dish but a typical Kyoto meal comprising of a collection of dishes and courses designed to appeal to both the taste buds and the eyes. While I had enjoyed a small introduction to this type of meal at my welcome to the Sahashi home, to taste a full meal was just incredible. To say the food was excellent would be an understatement. Takahiro had ordered seafood so the restaurant took the spring sea as the theme by using seashells as vessels filled with wild greens and succulent abalone, prawns, scallops and various white fish, while sliced radish suggested waves on the shore. But first we enjoyed a seafood soup, followed by the above served with steamed rice and pickles. During our meal I was interested in listening to Kao and Takahiro discussing company business although they didn't hog the conversation. It was good to see them interacting and they appeared to have a strong relationship. Ikumi and I found plenty to talk about, particularly our respective lives in Australia. I was surprised to learn she was a corporate lawyer who worked four days a week from 8. 00 am to 6.00 pm while the children had a live-in nanny. Takahiro and Ikumi also employed a housekeeper and a gardener, the latter doubled as a chauffeur. I discussed my working life with Ikumi and since retirement. She was interested in my artwork as she was a watercolour artist, so we had quite a bit in common. We both could discuss art until the cows came home!

Takahiro was also interesting as he collected traditional Japanese musical instruments mainly of the stringed variety and he was apparent quite adept at playing them. He revealed that he was in a rock band while at University. This amazed his father who had no idea. We all laughed at this revelation. I was surprised but touched when Takahiro thanked me for helping to take the stress out of his father's life. Takahiro went on to explain how Kao had changed since he had met me. He was more relaxed, certainly laughed and smiled more, and considered carefully what decisions had to made, whether business or private, consulting business partners or relevant family members, whereas previously he had quickly made decisions without any consultations. While his father's decisions were always sound, Takahiro added, he and others in the Company as well as the family appreciated being consulted, even if the decision had the same outcome. Embarrassed Kao put his arm around me saying,

"See what I mean when I say I owe you much for opening my eyes to many things - but especially for your infuriating obstinacy." He kissed me on the forehead and we all laughed. Kao went on to say that, seriously, he found my unwavering point of view would eat into his brain until he was forced to consider my arguments, and 'quite often' he would have to admit that they were valid and he needed to soften his approach to all things except those that were fundamental to his belief and value systems. We all nodded.

The waiter returned with dessert, a selection of confections all looking and tasting great. I found it amusing that we never missed the dessert course of any meal, so everyone had a sweet tooth, although it didn't seem to make much difference to Japanese waistlines. We discussed the dessert dishes as we ate, then the order for Kyoto sake was placed. It was a very pleasant luncheon, I had enjoyed the company of Takahiro and Ikumi and being able to get to know them better. When we had finished lunch Kao suggested we went for a walk and we all enthusiastically agreed. We strolled down *Saga-Toriimoto* Preserved Street which turns back time to the Meiji Period where the old homes have been transformed into tea houses and restaurants. We watched the various picturesque boats serenely drift down the Oi River and under wooden bridges. It was very relaxing and we all enjoyed the brief walk to the *Saga Arashiyama Museum of Arts & Culture*. I admired the traditional buildings along the way. The Museum opened on 01 November 2018, the main exhibition changing four times per year. Currently, *We Love Arashiyama* is an exhibition with various Japanese paintings from the 17th to the 19th century associated with the region. The permanent exhibition is about *Hyakunin Isshu* (one hundred poets, one poem each), which is the most famous anthology of *Waka* poems, that were born in Arashiyama. It was a fascinating exhibition with Kao explaining its highlights. A cafe attached serves light lunches and beverages. The *Arashiyama Omokage Terrace* faces a calm garden and is generally viewed by locals as a hidden gem, however, we were not tempted by its fare and moved on. We arrived back home around 4.00pm and retired to our respective quarters to freshen up for the musical evening before supper.

As organized, all family members including Kao and I were in the downstairs room adjacent to Chieko's apartment, the area I call the old house due to the traditional furnishings and paper sliding doors. Some of the family sat on big cushions on the floor while Chieko, Kao and I sat on low chairs. We were all facing a low dais where various musical instruments sat: *biwa* and *koto,* both traditional stringed musical instruments and a set of *wadaiko,* or *taikos* for short, which are drums. The evening began with Akiko singing and dancing with a colourful fan. I thought her voice was very melodic. She was accompanied by another young woman playing a three-stringed instrument which Kao explained was a traditional Japanese instrument called a *shamisen.* Kao continued that fan dancing involved slow, deliberate movements and poses, which Akiko demonstrated beautifully.

Kao explained "The song is about a lost love and the earliest recorded fan dances in Japan took place in 6th century AD, during the reign of *Emperor Jimmu.* Fan dancing was a dance of high social status, and only performed at court among aristocrats and many of the gestures are symbolic of the story line. Hand-painted fans were originally made from ivory, mother-of-pearl and sandalwood for those of high rank, and the use of *hinoku* (Japanese cypress) in the decoration of fans was regulated according to the social standing of the fan's owner. Today, Japanese fans no longer represent social significance and they are usually made from paper and are brightly painted. They represent friendship or loyalty and are often exchanged as symbols of good will". I found the singing and the dance with the musical accompaniment, together with Kao's enlightenment, most enjoyable. Next a conjurer displayed various tricks which the children enjoyed, often shrieking with pleasure – a lot of fun for all of us. I was interested to see what would happen next when Kao asked if I was bored. I was amazed and quickly let him know how much I was enjoying the evening. He was pleased, squeezed my hand and advised that Hiroto and Haruki were on next. When the young men took centre stage it was interesting to see that Hiroto picked up the *koto* and Haruki knelt behind the set of *taikos*. The music they played had a haunting quality with emphasis provided by the drums which sounded like thunder and echoed around the room. I found all this quite emotional and I was blown away by the talent of these two. I guess they played for about 20 minutes then a short interval was announced. We all clapped then enjoyed the refreshments served. It was good to stand up as I found I had become quite stiff sitting on the low chairs but silently thanked them for I couldn't imagine myself sitting on cushions on the floor – I would never have been able to stand again! Oh, the joys of getting old!!

After the interval we returned to our seats and I was surprised to find I was sitting between Hiroto and Haruki while Kao, Chieko, Takahiro and Ikumi had positioned themselves on the dais. Kao gave me a slow smile, knelt and picked up the *biwa*, Chieko also knelt and placed the *kokyū*, a traditional string instrument played with a bow, on her knee, Ikumi also knelt and placed a flute like instrument to her lips. She told me later that this was a *shinobue*, or *fue*, which she played sideways. It had a high-pitched sound. Takahiro had knelt behind the *taikos*. The music was exceptional and I was moved to tears. The sounds emanated by these instruments was absolutely magnificent. I lost all sense of time as I listened and thoroughly enjoyed this unusual but beautiful music – I was spellbound by the sound. The quartet played several tunes which resulted in polite applause when each one came to an end. Kao then gave a solo on his *biwa*. He played several haunting melodies which I thought were particularly nostalgic of older times in Japan. When he stood everyone politely clapped but I thought he deserved more than that, even though I knew that the Japanese were always modest in their praise however, I was enchanted by the whole evening - especially with Kao's playing. We all ventured into the dining room and supper was traditional Japanese fare which I really enjoyed and, during the meal, I spoke to Kao and other family members regarding the musical evening. Chieko was especially pleased I had enjoyed it as she had chosen the music and had made sure that everyone was well rehearsed. I expressed how much I had enjoyed the talents of everyone and thanked them. Everyone appeared delighted that I had enjoyed the experience of hearing traditional music.

Kao was as good as his word for the next day we explored Kyoto, visiting the wonderful kimono textile warehouse, witnessing sumo wrestling, a traditional sword match, and we were also involved in two Kyoto festivals. I especially enjoyed a visit to *Ninna-ji Reihokan* (Sacred Treasure Hall) for its special autumn opening. We joined the morning service which was held in the *Kon-do Hall*, a temple hall and National Treasure generally not open to the public so I was thrilled to be able to attend it this day. This had originally been a part of the Imperial Palace. The Buddhist monks chanting resonated throughout the hall and created a spiritual feeling which was very calming. The path in the precinct connecting the main gate and the *Kon-do Hall* is called the "Path of Purifying Soul." Kao explained that walking on this path is believed to get rid of ambivalences in the mind so that your stresses and concerns are minimised or relieved completely. The whole site was quite spectacular with the gardens especially colourful yet constrained in true Buddhist fashion.

The *Kinkaku-ji* Temple (Golden Pavilion) was also beautiful and very interesting. It is a Zen Buddhist temple with the two top floors completely covered in gold leaf and a lovely golden floor. Its reflection in the *Anmintaku Pond*, on which it sits, is most impressive. The temple's gardens, which have retained their original design from *Yoshimitsu's* days, hold a few other spots of interest including the Pond that is said to never dry up and, at its center, a small island compete with a Zen style tree giving the site an air of serenity. There are also statues that people throw coins at for good luck. Kao and I thought we needed all the luck we could get so threw lots of coins! Formally known as *Rokuonji*, the temple was the retirement villa of the shogun *Ashikaga Yoshimitsu*, and according to his will it became a Zen temple of the *Rinzai* sect after his death in 1408. Kao explained that *Kinkakuji* was the inspiration for the similarly named *Ginkakuji* (Silver Pavilion), built by *Yoshimitsu's* grandson, *Ashikaga Yoshimasa*, on the other side of the city a few decades later. While I loved all Kao showed me it was perhaps the *Onshukai* presented in Gion Kobu, Kyoto's largest and most spectacular geisha district, that I found quite enchanting - an event not to be missed. The songs and dances performed by the geisha girls are rated highly by local connoisseurs of the geisha world. The graceful dancers told stories of love, jealousy, or happiness through their dance steps and hand movements. Their voices were a bit tinny to this Westerner's ears, but not unpleasant, and their kimono's were outstandingly beautiful.

CHAPTER 16

EXPLORATIONS

Anyone who knows me understands my interest in anything second-hand, particularly if it has historical significance, so it would come no surprise to them when I say I had a great time at the *Tezukuri-ichi Market* which is held monthly at *Chionji Shrine*! Sometimes called a flea market – but whatever it was called it was fantastic! Kao was captivated by my interest, which he described as childlike! Everything delighted me. There was everything from very old earthenware bowls to furnishings, clothing, various ancient documents, with ornaments representing all the deities and some wonderful ancient furniture, plus a world of other paraphernalia. I could have explored for years!! Best of all was the food and I just had to try *ichigo-daifuku* popular Japanese sweets made of soft mochi with bean jam and fresh strawberry as fillings. Kao warned me of eating too many as, he said, they would spoil my appetite for dinner. I laughed but accepted his cautious words as they really were very addictive! With all these experiences perhaps the one which resonates the best for me was the Jidai Festival. This happens every year on 22 October, the anniversary of the foundation of Kyoto. A procession starts from Kyoto Imperial Palace to Heian Shrine. What I found delightful about this parade were the people dressed in costumes representing various periods of Japanese history. It was all very colourful and accompanied by traditional Japanese music. As we walked out of the flea market Kao said he thought that, as it was getting late, he would like to take me out for dinner. I answered that I thought that was a charming idea, which pleased him.

We caught a taxi to what Kao described one of the oldest *ryokan* inns in Kyoto serving authentic food for over 300 years, *Tamarama Ryokan*. He said normally we would have to book in for an overnight stay but as he knew the owners that had not been necessary which meant we could just eat dinner then return home. We were shown to a small room with a table that looked out onto the small garden. The garden was festooned with coloured lights and I could hear water running. Kao explained that a small waterfall fell into a stream running through the garden. Kao ordered *Kaiseki* which, he explained, "You may believe you have eaten this meal previously, at the dinner at our house, but that was only a part of the whole dining experience you will receive this evening". Kao explained further that due to seasonal changes and the chef's preferences each meal would be different. This elaborate dining style developed out of the refined meals served to the aristocracy and imperial court in Kyoto. Ttue to the custom we thanked the chef by saying, "*Arigato - tabe masho u*" or "Thank you – let's eat".

I understood that k*aiseki* was renowned in Kyoto, and while helpings are small, each dish was a gourmet's delight. After a tasting everything I just wanted to die and go to heaven. Kao was delighted by my state of health, even though I said he would have to carry me home. Unfortunately he refused and said I would be left to my own devices if I didn't move – Oh, what a heartless soul! We remembered to show thanks to the chef at the end of the meal by saying, '*Gochiso sama deshita*' (thank you for the meal) and bowing, then I waddled my way outside to where a cab waited to take us back home. We took the lift up to Kao's apartment – I just couldn't manage the stairs! Kao helped me undress but I told him in no uncertain terms that I was only fit for going to sleep so not to expect anything else. He was most amused but I was soooo full!

We kissed and went to bed where Kao respected my wishes and hugged me as I settled onto his shoulder. I fell asleep almost straight away then in the night I awoke suddenly.

I felt for Kao but the bed was empty and cold. I looked around but could not see where he might be. After seeing the sliding door to the balcony open, I grabbed my gown and padded over where I saw Kao highlighted by the moonshine leaning on the balustrade looking at the garden and beyond. I asked if there was anything wrong. He answered no but did not turn towards me as I thought he would. I went to him and put my arms around him. He shivered. I asked if he was cold but he shook his head. I hugged him to me and thought I felt a stifled sob. I asked Kao if there was something he would like to share with me. He didn't answer.

Suddenly he turned towards me, taking both of my hands in his, he led me to the day bed where we both sat, knee to knee, on its edge. I knew there was something serious he had to say so waited for him to speak.

"Caroline we have spent a wonderful day and a lovely evening together. You have made me very happy. I have enjoyed your facial expressions as you have experienced the sites and tastes of Kyoto. It is as if I too were experiencing these for the first time. At times you have that childlike exuberance which I find so charming that I feel my heart breaking. I love you so very much. I still see you as I did that first time on the ship as my Venus. You know that painting by Botticelli *Birth of Venus*. Everything you see and feel you do so from the heart, but I have but one regret – and I think of this often - we met too late, too late for us to have children and when we couple I so much want to impregnate you. You would have made a wonderful mother but that is all beyond us now, so we must look to the future". Kao looked at me earnestly, his eyes pleading.

"I don't want to go on alone, without you. I cannot envision a life with you one side of the world and me on the other, so I wish you to seriously consider what I asked you earlier. I know and understand how things are with you in

Tasmania and I accept that however, my dearest wish my lovely lady is that before you return home you honour this humble man by becoming my legal wife. We would do this in a simple Shinto ceremony. As I have said before, I have checked and this would not infringe any Australia laws. Now I know you do not want anything from me, but please humour an old man. We are both nearing the end of our earthly lives and I want to get my affairs in order so please, I wish to leave you some reminder of the happiness you have brought to me and also to my family". He paused, ran his fingers through his hair.

"I would leave you everything I have but I know you do not want this however, what I want to give you is the farm and the cottage in Tasmania where I look forward to sharing many moments of joy with you. I also want to leave you a few shares in our Company. I have Hiroto checking into how much I can leave you without this affecting your Pension, although you know I would leave you much more so that this Pension was not necessary however, you are a proud woman and I know you would not like this. Please consider my supplication and, when you are ready, give me your answer. Whatever it may be, your answer will not change my mind about my plans for the future". He raised my hand to his lips and gently kissed my fingers then placing my palm against his cheek he tenderly caressed it. To say I was surprised with Kao's plans would be an understatement. I was speechless as I had no knowledge of what had been on his mind and, from what he had said, for some considerable time.

I breathed, "Oh, Kao", before saying, "You have honoured me greatly with your words, which were spoken from the heart. I understand your desire to have children with me as this is part of your inherent values and beliefs taught to you from a young child, while I see our coupling as a wonderful way to show each other how much we care – part of my own value system – so this urge is not with me. I accept that we are what we are. Had we met years ago maybe we would not have been compatible or even attracted each to the other but we have found something so unique and I feel truly blessed that you are now part of my life. I shall indeed consider your desire for me to become your wife but not for the financial reasons you give but because we love each other. I find your kindness and consideration most generous and I thank you. While I understand that you must organise your affairs before you are called to stand before your ancestors, I do not wish to linger on this sad prospect, rather I wish to look to a long and happy future that wherever we are - either together or apart - our love is steadfast and true. I too had a very enjoyable day and evening with you and I could not be happier. You have brought much joy into my life for many reasons: for your body, which gives me great pleasure and our lovemaking is perfect, for your mind - I love our debates and learning new things about your world and the world in general, for your creative abilities – your beautiful poetry which I love to listen to as you read to me, and I love it when you play your biwa and sing to me. I love the way you smile, not only to me, but when you think I am not watching. Your smile reaches into the corners of your eyes and makes them twinkle and crinkle. Oh, and I do love your eyes. They are so expressive and can be liquid dark chocolate or as black as the thunder clouds in the mountains. I love your incredible generosity of spirit and your love of all things. It has been and will continue to be my pleasure to watch and learn from you, and to attempt to have the infinite patience that you exhibit without knowing you are doing so. There is still so much of you I need to discover and I will take much pleasure in doing so, so whether I agree to be your wife or not, know this Kao we shall be together for very long time." I leaned forward and kissed him lightly on his lips.

Kao looked at me through misty eyes then gently tucked his hand under my chin and brought it forward wherein he kissed me lovingly on the lips. It was such a pure kiss full of love. My eyes filled with unshed tears. His arms came around me and he held me close. "Thank you" he said, "you are the wisest of the wise and your words always heal my soul when I am at my lowest", then "Let's go to bed" he whispered. We rose together, retraced our steps into the bedroom and lay together saying things that lovers say before making love. Kao was so tender and I knew I would miss him terribly when I returned to Tassie. It wasn't long before I felt myself melt into him and we moved as one. What an experience. I just couldn't believe that in the twilight of our lives we could delight in each other not only in our daily experiences but also in the bedroom and obtain much joy just in being together. We climaxed then I lay in his arms. He caressed my skin and kissed me and told me over and over how much he loved me.

I contemplated Kao's proposal before I fell asleep and wondered how being Kao's wife in Japan would affect my life in Tasmania. I knew it would mean a lot to him, but what would it mean for me? How complicated? Would I become confused and answer to Mrs Sahashi in Ulverstone? Could I trust Kao not to embarrass me again in front of people I knew and people who knew Phil? All perplexing questions. I eventually fell asleep but my mind was full of questions so I slept fitfully.

CHAPTER 17

A NEW LIFE

The morning dawned bright and sharp for although it was sunny the wind sent clouds scurrying across the sky like large Samoyed dogs enjoying a chase, and there was a chill in the air. Kao's side of the bed was empty and he had gone to the gym I supposed so I arose, showered and dressed. Kao arrived as I was completing my makeup and kissed me sweetly before taking his shower. While drying his hair with a towel, Kao advised that he and the boys were going into Kyoto today to see that everything was in place before the hurricane arrived. He expected they would be gone for most of the day but would return as soon as he could. Kao said that Chieko would like me to join her, Ikumi and the two children for a picnic lunch in the pavilion today if I would be interested. I said of course I would be, so Kao kissed me and said he would see me later. As an afterthought, he poked his head around the door and asked whether I minded eating at home tonight with the family and I answered that I would love to and he happily went on his way. I checked the time and found it was only 8.30 am so I had plenty of time before lunch, which I knew would be at noon sharp! I decided to sit on the lounge balcony, where they were several chairs and a table, and read some of Kao's poems. I was intent in my book when Masaya, Kao's man servant, excused himself and asked whether I would like coffee. I thanked him and said yes I would. He brought in a silver tray with a delightful coffee pot, matching sugar bowl and milk jug, complete with a dish of Japanese cakes. When he was satisfied there was nothing more he could do Masaya left closing the sliding doors behind him. I returned to the poems and sipped my coffee – which was most enjoyable. When I next looked at my watch it was 11.30 am and I thought that I had better make a move as being late for an appointment was viewed as tardiness by Chieko. I opened the door and went through the bedroom to the bathroom and retouched my makeup and combed my hair.

As I walked through the garden to the pavilion, I thought how the day had warmed up as I enjoyed the sun on my face. There were cries of joy from the children as they ran towards me grabbing my hands and pulling me forward. Their mother rebuked them but it didn't make any difference! Both Chikako and Kimiya could speak pretty good English so we were able to chatter about things kids liked to chatter about. We were served coffee and there were a range of wonderful delicacies to taste which quickly disappeared into the children's stomachs! The two hours spent over lunch passed very quickly. Eventually Ikumi advised Chikako and Kimiya that it was time to go and they kissed both Chieko and myself before running off in front of their mother. Chieko said she was pleased to have me join her and spoke about the garden and how Kao had planned most of it while further developing the ancient garden of his forefathers, which was the garden directly to the rear of the house with its waterways and cherry blossoms. She then turned to me and said, "*Kyarorain san, Aanata ga furui hone ni atarashī inochi o fukikonde iru koto no o jikakushite kudasai*". ("Caroline, be aware that you breathe new life into old bones"). I smiled and said I understood. I kissed her cheek and left her to snooze in the garden she loved so much.

Walking back to Kao's rooms I thought about the homily voiced by Chieko and wondered whether she meant it as a compliment, or maybe she was jealous, or perhaps she was just being sarcastic. I rejected the last two as Chieko wasn't like that, she said what she thought, so perhaps it was a compliment. Then I wondered whether it was a warning as Kao has a heart problem. Maybe she was urging caution. I was unsure of just what she meant but decided I would not let Kao over-exert himself. By the time I settled back into my chair it was a little after 3.00 pm. The sun had moved so that the balcony was in shadow and a cool breeze had sprung up, necessitating my moving inside and closing the sliding doors behind me. I did not think Kao would be long as he said he expected to be back late afternoon, so I picked up the crime novel I had begun a few days ago and started reading.

I heard Kao return and checked the clock. He was early which was good as it was only twenty past four. As I looked up to welcome him I was shocked by his appearance. He really looked very ill with his grey face and tired demeanor. I immediately jumped up and put my arms around him. I led him to the bed and I took off his slippers. My concern was obvious, but he smiled wanly and told me he was OK and that he if he had a rest before dinner he would be refreshed. A few minutes later Takahiro arrived and I heard Hiroto and Haruki in the hall outside the room. Takahiro informed us that the Doctor had been called and was on his way. Kao snapped at him in Japanese but without any energy and Takahiro carefully and slowly answered him. I thought Takahiro showed great restraint. Takahiro called for Masaya advising me that Masaya would make Kao comfortable for the doctor. Kao had given up arguing and when Masaya arrived Takahiro ushered me into the lounge room.

"Father just did far too much. I warned him to stop but he is intractable when he has his mind set on something", Takahiro advised. He looked worried so I asked what this meant for his father. "It is not good. He wouldn't be told. Episodes like this are very bad for him", Takahiro continued, "I am sorry Caroline but he should rest now. The Doctor will banish you so I will get Masaya to make up the day bed on the balcony for you if that is satisfactory. I know you will want to be near Father". I was thanking Takahiro for his consideration when the Doctor arrived. He waved his arms around and shouted in Japanese, "Dero, dero" (Out, out). Takahiro cupped his hand under my elbow and manoeuvred me through the doorway and into the passage telling me the Doctor would probably need half an hour and suggested that we walk in the garden so he could talk to me about his Father's illness. The sun had disappeared behind a cloud and I noticed that clouds were quickly gathering. I sensed the smell of rain – the typhoon was approaching.

Takahiro informed me that Kao had been ill for as long as Takahiro could remember suffering similar episodes of exhaustion from time to time. He had been treated for a congenital heart problem which had worsened over time. Any strain on the heart was potentially dangerous, meaning that he could die, so all family members were seriously worried over his last attack. Takahiro explained that his Father had probably suffered a mini heart attack as he had complained of chest pains and of swelling in his legs, ankles and feet. Takahiro looked worried so I asked what this meant for his Father. "It is not good. He wouldn't be told. Episodes like this are not good for him" he continued. "My Father has always followed the Doctors orders for his prescribed medication to the letter. He follows a balanced diet and drinks alcohol only in moderation as you would have noticed. He undertakes mild exercise everyday which the Doctor advised has been proved to improve the overall ability of the heart to function. Our family believes that having followed all this has helped Father enjoy a long and fruitful life to date. I wish no disrespect Caroline, as we all have affection for you for the happiness you have brought Father and when I say that I wonder whether he is perhaps over-exerting himself at times however, I am anxious to state that it was the work in Kyoto today that caused his latest collapse and not anything you have done or encouraged Father to do". He paused before taking a deep breath and continuing.

"I speak on behalf of my family as we are all concerned for Father's continuing health and, with moderation, we are sure he can continue to live a rewarding life for some years yet". He finished with, "I hope I have not offended you for speaking so openly". Takahiro stopped and looked at me questioningly. I smiled saying that he had not offended me for I was appreciative of his honestly and for explaining Kao's illness. I asked him to reassure the family that I would be mindful of his Father's health and that I would indeed take care of it from now on. Thanking me he squeezed my arm. We walked back to the house discussing the garden and Kao's major role in its development. The Doctor was just taking his leave as we entered Kao's apartment. He told me in no uncertain terms that Kao needed completed bed rest – with no exertion for at least 24 hours. His English was good and I answered that I completely understood. I got the impression that he thought I was a barbaric Westerner obsessed with sex, but I let it go as I was grateful for his quick response to attend Kao. When I first saw Kao on his return home I was so frightened that he was going to die, so I was thankful that the Doctor, who knew Kao well, had done everything necessary to ease his suffering and point Kao in the right direction towards better health.

I looked in on Kao but he was resting however, I was pleased to see some colour had returned to his cheeks. I walked out onto the balcony and found that Masaya had already made up the day bed. It looked very comfortable with pale yellow silk sheets and a brocade cover on the quilt. While I was saddened by the thought of sleeping alone, I knew this would be good for Kao. A good rest was what he needed and anyway I would be in ear shot if I was wanted. I thought of our previous conversation when Kao wanted me to return to Tassie earlier than I had planned, due to the typhoon, but I had wanted to stay. On reflection I thought that I may be a source of distraction for Kao when he had so much to think about and organise before the typhoon, and its aftermath. I decided I would return to Tasmania Thursday morning, as recommended by Kao. I knew that he would be watched by his two younger sons so he didn't overdue things – Takahiro and his family were returning to Sydney on Wednesday which was only 4 days away. I suddenly thought about dinner and my watch said that I wasn't late – yet – but I had better get a move on.

I walked quickly and quietly through the bedroom to the bathroom where I had a quick shower. Drying myself quickly I brushed my hair (having managed to avoid getting it wet) and applied fresh makeup. I then picked out my pale blue cotton kimono with matching obi which I slipped on. I also put my feet into slippers, glancing at my watch I saw that it was just 6.00 pm so I walked to the lift which would take me downstairs for dinner. Family members were already assembled in the dining room and Chieko indicated I should sit next to her, which I did. Takahiro had obviously advised her of our conversation because she thanked me for being so understanding. I told her that Kao's welfare was also my concern and she patted my hand and smiled. I did not eat much as I wasn't hungry; I was still worried about Kao. I excused myself when I thought it was polite to do so and returned to the apartment.

Kao was still fast asleep and I assumed he had been sedated. It was 8.15 pm, too early for bed so I read my crime book in the lounge room until 10 pm then I undressed, checked on Kao – making sure he had water within his reach should be become thirsty – and went to the day lounge on the balcony. It was surprisingly warm outside as the wind had turned and the house was now protecting the balcony. It took me a while to fall asleep, I kept listening to hear if Kao had moved or was wanting something, but all was quiet. I awoke suddenly and the clock said 3.00 am. I went in to look at Kao but he hadn't moved. His breathing was regular and the water had not been touched. I went back to bed and fell asleep almost immediately.

When I awoke again dawn was just breaking and at first I couldn't understand where I was, then I remembered the events of yesterday evening. I sat on the edge of the bed and put on my robe. I tiptoed into the bedroom to find Kao still sleeping. He hadn't moved all night. I left him to rest and had a shower, dried myself and my hair then applied makeup. I quietly walked into the bedroom and chose my lavender kimono and began dressing. Kao stirred but didn't awaken. Just then there was a quiet tap on the lounge room door and when I opened it Masaya stood there holding a tray. I ushered him in and he placed the tray on the small round table by the balcony doors. He said he thought I might like breakfast and I thanked him for his thoughtfulness. He quietly left and I discovered that the tray comprised of a pot of green tea with two soft boiled eggs and two slices of toast. I was touched to think he would make me a Western breakfast. I enjoyed the change although I loved the Japanese breakfasts I had been having.

I was just finishing when I heard a noise from the bedroom. I found Kao, bleary eyed but awake – well almost! I helped Kao to sit up, placing extra pillows behind him to give him some stability and asked him how he was. He certainly looked much better and he said he felt so. We held hands and to my query he said he wasn't hungry. I kissed him gently and told him how worried I had been. He admitted to being wrong in wanting to do everything at once but countered this by saying he was anxious to return to me. I thought of the decision I had made to leave early, according to Kao's wishes, and told him of this. He looked relieved and said he was pleased I would be out of danger although he would miss me. He squeezed then kissed my hand. I kissed him gently on the lips and said the Doctor had ordered completed bed rest for him. Kao smiled and there was a glint in his eye which I knew only too well before he said that I could join him if I liked. I laughed and said rest meant just that and I would be doing other things today.

"What would be more important than attending to the needs of the sick, Madam?" he asked with mock indignation. I told him he was wicked and ruffled his hair!

During my wakeful moments in the night I had thought over Kao's proposal of becoming his wife. I had considered his assurances that I would not be violating any Australia laws and being his wife would make it easier for me to benefit from his Estate should he die before me. The latter was not important for me but I understood it was for Kao. I knew he loved me, probably more deeply than I loved him, but he understood my position in Tasmania and I loved him as much as I was capable of – which was lots. I shifted my position on Kao's bed and told Kao I wished to talk to him. He fixed me with his 'attention' stare so I raised the subject of his prior proposition and asked him if this is what he still wanted. Kao's grasp on my hands tightened.

"Oh my dear sweet lady, it is my dearest wish that you agree to be my wife before you return to Tasmania. This would make me the happiest man in the universe". The love in Kao's eyes was further testament to his voiced desire and I could have wept with the love I felt for him then. He looked at me expectantly, with hope in his eyes. I cleared my throat and met his gaze.

"Kao you know this has been far from my thoughts and that I have been more than happy with our relationship as it stands". I paused, my eyes still holding Kao's. I noticed that he was attempting to hide his disappointment so I continued, "I have seriously considered your proposal which you have honoured me with. I am humbled that you wish to sanctify our relationship with a Shinto ceremony. I have faith our love is strong and lasting without any ceremonies, but I know this is important to you and, because making me your officially recognisable wife is important to you so it is for me - I accept your proposal. Kao I accept your proposal because I really do want to become your wife". Kao was silent. He looked stunned. Suddenly he was crying, the tears running down his face. I moved closer to him and hugged him. Kao wiped his eyes and gave a wan smile.

"I thought you were going to refuse", he admitted "but I am very, very happy you have agreed". We held each other for a long time without saying a word, just enjoying the moment. Eventually, we drew apart and kissed. Kao said there was much to be done and he had to inform Chieko who would help me get organised. He said he had to see the Priest and made to get out of bed.

"No", I said forcefully, "Stop, you will stay here in bed – for 24 hours". Kao looked shocked and I folded the quilt back over him. "Tell me who you want to see and I shall send them to you. You are to remain in bed". He appeared bemused but answered, "Well, I shall need to ask Takahiro to complete the arrangements. He will have lots to do, and you will need to consult Chieko, but we cannot do anything until everyone has been advised and that requires an appropriate ceremony, my dear lady", Kao spoke seriously. I enquired about the format and Kao said that we should plan this together but felt that it would be appropriate to announce our marriage at a cocktail party which could be arranged to take place in his lounge. Kao expressed his desire to have the wedding ceremony as soon as possible. I asked when the announcement should be made and he replied that he wanted to announce it this evening. He must have seen the look on my face for he said that he had suggested his apartment for the cocktail party as this would take little effort on his part to attend. I still was far from convinced but Kao added that he would get Masaya to organise everything so all he had to do was have a shower and present himself. He looked at me so appealingly that I had to smile and nod my acceptance. I then asked when he would like the wedding ceremony to take place and he asked me if the day after tomorrow would be OK with me. Kao watched me anxiously as I thought about the step I was about to take. Was this really what I wanted, I asked myself. I stood and walked to the balcony doors then walked outside and looked along the balcony towards the lounge room doors. I walked over to them, entering the lounge and closing the doors behind me as the breeze had sharpened. I walked back into the bedroom and reclaimed my previous seat on Kao's bed.

"Will you be well enough?" I asked. Our eyes locked and I could see that Kao understood this was not my only concern. "Caroline, we don't have to do this if you are unsure. I want you to be absolutely certain that this is right for you". Having said that Kao took my hand, "I can wait until you are sure, whether it takes weeks or years. My love will never change. I am a patient man Caroline, and I can wait for eternity alongside my ancestors if necessary, for in life you belong to Phil but in death you will belong to me". I saw how sad he was and my heart went out to him. I knew that I loved him dearly and I did want to be his wife. I leant over to him kissing him gently then lay beside him. He kissed my forehead and stroked my hair.

"Kao I think your idea of the day after tomorrow has merit, as long as you think you will be well enough, my dear" I whispered. I know this sounds soppy but we both cried silent tears of joy, of relief, of commitment to each other, who knows what but we hugged each other and kissed. I guess we lay like that for half an hour or more, but I knew there was much to be done and so little time to do it in and I said as much to Kao. I sat up and we smiled at each other before I kissed Kao gently and stood. He asked me to press the bell to summon Masaya to begin preparations for the party that evening.

I left Kao to make arrangements and retired to the lounge room where I searched the writing desk for suitable stationary on which to write the invitations. I found some lovely parchment-like stationery embossed with the family crest which I thought would do very well and took a sheet into Kao for his advice. He had finished giving instructions to Masaya so he examined the paper and agreed with me that it would be perfect. He asked if would be happy for him to write out the invitations to family members. I said I would be. Kao then asked would I mind if the invitations were written in Japanese not English. If course I didn't mind and told him so. I retraced my steps back to the writing desk, returning to Kao with enough paper, a pen and writing board to lean on. These I placed on the table near the bed and Kao asked if he could sit at the table to write the invitations. I said he could if he ate some breakfast and he capitulated, much to my delight. Right on cue Masaya tapped at the door and on Kao's 'come' he entered. I relayed Kao's need for food and Masaya departed to tend to his needs.

Kao said how excited he was of our impending wedding adding, "You know you will be my number one wife don't you Caroline?" I must confess I hadn't even thought about this and told Kao so, but he said that it was important for me to know my rightful place in the family. I argued that Chieko, being the mother of his sons and having run the household very efficient for over 40 years, should surely remain in number one position. Kao argued that Chieko would understand, accept and approve. I had my doubts but there was no arguing with Kao once he had his mind made up, so I left it there for the moment. Masaya wasn't long before he returned with a tray containing breakfast for Kao. Kao ate with relish and I was so pleased to see him looking well again so quickly

I ruminated on our forthcoming ceremony and had butterflies in my stomach, as I didn't know what the Shinto ceremony would involve, but I did want to be Kao's wife – in Japan. I didn't think I would feel I was his wife once I returned to Phil. Strangely, I didn't feel any guilt over what was about happen, as I had always felt a disconnection between my two loves and my life with each of them. I brushed these thoughts from my mind as I was aware that Kao had paused in eating and was looking at me.

"You have been lost in thought", he said "Do I have anything to be worried about?" he queried. I shook my head and answered "No, I was thinking of all the planning ahead" I lied, "For a start what will I wear for the ceremony?" I asked. Kao laughed and said Chieko and Ikumi would help me there, before returning to his breakfast. When he could eat no more I took the tray and placed it on the table nearby. I then handed him the three bottles of pills the Doctor had left and a glass of water. He chose the pills he wanted, swallowed them with water and I replaced everything back onto the table.

"Now you have to rest. I shall see you later this afternoon". I tried to sound authoritative but Kao only grinned, saying that he had four invitations to complete and THEN he would rest. I shook my head – and he had the cheek to call me stubborn!

CHAPTER 18

FAMILY CONCERNS

I was wondering what to wear this evening when Kao looked up from his task of invitation writing, at the table near the bed, cloaked in his dressing gown. As I passed him on the way to my wardrobe, Kao touched my hand and we exchanged smiles. I checked the hangers in the wardrobe, having made up my mind that a kimono would be appropriate – but which one? I finally settled on a pale aquamarine kimono patterned with sprays of pink *sakura* (cherry blossoms). The obi was pink with aquamarine decorations. I was pleased with my selection and speculated that as *sakura* symbolized chastity, love, affection, purity, and good luck that Kao would also be pleased. I returned to the lounge, picked up my book settled myself in the chair and commenced to read. I hadn't been reading for very long when Kao came into the room and sat on the arm of my chair.

"My dear lady I am going to do as ordered, I am going back to bed to have a rest. I must confess I am feeling quite weary so I am sure I shall be soon asleep. I would very much like you beside me if I can tear you away from that book" he declared while producing his more winsome smile. I returned his smile but declined his offer. He looked crestfallen and I could see in his eyes what he had in mind but I reiterated that he was going to bed to rest and my being beside him may distract him from this. He patted my shoulder and said I was quite correct on all counts and that he was duly chastised so he would return to bed alone (emphasised) and try to sleep. He actually did look tired and I thought this was probably due to the medication he had taken. I stood and took his hand saying that I would tuck him up in bed and kiss him to ensure he would have pleasant dreams. He placed his arm around my shoulders as we walked into the bedroom. Kao quickly removed his dressing gown and slipped into bed. I kissed him gently on the lips and tucked him in. He held onto my hand for a little while but he could see I was not going to weaken. I walked to the door, gave Kao a wave then closed the door behind me. I settled down to read my book. I heard the door of the bedroom open and close a few moments later, assuming that Masaya had picked up the invitations for tonight's cocktail party and was on his way to deliver them. I checked my watch and was surprised to realise that it was only just after 11.00am so there was plenty of time before the party. I returned to my book.

I was lost in my story with only a few pages left when I heard a discreet knock on the lounge door. My watch said it was 1.15pm. I said 'come' and Masaya came in asking whether I desired lunch. I said I did and he asked me what I would like. I thought for a moment and would have loved a baked bean sandwich, but this was unknown in Japan so I asked if I could have *Tamagoyaki* (egg omelette) followed by *Manju* (small round steamed cake stuffed with mashed sweet red beans). Masaya smiled, bowed and retreated. I knew I had half an hour before Masaya returned with my meal so I was determined the finish my book. I had just read the last few words and was closing the book when Masaya knocked and entered with my meal. He placed it on the table, arranging the chopsticks, napkin and a glass of wine (?) on the small dining table. He then pulled out a chair, placed the napkin on my knees then, making sure I was comfortably seated he bowed and left the room. I took a sip from the glass and found that it was indeed a lovely rice wine made not far away from the house in Kyoto – it was delicious. I ate the meal slowly enjoying every mouthful and washed it down with the wine. Everything was superb except that Kao was not with me. Well, I sighed, I had finally finished my book, had enjoyed a lovely meal and I was feeling a little tired. I walked to the balcony doors and opened them stepping out onto the balcony. The wind had dropped and while it wasn't overly warm the sun shone bleakly in a cloudy sky so it was a comfortable temperature. I sat on the day bed wrapping the blankets around me. I decided to have a nap so made myself comfortable.

I must have slept for a couple of hours because when I awoke the breeze had risen to a cold wind. I walked inside closing the doors behind me. The clock said it was almost 4.00 pm and I could hear voices coming from the bedroom. I straightened my hair and checked my makeup then knocked on the door. I heard Kao say 'come' so entered the bedroom. He smiled as I did so and beckoned me over. He was propped up in bed with several pillows behind him and he looked well and rested. Masaya was with him and he bowed as I joined Kao and sat next to him on the bed. Kao explained that everything was in order and everyone said they would be in his apartment by 5.30pm that evening. The food and drinks would be set up in the lounge shortly and, he announced, he had decided that he would play a couple of traditional tunes on his *biwa*. He added that this was not an overly strenuous task and everyone would enjoy it, also, that it would set the tone of the evening. I just accepted that all the arrangements had been made and made no comment other than I would love to hear him play the *biwa*. We decided that I would shower first and did so after which I dried my hair and put on fresh makeup while Kao was in the shower. I dressed in the kimono I had chosen, took out Kao's gifts placing the necklace around my neck and the earrings on my ears, just as Kao came out of the bathroom. He stopped and his look said everything. He came over and gave me a sweet kiss and said I looked wonderful.

I reminded him of the time so Kao responded by dressing quickly in a dark blue male kimono, emblazoned with the family crest, with a matching sash tied around his waist.

He looked magnificent. We walked into the lounge just as Masaya entered the bedroom closing the door behind us. Kao poured me a drink assuring me that it was non-alcoholic wine. It tasted like the wine that Masaya had served at lunchtime. It was beautifully chilled and absolutely delicious. Kao opened the lounge door to the hallway and took the *biwa* from the wall. He ran his fingers along the strings which he adjusted then leaned it against the side wall, where there had been placed a low stool. I assumed that was where he would sit and play for our guests. Talking of guests, I checked my watch and saw that it was 5.28 pm precisely, and it was then I heard voices coming from the hall. Soon Kao's lounge was filled with people. While there were only a few guests – all family members – yet they seemed to fill the room, even though it was quite large. There was Chieko and their three sons, Takahiro's wife Ikumi and their two children Chikako and Kimiya, Chieko's father Gentarō, Kao's uncle Katsumoto (Managing Director of the Kyoto office) and his wife Mayako.

Masaya served everyone drinks from a tray and Akiko circulated with various dishes of exquisite finger food. The small dining table was decorated with red candles burning in wooden bowls. Blossoms of Chrysanthemum, Cosmos and Spider lily, together with autumn toned leaves in various shades of red and yellow were, strewn across the table. The electric lights burned low creating an ambiance of tranquility, although there was a feeling of restrained enjoyment in the room as I am sure everyone wished to know why they had been summoned. Kao walked over to me and took my hand then, in Japanese, he welcomed everyone and said how honoured he was that they could join him and his companion Caroline, who everyone had previously met. Everyone smiled, nodded and bowed in my direction. He said he would like to play his *biwa* in honour of this occasion and everyone was invited to enjoy the wine and the food while he did so. Kao then sat on the stool and played two lovely haunting melodies. The assembled company appeared to enjoy this greatly and politely clapped while Kao returned his *biwa* to the wall. He rejoined me and again took my hand. In Japanese he asked that glasses be refreshed and Masaya ensured that everyone had a fresh glass of rice wine. When this was done, Kao looked at me and smiled, then he said in English.

"This is a very special and serious occasion to which you, my dearest family, have been invited. I want you to know how very happy I am to have Caroline standing with me tonight. I have loved her visit and I thank you for having made her feel very welcome. Caroline is very grateful for your kindness". Kao squeezed my hand then continued, "So tonight I take great pleasure in announcing that Caroline has honoured me by agreeing to be my wife". There were gasps from the audience and everyone started clapping and there appeared to be a lot of excitement in the room. Kao placed his arm around my shoulder and gave me a gentle squeeze then, he held up his hand to capture everyone's attention again.

"We are to be married before Caroline returns to Tasmania and this has been arranged for the day after tomorrow at 11.00 am". Everyone began to smile and talk again so Kao put his hand up to restore order before continuing. "I wish to give out your invitations before you leave tonight but, for the time being, enjoy yourselves and join Caroline and I as we celebrate our happiness tonight". Everyone crowded around to congratulate us and wish us well. Takahiro advised Kao that he would be happy to organise the details of the wedding with the Shinto Priest due to Kao's illness, while his wife Ikumi and Chieko both offered to guide me through the correct procedures involving choosing my dress and in understanding the format of the ceremony. They also chattered on about the food, the drink and where it would be best to hold the luncheon – and I thought it was going to be a simple affair! How naive I was! Anyway, everyone appeared to be happy for us and I felt part of a large and loving family. By 7.00pm Kao was looking tired and I quietly suggested to Takahiro that he may like to politely ask everyone to leave. He agreed as he had also been watching Kao closely. The group gradually dispersed after bowing and shaking hands and Chieko and Ikumi giving me a hug.

At last Kao and I were on our own. Kao kissed me tenderly and held me close. I could feel his heart beating. I was so happy and Kao looked happy also. I took his hand and led him into the bedroom. He looked expectantly at me and I laughed, telling him that I intended to sleep again on the day bed on the balcony. "Oh, Caroline do not do this to me. I have missed not having you lay beside me. Please keep me warm tonight". But I remained strong telling him that in two day's I would be his wife and he would need all his energy for our wedding night. We laughed together but he could not dissuade me. We kissed again before I left him, returning to the lounge room where Masaya was placing used wine glasses onto a tray. I told him that Kao was ready to retire and required his assistance. Masaya immediately went through to the bedroom.

I moved onto the balcony and found Akiko waiting for me. She helped me undress then dress in the red silk nightdress, that Kao had given me, and my pink bathrobe. She had made up the bed but I just sat on its edge and thought that I would read for a while. Kao had given me an English translation of the recent publication of his new book of poems - it was literally 'hot off the press.' Akiko asked if I wished for something to eat but I had eaten quite a bit at the Cocktail Party so didn't feel hungry. I asked if she could bring me Ramen Soup in about two hours with a glass of sake and she bowed as she left me. Ramen Soup is generally made from chicken or pork stock basically with noodles of wheat, combined with a various ingredients: *kombu* (kelp), *katsuobushi* (skipjack tuna flakes), *niboshi* (dried baby sardines), beef bones, pork bones, shiitake mushrooms, and onions and it is absolutely delicious.

There was a knock on my door and Masaya answered my 'come'. He advised me that Kao had invited me to join him for chocolate and liquor before bed. I smiled and said I would be with Kao shortly. Kao smiled as I entered his room and patted the edge of the bed beside him. I duly sat and he gave me a mug of hot chocolate, and a glass of the wonderful Japanese liquor stood on the table close to me. Kao kissed me gently and expressed his delight that I could join him. I also expressed my delight that he had invited me but left him no doubt that I was there to enjoy the drinks and his company for a short time. He said I was a cruel woman to leave a sick person overnight on his own when who knows what may happen. I said he was a cunning man who wanted me in his bed only so that he could seduce me - AND against Doctor's orders. We laughed together and Kao put his arm around me. I was so pleased he was feeling better and on his way to being his old self again, but I was determined that he would get his much needed rest overnight so that tomorrow he would be feeling even better health wise. I finished both the chocolate and the liquor and kissed Kao goodnight. The kiss was long and bordering on passionate so I pulled away from Kao and kissed him on his nose saying that I would see him in the morning. He had a wicked gleam in his eyes when he said he could hardly wait. I shook my head and smiled and left him to his dreams. I returned to my day bed.

I was not disappointed. All too soon Akiko returned with my meal which I devoured. I am going to miss all this wonderful food when I return to Tasmania. The evening was getting cooler and I pulled the bedclothes over me before I became chilled. It had been an exhausting day but one of extreme enjoyment so I was tired enough to sleep well. I had heard nothing from Kao's room so envisioned him being curled up and fast asleep. I was pleased as he needed his sleep to renew his strength and hoped that he would soon be his old self again. I was worried that even though he had enjoyed the Cocktail Party it had taken its toll and Kao had looked very tired at its conclusion. I hoped that all was well for him during the next few days as I was fearful for his health. Neither of us were getting any younger and I thought that, potentially, either one of us could die at any time. Only the good Lord or Kao's ancestors knew what was in our destinies, so we were literally in the hands of the Gods. We must make each moment count, collecting memories as we enjoyed the company of each other for the short time we had together.

I awoke to a dull and drizzly morning. I felt cold so quickly put on my bathrobe and moved inside closing the double doors behind me. It was 7 o'clock and I wondered what was in store for us today. There was no noise from Kao's room so I presumed he must still be asleep. I slipped through and had a quick shower then dressed in my usual cotton *yukata*, this one was of pale lemon with a design of green foliage embroidered on it. As I moved silently through Kao's room I saw him stir. I stopped as he turned over and opened his eyes.

"Oh it is you my lovely lady", he exclaimed. I walked over to his bed and gave him a quick morning kiss, but he demanded more, so after a longer kiss I finally was able to disengage and discuss any plans or possible plans for today. Apparently the Doctor was due at 9.00 am and Kao was anxious that he be allowed to get out of bed and get dressed so that we could do something together. I said I would abide by the Doctor's decision, whatever that was, and I would make sure that Kao would also. Kao frowned saying he hoped all would be well so that we could plan our wedding and visit the Shinto Priest together later that day.

Masaya arrived with breakfast for the two of us which, as usual, was delicious. I was beginning to understand the relationship between Masaya and Kao. Masaya had been in the family's service since a young boy and had become Kao personal assistant some 30 years before. They knew each other well and Masaya was treasured as more than just a servant. There was a deep respect between the two of them. Masaya would know just what Kao wanted at any time of the day and Kao had shown his appreciation by doing everything possible for Masaya and his family members to ensure that they could enjoy a good quality of life. I understood that Kao, like all Shinto followers, believed in living in harmony with all things – everything in nature and everyone he came into contact with.

As well as harmony, Kao believed in patience, kindness, responsibility towards others, appreciation and, most of all, not being judgemental. I know he often questioned me when I passed judgement on someone I knew, which had made me question myself as to why I would judge them so, based on what grounds? He made me question many things that in my Western world I accepted. I had learnt so much from him. I guess I had begun to acknowledge Kao as my sounding board, someone I could use to reassess my values and beliefs and to make sense of who I was. I think I had a similar effect on Kao and I thought this was a very healthy outlook for as we learnt from each other we did not take our cultural heritage for granted anymore but questioned many things we had just accepted in the past.

We finished breakfast just before 8 o'clock and put the dishes aside for Masaya to collect later. Kao was holding my hand when there was a knock on his door. He said 'come' and Takahiro entered giving me a bow and checking what plans his father had for the day. He was pleased that Kao was planning nothing until he had seen the Doctor. Takahiro had offered his services to assist in the organisation of our wedding ceremony and had already visited the kannushi to arrange the ceremony. He also advised that Chieko had offered to help me with my wedding attire and plan the organisation of the food. He added that Chieko would be waiting for me in her apartment at 10 o'clock this morning to discuss the format of the ceremony and the type of dress I would like to wear. I thanked Takahiro and confirmed that I would meet with Chieko. Kao had remained in bed and was sitting up with his back propped against several pillows. He looked comfortable but said he was feeling very lazy. Takahiro and I both agreed this was the best place for him to regain his strength, but Kao just smiled sadly and answered that he really should be spending as much time with me as possible as I would soon be returning home.

"Quality time is what really matters Kao" I replied, "and we shall have that during our ceremony and afterwards". I squeezed his hand and sat on the bed. He nodded. Takahiro said he would check with the Doctor after he had seen Kao and then come back. He said his goodbyes and departed.

Kao remarked "Oh, my lovely lady I fear I am a disappointment to you". He kissed my hand and continued "I hope you will forgive my inability to be a better host". I reassured him that he had been a perfect host and that he couldn't help becoming ill, but he smiled sadly again and pulled me closer. We kissed gently then I kissed him on the forehead, telling him that we could still have quality time together even if he was confined to bed for the day. Kao gave a wicked smile and said "Yes". I had to laugh. He was so incorrigible. I disentangled my hand from his and advised I was going to put on my makeup. As I walked into the bathroom Kao settled down into bed and closed his eyes. I realised that he was more tired than he cared to admit and thought a day in bed would be so good for him. I hoped he would be well enough for our ceremony the following day as I knew this was something he really wanted, as I did however, if he wasn't well ….

When I had completed my makeup I found Kao had slipped back to sleep so I left him and walked quietly back into the lounge room. I checked my watch and found that I had 20 minutes before I had to meet with Chieko. I picked up my book and put it onto the table, making sure I had placed a bookmark in the page I was reading. I picked up a small notebook I recorded all appointments etc. and for which I could make notes about our wedding ceremony whilst talking to Chieko and Ikumi. I checked that I had everything I might require then quietly left the room.

CHAPTER 19

FAMILY GATHERINGS

Chieko had organised coffee and a range of Japanese delicacies which the three of us enjoyed while discussing the next days' celebrations. Chieko informed me that I should understand that Shinto has no known founder or single sacred scripture, explaining that it is wholly devoted to life in this world, emphasising the essential goodness of men and women. Shinto is an optimistic faith as humans are thought to be fundamentally good, and evil is believed to be caused by evil spirits. Consequently, the purpose of most Shinto rituals is to keep away evil spirits by purification, prayers and offerings to the kami. All things are considered sacred and given homage: trees, stones, flowers, animals and even bugs.

She continued "A Shinto wedding is a small-scale affair involving the couple, their families and their close friends, but it is a sacred ceremony. The bride normally wears a *shiromuku* (white kimono) with a white scarf. This colour symbolises purity. This ceremony must not to be taken lightly" she emphasized "it is highly spiritual, and we pray to the *kami* for your good health and happiness, but also for protection. Every Shinto ritual should be carried out in a spirit of sincerity, cheerfulness and purity" she resumed, "The wedding ceremony begins with ritual purification, that is, the use of water to wash hands and faces. Next prayers are offered after which you will drink sake, taking three sips from each of the three cups poured by the *miko* (shrine maiden) then Kao will say words of commitment to you. In many weddings rings are exchanged although this is not essential. A sacred dance is performed by the miko. The ceremony ends with an offering of *tamagushi* (a sacred branch) and a ritual sharing of sake by everyone present. It is then time for photographs and everyone will want one with the Bride and Groom", Chieko and Ikumi smiled then Ikumi informed me that Shinto weddings were much less popular today than a generation ago when 70% of Japanese chose a Shinto ceremony, now the number is less than 20%. The standardised Shinto wedding ritual is based on the ceremony used for the wedding of Crown Prince Yoshihito and Princess Sado in 1900. Ceremonies varied greatly before this time depending on the culture of the prefecture and the financial situations of the families involved. Both Chieko and Ikumi advised that it was traditional for brides to wear a shiromuku and that a wedding fitter in Kyoto will bring out several for me to choose from.

"The wedding kimono is not bought but rented for the day and brides may have several changes of dress. For instance, a traditional kimono for the ceremony and a modern evening dress for the meal and the dancing afterwards," Chieko offered. Ikumi insisted that I would also have to wear a headdress – either a traditional scarf or, at least, some flowers in my hair. I made notes frantically – it was becoming more complicated by the minute! Chieko and Ikumi laughed at my confusion and said that I had not to worry but just to leave everything to them however, I was determined to have the final say on what I would wear as it was my wedding after all! I left Ikumi ringing the wedding dresser with Chieko giving her instructions. I shook my head as I said goodbye and left them laughing. At least they were having fun and thoroughly enjoying themselves. I had to admit, I too was enjoying the planning, and very much looking forward to the ceremony.

I arrived back at Kao's apartment just after 12 noon and found Kao still asleep. I quietly walked through into the lounge and closed the intervening door. I found a note left to me by Takahiro advising the Doctor had been and all was well with Kao but the Doctor had recommended more rest for Kao with short intervals out of bed. A walk in the garden was recommended. Takahiro also advised that he had spoken to the

Shinto priest and had organised the wedding ceremony which he believed would please both Kao and myself. The Priest had ordained that, due to our circumstances, Kao and I should have no contact until the wedding ceremony. No sightings, no sitting, no communication on any level. The Priest had apparently stated that our meeting and melding would be incorporated within the ceremony itself. I sat and mulled this over. This was a spiritual message from Kao's spiritual leader, something we couldn't ignore. I wondered how Kao would take this, but I knew I would honour this directive no matter what Kao may or may not want. I rang the bell for Akiko who arrived promptly. I informed her that I would be sleeping in the spare bedroom of Kao's apartment prior to the wedding so could she please see that everything would be ready for me. She bowed and we worked out what I would need for the next 24 hours. I also advised that the wedding kimono should be delivered to that room when they arrived in the morning. She indicated that she understood and left taking a range of items with her to place in the next room: underwear, two *yukata*, and sleepwear. I collected my makeup, and several books to read then I left Kao's lounge and walked to the spare bedroom. I locked the door behind me – I was taking no chances for Kao's cogent spirit to get his own way!

After arranging my clothes and toiletries I left the bedroom in search of Takahiro, locking the bedroom door behind me. Eventually I found him in the garden with his family. The children ran up to me when they saw me and I hugged them. They led me to where their parents were sitting under the pagoda. We discussed the Priests' directive and I explained where I would be sleeping. Both agreed I had taken a wise path. I sought more information about the wedding ceremony which they were able to provide. Takahiro explained that many couples choose to marry 'before the gods' (*Shinzenshiki*) in a Shinto wedding ceremony. Both parties should be in traditional dress. Kao would be wearing a *montsuki hakama* which is comprised of a *motsuki* (black formal kimono) and a *haori* (black kimono jacket) and *hakama* (kimono pants) both embroidered with the Sahashi family crest. He would also be wearing a fine brocade obi, carrying a fan and wearing white split-toed *tabi* socks and *zori* sandals. I confirmed that I would be traditionally dressed in a white kimono. Ikumi nodded. She informed me that, guided by a shrine maiden, I would walk into the Main Hall where family and friends would be waiting. The Priest would use *Norito soujyo (norito)* being the language of the gods) to report Kao and I to the kami as becoming married and to pray for our enduring happiness.

Takahiro explained that Kao would make a declaration of his commitment to me then we would drink and exchange sacred sake in turn from three small, medium, and large sized cups, as an exchange of eternal vows of marriage. Kao will then read out the formal language of an oath from husband to wife, after bowing in front of the shrine and before he signs his name to the documentation. I will follow Kao reading the oath and adding my name after his. Takahiro then explained about the *tamagushi* (literally means the jewel skewer) which is a form of Shinto offering made from a branch of a *sakaki* tree, a Japanese evergreen tree, decorated with thin strips of *washi* paper, silk, or cotton and made by the Shinto Priest in front of the shrine.

"In the Supreme Court of Japan in April 1997 a landmark ruling was made that *tamagushi* offerings were unconstitutional however, this ritual is still attached to many weddings and funerals today", Takahiro stated. He went on to explain that this leafed twig represented the deepening spiritual relation between kami and man when offered before a shrine and it cemented the marriage vows made. The shrine maiden dances the shaman dance to traditional Japanese court music before she serves sake to all family members. The ceremony is over when the Shinto Priest issues words of congratulations.

Having been taken through the ceremony twice now, first by Chieko and Ikumi and now by Takahiro and Ikumi, I believed I was fully conversant with the procedures and - fingers crossed - I would have no difficulties on the day! Ikumi appeared worried about Kao's endurance as she advised me that the ceremony could take over an hour but Takahiro reassured us both saying the Priest had agreed that it would be reduced as both of us having being married previously. Takahiro explained that there usually is a procession led by two priests and two shrine maidens, the couple then follows under a large, red parasol and then the couple is followed by their family and friends however, in order to shorten the ceremony – largely due to our ages and assessment of our endurance to stand – but not distracting from the spiritual nature of the ceremony, it had been reduced to half an hour due to ruling out the procession. It was more in keeping, according to the Priest, that I should come to Kao because that had spiritual significance being his second wife. Ikumi asked about the bride's head dress and Takahiro said a simple one would suffice as the reason for elaborate head dresses were to ensure that the bride saw only the groom, for purity's sake, and this did not apply to a woman who had been previously married. Takahiro also informed me that the normal monetary gifts that guests would be expected to present to us had been waived as this was a second marriage for us both and, I thought, Kao wasn't short of a bob or two! We sipped coffee and enjoyed the usual delights of Japanese *wagashi* (desserts) as I received more insights into Shintoism. It was all very interesting and, the more I learnt about it, the more I began to affiliate with this belief system. It was past 3 o'clock and at last it was time for us to move on to our respective family responsibilities, so we bade our goodbyes and went our separate ways.

I entered my bedroom and picked up my book and decided that I would read it until I became sleepy. I read for some hours and just after 5.00pm Masaya knocked at the door and asked whether I would be joining the family for dinner at 6.00pm or having a tray with Kao when he awoke. I chose the former and thanked him. Just after he left my mobile phone rang which surprised me, and I found myself talking to the Project Manager of the house we were having built on the farm in Gawler. I had completely forgotten all about the project - and about Bill the Manager. He just wanted to update me on the latest developments. It was pleasing to hear he was on budget and work was progressing within the proposed framework. I was aware the plumbing and floors had been completed prior to my leaving Tasmania however, Bob informed me that the wall framing was now finished and standing, along with the completion of the roof. The weather had been kind and work had been able to continue without too many missed days. Bill explained that he expected the inside wall cladding to be accomplished during the next week, also the electrical wiring to be finished together with the insertion of all the windows. Once all this was done the house would be weatherproof, which would be a great relief. I crossed my fingers and hoped that the weather would remain kind and allow these tasks to be completed. Bill asked some questions in regard to power points. Fortunately, I had brought the house plans with me – including the wiring diagrams so, asking Bill to hold, I dug these out of my case and was able to ascertain the point Bill was making. He suggested moving a couple and his suggestions had merit so I readily agreed so making the power points more accessible. Bill rang off promising to contact me the following week with more up to date information on progress, or otherwise, of the build. I sat for a long time going over the plans and I was quite excited as Kao had not seen these; leaving everything to me regarding the our new house. I had gained Hiroto as my 'partner in crime', in other words someone who could help me furnish our new home, in particular the Master Bedroom. I wanted this room to be in pure Japanese style as the rest of the house would echo the turn of the century Australian. I could envision the deco including the type of furniture required, the special features of each room, the artifacts, and the books. I sketched onto the plans where I wanted the kitchenette to be, where the computer should be placed, and considered the colour scheme required. Enough, I thought and folded away the plans. I checked the time and realized that it was later than I had thought. I renewed my makeup and made sure my dress wasn't crumpled, washed my hands and smoothed my hair. I found that in the dining room most of the family was assembled and, as I sat next to Chieko, she smiled and asked after Kao. I brought her up to date and she seemed satisfied with Kao's improvement. I found that I was quite hungry so turned my attention to my favourite, *milo* soup. Several complementary toppings had been added including green onion, *wakame* seaweed, and firm tofu. It was truly delicious. Also served was *soba* with toppings of spring onions, *agetama* tempura flakes, *kamaboko* fish cakes and grilled *mochi*. I saw that my favourite, *tonkatsu*, was also served. This is made by coating pork chops with crisp *panko* breadcrumbs and deep-frying them until they are golden brown in colour. They had fruit and vegetable based *tonkatsu* sauce drizzled over them with shredded cabbage and other crisp salad greens served on the side. Last, but not least, tamagoyaki (cooked egg), which has a slight sweetness that makes it almost dessert-like, is a Japanese omelet made by sequentially cooking and rolling several layers of beaten egg. These look like a rolled up crêpe, and when sugar is added and they are sliced up and eaten alone they make a fitting end to a wonderful meal however, varieties of my favorite fruits of kiwi, strawberries, oranges, watermelon, melon and grapes were in abundance much to my delight. Yet again I had indulged and thoroughly enjoyed my Japanese meal with my Japanese family. I enjoyed the repartee between family members and between them and myself. It was a pleasant two hours. Chieko asked whether I wanted to join her in her apartment for chocolate and liqueurs and I said that would be nice. I am sure she knew that this is what Kao and I would do after dinner and I was touched by her kindness and understanding. We retired to Chieko's apartment and were served and enjoyed our drinks. We discussed the state of Kao's health and we both hoped that he would be well enough to go through with the ceremony in the morning.

It was past 9 o'clock when I took my leave of Chieko. We hugged and I promised to join the family for breakfast at 8 am the next day. She revealed that Takahiro has spoken to his father about the Priest's directive of no contact between us and she expressed her confidence that Kao would not violate this request. I thanked her for the drinks and for this information as I left. I wandered back to my bedroom and went directly to the bathroom. I needed a shower to relax me and put me in the mood for sleep. The water was lovely and hot and I felt very relaxed as I reached for my towel. The only thing that was missing was Kao. I loved the feeling of him rubbing me dry with the towel and I missed him very much. I wouldn't see him tomorrow before the ceremony either so I was looking forward to getting the formalities over so we could be together again. I really could do with a hug but I had to wait for tomorrow for that. I put on my nightie, turned back the bedcovers and got into bed. I had intended to read but I was suddenly very weary so turned out the light and lay down. I thought about the next day and hoped that I would be able to say all the special things that were necessary. The Shinto ceremony appeared very complex and I did so hope I would get all the Japanese words right as they were so very beautiful. I also ruminated on what *hikidemono* or wedding souvenir that Kao and I would give to each of our guests. The 'little trinkets' as Takahiro had called them are usually small and elegant gifts. I hoped that Kao had discussed this with Takahiro as I hadn't thought of doing so. I imaged they would be some small silver object to remind them of our ceremony. Eventually I fell asleep and had some dreams about our wedding but they were all jumbled, as dreams often are, so I really couldn't make any sense out of them. At last I fell into a deep sleep.

CHAPTER 20

SHINTO CELEBRATIONS

I awoke to a day that was overcast and cool. It had rained overnight and the clouds looked heavy signifying more rain that day. The sky was just becoming light and the birds were starting their morning chorus while the clock showed it was just after 6 am. I stretched and lay comfortably in the big bed, in no hurry to start the new day. It was going to be a big day for both Kao and I. I thought of the commitment we were both going to make, each to the other, and asked myself whether this is what I really wanted or was I being swept away by Kao's emotions and his recent brush with death. It wasn't too late to inform everyone that I had changed my mind – if indeed I had. Gosh I was self-analyzing again! Not a bad thing though as I had to be confident in what I was doing and that I was doing it for the right reason. Yes, I loved Kao and yes, I wanted to be his wife, but how would that make me feel when I returned to Tasmania. I couldn't answer that now but I would know when I returned to Tassie! I sighed, stretched again and sat up.

Throwing back the doona, I swung my legs over the side of the bed and stood. Just then a gentle knock came at the door. I grabbed my robe and said 'come'. Akiko entered and asked whether I required some assistance to get ready for the family breakfast. I smiled and said 'yes please'. She readied the shower and helped me into it, allowing me the time to wash myself and shampoo my hair. She then stepped forward with a towel and helped to dry me. I put on my robe and sat on the stool while she hung the towel on the rail then she gently brushed my hair. After checking with me, Akiko took the hair dryer and dried my hair. Then she left the bathroom to organize my clothes for the day while I bushed my teeth and put on my makeup. I was soon dressed with Akiko's help, choosing the yellow kimono to wear. It was still early but Akiko wanted to paint my nails. She picked out a pale pink nail varnish, one that she knew I liked, and expertly coloured the nails on each hand, finishing them off with the hair dryer. She wanted to paint my toe nails next and I thought 'why not'.

Akiko seemed happy enough doing this chore and we chattered on in English as I knew she wanted to improve her pronunciation and general knowledge of the language. It was interesting listening to her talk of her family and of her early life, and how she came to be working for the Sahashi family. Making sure all my toes were dry Akiko asked if I would be wearing the wooden shoes for the ceremony and when I said I would be she wondered if I wanted to wear them now so I would get used to them. I agreed this was a good idea so she fetched the shoes and the socks and showed me how to put them on. They felt very different from my normal shoes but not uncomfortable and I wondered whether I could wear them for the best part of the day. Akiko gave me a smile of encouragement as I left for breakfast.

I arrived at the dining room just before 8 o'clock and found Chieko, Ikumi and the children assembled. I took the vacant seat next to Chieko who advised that Kao and the boys would be having breakfast together in Kao's apartment. My enquiry revealed that Kao had slept well and was looking forward to his breakfast. I smiled at this as it meant the Kao was feeling very much better. The men's breakfast was going to be similar to ours: a hot bowl of miso soup and some grilled fish, Kyoto's famous tsukemono pickles and tofu with a *miso-matcha* sauce poured over it and lastly a bowl of brown rice and oats. All this followed by green tea or coffee. I thought this should sustain me until the evening meal which, I believed, we would be partaking around 4.00 pm. Chieko told me with a blush that it was traditional that the newly married couple retired early however, nowadays it was more usual for both the ceremony and the dinner to be later, which included dancing until maybe midnight. Chieko sounded slightly shocked at such antics.

I agreed, "Retiring early was just what Kao and I wanted" – and Chieko giggled into her fan at this. I squeezed her hand and we laughed together. She suggested that I should get plenty of rest before I left for the shrine as I would be on my feet for most of the day both during and after the ceremony. I felt that these were wise words and I nodded in agreement. She also reminded me that the shiromuku was to be delivered at 9 am and it would take at least two hours to have me dressed in the traditional kimono but said that Akiko would be there to help me. She, Ikumi and the children would not see me again until the ceremony began, and Kao would be accompanied by their three boys. The rest of the family would also be seated and I would be the last person to enter. Chieko reminded me that lateness by me would not be tolerated. She added that the shrine maiden would assist me when I entered the shrine. I was a bit worried about how I would manage in the shoes, so far had been OK being in the house, but I had to walk down underneath the avenue of cherry trees, pass under the torii, then wash my hands and mouth before entering the shrine it was all a bit nerve racking. I took a deep breath and decided I would just deal with any issues as and when they arose as it would do no good to try and presuppose what these might be.

Back in my room I decided to put my feet up until my shiromuku arrived. I grabbed a book and lay on the bed reading until a knock on the door announced the arrival of the 'bridal' man. Akiko ushered him and his two helpers, women who looked like mother and daughter. They brought in with them several shiromuku on a clothing hanger on wheels. I was amazed at the beauty of these kimono, they were dazzling. Akiko indicated she would help me try them on. The 'bridal' man, Jūzō, was very helpful and spoke reasonably good

English which I found great. He turned his back as I chose a beautiful silk brocade white kimono. Akiko helped slip my arms through the *shiromuko*. It had silver and very pale pink cherry blossoms strewn subtlety throughout the fabric. The obo was very pale pink and silver. I was made aware that some wedding kimono took up to 3 hours to be dressed in due to some having three layers. I thought 3 hours was too long and said so, but I thought the shiromuku was so very beautiful. Akiko was so delighted with my choice she was almost beside herself and kept saying "beautiful, beautiful". Jūzō was also suitably impressed especially when I chose a delicate white sheer cloak with sprigs of pink cherry blossom embroidered on it, to complete my outfit. He appeared very pleased with my choice, waiving my request for the bill for the hire of the shiromuku, saying that it would be sent to the Master (Kao I guessed). Jūzō also had several head dresses, he had obviously been advised that hoods were not necessary. He had one which was of fresh cherry blossoms, the smell was wonderful, and when Akiko placed this on my hair, over my left ear, I felt it just completed the picture. I was very happy and so was Akiko and so was Jūzō. He gathered up the rest of his wares saying he would leave the two female helpers to assist with my dressing. I sighed a sigh of relief, at last I was organized for the wedding – at least dress wise!

Akiko asked how the shoes were and I felt I could continue to wear them for the duration of the ceremony. She pointed out that, if need be, I could change into slippers when I returned to the house before the meal which appeared a good suggestion if I needed this. This also made me wonder what we were going to eat. I am sure Chieko and Ikumi had arranged everything to suit the occasion, but I had no knowledge of what this might entail and hoped it contained at least some of the dishes I enjoyed, as there were a lot of Japanese dishes that I did not like, for example *sushi,* so I hoped at least Chieko would run the menu passed Kao. My stomach fluttered as time was fast approaching to get ready for the big occasion. Akiko apparently sensed my apprehension.

"Everything will be OK, and you will be a beautiful bride". I appreciated her support and her concerns for my nerves! It was almost 9.35 am and the time had come to get ready. Akiko suggested I may require to adjust my makeup and I agreed. I allowed her remove the makeup I had put on only a few hours earlier and apply new makeup. She was very quick and understood what I wanted. She knew I did not want to look like a geisha and when she had finished I must admit she had done a marvelous job. I looked almost pretty!! The eyeshadow was subtle but nevertheless brought out the blue of my eyes and the lipstick she had chosen was a lovely pink which complemented the pink flowers in my shiromuku. She had added a faint blush to my cheeks. I could see no signs of the dark patches that age had brought to my cheeks, so I was happy. I thanked her and she help as the two women helped me on with the kimono.

Both expertly arranged and fastened it then wound on the obi with its obviously intricate knotting and fastening in bows at the back and finally adjusting the collar and sleeves. Lastly, Akiko tucked my fan and curved dagger (in its holster) into the obi. Akiko fastened the flowers, on a tortoiseshell head band, securely in my hair. I didn't look too bad for an old chick, I thought and had to smile. Akiko smiled also and touched my hand, which just visible beyond the sleeve. She helped me put my feet back into the wooden shoes and I was glad to have taken them off when trying on the kimono. It was ten minutes to 11 and time for me to begin my journey to the Shinto shrine.

Akiko squeezed my hand and ran off as she revealed that she was to be seated prior to my arrival at the shrine – so I was all alone. As I walked to the door I realised there was a glass of Kao's wonderful liquor waiting on the table near the door. How I didn't see this before I really don't know, but I certainly need some Dutch courage so took a long sip, then finished it off. It was delicious and just what I needed. I believed this to be a message from Kao, how lovely I thought. I took a deep breath as I opened the door and went into the hallway making for the lift.

As I walked through the beautiful garden, along the avenue of cherry trees and under the imposing Torii, I really felt the transition from the mundane to the spiritual. The shrine stood in front of me and I turned to where I had to rinse my mouth and hands with pure water in the *temizu* ritual, which was necessary prior to a shrine visit in order to make me pure enough to approach the kami. This done, I mounted the steps and walked through the shrine's worship hall and into the main sanctuary. I was met by the shrine maiden as I paused to take in the scene. Everyone was present and sat each side of the hall facing the middle of the room. Chieko met my eyes and smiled. The scene was very emotional but I was able to return her smile. The miko made sure I was OK then she smiled and left me, moving behind the family members on my left to join the Priest on the dais. I took a deep breath before I continued my walk towards where Kao was standing in front of the *Shinshoku*. He glanced over his shoulder and our eyes met. Oh, that was so wonderful and made me confident to continue as my legs were shaking and I thought they may let me down. This was not the occasion for me to fall or faint.

I joined Kao and the Priest began the ceremony. While it was all in Japanese the Priest had thoughtfully supplied an English translation so I was able to follow the ceremony and feel the full spirituality of the moment. I had been tutored by the Priest to make my vow of commitment in Japanese. This I did and I was pleased I was able to pronounce everything the way it should be. After several prayers and entreaties to the various gods we were soon partaking in the sake ceremony, with the rest of the family following. We watched the miko complete her ritual dance, she then sang a melodic song before the Priest motioned us to sign all the documentation, after which he made the declaration that we were (at last) married. I was surprised that Kao took me by the shoulders and kissed me gently. His eyes were dewy, as were mine, and they told me just how he felt. It was a lovely moment; one I would remember all my life. We bowed to the Priest, turned and walked into the worship hall with the rest of the family following. They all congratulated us and crowded around while we cut the cake which the miko handed around to everyone. Even Kao and I received a piece which was delicious.

We had a few moments on our own when he told me how much he loved me and how beautiful I looked. He said he would remember this day until the end of time. Takahiro approached us and suggested we lead everyone towards the lake, which was just behind the shrine. We did so and was surprised that everything had been organised. Tables to the right literally groaned with food and there was a drink stall to the left. In between tables and seating for 6 or 8 were set between these. Even though it was still early tiny coloured lights twinkled amongst the trees which established a very tranquil scene helped by the sound of the small waterfall and a slight breeze which felt very cool and pleasant. The rain, which had threatened earlier, had not eventuated and the day had turned out warm and sunny. Kao handed me a glass of wine and we clinked glasses to each other, then Takahiro asked everyone to drink to the 'bride and groom'. We both laughed at that. Nothing but happiness shone out of Kao's eyes, and mine too I hoped. I thought Kao looked very majestic in his wedding outfit and told him so. He smiled when he said he hoped I would like him more without his wedding outfit. I said "decidedly so Master" and he grinned. Chieko came up and said we were acting as if we were shy young things. We declared that was just what we were and she giggled behind her fan and shook her head. The grandchildren came up and said I looked like a princess before Ikumi came up and tried to pull them away. I said not to bother but she was concerned they may dirty my dress. I said it didn't matter as I just loved having them around. She sighed and shrugged her shoulders saying I was as bad as they were, with a smile. We hugged and she said how lovely I looked and how proud the family was to have me officially join them as a member. Everyone was so nice. I excused myself and walked towards the house with Akiko following close behind.

Akiko opened the door to the spare bedroom I had been occupying in Kao's apartment and she helped me to negotiate the removal of my shiromuko. Even though the shiromuko had only three layers it was still impossible to negotiate the intimate use of the bathroom while wearing it! After attending to my needs, I returned to the bedroom where Akiko helped me into a lovely vermillion satin kimono which I had purchased when Kao had taken me on a tour of Kyoto just a few days ago. The kimono had a stork embroidered in silver thread on the back and on the front. The obi was of silver satin but with the Sahashi family crest embroidered in gold and red in its center. Akiko fastened the diamond necklace around my neck and I put on the earrings. I also had the opportunity to change my shoes, discarding the *geta* for sandals, thinking I couldn't stand for much longer in these. I returned to the party with Akiko following. I rejoined Kao who looked lovingly at me, saying I looked 'divine'. Akiko approached me with a platter of finger food and I happily choose a piece of pickled eel, one of my favourate foods. I was sure Kao had been consulted regarding the meal as most of it was sushi but there were enough variety for my appetite to be satisfied. I was so happy to be standing next to the man I loved – as his wife – and to be surrounded by my new family. We managed to eat a little and drink lots. I wasn't worried about the drink as I was sure it was all non-alcoholic so I drank copious amounts as I was very thirsty.

First the champagne for the toasts – of which there were many – and then the absolutely delicious Kyoto wine. I received a kiss on both cheeks from Takahiro and the two younger boys, and even from Gentarō's, Cheiko's father, while welcoming me into the family. His speech was long and I could understand only some of what he had to say but I bowed low when he had finished and said, "Arigatou". Kao was kind enough to translate the gist of Gentarō' speech which I had guessed at anyway. The whole family had welcomed me from the start with no jealousies or conflicts. I had previously thought that maybe it was politeness on the part of Japanese which prevented them from showing their true feelings but I had learnt that they were showing their true feelings and really liked and accepted me. As the sun began to sink the fairy lights twinkled on the lake and Kao took me by the hand and led me to the water. He had a boat standing by and both Kao and the Captain helped me into it.

The boat moved away from the shore while everyone cheered. We waved, then Kao opened a bottle of champagne. There was a silver platter of nibbles with a variety of cheeses. including Cheddar and Brie with biscuits, sliced pickled dill cucumbers, sliced cabana and green pitted olives. I was amazed and said so. Kao smiled and said, "I thought a bit of Aussie fare would suit you tonight my dear lady". I hugged him and thought what a very special man he was to have thought that I may like something a little plainer than all Japanese food today. The Captain took us around the Lake, which was quite large and, I hadn't noticed before, it had a small island it its middle with a solitary tree planted on it. This also was lit with fairy lights although these were all white.

It was such a magical moment and I shall never forget it. The merriment from the family echoed across the lake to us and we laughed together and commented on the wonderful experiences of the day. Kao whispered words of love to me and I to him. He held me close and I felt the hardness of him. I wanted him too and couldn't wait to be in bed with him. All too soon we returned to shore where everyone wanted to help us ashore so we nearly didn't make it! Ashore at last, glasses of wine thrust in our hands and everyone talking at once. I was amazed when Chieko, very seriously, related the time to me. It was almost 6 o'clock and Chieko obviously thought it was time for us to move on.

Kao then asked for photographs and we eventually had a group photograph, with lots of other photographs with all the other members of the family. Chieko again urged us to be on our way, and I realized that she hadn't stuck to the non-alcoholic wines as she was more than a little tipsy. Kao humoured her and said we would be leaving shortly, wherein she sat down heavily on a nearby chair. I hoped she would be Ok but I could see Ikumi had everything under control as she was giving Chieko a glass of water to drink. She smiled and I waived to her just as Takahiro approached Kao and had a few words. I couldn't hear what was being said but Takahiro banged a small silver gong which caught everyone's attention. He announced that Kao and his wife Caroline were about to depart for the night and, he paused as everyone cheered, we would like to say goodnight.

Kao gave a lovely speech the gist of which was to thank everyone for cementing our happiness with their presence today, to wishing their ancestors smile on everyone and to ensure they walked safely through life. We walked hand in hand back towards the house and I realised just how tired I was. I asked Kao how he was feeling and he admitted he was tired and ready for bed, but he smiled when he said it and I knew what was on his mind because it was on my mind also. We caught the lift up to his apartment where Masaya and Akiko were waiting for us. Akiko took me into the spare bedroom where she helped me undress. She unclipped the hairpiece and laid it on the table. I said I would have a shower to freshen up so she prepared the shower for me and helped dry me afterwards. She brushed my hair, which I had managed to keep dry then she indicated a box on the bed fastened with a white satin bow and said it was from 'the Master'. I opened it and parted the white tissue paper to reveal a beautiful white silk negligee set. The nightdress had a deep vee lace insert in the front which was set with diamantes. The sheer peignoir (outer garment) had three diamante buttons down the front. The set was absolutely beautiful and I overwhelmed. As I was examining the peignoir, a piece of paper fell to the floor – it was a note from Kao. It read:

To My Lovely Wife,
I cannot express how much you have honoured me today by becoming my wife. I am so very happy. I hope you like this small token of my love. There is not enough of anything in this world to show you how much you mean to me but I hope to show you tonight in some small way. You have a choice to wear this or not. Whatever you decide, I await your presence with longing.

Eternally Yours, Kao

I wiped my eyes and Akiko took my hand, she also had tears in her eyes. I thought what a soppy lot we all were. I stood and Akiko helped me into the nightie and then the peignoir. To her query I said I would leave on jewellery on for the time being. She nodded and, satisfied she was no longer required, she bowed wished me goodnight and left. I checked my watch and realised that it had been almost an hour since I had left Kao so I imagined that he too was changed and ready for bed. I felt nervous, which surprised me, as I left my room and knocked gently on his door.

He opened it and his eyes travelled down by body. "Ah, come in my lovely lady," he said and took my hand "You are looking especially lovely tonight" he whispered. "Thank you so much Kao, you really spoil me you know. I really love this and feel like a princess." I answered. "That is because you are a Princess, and I am your Prince. I want you to believe that I will always treat you thus. I vow that your happiness will always be my top priority. Whatever you desire will be my delight to give this to you, if I can," he smiled and kissed my hand and handed me glass of his famous liqueur.

"Kao you have no need to make any more vows to me today. We shall both work towards the happiness of each other but sometimes other people or events get in the way and this just is not possible. We will do what can and no more can be asked of us. I know you want the best for me as I do for you this just means us both working together to reach that distant horizon called tranquillity. Happiness, like sorrow, is fleeting but tranquillity of spirit is eternal".

Kao gazed at me unspeaking. We sipped our liqueurs and at last he said, "Oh, Caroline you speak such words of wisdom, always. You just say in a nutshell what I want, but can't find the words, to say".

We hugged and he led me towards the bed. He helped me off with the necklace and I removed my earrings, he then kissed me long and sweet, gently slipping first the peignoir then the nightie over my shoulders and onto the floor. I stepped out of these as Kao dropped his robe. We climbed into bed and he kissed me again this time with an urgency which raised my passion to his. He caressed me, told me he loved me and kissed me again and again. I couldn't keep my hands off him and felt his swelling in my hand. He was soon inside me and we moved together as one as I felt myself dissolve into his physical being. Our lovemaking was unbelievable and seemed to last forever. We eventually climaxed together, exhausted but very satisfied. Kao continued to caress and kiss me which aroused us both. We made love again. This time it was slower, gentler but just as amazing. I was totally overcome by the knowledge that this man was now my husband - forever. I thanked our ancestors and the gods for allowing us to meet and to enjoy our golden years together. Kao was watching me and we both smiled together. I thanked him for the beautiful day we had shared: the ceremony, the boat trip, the lovely food and drinks, for his family and for his love. He nuzzled my hair and said he was very proud to be my husband and very proud that I had married him in front of his family. He said he would always be grateful and that he would love me forever. I must have been tired because I remember no more.

I woke during the night to hear Kao snoring softly alongside me. I smiled and snuggled up to him. He felt so good. He smelt so good. I had missed not being with him when he had been ill and hoped that our lovemaking had not put too much strain on his heart. I felt so lucky to have found him. He was very precious to me and I vowed to watch over him when I was with him to ensure he wouldn't become exhausted due to our being together. I fell quickly back to sleep and when I awoke it was still dark and the wind was cold coming through the half open doors of the balcony. I got out of bed and closed the door, went to the bathroom then slipped back into bed. Kao had not stirred. I kept my distance in case I woke him but put my leg across his. I was soon asleep. When I next awoke Kao's side of the bed was empty. I hoped he hadn't gone to the gym this morning as I wanted him all to myself. I rolled onto my back and stretched. From what I could see the day looked fine and I hoped we wouldn't get any rain today.

Kao suddenly appeared from the kitchen with a tray. "How are you my lovely wife", he said with a smile. I smiled in return and said I was wonderfully well, all things considered. It was still early but he thought I may like something to eat, he said as he placed the tray on the table next to the bed. I sat up and he pushed pillows behind me to enable me to sit comfortably. I rearranged his pillows also. Kao climbed into bed and placed the tray on his knees.

"First for Madam a nice cup of green tea" he said and passed me over a cup. "Next" he said, "boiled eggs to Madams explicit instructions" and passed over a plate containing two lightly boiled eggs in egg cups and buttered toast, complete with marmalade in a small dish. I exclaimed my delight and surprise, and he said I would make an Aussie of him after all. We giggled together as I began eating. Oh, what a wonderful day this was going to be.

CHAPTER 21

GOODBYE KYOTO

I had been planning a surprise for Kao and his, now our, family for some time and had gained Chieko's permission to use the music room, which was just off the traditional room at the front of the house and where most of the entertainment was held. We had eaten a late breakfast and Kao was now at the gym – doing only a minor exercise program – so I went down to this room. I silently slid open the paper door and entered closing the door behind me. I sat at the piano and ran my fingers across the keys. I had picked out several of Chopin's piano pieces which I had been practicing for several days as I wished to play for the family before I left, a sort of mini concert. It was a 'goodbye and thank you' gift to them for their kindnesses, their support and the entertainment while I had been visiting them. I played through the pieces and was pleased that I made no mistakes. I hoped my effort would please them. No one knew what I had planned but I supposed Chieko would have an inkling. She had promised to organise drinks and nibbles for 4.30 that afternoon and casual invitations were extended to those members of the family who were free to come along. I envisioned that the concert would take less than an hour and the socialising would take about the same time. This meant Kao and I would still have plenty of time together before the plane took off for Melbourne around 9 o'clock. I walked back to Kao's apartment thinking that I would wear the vermillion satin kimono, complete with the diamonds, as I saw last evening that Kao really appreciated me wearing this.

Kao hadn't returned when I reached the apartment. I looked out onto the balcony and found the day dark and grey, and raining quite heavily. The tornado wasn't far away. I was glad I had heeded Kao's warning and would be gone before it arrived. Just then Kao entered saying he would have a quick shower and I was to think what I wanted to do today. He disappeared into the bathroom and I heard the water running. He had looked well and rested and I was so pleased he had recovered from the suspected mini heart attack he had suffered.

I reminded him of Chieko's invitation for this afternoon and he replied, "I have not forgotten but the rest of the day is ours". I ruminated over how we should occupy ourselves. It was too wet to wander around the garden or to go into Kyoto. 0We could read our respective books, play chess or he could read some of his poems to me, but I thought that perhaps we could do something with the family as it was my last day in Kyoto. I suggested this to Kao as he emerged from the shower. He looked pleased and said it was a wonderful idea. When Kao vacated the bathroom to get dressed I took over and applied my makeup then returned to bedroom. We kissed and he said how sad it was that we only had a few short hours together. I had persuaded him not to come with me on the flight as it was 12 hours to Australia then 12 hours return, quite a long journey for him. Also, the plane would be a bit overloaded with Takahiro and his family aboard, as they were also returning to their home in Sydney. I added that we would have little privacy and the sleeping arrangements would be cramped. Kao agreed to the wisdom of my words although I knew he would want to be with me on the trip, just to spend a little more time together. Kao hugged me and said we had better check to see what the family were doing for lunch and afterwards, so we made our way to lift.

We met Masaya in the hall who informed us that the family had no plans, apart from lunch at noon but he reminded us of Chieko's afternoon soiree at 4.30 pm, for which we thanked him. We stopped outside Chieko's apartment and knocked. Masco opened the door and bade us enter. Chieko was delighted to see us and offered us tea, which we accepted.

We discussed what we could do as a family after lunch and Chieko suggested that they had some old 8mm film showing Kao's grandmother and grandfather with his very young aunts and uncles, and there were also film of his parents and even of Kao when he was growing up. It sounded delightful and we agree to convene in the entertainment at room at 2.00 when Chieko said she would have the necessary equipment all arranged. I was excited to see these old films and Kao admitted that he hadn't seen them for many years. We withdrew from Chieko about an hour later so we could tidy up prior to lunch. Kao thanked me for wanting to spend time with the family and I told him how much I enjoyed their company, particularly as they were my family now. We both smiled happily as we entered his apartment. Kao checked his watch and said there was no hurry as we would have plenty of time before lunch. I knew what was on his mind so taking his hand I walked with him into the bedroom. We were in bed and enjoying being together and making love. Afterwards I lay in his arms and we reminisced about our experiences over the last few days and everything we had packed into them.

Kao told me again how beautiful I had looked on our wedding day, how he had loved the outfits I had chosen and especially of my wearing the diamonds he had bought for me. I said I thought he had preferred the outfit I had worn after the wedding, and he had to agree that he had enjoyed removing the silken material from my shoulders to the floor. We kissed and I reminded him of the time but he said he would enjoy being late on this occasion. He stifled my protests with another kiss and we made love again. I clung to him afterward thinking that this may be the last time we made love for a long, long time. Eventually we had to make a move and I bagged the shower first. Kao, as always, was waiting for me with a large fluffy towel and quickly dried me. He then stepped into the shower and I was left to dry my hair and renew my makeup. He refused my assistance saying when I dried him it always took three times as long as when he dried himself. I countered that was my complaint also and we both laughed.

I had dressed in the magenta kimono and Kao helped me with the necklace, I added the earrings as he was slipping into his kimono. This was royal blue with matching obi. He looked so good! Blue was definitely his colour. He said how proud he had been when he saw me last evening and realised that I had the family crest embroidered onto my obi. I said I hoped that it had pleased him and he said he had thought it was wonderful. He took my hand and revealed that he felt humbled in my company as I did everything with such enthusiasm and with a big heart, and I said I was humbled by his appreciation and his love for me. We kissed a gentle but wonderful kiss then I dabbed my eyes and we left for Chieko's film afternoon, our hands entwined.

Hiroto and Haruki were the last to arrive. There was green tea in beautiful Japanese tea pots and various delicacies for our enjoyment. Kao and I helped ourselves to a cup of tea and settled into our seats. Chieko had been as good as her word as a table stood behind us on which sat the projector. In front of us was a drop down screen. When we were all settled the lights were turned down and the movies began. As there was no sound, Masaya ran a commentary advising who the people were in the movies and their relationship to Kao. These first two were black and white so after the second reel there was an interval when more tea was circulated as well as more desserts and cakes. We then settled for the rest of the films now in colour. The first film covered the lives of Kao's grandparents and their children, the second was of the aftermath of the American nuclear bombings

The devastation of the bombing was really brutal and I felt for the Japanese people at that time, and their incredible fortitude to survive and build up their society and their communities during the recovery process. The last film was of Kao's parents and their children. It was interesting to see the makeup of Kao's family, especially of Kao and his brother when they were young. Some of this was quite funny and I imagined Kao would have been somewhat embarrassed by it all, but it was all in good fun and for family members. I felt as if I was well and truly ensconced into the bosom of this family. The last of the movies deposited back into the library with the screen and project removed, more refreshments were served.

As it was just after 4.15 pm Chieko asked Masaya to announce that the soiree would take place in 15 minutes. There was a scurrying two and fro as, I expect, everyone wanted to use the bathroom prior to the soiree. Masaya had organised to have the chairs rearranged so there was seating around the room rather than in rows. Tables had been brought in which held beer, wine, sake and a collection of savoury delights. Family members were moving around talking to each other while the children ran in and out of everyone. Eventually Ikumi gained some sort of control and they sat eating. Family members began gravitating towards the chairs and there was a lull in the room, so I thought it would be expedient if I said a few words then started the concert.

Much to Kao's consternation, I walked to the centre of the room where the grand piano now stood. In shaky Japanese I thanked everyone for responding to Chieko's kind invitation which was at my request. I thanked everyone for welcoming me into the family. I was honoured by their kindness and appreciated their presence at my marriage to Kao. I also expressed how honoured I was that Kao had chosen me to be his wife and I hoped to prove myself worthy of his love and trust. I explained that today was a small expression of what they all meant to me and to thank them again. I said Frederick Chopin was my favourite composer and I had chosen several pieces by him which were my favourites and I hoped that they would enjoy his music as much as I. There was stunned silence then polite clapping started.

To say I was nervous would be an understatement, but I started the program with Chopin's Polonaise No: 3 which gave me confidence as I knew this was the one piece I could play without mistakes! I followed this with Piano Concerto No; 2 in F minor, Etude in E, then Cherzo No: 2 in B Flat Minor. When I finished playing I stood and bowed then polite clapping began. I was happy that I had not made any obvious mistakes. I thought, *Well I hoped they liked it,* but I knew Japanese were very sparse in their enthusiasm. As I joined Kao he certainly wasn't sparse in his praise. He appeared quite overwhelmed. Kao expressed his delight again and said what a wonderful surprise and lovely gift I had given the family. Everyone appeared pleased and I was happy to have been able to give them something unique and personal. Chieko was also impressed and soon other members of the family were joining in and saying how much they enjoyed it and what a musical family we all were – and that was the best praise ever. I felt as if I was indeed a real member of the family.

The rain had stopped and there was a watery sun in the sky so Kao suggested a short walk in the garden. We donned jackets and shoes and found that Takahiro, Ikumi, Chikako and Kimiya doing the same so we all joined in the walk. Although a bit chilly the air smelt fresh and full of the smell of blossoms. It was lovely. It was difficult to compare last evening with tonight. Yesterday the air had been balmy and it was very pleasant down by the lake with all the fairy lights reflected in it. We walked through the rose garden and down the steps passed the three pools of water and their respective waterfalls. The children were playing with the carp in one of the pools and we all had to go over and have a look. We laughed at their antics. I was going to miss this place along with all the family but especially Kao who always treated me so well. As if he could read my thoughts, Kao squeezed my hand. I squeezed his back and we smiled at each other.

It was getting dark when we walked through the pavilion and back into the house. We removed our jackets and shoes and Kao invited them all upstairs to have some hot chocolate in our apartment, which delighted the children. The chocolate soon made and distributed, together with liqueurs for the adults, we were soon settled and discussing the events of the last week, along with the forthcoming tornado, which was concerning some of the townspeople. Takahiro agreed with Kao that they had done everything possible to protect the old town and its businesses and they had made appropriate offerings to the relative gods, so now the fate of Kyoto lay in their hands. It seemed the combination of practicality and fatalism was very much universal to all cultures, although expressed in different ways. You did what you could then it was left in the hands of the gods!

Ikumi had found some travel books containing lots of colour photographs for the children to look at. They were asking me where this place or that place was. One of the books was about Tasmania so I was able to point out some of countryside that was around the North West Coast and there was even a picture of Ulverstone where I told them I lived. Then the question arose, why I didn't live with Papa. That was a curly one which their mother was able to explain – far better than I could! All in all it was a lovely way to relax and I thoroughly enjoyed their company. Ikumi then pointed to the two pictures of mine that Kao had purchased and hung in the lounge room. They were of animals, a Spotted Tailed Quoll and a Bandicoot. Both children were enamoured and wanted to know how I had painted them. I explained this as simply as I could then they wanted to see more of my artwork. Laughing I said they would have to visit me in Tasmania to see more, so of course that was all they talked about until Ikumi called it time to return to their quarters to pack. Of course there was resistance but mother got her way and they all left.

As the door closed I conveyed my enjoyment of their company to Kao, he also was pleased and thanked me for entertaining Takahiro, Ikumi and their children. I said I found them to be great company. We hugged and kissed then sat on the couch together, Kao with his arm around my shoulders. I leant back on him and thought how blessed I was and that I would remember this time all my life. I wondered when I would see them all again and sighed. Kao squeezed me and asked why the sigh. I told him and he reassured me that we should all be together 'soon', and I hoped so - but our lives were also in the lap of the gods! I said I had better pack and with a quick kiss I left Kao and placed my suitcase on the table next to the bed. Kao followed me into the bedroom and sat on the bed. There wasn't much to pack as the various kimono would be staying and I had brought few western clothes with me. I went to the bathroom and packed up my makeup, placing it into the suitcase. Kao asked if I could leave my perfume behind so he could smell it when he missed me – so how could I refuse? Every item packed there was little else I had to do so I turned to Kao who caught my hand asking me to come to bed. We made love and it was as wonderful as ever, tinged with a little sadness that this would be last time until goodness knows when. I clung to Kao and he held me close. We both knew that the time had come to get ready for the long journey to Melbourne, where I would catch a commercial flight to Tasmania.

I had first shower and had just finished drying my hair when Kao emerged from the shower. I helped him to dry with some kisses and laughter then, while he dressed, I put on makeup and went into the bedroom and dressed in western clothes, slacks and top. It felt strange wearing these again as I had found the kimono very comfortable. At last we were ready and it was almost 8 o'clock, time to be moving. Kao expressed his desire to accompany me on the trip but my arguments against this were valid, he agreed. Summoned by Kao, Masaya took my bag downstairs where the rest of the family gathered. We said our goodbyes. Takahiro and his family got into the first car and Kao and I in the second car. After waving our goodbyes to everyone we drove down the driveway out onto the road and towards Itami Airport, the airport servicing the Kyoto region along with Osaka Airport. We drove straight to the aeroplane and Takahiro took his family aboard. Kao and I said our goodbyes, we kissed and hugged and he saw me safely aboard. He checked with the Pilot that all was well, we kissed again – a long kiss this time – then reluctantly parted. I sat and watched him as he walked down the steps. He turned and waved then got back into the car. The plane door was closed and the engine revved. As the car drove away the plane started to move. Thankfully the children were otherwise occupied as I didn't want them to see me upset, and I was.

We were soon taking off just after 9.00 pm. Ikumi had settled the children in the double bed in the master bedroom and was turning the two couches into a second double bed for her and Takahiro. I would be sleeping in the single quarters towards the rear of the plane. She asked me if I was OK and if I wanted anything before she turned in. I answered no and said goodnight. I sat on the large single bed and wished Kao was with me, feeling foolish that I had denied his company, but then I thought that the 24 hours of travelling may well have been too much for him, as he was still recuperating from his mini heart attack and I was thankful he would be home soon. I undressed and got into bed, suddenly aware how weary I felt. I settled down and turned out the light wanting Kao desperately. I lay there for a while thinking of the wonderful things we had done together over the last few days, but eventually sleep claimed me.

CHAPTER 22

FROM ONE LIFE TO ANOTHER

I awoke being jumped on and by excited cries - the children! Ikumi apologised and hustled the children into the shower. I laughed and said it was OK as I was awake anyway. I checked my watch which read 7.45 am, time to get up. I would forego the shower and just get dressed. This done I applied makeup and brushed my hair. Feeling better, I brushed my teeth once the shower was vacated and accepted the coffee that Ikumi offered but refused breakfast as I wasn't hungry. We all sat around on the couches which had been transformed to their original condition and discussed what each was to do when landing in Melbourne. I would be leaving the plane which would then take off for Sydney. I said how much I had enjoyed their company and we promised to keep in touch. The Pilot informed us that we had the wind behind us overnight and were due to touch down earlier than expected. I gathered my bag and coat ready to disembark at Melbourne. I thanked Ikumi, Takahiro and the children for their company and we wished each other well. The plane landed without difficulty and I walked down the steps to a wet and windy Melbourne, waving to Ikumi and the children.

Entering the terminal I checked my ticket and found I had nearly 2 hours to wait before the plane to Devonport took off. I decided I would like a coffee and a sandwich so made my way to one of the coffee places. I also purchased a magazine and settled myself into a corner table to relax. Time soon passed and I found myself walking up the steps to my Devonport flight. I sat and clipped on my seat belt. Next stop Devonport and Phil. I had mixed feelings and wondered how I would feel seeing him again and slipping back into my old lifestyle. The flight wasn't long, less than an hour. It was an uneventful journey, broken only by light refreshments served by pleasant flight attendants. There was much activity when the plane stopped outside the transit lounge of Devonport airport with everyone appearing keen to disembark for their next journey home, or to start their holiday or whatever. I sat watching and waiting for the passengers to disembark. I then stood, retrieved my hand luggage from the overhead locker and walked towards the exit and the steps to the tarmac. As I walked into the lounge I immediately saw Phil. He was beaming! We kissed and hugged then walked to the carousel to claim my other suitcase. Phil brought me up to date with all the local news and what he had been doing while I was away, and I gave him my sisters' regards. Phil picked up my suitcase and we walked to the car parked just outside of the exit doors. It was a mild evening and the sun was just beginning to set, casting a rosy glow over the landscape. It looked really beautiful and I couldn't have wished for a better welcome home – Phil and a sunset.

I pushed thoughts of Kao from my mind and concentrated on what Phil was telling me, about an invitation to have lunch with friends the following day if I wouldn't be too tired. I said that sounded nice and no I wouldn't be too tired. I thought the busier I was the less likely I would fill my thoughts with Kao (?). Phil also reminded me of a dental appointment I had on the following Monday, which I had forgotten, so I thanked him for the reminder. We were soon turning into our driveway and Phil helped me out of the car then took the suitcase out of the boot while I took the hand luggage. These were placed in the spare bedroom and I advised that I would unpack in the morning. Phil made coffee and we sat, chattered and relaxed. I could smell something cooking and to my query Phil said it was a surprise – a special meal for a special lady to welcome her home. Phil smiled while he announced he had also made a dessert. I smiled and thanked him and said I could hardly wait as I was hungry. At

Phil's request I sat at the table whereupon he served up Roast Lamb and the vegetables. I could have cried, as I remembered that first meal at Kao's house when he surprised me with the Japanese version of a roast lamb dinner.

I asked for a small helping to start with as I could ask for seconds, but I feigned tiredness which had curbed my appetite. I hoped my memories of Kyoto would not inhibit my relationship with Phil, but my heart ached so for the sight of Kao and to be in his warm embrace. I must have closed my eyes for Phil was asking if I was OK and perhaps an early night was called for. "You are probably right Phil, but it was that wait in Melbourne that really got to me" I said. I helped with the dishes and in making the kitchen tidy then, as we walked to the bedroom, I related some of my excursions with Margaret and how we had enjoyed our time with Joanne and Artie, laughing at some of the things we had said and done. I told him of my shopping spree into the second hand market (flea market in Kyoto) and the very old Japanese pot I was able to purchase, which I thought may interest him. He showed interest and said he would like to examine it the next morning when I had unpacked. I had a quick shower then joined him in bed. It wasn't 10 o'clock, but I was suddenly aware of how weary I was. We kissed goodnight and I was surprised when Phil pulled me over and cuddled me. I couldn't remember the last time he had done this. My head on his shoulder I closed my eyes, but then Phil turned over and was soon breathing softy and evenly, but sleep alluded me. I couldn't stop thinking of Kao and wondering what he was doing. I guessed he was doing much as we were, trying to get some sleep. I lay there for a while thinking of the wonderful things Kao and I had done together over the last few days. Eventually I had to force thoughts of him from my mind but it still took a while for sleep to claim me.

I awoke about 6 am to a sunny day, which promised to be warm if a little breezy. Phil was still asleep so I carefully got up and padded into the kitchen, switching on the electric jug to make tea – green of course. Phil only had cereal for breakfast but I chose a variety of fresh fruit to cut into a bowl with a large spoon of yoghurt over my fruit. I switched off the jug, made the tea and placed these two mugs on the tray.

I took the tray back into the bedroom and as I opened the blinds I called a cheery "Wakey, wakey". Phil answered with a bleary "Good morning" as I deposited my mug and bowl on my bedside table. I helped him sit, adjusting his pillows before placing the tray on his knees. "This is a nice surprise, thank you Caroline but I had intended to give you breakfast in bed for your first morning home, and I feel guilty". I laughed and said this was to reward him for the lovely meal last night. We watched the morning news on the television and I learnt a little more about our luncheon rendezvous today.

We had known Marion and Bob since we had moved to Ulverstone some 8 or 9 years earlier. They had been almost the first people we had met, when they had leaned over the garden fence as we were renovating the house. We had been to their home countless times for lunch, dinner and coffee, as they had been to ours. I always enjoyed seeing them as they had news to tell often relating, very amusing incidents that had happened to one or the other. They were much the same age as us, liking similar music and enjoying similar activities so we were pretty compatible. We had formed a habit of, regardless what else happened, each couple choosing and booking a cafe or restaurant for lunch one day a month. It was Marion and Bob's turn to choose today's restaurant and they had decided on *Mystic Delights,* a new restaurant opened recently in East Devonport. It had already gained a reputation for good food at a good price. The decor was reminiscent of a Bedouins tent, without going overboard, but quite exotic. We were intrigued and quite excited to taste its food and enjoy its ambience!

After breakfast we discussed the rest of today's plans. Phil wanted to prune some bushes close to my studio before lunch while I needed to unpack and do some washing after my holiday. Phil reminded me again of the dentist appointment which I said I would put in my diary. We both arose and I quickly brushed my hair and put on a pair of jeans and a tee shirt. I washed the breakfast dishes and made the kitchen ship shape again by storing them away. I quickly unpacked my cases and put my soiled clothes into the washing machine, switching it on I then unwrapped the Japanese pot and placed it carefully on the bureau. It looked beautiful and I felt my heart lurch as I remembered where I had bought it and who I was with. I watched Phil through the window as he was clearing the debris from the two bushes he had just pruned into the green waste bin. I switched on the jug and prepared coffee for two. After pouring two cups, I placed these on a tray and took them out into the garden just as Phil was coming in to wash his hands.

"Oh great. I smelt the coffee and thought good oh I could really do with one". I laughed as I placed the tray down on the occasional table on the lawn. It was a lovely spot for a cuppa or for reading as it was sheltered from the sun by a broad Ash tree. Phil sank down and picked up his mug, taking a big swig of coffee. It was 10 minutes to 11 and we would have to get ready soon for our trip to Devonport. The trip would take half an hour and the booking had been made for 12.30 pm so we each had time for a shower and to look a bit more presentable than we did at this moment. I collected the coffee mugs and, sprucing ourselves up, we were ready for lunch.

It was almost half past three when we returned home discussed how pleasant the meal and company had been. Marion and Bob had not disappointed us with the restaurant.

The ambiance, food and service were all very good and we made a mental note to return. Phil announced that it was now 'Scotch o'clock' and poured us both a generous glass each. We enjoyed sipping this as we discussed the afternoon, and how we may occupy ourselves in the following days. I drifted off as thoughts of Kao intruded. I ached to be in his arms but I pushed thoughts of him from my mind as became aware of Phil with a question in his voice. I surmised correctly that he was discussing tonight's TV viewing, so I shrugged and answered I didn't mind what I watched. I made us a platter of cheese and biscuits and mugs of coffee while Phil turned on the TV. We watched *New Tricks* then *Midsommer Murders* before calling it a night around 10.30 pm.

As I lay there next to Phil in the dark my thoughts turned to Kao. Phil was soon asleep but sleep for me was a long time coming. Kao had made it obvious that he would like me solely to himself and had mentioned several times that I should tell Phil about our relationship. While I missed Kao I could not, nor would not, desert Phil when he needed me more than ever. Phil and I had shared so much in the time we had been married and I knew that if I explained Kao to Phil he would immediately finish our marriage. I still loved Phil and I appreciated everything he did, which he did with a kind heart. He was also thoughtful and considerate and I felt how lucky I was to be married to him. In fact I was twice blessed, as both Phil and Kao were great guys and I was pleased that I was able to keep both relationships with my Japanese and Aussie husbands separate.

The next day was cool, windy and overcast. It smelt of rain. Church today and it was good to catch up with everyone at morning tea after the service. I shared some memories of my time in WA with members of the congregation I found myself sitting with. Lunch was well in hand when I arrived home. Phil had cooked Roast Pork and it was absolutely wonderful – the crackling perfect! After lunch we discussed, over coffee, the next day's activities as Phil had to visit a heart specialist in Launceston. We agreed on a picnic lunch on the way home so Phil volunteered to make pork sandwiches and a flask of coffee. On such occasions we always found a great site to have our picnic so I was looking forward to this one. I had also arranged to see old friends living in Launceston on the way home. I had known Andrew and June for over 20 years but hadn't seen them for almost 6 months so we have lots of news to catch up on. They were equally looking forward to seeing us again after such a long time. Our trip was well organised and would be a full day but we would drive back to Ulverstone within an hour for my 4.00 pm dental appointment, if the dentist was on time and didn't have any delays during the day. I had already decided to cook Laksa, one of Phil's favourite meals, for dinner that night. While thoughts of Kao intruded from time to time I found it easier to keep my mind on my Tasmanian responsibilities and push thoughts of him to one side. It was only fair to be totally with Phil now I was back in Tasmania, as I had been with Kao while in Kyoto.

An e-mail from Kao saying how much he was missing me and asking when he could come over again unsettled me however, and I felt such pain in my heart. I wish he hadn't sent it. I asked him to please not email me for a few weeks as I had to honour my responsibilities here in Ulverstone, but not to think that I didn't want to hear from him, or that I didn't miss him. He complied and he was silent for several weeks.

Life continued and the months passed as I resumed many of my old community routines. Phil and I had arranged a joint exhibition in Wynyard, a 30-minute drive from home, for all of December. We both rallied ourselves so that we had necessary information printed about what we had to display. I printed the name tags for each painting, the catalogues and the fliers while Phil printed out the price tags and other information relevant to his display of leatherwork and bone jewellery. On the 1st December we drove to Wynyard and set up the exhibition. With the opening the following day, we had to organise wine and nibbles and ensured that the gallery was tidy and organised. I made sure that vases of flowers were suitably arranged and that everything was in order. Nibbles and glasses organised, we discussed the timetable for manning the exhibition. I had received an e-mail from Kao wishing me well with the opening. I always kept him up to date with exhibitions I had organised and he was always supportive and wished me good luck.

Phil and I had spread the timetable for attending the exhibition between us. The Exhibition opening went well and the ensuing two weeks was a busy time. Some of the patrons had been attending my Art Exhibitions since I started at the Wynyard Art Gallery several years previously. I had sold approximately six paintings in this exhibition, with interest in several more, so this looked like being great exhibition for me. We returned home happy and content. I particularly enjoyed manning an exhibition at this venue because I was able to paint while I was there. This caused quite a bit of interest amongst patrons, some of whom had no previous knowledge of pastel art. I found it easier to keep my mind on my Tasmanian responsibilities and push thoughts of Kao to one side. It was only fair to be totally with Phil now I was back in Tasmania, as I had been with Kao while in Kyoto.

I was painting one Thursday morning in the Wynyard gallery when a gentleman dressed in a red Santa Hat and a red polar shirt arrived and walked towards me. I could hardly contain myself – it was Kao. We hugged and kissed and he explained that he missed me so much he just had to come and wish me Merry Christmas in person. How wonderful. Kao disclosed that he had to return to Kyoto on Sunday afternoon but this meant that we had 4 days together. He took me out to lunch, which meant I had to close the gallery but, during that afternoon I had no interest in painting. Kao and I just talked and talked. Later, we returned to Wynyard airport where his plane was parked. We had hot chocolate and a liqueur – and we made love - truly wonderful. After a quick shower I had to return home but Kao said he would see me the next morning as Phil was manning the exhibition and I was free. Wow I thought, a whole day together.

The next few days were amazing. It was so good to be with Kao and we made very moment count. I asked about the Climate Conference but Kao was non-committal, saying that he had heard much of the arguments previously. I could not put my finger on it but I thought there was more to it than this and Kao was not being open with me. I could not shake off this feeling and felt Kao was a little reserved in some way, just not the same. I thought that this was perhaps due to his rush over to see me and maybe he was a little stressed. The plane had flown to Devonport airport in the intervening period, so on Sunday I drove him there and saw him aboard. We kissed and hugged. Holding me close with tears in his eyes, he said,

"No matter what, my dear sweet wife, I love you with all my heart and would not wish to do anything to hurt you - you understand that don't you?"

I looked at him strangely and said "Yes, I did know that". We kissed again as the engine revved, I went down the steps. The machine turned right and moved away along the tarmac. I waited until I could see the plane no more then I got into the car and drove home.

Kao's attitude had puzzled me and left me with an uneasy feeling. I never doubted for one moment that he loved me. Something was troubling him and I couldn't help him if I didn't know what it was.

CHAPTER 23

DISASTER

Caroline surprised me when she came into the library unexpectedly. I had been wondering how she was getting on and whether she had visited Japan as she had planned when she left Tassie on her WA trip, but that was before she knew about the typhoon that was forecast.

"Connie, how are you?" she said. I explained that I had just been thinking of her and here she was. She explained that she had lots to tell me, and she certainly had. I was overwhelmed when Caroline informed me that she and Kao had been married in a Shinto ceremony at the family's Shinto shrine! Between serving community members returning or taking out books or wanting help with the computers or printers, I heard just about everything Caroline did in Kyoto. I thought how wonderful it had been for her, especially as Kao's family accepted her and treated her as one of them. We discussed her recent Art exhibition and that both she and Phil had sold several pieces, also that Kao had surprised her with a visit and they had enjoyed four days together. She seemed so happy. I asked about Phil and Caroline confided that she found she still loved him and enjoyed being with him again, but her thoughts often turned to Kao and the happy times they had spent together.

I asked, "What are you going to do? Do you want to join Kao in Japan eventually?" Caroline looked thoughtful, and sighed.

"I don't know Connie. Whichever guy I am with I want to stay with him. The only difference is when I am with Kao I think of no-one else, but when I am with Phil I find it difficult not to think of Kao". I felt sad for her – and for her two men.

Someone had to get hurt eventually and I said this to her, and Caroline nodded her agreement.

Caroline was silent for a moment but her next words sent a shiver down my spine.

"What do you know about vaginal discharge?" she asked quietly, making sure she wasn't overheard. I didn't know much about it at all and asked what was worrying her. Caroline explained that all had been well when she returned home after the holiday in October but several days ago she noticed she had a discharge and having a wee often stung or was painful. I suggested she visit her GP or sought information from the internet's Google. I inferred that she may have something innocuous as thrush but she should have it checked out because if it's something more serious this could have long-time ramifications on her health. I next asked whether she thought she may have caught something from Kao.

"Well Connie I don't believe I have done so as we have been having sex for a long term now without any problems. I'm hoping it is something like thrush but you are right that I should have it checked out. Perhaps I shall Google it and get some information about what the options might be".

After Caroline left the library I couldn't help worrying about her situation. I didn't know anything about Kao or of his life in Japan and thought that maybe he was seeing someone else. Caroline was convinced that she was the only one in his life, but was she? I turned my attention to a woman wanting help with a computer and hoped all would be well with Caroline.

Connie had given me food for thought and an avenue to check on just what I may have contracted. When I returned home I went straight to the computer and searched 'Virginal Discharge'. This opened a Pandora's Box with a galaxy of information. I hadn't realised how ignorant I was. I learnt that this could be a normal phase of being a woman causing no health problems to being very serious indeed, involving some very dangerous sexually transmitted diseases which could lead to death if untreated. I devoured all this information, but I was none the wiser what my symptoms related to. I joined another website which told me much the same as the last. Thinking over all this I had the terrible thought that maybe – just maybe – I had contracted a venereal disease along the way somehow. I had to visit my GP. I felt ashamed and degraded after I rang my Doctor but relieved that I would see him the day after tomorrow.

After the early morning consultation, and having swabs taken from just about everywhere plus blood and urinary tests, I was assured I would have an initial result with 24 hours and a fairly detailed analysis of the provided specimens within three days. It was three days of hell waiting to hear, although within 24 hours I was advised it was possibly gonorrhoea. After 3 days this diagnosis was confirmed and I received a prescription for an antibiotic, ceftriaxone, which would be a one-off injection into the buttocks, together with a prescription for azithromycin, to be taken orally for 7 days. These medications would also treat chlamydia, as this was apparently often related to the gonorrhoea virus, and further tests would be necessary to ensure I was cured of both bacterial infections thus preventing pelvic inflammatory disease. It was stressed that these medications had to be taken strictly as directed otherwise serious side effects may result. I had to state the name and whereabouts of my sexual partner to check that he also had been treated and cured and, of course, the correct authorities had to be notified.

I left the surgery with the two prescriptions and a further appointment for that afternoon for the injection. While satisfied that all was being done that could be done I was still upset. I felt ashamed, humiliated and violated – both with contracting this disease and in the collection of the swabs.

While my Doctor was gentle, understanding and non-judgemental I was embarrassed with the process I had to go through. My one and only partner had been Kao. What had he been up to? Well I actually knew what he's been up to! I was hurt and angry, and I felt dishonoured by Kao. I had to see him. I had to talk to him. I reached for my mobile 'phone and rang Kao in Kyoto. He answered almost straightaway and was delighted that I should ring him. I suddenly found I was crying and it took some time before I could compose myself and speak.

His voice was full of concern and his words comforting, but I was still angry. "I have to see you, this is urgent. When can you come?" I blurted quickly.

He just said, "My dear lady, what is wrong?" but I just asked again when could he come over. Kao said he would leave immediately, but to tell him what was wrong. I couldn't tell him over the 'phone. Kao said he would leave within the hour but wished I would tell him what was upsetting me. When I remained silent Kao said he would ring me when he arrived in Devonport, and he would send a car for me. I said 'good' and rang off. Now I had to clear it with Phil and worried what I might say about going to Japan, as this is what I intended to do. For the first time I would have to lie to Phil as I couldn't tell him the truth.

Just at that moment I heard Phil's cheery 'Hello' as he walked in the back door. He took one look at me and asked me what was wrong. I cleared my throat before speaking.

"I have just spoken on the phone to John in Japan and Chieko is very ill and has been asking for me". Phil asked why she would do that. I shook my head and continued, "They are sending the plane to Devonport for me and a car will collect me at the house. The flight will take approximately 12 hours. As it is now 9 o'clock I would expect the car to arrive around 10 pm tonight so there is plenty of time to sort everything out".

Phil looked aghast. "Why are you rushing over there?" he asked "You hardly know the woman and it is such a long way. You don't know anything about this family. What if something happens to you? You have only just got home after your WA trip and now you want to leave me again!"
I could understand him being upset and I tried to calm him down, but he was confused and hurt. I said I had no idea what the problem was with Chieko but she had treated me kindly on the cruise ship and, while I thought it was unusual for her to ask for me, I had to go to her the same as I would answer the call of a good friend here in Ulverstone, or the call of one of my sisters in WA. Phil just shook his head and walked into the bedroom. I followed him. He sat on the bed shaking his head.

"You do some amazing things and I sometimes wonder if you like other people better than me" he glanced at me as he said this. I couldn't help thinking how selfish Phil could be at times – and then I thought, isn't that just what I am being. I sat next to him reassuring him that I would be home as soon as I could and that I expected I would be only gone a few days.

"No" Phil said shortly "I know how much you have wanted to visit Japan so take some time and have a few days looking around the place. I imagine you will be staying with John and his family so you should be well looked after". I said I would see how it all went, but thought yes I would be well looked after.

I grabbed a small suitcase from the spare bedroom and packed some underwear, a nightie, a couple pair of slacks, three jumpers and a pair of shoes. I said I would change into jeans, jumper and boots before I left as it would be cold in Japan at this time of the year. Phil just said "whatever" and stood, retracing his steps to the kitchen. He switched on the electric jug and asked whether I wanted coffee. I said that would be nice. We sat at the table, Phil reading the newspaper he had bought while I fiddled with my coffee.

I broached the subject again stating I wouldn't go but Phil glanced at me and saying harshly "Of course you will go" before returning to his paper. I wished to prune some roses in the front garden so, armed with secateurs, I was soon involved in the task. Clearing up the cuttings into the Council's green waste bin, I reflected that life was becoming more and more complicated. I hoped this infection wouldn't take long to clear up, that Kao and I could sort things out and that everything would return to normal soon. Normal! I laughed to myself. *Just what was 'normal'?* I queried. I returned to the house and washed my hands. Phil had left his seat so I picked up the newspaper and glanced through it, but I couldn't concentrate so decided to go for a walk. I found Phil in his workshop who expressed disinterest in joining me so I ventured out on my own along the path by the river. I enjoyed the warmth of the sun on my back and the slight breeze carrying the smell of seaweed along with it. I leaned on the rail gazing at the water as the tide came in, and at the antics of the seagulls along the foreshore. I wondered what Kao's explanation might be. I thought of my unease when we met last. Had he been feeling guilty due to his infidelity? No doubt Kao would answer all my queries, but I couldn't help feeling l betrayed. I held my head in my hands. I didn't know what to do. My head was spinning. I felt sick. I felt as if my whole world was collapsing around me. I wanted so much to feel Kao's arms around me, to feel his lips on mine, to hear him murmur that he loved me. I ached so much for him. I sighed and continued my walk, arriving home some 20 minutes later.

While Phil was in the shower I began preparing dinner. I had made some Carrot and Orange Soup yesterday and I planned Beef Cheeks for this evening's meal followed by fruit trifle for dessert, so an easy enough menu. I soon had the meal organised with the trifle in the refrigerator. I set the table for the two of us, opened a Peter Lehman Shiraz and placed the bottle on the table. I picked up the secateurs and checked the garden for appropriate flowers, choosing the lovely orange roses for the table setting. These displayed in a chrystal vase gave the table a lift and, I hoped, our spirits over dinner. The smell of cooking filled the house and Phil commented favourably as he left the bathroom. I had enjoyed cooking tonight's meal – perhaps I was feeling guilty – but I just wanted to make Phil a really good meal and I thought coffee and Grand Marnier liqueur would complete it. I hoped the meal would soothe Phil's mood so he wouldn't think too badly of me going to Japan. After dinner Phil expressed his appreciation for the meal stating that it had been 'outstanding'. Together we cleared the table, washed the dishes and stowed everything away. We sat in the lounge room discussing my trip and expected length I may be away. He had calmed down and appeared to be genuinely interested in my trip. I promised I would return as soon as I could.

In due course we saw car lights coming up the driveway which signalled the time had come for me to leave. I gave Phil a big hug and promised to text him when I arrived in Kyoto. He picked up my suitcase and we walked down the steps together to the waiting car. The driver opened the passenger door for me before stowing my case in the boot. Phil closed the door telling me to take care, then the car reversed down the drive and out onto the road. We were soon speeding towards Devonport and the airport where I would be reunited with Kao. It was a little after 10 o'clock and I surmised that the plane would be close to landing. I imagined Kao's surprise to find me ready to fly to Japan with him but how would he answer my questions.

I had found cooking and serving the meal to Phil had been a healing process and I was much calmer now and better able to think more clearly. If Kao had met someone at the conference, and it was only a one off occasion, then we should be able to sort things out between us but if it was more than this. I just didn't know how I would cope and whether this would mean the end of our relationship. I knew I had to keep an open mind until I had heard all the facts from Kao. I sat back and allowed the car seat to envelop me. It did no good to try and guess Kao's motives. He had no knowledge of sex except from my own lips. He wouldn't understand the ramifications of his actions especially when it involved sexually transmitted infections. I just hadn't thought to pass this information onto him. Was she the love of his life? I had often said I would be happy if Kao could find someone closer to home, but I had been lying.

I had butterflies in my stomach as the car turned into Devonport Airport. We stopped at Arrivals and the driver opened the door for me. I alighted and retrieved my bag from the boot. I thanked him, took my bag and walked into the lounge. It was completely empty except for Kao. His face was white making his eyes even darker. He was not happy – nor was I. Kao slowly walked towards me and took my hands in his. He slowly slid an arm around my shoulder and held me close, kissing my hair.

"How are you?" he asked gently. I answered OK and told him I would be flying to Japan with him. If Kao was surprised he made no comment as we walked into the Departure lounge, had my bags examined through the x-ray machine, then walked towards the plane. He sat me down and helped fasten my seatbelt as the Pilot revved the engines. Kao sat next to me on the couch and fastened his belt then held my hand. The plane taxied, gathered speed then we were airborne. I realised I was crying and Kao must have seen this too.

"Oh my dear sweet woman, what is making you so very sad", he murmured softly "Please tell me so I can help you in your sorrow". I swallowed but could not find my voice. Kao gave me space to collect my thoughts and to calm myself. We undid our seatbelts and I turned towards him. There was pain in his eyes and I thought, *How could I ever doubt his love for me?* Our eyes met. "Who was she?" I blurted out. His eyes widened. His flesh paled. I felt his hands go cold.

"What do you mean?" he asked slowly. "Oh, Kao please let us be honest with each other. Please don't mess me about" I begged and turned from him. He moved closer, turning my face towards him.

"Forgive me Caroline" he said, "You are correct as always, we should always be honest with one another". He paused then asked, "How did you know?" "Because she gave you more than sex" I answered.

Kao looked bewildered. "Have you any discharge from your penis? Does it hurt when you urinate? Do you suffer any pain or fever or are you feeling different from normal?" Kao's mouth dropped open and it seemed as if a light had gone on. "What do you mean?" he asked. I sighed and said, "Please just answer the questions Kao". He nodded and admitted that he had some of these symptoms. I had to remind myself that I was dealing with a very sophisticated man who was totally ignorant of sexual matters, as we know and accept in the West, due to his cultural inheritance. All Kao knew was that which he had learnt from me, so I could hardly expect him to know about venereal diseases or sexually transmitted infections.

I sighed again and realised how tired I was. "Kao you have caught a sexually transmitted disease from this woman which you have passed onto me. I have seen my doctor and I felt so ashamed both with this diagnosis and with the treatment. I felt humiliated and violated but, worse of all, I feel you have dishonoured me". Kao looked devastated, horrified even.

"Oh, my lovely wife, how could such a thing have happened? I would not wish to do this to you. You are my life, my joy. I live to see you, to be with you". He had tears in his eyes. I retorted that he knew how it happened – he'd had sex with this woman. "How could you do such a thing?" I asked. A sob escaped me and Kao's eyes met mine, they said so much; regret, love, guilt.

Kao explained that when I had returned to Tasmania he had missed me so very much. He wanted me and had ached for me. He said that it was so bad that he'd had an erection for days. He thought the Climate Conference would distract him and it had, marginally, but he couldn't get me out of his mind. Over afternoon coffee, Kao said he had been talking to one of the speakers, American Ivan Hunter, Professor of Climatology at the Tokyo University, when a woman joined them. She turned out to be a colleague of Ivan's, an American, who introduced herself as Sandy. The three subsequently agreed to meet for dinner that evening. When Kao presented himself at the meeting place at the appointed time he found only Sandy waiting for him with Ivan's apology as he had met an old colleague. She had suggested they could still have dinner together and, while Kao expressed reservations due to an early breakfast conference session, Sandy had laughed these aside and promised an early night.

Kao said he had still felt a bit awkward but thought some company may help get his mind off me for a while. After the meal they left the restaurant together with Kao thinking of nothing more than retiring to his room to read though the breakfast sessions' agenda before sleeping. When they reached the lift Sandy casually offered coffee and a liqueur. Kao said he initially refused citing the working breakfast and that he had already drunk more wine that he would normally. Sandy had laughed and said that one drink wouldn't hurt, and it would be a nice end to the evening. He relented as he didn't want to appear rude. The way she had laughed reminded him of me and his heart ached however, Kao emphasized he had no thoughts of compromising our relationship. Sandy had made coffee and poured the liqueurs, and they talked about work, then the conference and then she had apparently come on to him. His resistance was met with heated kisses and my face superimposed on hers. Before he knew it he was on the bed, she was on top of him, his zip open and Sandy pushing his penis into her. Kao said he suddenly came to his senses and pushed her off apologising and saying it was a mistake and he had to go. He had gathered his belongings, adjusted his clothing and returned to his room. He said he was feeling woozy due to the wine and liqueur, so had a long hot shower, went straight to bed and slept until 6 am. He felt ashamed of his reactions to this woman and what he had experienced but managed to avoid Sandy during the Conference the following day. He was relieved when he returned home.

To my query, Kao said that he thought his symptoms were due to his strong desire for me but emphasized he had not ejaculated. I sighed. "I don't expect you to forgive me. How could you? I have dishonoured you. I have dishonoured our relationship. I do not deserve to have such a lovely lady by my side". He sat with his head in his hands. I watched the moonlit clouds through the window and wondered how we could return from this. I put my face in my hands.

"Kao you will have to summon Doctor Fujiwara to be at the house as soon as we arrive". He nodded. "You will have to be examined, your symptoms analyzed, and he will have to provide you with his diagnosis. This will take 24 hours and confirmation will take a further 3 days. I intend staying until this time". Kao said nothing. "Kao did you hear what I said", I asked. He nodded again. I didn't want to sit any longer with him. I needed sleep. I could see I had to be the rational one. I released my seat belt and stood, informing Kao that I intended going to bed. He didn't move. I went into the bedroom, undressed and got into bed. I couldn't hear anything from Kao so I turned off the light and rolled towards the window watching the moonlit clouds again. I heard Kao enter the cabin. "Caroline" he said softly, "would you mind if I joined you? I said no and I heard him undressing and felt him slip into bed beside me. He put his arm over me and kissed my shoulder. I murmured goodnight and Kao answered by kissing the nape of my neck. My heart ached as I shed silent tears into my pillow.

CHAPTER 24

THE TRUTH REVEALED

I awoke early to find the bed empty and cold. I lay there thinking of Kao and how he would cope with all the prodding while the swabs were taken. I had found it humiliating and embarrassing and, even though my Doctor had been gentle and sensitive, I had felt ashamed of having to go through this process. The light from the corridor was momentarily blocked as Kao came into the room.

"I thought you might like a cup of tea" he said softly.

"Thank you Kao that's very thoughtful" I returned. I sat up. Kao pushed his pillow behind me and handed me the cup. He sat on the side of the bed. We both sipped our tea.

"I have told the Pilot to contact Doctor Fujiwara and have him meet us at the house as soon as he can. He will hear the plane as it goes directly over his house and, as he is retired, he will probably leave immediately". Kao informed me. I said that was good and thought *Now I knew why the good doctor was always available for Kao.* I finished my tea and Kao took the cup, placing it on the bedside table next to his.

"You probably don't want to hear this but it is only you I love, no other person, and I have been a miserable fool. I lay awake for most of the night thinking of all pain and suffering I have caused you and wondering how I can make this better. I can't begin to tell you how sorry I am and how much I regret what has happened. I cannot think of any way in which I can make everything better and for us to return to how we were, I realise that you can't and won't forgive me. I don't deserve to be forgiven, this I also realise, so I release you from your wedding vows. I cannot tell you how much I shall miss you, how much I have come to depend on you. I shall remember the smell of you always – your hair of honeysuckle and your perfume melts my heart. I shall miss your pools of blue which are so expressive, your smile, your laughter – in fact everything about you. I don't know how I shall exist without you, but this is what I must bear now I have hurt you so, and this is now my punishment. After you receive the Doctors verdict on my symptoms you will be free of me, free to return to your life in Tasmania. I will not bother you again".

I was looking out of the window as Kao spoke. I made not sound but the tears ran down my face. He left the cabin then, closing the door behind him. I was shattered. Kao had made up my mind without giving me a chance to speak. I had been sure we could find a way to work through this difficult time by talking and supporting each other, but he had left me nothing.I got out of bed and had a shower. The hot water felt good on my body but inside I was empty. I felt nothing. I missed Kao standing by with the towel to dry me and I realized this would never happen again. Methodically I dried my hair, dressed and applied makeup. I went into the galley and made myself a mug of coffee.

Kao was nowhere to be seen so assumed he was with the Pilot and Co-Pilot in the cockpit. I sat on the couch in the lounge with my coffee. We would be landing in a couple of hours and I needed time to sort myself out and gain some control over my feelings. I couldn't believe that it was over between Kao and myself and wondered why I was feeling guilty. If there was any guilt or blame to be laid then it shouldn't be at my feet. I felt a prickle of anger. Where had Kao's sympathy been? Shouldn't he feel something for me? He had cast me aside instead and was wallowing – yes, wallowing - his own grief, but what about mine? I felt as if I had been penalised twice – one for getting this damned disease and then for making Kao aware of what he had done! I picked up the nearest magazine and flipped through it. I picked up the next one and did the same, just glancing at the pictures. Then I realized that they were both in Japanese. I threw the magazines down and they hit the wall of the plane. I wanted to cry again but didn't. I was not going to let this affect me (!!??). I continued looking out of the window thinking of Phil. I made a mental note to text him as soon as we landed. The noise from the engine had changed and the Pilot requested that seat belts should be fastened. I fastened mine and concluded that Kao was staying where he was until we landed. I thought, *Fine if he doesn't want to see me then I don't want to see him.* Within half an hour we had landed and the plane taxied to the Airport building.

The Co-Pilot opened the door and the steps automatically descended. I grabbed my overnight case and coat and made for the stairs just as Kao appeared from the flight deck. He didn't speak but took my case and followed me down the steps. There was a car waiting and the driver held the door open for me, Kao went around the car and stepped into it, sitting on my left. The boot closed with the driver assuming his seat as we drove in silence to the Sahashi home. I thought how different this was to when I came to this house the last time. I swallowed hard - no tears! Kao helped me out of the car and I thanked him. Chieko met us at the door, linking her arm in mine and looking from me to Kao then back to me. She asked him what was happening but Kao only shook his head. I told her that I would like to occupy a spare bedroom for the next 4 or 5 nights. She tried to make light of it by making reference to his snoring, but I said nothing. Kao disappeared. Chieko took me to her apartment, sitting me down and pouring two cups of green tea, and offering me a sticky rice cake. I burst into tears.

Chieko tried to console me but it took a few moments to control myself. She caught my hand holding it to her heart. "Kao has hurt you big time Caroline and I am so sorry". I nodded and gave her a weak smile. I told her that Kao would need to speak to her and the boys, and she nodded.

I wondered what she would say to Kao when he told her his news! I also wondered what sort of testing would be done on the extended family members, if any, who weren't Kao's sexual partners.

I finished the tea and thanked Chieko for her kindness. She said I could have the room next to hers if I wanted it and I said, yes I did. I wanted to be as far away from Kao as I could be but I didn't say this to her. She said I could have lunch with her in her apartment if I liked and I smiled my agreement. Chieko really was a lovely lady, I thought, and the tears welled in my eyes again but I managed to stop them from falling. Chieko squeezed my hand, stood and led me to the room next to hers.

I placed my bag on the bed and as she went to the door she said, "Now Caroline you know where I am. I thought you may want some time to yourself to rest if you feel like it, lunch is at 12 but you can come to me at any time". I thanked her and gave her a hug. She closed the door behind her and I sat on the bed. The room was decorated in yellow and gold. It was very feminine and pretty. I felt safe and cosseted, but my heart ached for Kao. I texted Phil that I had arrived and would contact him again the next day.

There was a knock at the door and Masaya stood there informing me that the Doctor had arrived and I was required in Kao's apartment. I followed him and was ushered into Kao's rooms, nodding a hello to the Doctor. I produced the medical information from my own Doctor and informed Doctor Fujiwara that this should be sent to the Japanese Heath Department together with his own report. He thanked me and turned his attention to Kao. I walked out onto the balcony. Doctor Fujiwara called me after 45 minutes and said he had taken all the required swabs and the urine and blood specimens. These would be sent away today to be analyzed. He said he expected diagnostic information within 3 days. He queried the process I went through and as this appeared to mirror his own medical procedures, he was satisfied. The Doctor picked up his bag, bowed to us both and left.

I looked at Kao. He was sitting on the couch at the end of the bed. He didn't look at me but said, "Is that what you went through," meaning the taking of swabs and urine, and I answered yes. Kao closed his eyes and said softly, "Forgive me". I answered that I did, but he shook his head. "I am sorry I shouldn't have asked. I have no right to be forgiven. I have treated you badly and now I am lost – forever", he moaned.

"Oh Kao", I said "We can work through this and be stronger for it. I do understand. Please don't shut me out. We need each other now more than ever. I know you love me as I love you. We can do this". But Kao shook his head again and stood. "I cannot make this up to you" he began haltingly, "I don't know how to put this right. You are better off without me. This is my burden to bear alone".

"How selfish can you be" I shouted. "I am hurting too but you are so wrapped up in yourself that you cannot see beyond your pain. I am hurting, your whole family is hurting, but you are so self-absorbed that you cannot see any of this. You promised after that time in Paradise, when you were offended because I didn't want you to call me your wife in front of Phil's friends, that you would try to understand another's, mainly my, feelings. So what are you doing now? Where is that understanding now?" I entreated.

Kao still did not look at me but just stood there with his eyes downcast. There was a soft knock on the door and Chieko came in asking what was happening. I explained that Kao was so involved in his own grief that he couldn't see mine or anyone else's and, if that's the way it is going to be, I was better off out of the relationship and back where I belonged in Tasmania. Chieko was visibly distressed and wanted Kao to comfort me but he just stood there. I left the room, excusing myself to Chieko, and went back to my room. How long I cried I do not know but I awoke some time later with the doona flung across me. My watch said 11.55 and I felt terrible. I didn't feel like eating or being sociable, but Chieko had always been kind and today was no exception so I thought I should make the effort for her sake. I went to the bathroom and powered my nose, reapplying lipstick and brushing my hair. I still felt terrible. Chieko welcomed me and encouraged me to eat something, and to drink some wine. I endeavoured to do as she bid and although she wasn't totally happy she accepted that I had made the effort. She picked up her embroidery, showing me what she was making and how much she had undertaken and asked if I would like to read. She pointed her bookcase out to me and I chose a book by Hammond Inness, *The Angry Mountain*.

I curled up on the couch and began to read. At first it was difficult to concentrate but the book, as always, was well written by Innes. He was a great storyteller, one of my favourites, so I soon became entrenched in his weaving of the story around its characters, and time passed. I became aware of muted voices and realised I must have fallen asleep. When I opened my eyes Chieko was just closing the passage door. She apologised for wakening me while I apologised for falling asleep and we smiled at each other. She informed me that she had just been with Kao who had explained his health issues and that the Doctor would be attending later that evening to talk to them about the ramifications for them. Chieko said she admonished Kao for his behaviour especially his disregard for my feelings, but he had made no comment. She took my hand and said she wished she had a magic wand to make all the nasty things in life disappear, but it just wasn't that easy was it? I said 'no it wasn't'. Chieko offered me refreshments but I declined.

I excused myself saying I was exhausted and wanted to

sleep. I didn't know nor cared what the time was, I just wanted to blank out the last few days and sleep. Eventually sleep came, but I slept fitfully awaking in the early hours of the morning. I put on my robe and opened the balcony doors. The room overlooked the rear garden and I sat and enjoyed the view in the moonlight. The gentle breeze was cool and smelt of rain and the garden plants perfumed the night. It was just beautiful and, I thought with sadness, this was probably the last time I would be here. I would miss Chieko and the boys, as well as the servants. They were all part of this wonderful place – my second home. I remembered all the happy moments and although I was all choked up, I was all cried out. I don't know how long I sat there thinking but I returned to bed when I began to feel the chill of the night. I remained thinking of all the wonderful times Kao and I had shared, and I still couldn't believe that he would give up on me and our relationship so quickly – and not even listen to what I had wanted, needed even, to say.

I remember the night becoming lighter but then fell asleep, only to be woken around 9 o'clock by raised voices. I grabbed my robe and got out of bed. In the hallway there was Chieko and Takahiro with Kao. Chieko looked as if she was trying to calm down both Takahiro and Kao. Both men looked very agitated. It appeared that Takahiro was attempting to impress his point of view on Kao who was refusing to listen. Well, Kao was shaking his head with his hands over his ears. I asked Chieko what was happening and Chieko, visibly distressed, apologised for disturbing me saying that Kao was refusing to listen to some serious common sense from Takahiro. I could see Takahiro was angry with his father. The argument had apparently started in Chieko's apartment and continued in the corridor when Kao had attempted to leave.

"Please stop" I cried "I am sorry to be the cause of this ill feeling between you both. This is between Kao and I – Kao has made his decision. He doesn't want to hear what I have to say. He is so full of self-pity that he has no room for anyone else's feelings. Unfortunately, this is a failing of Kao's. He internalizes everything because he has been so used to being a spoilt brat that he sees this as his right, his right to use his own failings, his own weaknesses to discard everyone. This is the man I do not like, nor wish to be with. I long for the return of my Kao. The man who was caring, loving, tender and considerate, but I am left with his twin brother a man who is egotistical and wallowing in his own despair - the despair of his own doing. No one else was to blame. Yes, Kao you should feel guilty, but you should also attempt to make amends. This does not include shutting me out. I have a voice in this too but you don't want to listen to what I have to say. We should be working together, comforting each other, caring for each other's welfare, but you are too self-absorbed to be bothered. In your life there is only you. What a pathetic and lonely life you are going to lead. I feel sorry for you. Initially, I was angry because you had ordained that I had no voice, no voice worth listening to. Now I am sorry for the worthless piece of shit you really are. I apologise for my language Chieko, but how I could ever love this guy beats me! Let him wallow if that is what he wants. I don't care anymore and the sooner I can return home to a guy who truly loves me the better. My only regret is that I shall never see you again Chieko nor the boys and, of course, your lovely children Takahiro. I love you all and shall miss you terribly. I shall stop now before I say something I may regret", with that I returned to my room and closed the door.

Silence reigned for a few moments then I heard Takahiro say something in Japanese and Kao answered him. Then Chieko asked a question in Japanese and Kao answered her. *Well,* I thought, *at least Kao is talking to someone.* I turned on the shower and stood beneath the hot jet allowing the water to drain away all my anger and my sadness. I washed my hair as if it hadn't been washed for months. I had decided that now Kao wasn't on the scene I could forget him, put my relationship with him behind me. I would take care in drying my hair so it would look as good as it could be. I would dress in my finest, slowly apply makeup and put on a happy face. I rang for Masco, Chieko's maid, and asked her to send Akiko to me. Akiko arrived several minutes later and giggled when I asked her to make me look beautiful saying she would be proud to do so. When she had finished, my hair looked wonderful, and she had applied her magic to my face so my makeup was as good as on the day of my wedding to Kao. I fought back memories of that day and allowed Akiko to dress me in a kimono that Chieko had thoughtfully brought in from Kao's apartment, probably as I slept. It was pale emerald green with a dark green obi. I had no jewelry to wear and Akiko had suggested flowers in my hair, but I thought this was a bit too festive so refused politely. I thanked Akiko, we bowed to each other then, smiling she left me. It was ten to five when I knocked on Chieko's door.

I entered on her 'come' and she welcomed me. "Oh Caroline you look lovely" she complimented me, "Would you like a drink before dinner?' I said I would be honoured and Masco poured two large whiskies. I showed surprise, and Chieko laughed saying this was her secret vice. I countered by saying her secret was safe with me. We giggled. Chieko declared she was pleased I was feeling better and that I certainly looked better. She congratulated me on my speech to Kao. I felt I had to apologise to her for my language but she waived this aside. She said I had spoken truths that no one else had the courage to say and it was time Kao stopped behaving like a baby. I said I had been surprised to see Takahiro. Chieko admitted she had called him home because she thought Kao might listen to him, but Kao could be very stubborn at times, she added. We sipped our scotch and then Chieko excused herself saying she had to see someone, but wouldn't be long. I said OK and sat on the couch enjoying my drink.

About 5 minutes later there was a hesitant knock at the door. As Chieko had not yet returned I called 'come' and was surprised when Kao put his head around the door.

"Chieko is not here" I said. He came into the room and asked if he could sit. I said yes but I didn't know how long Chieko would be. He cleared his throat and surprised me by saying he had come to see me. I just said 'oh' and waited. He focused on the carpet then raised his eyes to meet mine. "Please do not stop me as I have something very serious to say to you", he paused. Then, clearing his throat again, Kao continued.

"Everyone has told me that I have done you a great disservice, then you told me yourself – so eloquently", he paused again. When I remained silent he resumed. "Sorry is such a small word but has a big meaning. I am sorry more than I can say for everything that has happened. I am sorry for Sandy and yes I know I have said this before but there is a lot I have to say and time isn't with me now. I am sorry for the infection I have given you. I am so ashamed of my behaviour with her". He closed his eyes and shook his head slowly, "but I am so ashamed of my behaviour to you, lovely lady. As usual you are quite correct. I didn't listen to what you had to say, and yes I was full of remorse and sorrow and I didn't know how to repair what I had done – to make things right between us. I was terrified you no longer loved me, wouldn't want anything more to do with me and that was why I finished it. Both Takahiro and Chieko told me what a fool I was and to think about how I was before I met you, but I was blinded by my own remorse, my own feelings", Kao paused and shook his head.

"Wallowing I think you called it, and so correct. It wasn't until the Doctor took those terribly invasive swabs that it came home to me what I had to put you through. How you must have felt – 10 times worse than I did I am sure. Yes, I too felt humiliated and ashamed but this was of my own doing. You had only loved me, but I had cursed you, I wanted to die. How could anyone love another person who had done that to them? I thought my world was over, yet I came to understand – was persuaded to understand – that I was indeed a cruel man. I was cruel to you, dear lady, because – you were quite correct – I didn't give you a voice. I had doubly condemned you – first with this terrible disease then by cutting you, your voice, your love, off. It was reprehensible of me to even contemplate this. You who have always given me wise counsel. A woman I respect and admire. Someone I love with all my being. How could I do this? Yes, I was self-absorbed because I felt as if I was in a corner with nowhere to go, no future without the one I love, and I was the one who had well and truly messed things up to the point that I honestly believed you would no longer want me. Perhaps I had talked myself into this belief, but I was frightened to face life without you. I wanted you to return to your home and happiness with Phil. I believed that this was the best place for you and that I would be out of your mind forever. Your words just a little while ago resonated with me", Kao paused again.

"In part, they echoed what Chieko and Takahiro had been saying to me" he revealed. "Last night, when I lay with you in the plane, I thought I would die. I loved you so much and I wanted you too. I couldn't remain with you so I settled on the couch but didn't sleep much. About 4 am I had a shower and went into the cockpit where the Co-Pilot Ben was flying, well, it was on auto-pilot but he was keeping a good watch on all the instruments and on the night sky. I hadn't done that for a while and enjoyed it. It took my mind off my problem. I just couldn't face you this morning but when I emerged I wanted to help. Then we sat in the car and I desperately wanted to hold your hand, to tell you how I felt about you and beg your forgiveness, but you looked so fierce, so composed and in charge that my courage failed me. It was later that I realised you were probably trying to remain in control, and not cry but it was too late then. I don't know how you feel now but I want to right this terrible wrong I have done you. I love you very, very much Caroline and I would like to call you MY dear lady again, if you would let me. Well, I think I have said all I wanted to say, although I expect I shall think of more to say when I have time to think more clearly. I am sure I have left something important out which I wanted to impart to you, but I hope I have been clear about how I felt and how I feel but, most of all, I am very sorry for the pain I have caused you. I cannot take this away but maybe, if you can forgive me and if we can work together, we can find a way to accept and forget, and renew our relationship. Oh yes, what I said about our wedding vows – please forget, if you can, that I said this, those vows are priceless to me and I shall treasure them until I die and beyond. Of course if you cannot find it in your heart to forgive me or if you no longer love me, I shall understand that I have caused you too much pain and I will accept your wishes if you no longer desire to have anything to do with me. It will be my one regret and I shall continue to love you to the end of my days". Kao paused, wiped his eyes, blew his nose and waited for me to speak. His eyes met mine.

Tears were in my eyes also, but I knew how persuasive Kao could be. His whole professional world was built on this. I always believed he could sell ice and snow to Eskimos! Nevertheless, I knew sincerity when I heard it and, deep down, I knew Kao loved me. I pondered on his words and I truly believed that our relationship was worth making an effort to recoup what we could, as we worked our way through the mire that we found ourselves in. I was concerned however, with Kao's regression into self-pity if something went wrong and felt this should be addressed.

"Well, Kao I thank you for your enlightenment" I said, "I accept what you have stated. I have never doubted that you loved me, and I have always loved you even though we find ourselves in this pickle however, I also believe that we can find a way through this by working together. I thank you for recognising, if belatedly, that I have a voice, something to say about this process, and that you respect my opinions. We have to put all the shit of the last 24 hours behind us and find a way through. We can only do this by sharing our thoughts and feelings, just as we have always done. Of course I forgive you. You were foolish but no one can say they have never been foolish. I hope you have learnt from your mistake. I have to emphasise though that I am not going to tolerate your terrible penchant for self-absorbance. Any hint of this and you won't see me for dust", I paused.

Kao had the sense to look embarrassed, but his eyes held hope. He stood then tentatively moved towards me. He sat down next to me on the couch and took my hands in his. "Can we do this?" he asked. "Do you want to stay with me and help me find my way out of this mess and I will help you to do the same?" My smile was shaky then I was crying for all the right reasons. Kao held me close whispered how much he loved me and wanted to be with me always. He kissed my ear, my cheek, my hair.

I pulled away before he could go further saying, "We shouldn't kiss or have any intimacy until we are both cured and cleared by our respective doctors". Kao nodded then asked if we could sleep together. I said yes, but with the aforesaid proviso. He agreed then said "I shall wait for that wonderful day when we can be together again, but I need to be close to you and have the smell of you in my bed again". We both stood and hugged, then Kao said we should go down for dinner.

As we opened the door we were surprised to see the corridor full of people all looking as if they were going somewhere. I grabbed Chieko and accused her of listening at the door. I laughed when she said she was just going 'somewhere'. I asked Takahiro whether he was going to this mythical place and he grinned ruefully, nodding. Hiroto and Haruki were also hovering in the background and I saw they had been joined by Masaya, Masco and Akiko. I turned to Kao who was laughing, saying we should have charged admission as it was probably the best entertainment they'd had all week. Everyone hugged us both saying how happy they were for us and that we should celebrate this evening. We all went downstairs to dinner with Kao's arm around my shoulders – the boys taking the stairs while us 'oldies' took the lift. Well, dinner was truly a wonderful celebration. I don't remember what we ate but we had lots of champagne and lots of laughter. We all retired early – no wonder – and we were all happy.

I was exhausted. It had been an emotional merry-go-round for the last 24 hours or so and I felt that I would sleep well tonight. Kao asked me very sweetly if I would join him that night and I nodded. He looked pleased and I felt so too. He helped me undress then took out the nightdress he had bought me, helping me slide into it. I got into bed while he undressed and put on a pair of cream silk pajamas. We both smiled as he got into bed and pulled me towards him. I placed my head on his shoulder and cuddled up to him. It was good to be lying close to him once more. I sighed with contentment and he kissed my forehead. "Goodnight my dear sweet wife. I am so pleased we are together again, even amongst all this misfortune I have caused we are united and can work through it. I love you with all that I am and I am this because of you. You have made me a better person and I shall be forever grateful to you. I am complete again now you are by my side". He kissed my forehead again then said, "but one question please Caroline. Am I really a useless piece of shit?" I couldn't help giggle as I answered, "No Kao, not all the time". I felt content as I said goodnight.

CHAPTER 25

RECONCILIATION

The next few days passed pleasantly. I rang Phil and brought him up to date on Chieko's health issues. I felt really terrible having to lie to him but I couldn't tell him the truth – this would have been far worse for him – and for me. Kao and I had lunch at a lovely Kyoto restaurant. He even took me to the movies and I found the Japanese film most interesting. Chieko and I had some time together too, which I really enjoyed. She was so pleased that Kao had 'come to his senses' and we were reconciled. I am very fond of her. Takahiro had returned to Sydney, Hiroto had resumed work at the Kyoto office, Haruki was back at University in Tokyo and Kao was going into the Kyoto office several hours a day so the house was pretty quiet. Chieko appeared to enjoy my company and she would discuss the boys with me. Her embroidery was exquisite. She was working on a tablecloth with a complex, but beautiful, traditional Japanese pattern. She believed she would complete it by the end of the week. I watched her work and commented on her delicate stitches. She seemed surprised with my interest but took delight in showing me her work, describing how she undertook the complicated stitches while relating the story of the pattern and how it was developed in order to pass the story on down the ages.

Doctor Fijiwara rang to advise that he would be arriving to check on Kao at 5.00 pm that evening. I passed on this message when Kao returned from work at 3.30 pm and he nodded and said he would be ready. He asked whether I would be with him and I said I would. The Doctor's news was expected – the tests proved positive to gonorrhea so treatment began immediately. I sat outside on the balcony while the Doctor administered the injection and Kao took his medication. The Doctor asked how I was feeling and whether I wanted a check-up. I declined saying I would be consulting my own GP within a few days. He nodded curtly, shook hands with Kao, bowed and left. Kao hugged me and said, "Well my dear lady, recovery has begun". I agreed stating "Yes Kao, recovery for us also". He kissed my hair, took my hand and we walked onto the balcony. We sat on the day bed together, Kao's arm around my shoulders. I leaned against him and he asked when I was thinking of returning to Tassie. I said I thought I would go back tomorrow. His arm tightened but he said nothing. I sat just thinking and putting the moment in my memory bank.

A light rain began to fall and Kao suggested we go inside. Closing the doors behind us he asked what I wanted to do.

"I just want to be with you Kao" I uttered.

"Oh Caroline, I don't want you to go. Why can't you stay with me? I love you so much and every parting is painful, can't you see that? I want you to be me with every day for always" he cried with a catch in his voice.

'It's just as painful for me Kao, but that is the way it is. You know I shall never leave Phil". He held me tight and I didn't want him to let me go. "What we need is a hot chocolate and a glass of your delightful liqueur" I said flippantly.

"Yes" he breathed "you are right Caroline". He kissed my forehead and released me. I heard clattering in the kitchen as I sat on the couch then Kao appeared with two mugs of hot chocolate which he placed on the table in front of me. He then turned to the side table and poured two glasses of his liqueur, handing one to me and, sipping from the other, he wished me good health. I wished him the same as he sat next to me. Slipping his free arm around my shoulders, I leant against him, closing my eyes.

"I will try to come over in February for our anniversary" he said softly.

"Oh Kao that would be wonderful' I smiled up at him.

"All this should be behind us and we should be well and happy to be together once more" he murmured, and I agreed.

"And" I declared with a grin "the house should be complete and waiting your arrival and, I hope, your stamp of approval". Kao smiled at me and expressed his excitement at seeing the finished house.

"I am sure your wonderful artistic talents will be obvious everywhere" he said generously. I hoped he would like everything I planned to do with the interior. I thought of Hiroto and the secrets we shared of the Japanese artifacts he was sourcing for me in Japan then sending them to me in Gawler as the plan to provide Kao with a Japanese inspired master bedroom developed.

"The house is at lock-up stage now and when I return the inside walls will be completed, also the wiring and plumbing, so not much longer now and the build will be complete". I hoped Kao would like the plans I had for the garden. I could just picture the finished result and crossed my fingers that all would go to plan with no delays.

"Caroline you are a remarkable woman and I thank you for doing so much. You add to my happiness every day" then "Let's go to bed for the last time my lovely" he said gently and, taking my hand, he helped me stand and walked me to the bedroom. We undressed and lay on bed together. His hands drifted over my body and he held me tightly.

"I am impatient for the time when I can know you again" then he kissed my cheek. I replied that I wanted that too. We wished each other good night and Kao switched off the light.

When I awoke, Kao was already up and dressed. I found a poem on his pillow. It read:

I love you more than the earth is round,
More than the sky is high,
More than the sea is deep.
I love you for your wisdom,
For your knowledge,
For your caring
And because you brought your love to me.

I am a taller man for knowing you.
You take me to new heights.
More than I realised I could go.
I am an understanding man
For knowing you -
A kinder man.
For you have taught me to love in so many ways.

You have shown me how to love a stranger
To show compassion to the underprivileged.
To empathize with those in despair,
To help those in need,
To love unconditionally
With everything that I am and have.
You are my Wise Goddess and I love you dearly.

Such a wonderful expression of Kao's love for me. I was overwhelmed. He never ceases to amaze me. I folded the poem and placed it between the covers of my Diary.

I wanted to leave early today as I didn't want to prolong goodbyes. Kao helped by providing a morning cup of tea - I declined breakfast. I thanked him for the poem as he ruffled my hair as he passed. I was both surprised and delighted that Chieko was there to give me a hug. The sky was leaden with the promise of rain and the wind was strong and blustery. Kao explained that his ancestors were emphasizing that they did not want me to leave. I made Kao promise to visit the shrine and make an offering to the gods later today, to thank them for our reunification. As we drove down the driveway leaving the house behind us my watch said 7.05 am. I should be in Tassie within 12 hours. Phil was looking forward to my return and I was eager to check on the house at Gawler to see what improvements had been made to the site since I left.

Kao sat beside me with a grim face. I tried to cheer him up by saying I could oversee the build when I got back and make sure it was on schedule. Kao managed a weak smile and squeezed my hand. All too soon we were at the plane. Kao helped me out of the car and the driver retrieved my bag from the boot. Kao took it and walked behind me up the steps into the plane. He desperately wanted to come with me but I told him that I needed this time to compose myself for Phil. Kao said he understood, but he wasn't happy, for if he came with me he could have 12 more hours with me. I clung to him as we said our goodbyes. Oh, I was so tempted to stay.

Kao stored my bag in the overhead locker before I walked with him to the steps as the engines revved. Walking down the steps Kao waved to me. He looked such a lonely figure as he stood on the airport apron. I suddenly thought what a lost old man he looked. It shocked me to think this but, after all, we were both old, and I guess you could say we would also be lost without each other. The steps folded and the door closed. Ben saw me to my seat and ensured my seat belt was fastened before returning to the flight deck. This would be the first time I had flown in daylight. I looked out of the window and saw that Kao had walked towards the airport building but was looking at the plane. We waved to each other, then the plane accelerated, turned and taxied along the tarmac. Halfway down the runway we were airborne. I saw Kyoto spread out before me. We were soon in the clouds and I saw nothing more. Some English books had been thoughtfully placed in the little bookcase next to the couch. I picked up *Winter Solstice* by Rosamunde Pilcher and I smiled at the thought that this must have come from Chieko. It was quite a heavy tome so I guessed it would take a good 12 hours to read - just the book I needed! I had read several other books by this writer and I had enjoyed them, so I settled down and tried not to miss Kao and all I was leaving behind.

I was deep in my book when I became aware that I had company. Ben, the Co-pilot, was standing next to me proffering a mug of coffee and a sticky rice cake. Taking these from him I thanked him. He asked what I would like for dinner, but I assured Ben that I would get my own as they both had enough to do with flying the plane. He said he didn't mind but there was plenty of food if and when I felt hungry. I thanked him and said I was really happy to help myself when the time came. He bowed and returned to the cockpit. I thought how kind everyone had been and I was overcome by Ben's offer. I returned to my book and was soon engrossed again.

I was feeling a bit sleepy and was surprised to see it was past 2 o'clock. I put down my book and thought this was a good time to raid the larder! I undid my seatbelt and made my way into the galley. There was certainly plenty of food. All sorts of pickles, fish, pork and rice of course. I was spoilt for choice. I took a plate and placed a little of each onto it then, pouring a glass of non-alcoholic wine, I picked up chopsticks and returned to my seat. I enjoyed the food and the wine. I read a little more of my book then returned everything to the kitchen. After I washed everything I tucked the dishes away then had another sticky rice cake returning to the couch with a hot chocolate and the inevitable liqueur! I enjoyed both very much - a fitting end to a delectable meal.

The sky outside had cleared. No clouds and a good view of the sea below with a touch of land visible to the far right. I thought I might have a snooze so took a blanket from the overhead locker and, using a cushion from the couch opposite, I lay down and I wasn't long before I was asleep. I slept soundly and awoke slowly finding I had slept for almost 4 hours. I stood and replaced the blanket in the locker and the borrowed cushion to its couch. I took my makeup bag into the bathroom where I touched up where required, finishing with a quick brush to the hair. The person looking back at me in the mirror looked old and tired. I wondered what on earth Kao saw in me? What on earth did Phil see in me? I shook my head. I was old and past it. I should know better.

I should just sit down with my knitting and wait to die, I thought. That is what everyone thinks you should do once you reach my age. But I wasn't ready for death yet. I still felt I had a life to live. Well, I was certainly doing that. I laughed to myself. However, I was certainly living life to the full – as full as I could at my age anyway. I thought how blessed I was having two great guys who loved me and who, each in their own way, brought me much happiness. I thought of all the women in the world who couldn't even find one man in their lifetime to care for them as each of my guys cared for me. I felt for these women. In my counselling profession I had seen many such women and I hoped that I had been able to help them make the necessary changes in their lives to enable them to find enrichment. Unless you receive feedback you, as a counsellor, always wonder if your intervention was positive or not.

I checked the time and continued to read. I was on the final pages when the Pilot requested that I fasten my seatbelt ready for landing. I couldn't see anything from the window but accepted he knew what he was talking about, then I saw the sparkle of the sea below and realised we would land at

Devonport shortly. I was just reading the final page when I felt a gentle bump as we landed. Replacing the book in the bookshelf I pulled my bag closer to me. Disentangling myself from the seatbelt I shrugged on my jacket. When the plane came to a halt Geoffrey, the Pilot, came out and asked whether I had a good flight. I thanked him and said yes. He pressed a button, the door opened, and the steps descended. We shook hands and I walked down the steps onto the tarmac and into the Devonport Terminal.

I saw Phil immediately. We hugged and I kissed his cheek saying I was pleased to be home. He said he had missed me and took my bag. The car was parked just outside the door. Phil helped me into it, sat next to me and drove us home. I tried to explain Chieko's illness and why she wanted me there. I said I was mystified but it appeared she had become attached to me during the cruise and had not made many lasting friendships in Kyoto, so wanted me by her side. Her health had much improved so I had been able to leave her. Whether Phil believed me or not I don't know but, on the surface, he appeared to accept my explanation. He asked whether I had eaten and when I replied 'no' he advised that he had made me a little something. I smiled as I thanked him and said he looked after me so well. That seemed to please him. We arrived home and Phil took my bag into the spare bedroom as I said I would unpack tomorrow. Phil had made some really thick soup out of left over chicken and vegetables. It was delicious and I said so. While eating, Phil brought me up to date with his movements while I was away. He had made some new jewelry which I loved. Our next joint exhibition was due soon and he had arranged its advertising. Thus satisfied we retired to bed. Phil said he expected I was tired and I said I was. He expressed his delight to have me home and hoped that nothing else would take me away in the near future. I said I hoped so too and settled down to sleep. Phil was soon asleep, but I lay awake for a while thinking of Kao and Chieko and wondering what they were doing. I reflected on the emotional time I'd had in Kyoto this time and decided I was getting too old for all of this!

Before I knew it dawn was washing stars across the sky like pebbles before the sea. I couldn't believe that I had slept through the night without waking. I went to the bathroom taking my medication as directed, then returned to bed. I lay there for some time wondering what today would bring - one thing was for sure, I had to text Kao. I arose again and went to the kitchen where I had left my phone. I quickly texted Kao that I was home and missing him terribly, but not to answer text me back as I couldn't accept this from him yet - perhaps next week? I signed off that he was always in my heart. I made breakfast for Phil and I and carried the tray back to bed. We said good morning and Phil thanked me for breakfast. He switched on the TV for the early ABC news. After breakfast I returned the tray to the kitchen and showered. As I was toweling dry Phil came into the bathroom asking what I wanted to do today, I answered I had no plans and Phil suggested a day at home to rest after my long trip and I agreed that was what I was looking forward to. We filled the day with a bit of gardening, well weeding really! We both read our books in the sunshine on the front veranda, and we made plans for the rest of the week. Phil suggested we take in a movie the following day and I thought this was a good idea, something concrete to do tomorrow.

The clouds that had threatened rain the previous evening had unburdened themselves over night, but dark thunderheads hovered, silhouetted against the horizon, and the sun was gaining in heat as the morning developed. It was unusual for Tasmania to suffer from humidity, but today the temperature was already 32 degrees (mid 80's F) with corresponding high humidity. Checking the refrigerator and pantry I found I needed a few items for dinner tonight so made a note of what was required. I would buy these after the movie which finished at 3.30pm. *At least the movie theatre would be cool*, I thought. The film, *1917,* was enjoyable but, while it was well made and directed, it really cemented my feelings against warfare. The major roles were played by Colin Firth and Benedict Cumberbatch, both actors I liked as they were good natural actors, so the story was believable and, I understand, was based on an amalgam of true stories. On the way home we called into the supermarket and bought what was required for dinner. I was cooking Pork and Fennel Pies.

In less than an hour the Pork and Fennel Pies were made and cooked. I placed a bottle of New Zealand Chardonnay on the table and completed setting the table before making dessert – strawberries and whipped cream. Phil complimented me on the meal, so it had been a good day, well spent.

CHAPTER 26

BACK TO OLD ROUTINES

When I awoke I made a quick breakfast for Phil and I then packed the car with pastels and paper, as I was due to run my Pastel Workshop today, and drove to the gallery. I enjoyed revealing the secrets of pastel painting to my students just as much as I was thrilled with their artistic development. I always returned home with a feeling of accomplishment. I usually took along an unfinished painting where I would teach the importance of some salient point of pastel art however, I made sure I had plenty of time to spend with each student.

On my way home I called into the library to see Connie. She was pleased to see me and to hear my news. I disclosed that I was finding it increasingly difficult to leave Kao and she asked again whether I intended to move over to Japan to be with him, but I shook my head stating I would never leave Phil. Connie then had news to tell me – that she was thinking of retiring at the end of the year. I expressed surprise but she disclosed that she had been thinking of this for some time. While she had no definite plans for her retirement, she shared that she would like to visit her brother and his family in Sydney as it had been several years since they had got together. She also suggested that a cruise could be on the cards as, who knows, who she may meet. We both laughed. Connie was keen to have me visit her again so we made plans for the following weekend.

I returned home and, as Phil was cooking tonight, I had no thoughts of preparing any food so I relaxed and unpacked the car into my studio. Phil was in the kitchen involved with dinner preparations so I set the table then poured us both a glass of scotch. We swopped stories of how our day had been, then watched the TV news. Phil served his specialty –

Spaghetti Bolognaise, which I always enjoyed, and I was not disappointed as it was cooked to perfection. We had strawberries and cream for dessert, then enjoyed a coffee. There wasn't anything we wanted to watch on the television. It always intrigued us that with all the additional channels we now have the TV schedules haven't improved – in fact the reverse! After we cleaned up after dinner we decided to watch a DVD and chose *Paint Your Wagon* which we had last viewed at a cinema a long time ago! We thoroughly enjoyed it as it embroiled every situation from comedy to drama. It was a well-made film with some great acting, singing and dancing. It was only 9.30 pm when we decided to call it a night as we were both weary.

Phil was still asleep when I awoke. It was almost 7 am. I lay there thinking of Kao, wondering if he would come to Tassie in February. I wanted to see him again, I missed him. I wished Phil would regain his health again so we could enjoy what we had before. No matter how much I felt for Kao I had always been honest with him and he was under no illusions. He knew his feelings for me were deeper than my feelings for him and, if my circumstances in Ulverstone changed, I would say goodbye to him. That was the theory anyway – how this would work out in reality was another thing as I was sure parting from Kao would involve an enormous jump of the heart and I didn't know whether I would be strong enough to do this. I knew enough about myself to know I would have problems serving two masters should Phil be able to make love to me again. Would Kao or Phil vie for my sexual favours? Neither deserved this. I knew I needed Kao but not at the expense of Phil nor did I want to be unfaithful to Phil. Deliberating on this I dozed until I heard Phil stir. I asked whether he had anything planned for the day.

Phil replied "I want to work on some bone carvings in the workshop, would you mind mowing the lawns if you feel up to this" he asked. I said that would be no problem if he would make sure the mower had enough petrol for the job. He agreed to do this straight after breakfast. The sun was shining through the window and it promised to be another hot day, and already the humidity was rising, so the sooner I cut the lawns the better as, like many people, I found the high humidity almost unbearable. With the mower ready to go I finally completed this task and placed the lawn cuttings in the compost bin. I showered and poured Phil and I a beer which we consumed under the trees on the back lawn. The rest of the day passed pleasantly enough with Phil returning to his carving while I started a new painting.

The following day I decided to visit the Gawler house to check on its progress. I was pleasantly surprised with the two major rooms already painted, the land surrounding the house cleared and landscaping well on the way. When I returned home Phil and I did some shopping and answered several e-mails, after which I prepared dinner. We were travelling to Launceston early the next morning for Phil's specialist appointment so an early night was called for. I slept well knowing that the house was on schedule and I refused to let thoughts of Kao intrude on my life with Phil. We were up at the crack of dawn with the trip to Launceston uneventful but, as was always, interesting noting the change in seasons each time we did this trip. The lovely scenery of the countryside with the changing colours of the trees and bushes and the bountiful wildflowers, created a wonderful panorama set against rolling hills and paddocks full of cattle, sheep and crops. It was all so picturesque especially when highlighted by the backdrop of mountains in the distance – it was an artists' dream with a painting waiting around every corner!

After examining Phil the specialist prognosis was positive. This was great but we were becoming tired of the seemingly constant travel to various specialists, either for consultations for Phil or myself and wondered when this would all end. But I was glad we were helping to educate their children up to university level or pay for their overseas holidays! We were happy to return home at last. It was usually a long and tiring trip and the humidity had made it more so. We both showered immediately we were home. I opened all the windows then, as the evening progressed, the air cooled and so did the house with a lovely breeze flowing through it.

I received an e-mail from Kao during the week informing me that he had been given a clean bill of health and cleared of any infection. He wrote that he missed me very much and was looking forward to being with me again in February. I was enthusiastic in regard to Kao's medical diagnosis, revealing I also was free of the infection so had a clean bill of health too. I added that I was missing him also and looking forward to seeing him again, but February seemed a long way away. I brought Kao up to date on the Gawler house build, that it was on schedule and I was satisfied with the workmanship. I shared my desire with Kao to show him around the completed house and its grounds and that I hoped he would like what I had done. Kao laughed and said he was sure he would like it. Well, I was very pleased with it, and it closely resembled the idea I had in my mind.

I wanted the house to look like a typical turn of the century Aussie homestead and I was pleased that it had settled well into land. It appeared to have been built in the early 1900's with a wide veranda and railings, together with a swing lounge. On the ground floor to the right of the front door there was a lounge room which looked out over the paddocks to the hills beyond. The second and third bedrooms were opposite on the left of the front door, with the bathroom between, and the kitchen and laundry beyond these near the back door. Outside the back door the Shinto style garden would be developed complete with pebble garden simulating mountains and oceans. There would be a pathway down to the creek and maybe, a new bridge over it. In front of the house a circular driveway was under construction and would have a central garden featuring a cherry tree. I had lots of plans. I could see the house competed and the garden landscaped. I was happy and hoped Kao would be happy also. It all looked lovely in my head; I just hoped it would do so in reality.

The first floor was to be our apartment, taking up the whole length and breadth of the house comprising of a large bedroom with bathroom, and lounge with small kitchenette and, of course, lots of storage space. I hoped this would be my masterpiece, as I wanted to both surprise and please Kao. I intended to embrace the Shinto style and have artifacts placed artistically around both rooms. I even had sent over to Kyoto for both Kao's and my wedding outfits, complete with appropriate supports so they would be tastefully displayed. I was grateful to Hiroto for his assistance as he had advised me of his father's passion for ancient collectables, accessing these in Japan and forwarding these onto Gawler also, advising me on the Shinto house shrine I wanted in the lounge. I had obtained a collection of ancient Japanese books and had managed to get a full collection of Kao's poetry books. I couldn't wait for the inside of the house to be completed so I could begin to furnish it. I had ordered a queen-sized bed plus large twin beds for the downstairs bedrooms, and a king-sized bed for our master suite upstairs. I had also ordered a lounge suit and other lounge furniture for the ground floor, reminiscent of the 1930's style, plus kitchen furniture and necessary white goods.

I was excited about the traditional Tatami matting I had ordered from Japan for our lounge and bedroom which would be laid as soon as the walls had been painted. The ground floor lounge and bedrooms would have carpet squares with matching drapes to suit each room's décor. Last, but not least, I wanted some paintings for the walls and would ask Kao for his input – I would like my paintings to hang in our home, but that would be up to Kao. I was getting excited and hoped Kao would like the finished product. Kao would be with me in less than 4 weeks, I hoped, and there was still so much to do.

The next few weeks were very busy. I was in constant consultation with Bill making sure everything was completed on time. The house was looking really lovely, and I was pleased with the professionalism of all the work. The gardens were getting their final watering and the gravel driveway was completed, as was the circular garden in its center. I was particularly pleased with the Shinto garden which Haruki had worked so hard on, and had made it so perfect, so beautiful. The pathway and garden down to the creek had also turned out well, but no time to reconstruct the bridge so this would be Kao's task.

Our house stood in its own grounds with a cattle grid installed at the junction where our drive separated from the drive leading to Brett and Barbara's farmhouse, and a further cattle grid had been installed at the junction of our drive as it entered the circular pebble driveway leading to the parking area, and the front door of our house. Most of the furniture I had ordered had arrived together with the carpet squares and drapes, so the downstairs rooms would be completed by the following day. As far as our apartment was concerned, in our Master bedroom the Tatami matting had been laid. This had been made by master mat maker Yoshiaki Kagami and had cost a small fortune, but it was well worth the expense. (Woven rush Tatami matting was a traditional element in Japanese homes, valued for their long wearing capability and the lovely smell of the outdoors they possess.) Very soft lamb skin rugs lay on the matting each side of the king-sized bed. The bed looked towards the balcony window, which was built over the ground floor French windows, with views across the paddocks to the distant hill beyond. The outside sliding doors of the balcony were regular aluminum and glass, while the inside sliding doors were of traditional paper. Behind the bed was a short headboard with a large gilded Japanese traditional painting attached to the wall from floor to ceiling depicting mountains in the distance with cedar trees framing the art. On the left side of the bed Kao's wedding kimono hung on the wall while on the right side of the bed my wedding kimono hung. I was particularly pleased with how this wall looked as I had spent a long time making sure each kimono was hung correctly on its support and that the whole wall looked artistically balanced.

In the lounge, the Tatami matting had also been laid with the furniture and Kao's antiquities arranged. The bookcase wasn't large but contained all the books I thought might interest Kao, and me of course. The walls were painted gunmetal grey and the *tokonoma* (a niche to display traditional ornaments), on the right hand side wall contained on the highest shelf, a small rough male figure and a larger male figure designated, according to his clothing, from the Royal household. Both were ancient artifacts that Kao loved. High quality silk sheets and a vermillion quilt adorned the bed, with lots of pillows and cushions coloured vermillion, green and gold added a bit of glamour to the rather austere décor. There was a padded bench at the foot of the bed, covered in gold velvet, as was the couch on the opposite wall. Traditional bamboo blinds covered the windows.

In the lounge two 3-seater couches and two armchairs were positioned to facilitate conversation. These had vermillion painted wood frames while the back and seat cushions were covered in grey woven fabric, which also surrounded a vermillion casual table/footrest. Vermillion scatter cushions with the Sahashi family crest embroidered by

Akiko at their centers covered the couches and chairs. These complemented the grey walls and cream woodwork and created what I thought was a charming lounge room. The ceiling was cream but patterned with a square towards its center which was surrounded by a frame of vermillion painted edges on its extreme and middle borders. Between these a circular design of black inlay in which was painted the Sahashi Coat of Arms. It looked very impressive.

As indoor plants and flowers are a critical part of Japanese-inspired interior design, I choose several plants for the lounge. First, I chose two *Kokedama* Bonsai, which are small balls of compost and soil wrapped in moss. They are suitable for a variety of plants and I chose Asparagus Fern, a very hardy plant which makes a beautiful display piece. These I placed on the occasional table and the top of the bookcase. I also bought a Black Pine bonsai, which I placed in the bedroom above the collectables, and a 1.7 metre Japanese bamboo which I found a home for in the corner next to the balcony doors. Oh, around the roof windows in both the bedroom and the lounge I had grey painted Japanese wooden screens installed. These had the traditional design of oblongs of wood attached throughout by vertical wooden slats. Artifacts were arranged on shelves, the bookcase and occasional table in the lounge as well as the coffee table in the bedroom, in front of the couch. I was even able to place several photographs of our wedding wherever there was a space. The furnishings and the house shrine were all now complete, as was the landscaping, circular drive and the entry off the main road. Everything was ready – the house and the gardens – all I needed was Kao.

I had tested and found the under floor heating system was effective and seemingly efficient. I was sure this central heating system would ensure the house was comfortably warm during the cooler days, with the kitchen's Aga supplementing the heating during colder days. With solar power panels on the roof to heat water in the summer, the Aga would also heat our water during the colder months. The open fire in the ground floor lounge had been tested, proving reliable and effective, so worked well. The kitchen was looking as good as any kitchen could with the white goods (actually stainless steel) in place and wooden table and chairs at its center. There were several televisions scattered around the house so Kao could catch the news wherever he was located. I believe I had thought of everything, but I am sure Kao would think of things I had forgotten or not thought of.

The stairs looked impressive rising from the front hall and the lift, just beyond the stairs, was large enough for four people. It had been tested and signed off as OK. The proviso that Kao had demanded, and I fully concurred, that we would have sole access to our apartment which meant that the lift, together with the wooden door under the stairs, would remain locked at all times – as would be the entry door at the top of the stairs. Any guest whether they were Company employees, friends or relatives would occupy the ground floor and have access to that part of the house only. The Master suite would be our touch of paradise.

We were blessed by Barbara agreeing to ensure that the house would be ready for any expected visitors, and to ensure that it was clean and tidy when they left. Our apartment would be my responsibility. Also, together with her husband, she had agreed to maintain the gardens, which wouldn't take much time. Brett would also be farm manager once the breeding program began. I thought the family had been well dealt with by Kao who had offered to educate the three girls to 4 years of University or alternative studies, as well as giving Barbara and Brett a cut of the profits once the wagyu beef were bred and sold off, so I was pleased when the couple refused additional compensation for the gardening. Kao believed that the breeding program at Gawler would extend the markets for wagyu beef in Australia, Japan and other counties because wagyu beef was popular round the world for having 300% monounsaturated fat than regular beef breeds, together with finer meat texture. This resulted in a more succulent eating experience. It also has the lowest cholesterol levels of all meats, even lower than fish or chicken, and it contains oleic acid which is for good for your heart having an incredibly high omega 3 and 6 content. Not only does wagyu beef have higher levels of intra-muscular fat or marbling, it is considered the tastiest beef on the market and is highly desirable. Kao had high hopes for his enterprise and said this venture was essential as the Company wanted to expand in Japan but had no available land, so Tasmania was the closest alternative for expanding their wagyu program. Kao was obviously aware breeding programs existed throughout the world including Australia, the UK and the USA as well as Asian countries however, he was confident that he would find new markets and even extend existing markets ensuring that the farm would be profitable. I understood that Kao had completed 2 years research prior to his Company's purchase of the farm and believed that Tasmania's climate was closest to Japan's, which would enhance the breeding of this type of beef. Having no knowledge of beef farming let alone wagyu farming I felt I had to bow to Kao's superior knowledge in this instance.

While I waited to hear confirmation of Kao's impending visit, life continued as normal in Ulverstone. From time to time we attended a specialist's or doctor's appointments for either Phil or myself, which were par for the course as one gets older. Lots of aches and pains as the body breaks down I suppose, but we won't go there! My involvement in the Seniors Group saw me attending the weekly meetings and social afternoons. I also had my responsibilities with various Art Groups to man galleries holding exhibitions. Some were general exhibitions while others were my solo exhibitions, all were held along the North West Coast of Tasmania. I enjoyed doing this as I met people from all over Australia and overseas. It was interesting talking to them about Tasmania and receiving feedback from the various towns they had visited and locations they had travelled to as well as learning about their lives back home. I enjoyed promoting Tasmania and our artists. Even better was when I was curating galleries in which I was able to paint. I loved explaining my work with visitors especially the techniques of pastel art. I guess, most of all, I gained a great deal of satisfaction from running pastel workshops in Ulverstone each Wednesday morning, passing on my knowledge of pastel art to students of all ages and experiences. I was appreciative of the hard work they put into developing skills and in producing incredible works of art. At home, I had my own studio where I was already painting for a new art exhibition. I had completed 14 paintings out of 20 required for this solo exhibition so pretty busy, but was well on the way to complete these.

The outbreak of the Coronavirus in China had concerned me for, although Japan had only a handful of reported and confirmed cases, this could make it difficult for Kao to get permission to travel to Australia. I hoped this would not be the case but as I had no word from Kao I grew increasingly worried. Everything was ready for him: the house, the garden and me! I wondered what influence Kao's ancestors had on world affairs and I prayed to them to assist Kao to come to me. I really needed to see him again and I would be terribly disappointed if he was prevented from travelling.

Two days later at last I received a text from Kao confirming that he would be in Tassie the following week. I thanked his ancestors for hearing my prayers and I needed to go to Gawler and make an offering to them and to the gods. The next day I found the opportunity to visit the house and give thanks at the house shrine. I turned on the central heating so the house would be welcoming to Kao, as I understood being a new unit it may take a couple of days to warm the whole house. I made a mental note that I should check the house the day prior to Kao's arrival and place fresh flowers in the downstairs lounge and kitchen as well as our lounge upstairs. I stood and examined all aspects of the house I had built. I saw it with renewed eyes as I hadn't had the time to see it complete in itself – a lovely little cottage built just for Kao and I. I was tingling with excitement and could hardly contain myself. Fortunately, I wasn't as obvious as thought I might have been as Phil made no comment and seemed not to suspect anything was in the wind. The following day Phil ran his Leather Workshop at the Ulverstone Gallery, so I was a free agent for most of the day.

Kao rang me from the airport saying he would see me in half an hour. I explained where to meet me in Ulverstone and nervously waited in the Quadrant carpark for his arrival. In due course a taxi drew up and Kao alighted. Oh, it was so good to see him again. He sat in the passenger seat of my car and told me how much he had missed me. We kissed and he placed my hand on his crotch, he was rock hard and desire flooded through my body. He told me that my eyes were inviting him to do all the things he wanted to do and, as he nuzzled my ear I squeezed him gently, he whispered "My dear Caroline it you do that again I shall explode". I thought prudence was required so I removed my hand, concentrating on starting the car.

Turning to Kao I said, "Well my dear Kao, my promise will have to wait. Now please fasten your seat belt because you have a house to inspect", to which Kao replied I was a cruel lady however, I didn't think the car park was conducive to sexual gratification, so I laughed and agreed with him. With that we drove off towards our new home.

CHAPTER 27

THE COTTAGE

When we reached the first cattle grid I stopped the vehicle and asked Kao to close his eyes. When I was sure he wouldn't cheat I continued onto the second cattle grid and stopped again. From here was a good view of the cottage, the circular garden and driveway could be had. I took a deep breath then asked Kao to open his eyes. He did so but remained silent.

I thought, *Oh no, he doesn't like it,* but after a few moments he turned to me with shining eyes.

"This it is truly wonderful" he breathed. We drove up to the house and parked. The agapanthus planted in front of the veranda railings were a sea of blue and a perfect setting for the house. Kao got out of the car, came around to my side and helped me out. I gave Kao the door key, he took my hand and we walked up the path, mounting the two steps to the veranda and walked to the front door. The house was painted pale grey, the door painted white with a blue panel in its center (echoing the agapanthus), setting off the frosted glass panels each side of the door. The windows were also painted white. Kao said the colours were perfect, then asked wasn't there a Western custom when the new husband carried his new bride across the threshold of their new home? I laughed and said this just wasn't going to happen as I didn't want to get a doctor for his heart attack or spinal injury. He laughed too, then opening the door he ushered me inside, following and closing the door behind him. We walked through every room on the ground floor then I showed Kao the lift under the stair-well but suggested we walked up the stairs. I was pleased the way the Tassie oak staircase had been made and fitted. Although not large it really looked most imposing, and the lift fitted well under the stairs which was a tidy way of dealing with what could have been a cumbersome item in a small space.

Kao reached the door which led into the lounge and glanced at me. So far he had made no comment about the ground floor and I was afraid that he hadn't liked the 1930's style of the furniture and fittings however, I was praying that he would like the décor of our apartment. Kao entered the lounge room, stopped looked around and took in every detail before he went through into the bedroom. Here he not just looked but examined everything. He sat on the bench at the foot of the bed and studied the Tatami matting. Kao walked around the room again examining everything. He smiled at the display of our wedding garments, the Japanese books and he handled the copies of his poetry books shaking his head. I told him I wanted his help to choosing pictures for the downstairs lounge and bedrooms and Kao agreed to this but surprised me with his next words.

"When can we view the paintings in your studio because I think it fitting that we choose your paintings to decorate the walls of our home and" he added "I shall be proud to pay the going price, no discounts or I shall be offended". I tried to object but Kao would have none of it. His mind was made up and there was nothing I could do but acquiesce. Kao then moved to the French window, examined the bamboo blinds then opened the inside paper sliding doors and the outside sliding doors to the balcony and stepped outside. The delicate perfume from the garden wafted in on the gentle breeze. I followed Kao out and watched Kao as he viewed the garden.

"Caroline I do not know what to say. You know I am a man of few words, but this house is even beyond me". I thought *Oh my God, he doesn't like it!* He held out his hand and took mine in his. He pulled me towards him and kissed me so sweetly. Our eyes locked.

"You like it then?" I ventured.

"No" he answered, "I do not like it – I love it". I was so relieved and we both grinned at each other. "I am so proud of you. You are so thoughtful. How did you source all those pots?" he asked, and I had to admit that there had been a spy in his family. Kao laughed at that, stating that the décor everywhere throughout the house was just perfect.

Kao then announced that it was time for a celebration. and he removed from his pocket a small bottle of that wonderful liqueur, asking to be pointed on the direction of the glasses. I showed him where the kitchenette was – behind a folding door in the lounge, where an array of glassware was hanging, slotted into shelving above our heads. We sat on the couch in the bedroom and drank to us and much happiness in our new home. After our drinks Kao stood and proffered his hand. I took it and he raised me to my feet.

"Now" he said with a smile "your eyes have made a promise which must be kept" and his eyes met mine "we have to christen our bed, don't we?" He swept me into his arms crushing me to him and his kisses were demanding while mine were needy. We stumbled to the bed with his mouth on mine and a hunger that dissolved my bones turning my legs to jelly.

Kao quickly disrobed me. I tried to assist him, but I was all fingers and thumbs, instead he ordered me into bed and slapped my bottom as I climbed in laughing. He swiftly joined me and ran his hand over my body saying he had been waiting all day when he could feel my skin as he longed to feel its silkiness again and admitted to dreaming of being skin-to-skin with me, smelling my hair and my perfumes, which he always found most sensual. I leaned over Kao, running my tongue over his lips before brushing them with mine. I pulled myself over his prone body and began caressing his body with my lips and tongue. I moved down kissing and nibbling until and heard Kao moan as I caressed his erection with my tongue. I took him in my mouth and my movement gained momentum. Kao's fingers ran through my hair. He was moaning with pleasure and suddenly announced that he couldn't last for much longer. I continued until Kao reached his peak, then I tasted him.

"Oh, Caroline" he moaned "that was exquisite" he said breathlessly "You are a very sexy lady, a wonderful lover. How I have missed you. You make me feel like a million dollars" he laughed as I worked my way up his body, caressing and kissing him as I went. Then I caught his lips. Kao's return kiss was passionate, his erection remained. He slipped into me and I felt his arms tighten around me as we moved together as one. Our lovemaking was urgent, making up for lost time due to our infections and the distance between us. Nothing else mattered at this moment. All I cared about was Kao being here, with me, and doing exactly what he was doing now. I gave way to the feelings I had, and we melded together. I was taken out of this world. Once more he possessed me completely.

I climaxed and felt an incredible release of the love I had held for the seven months or so of separation from Kao. Then, when I felt I had no more to give, I climaxed again with Kao following close behind. We lay back exhausted, the sweat running down our bodies.

"Oh, Caroline that is definitely not recommended for a person with a weak heart" he declared. We both chuckled together and, when we stopped, Kao kissed me tenderly. I checked that Kao was indeed OK and had not been overtaxed before tottering to the bathroom and showered. Kao was waiting for me with a towel, and we laughed some more during this episode before Kao had his shower. Back in bed we curled up together holding each other close, wrapped in each other's arms. We kissed several times then slept.

On awakening Kao kissed me, expressing his happiness at being in our house that I had made so beautiful. He said he hadn't envisioned anything like it and had been thrilled with the house design and the furnishings, which appeared to suit it so well. Kao was especially impressed with my ability to source Tatami matting so I told him I had commissioned Yoshiaki Kagami to complete the matting. He was impressed. I didn't tell him how much it had cost, although Kao probably wouldn't have blinked, but I had thought it was astronomical! He made favourable comments about the front, side and back gardens, and was particularly impressed with the Shinto garden saying he had been 'blown away' when he had seen it. I was pleased he was happy with everything I had done. We made love again, but slowly this time. Kao was tender and loving and he felt wonderful deep inside me, murmuring words of love in my ear. He stroked my hair and told me again how much he loved me. Our love making was gentle and tender and very spiritual. Every time with Kao was an amazing experience. He is a loving, caring man. I couldn't wish for a better mate. I must have dozed for a while because I was aware of Kao sitting on the bed shaking me gently.

"You will have to go soon" he said with regret in his eyes. "We just have time for a cup of tea and I want to sit with you downstairs in our kitchen". I saw he had just showered as a towel was wrapped around him so, reluctantly, I accessed the bathroom and let the hot water just run over me. I felt so good and very happy. I hadn't even asked how long Kao would be in Tassie but already I was hating the idea of him leaving me.

Kao was waiting with a towel as I emerged from the shower. He sort of dried me between hugs, kisses and laughter. Both dressed and looking reasonably well-presented we descended to the ground floor via the lift. Kao commented on how pleasant the kitchen was but queried where the sink was. I laughed and walked to an overhead cupboard pushing aside the double folding door, revealing the sink unit as the doors swung back against the kitchen walls. This also showcased windows into the sunroom, beyond which overlooked the deck and the pathway down to the creek. With the doors closed it just looked like the continuation of the cupboard system which also hid the dishwasher underneath the sink. There were plenty of other windows, so a win-win situation for neatness without losing precious light. Kao thought this design feature was a wonderful addition to the kitchen. I mentioned that it meant we could eat and not have to look at the sink at the same time. I made a pot of green tea and, while we talked, I had warmed up several scones I had baked that morning, placing strawberry jam and lightly whipped cream on the table. We munched, sipped and talked. I learnt that Kao was staying for a whole month! Wonderful news. He understood that I couldn't stay overnight with him but we checked my diary and I was able to see him almost every day for varying lengths of time.

He asked whether now we had our own home "a part of Japan" he asked "Could I not assume you are my wife here, at this cottage, our home" he queried and caught me by the arm. "What do you say Caroline, can't we truly belong to each other in our own home. Our little part of Japan, and I swear to you I shall not cause you any heartache within the communities we spend time in here in Tasmania. I shall be circumspect, discreet and respectful to you, and to Phil's name, at all times". He pleaded with me. I considered Kao's request, which sounded reasonable but only if he kept his word.

"Kao you must be true to your word. I can't afford any slip of the tongue, any remote association of being your wife", I insisted. "If I hear any hint of this then I shall dissolve our relationship instantly. Is that understood?" I demanded. "I understand completely and I shall keep my word. I will not let you down, my dear wife". He grinned with pleasure, and so it was.

Kao then shared his plans with me. He had to discuss the breeding program with Brett the farm manager, look at some land that was for sale close to the farm, check out on the computer where there may be breeding stock for sale, get in contact with other wagyu breeders in Tasmania and Australia and contact his sources in Japan. He queried whether there was a computer in the house, and I admitted that I had forgotten all about a computer. But seeing Kao's crestfallen look I silently rebuked myself and admitted to Kao that the computer was stored in a side cupboard in our lounge upstairs.

"Oh, Caroline my dear" he said with a smile "I am going to have such fun exploring all the cupboards in the house to see what may be hidden in them" and we both laughed. I cleared the table putting everything away. Kao said to leave everything to him as he would wash and dry the dishes, saying how domesticated he had become since knowing me. He put his arms around me advising that he could live like this forever. I felt very comfortable with him whatever we were doing, and I thought exactly the same, but said nothing. Kao walked me to the front door. We said our goodbyes and I arranged to see him the following day. As we walked down the steps to my car I turned to Kao saying, "Oh by the way Kao, there is a surprise in the garage for you. Have a look when I am gone, also explore the path to the creek". I placed the automatic garage door opener in his hand. Puzzled Kao nodded and we kissed. Settling into the car I started the engine. Kao kissed me through the open window, and I reversed. I hated to leave him but I knew he would be OK. I had made sure that the refrigerator and the walk-in pantry were well stocked with food and drink. There were books for him to read or television to watch and the computer to play on! AND I knew he would play with his new toy – the car I had persuaded Takahiro to purchase for Kao. I hoped Kao would like the car, a red Mercedes-Benz GLS 580S-Clas SUV with red stitched leather seats. I was sure he would enjoy driving this turbo-charged vehicle with all systems computer controlled so stress free driving. I was sure Kao would enjoy putting the car through its paces to find just what the computer systems would do. He was really into that sort of thing. I had loved the short test drive I had in it and found it to be quiet and responsive. Kao would have the independence to go wherever he wanted without borrowing the farm vehicle now. I smiled as I thought of Kao's first night in our new home and I knew that the bed was comfortable so he should sleep well. I sighed as I looked forward to seeing Kao again tomorrow.

Arriving home I found an empty house. It was just after 4.00pm so I had plenty of time to organize dinner. The fridge, freezer and pantry checked I decided to cook a casserole. Casseroles and stews were so easy to cook and full of nutrition so in no time at all I had completed this task and placed the dish in the oven to cook for a couple of hours. It was simmering gently when Phil returned saying the house smelt really good and he could hardly wait for dinner. While he showered, I opened a bottle of Peter Dennis Shiraz and placed it on the table which I had just finished setting. When Phil reappeared, I poured us both a whisky and we sat in the lounge discussing Phil's activities for the day and what he had planned for tomorrow. As usual, Phil was most appreciative of the meal and helped me get the kitchen back in order and dishes put away. I forced myself to concentrate as thoughts of Kao and I having afternoon tea kept intruding. Eventually we retired to bed, but I slept fitfully and awoke to a dismal day of dark clouds and heavy rain.

I couldn't see across the river for the heavy rain. It was a different world from yesterday which had been bright and clear. Phil still slept soundly so I made tea in the kitchen and took it into him with a bowl of cereal. He sleepily said good morning then gradually outlined what he wanted to achieve in this workshop today. I would be constructing the flyers for my next art exhibition, e-mailing them to art enthusiasts along the North West coast and printing out some for delivery for those in the Ulverstone area. The day passed without any dramas and ended with Phil cooking a delightful meal with apple cake and cream for dessert.

The next day I hurried through my chores and made coffee for Phil and I which we drank on the front veranda as the rain eased. Phil's schedule left me free for most of the day so, after Phil helped me compile a shopping list I rang Kao saying I could see him in about an hour's time after I had completed the shopping. I left shortly after Phil, visited the supermarket then drove to Gawler.

Kao met me at the door with a big kiss and a hug exclaiming how amazed he was to find what was in the garage and how wonderful the new car was. He then related all aspects of its design, performance and special features. He particularly loved the way it could extricate itself from boggy ground, e.g. sand, mud or snow, by shaking itself from side to side or corner to corner. He said it was 'unbelievable'. Kao really loved gadgets and I had been sure he would like this feature. Anyway, he gave me a hug and a kiss and thanked me for the gift which, I assured him, was from the Company and not me but he said it was my idea and he appreciated my thoughtfulness very much. Kao continued, revealing that he had investigated every nook and cranny of the house and was delighted at what he had discovered: a gym at the rear of the garage, the computer off the upstairs lounge, together with the kitchenette with a refrigerator, freezer and small pantry "stuffed with food and drink". I laughed at his enthusiasm and delight in all he had found.

Kao brought me up to date with the breeding program informed me that he had used the computer to locate several Australian breeders of wagyu cattle, several of whom were in

Tasmania, which he had contacted and would be visiting before returning to Kyoto. He had arranged a meeting with his farm manager in the morning to discuss strategies before meeting with these breeders. Kao's eyes shone as he discussed all this and I was pleased that his plans were coming to fruition and his dreams were becoming realities, as this meant that there was less emphasis on his being totally reliant on me. I wished Kao to be independent of me when in Tassie. Of course I wanted to be with him, but I didn't want to be the sole reason for him coming here. It was good for Kao to become quickly involved in the wagyu breeding program and getting the farm organized in this direction – and getting Brett up to speed as this was a completely new area for him to be managing. Brett appeared to be a capable individual – after all he ran his own very successful dairy business for over 20 years – so it was a matter of the two of them sharing their expertise and knowledge, together with any new information they may gain, and for Kao to instruct Brett of the direction he wanted the farm to go in.

Kao discussed impending developments in planning the early stages which included deciding whether he should purchase a bull, use AI or embryonic transference to breed wagyu. He had already decided that some of Brett's milkers could become surrogate mums. He elaborated on each topic at length, but I ended up brain dead – not the most inspiring conversation however, I attempted to look and sound interested as Kao as so enthusiastic. After we had drank and eaten I suggested a walk. We strolled along the cherry path down to the creek where I suggested Kao may like to design a better bridge than the one that existed – which was basically two planks of wood and a one bar railing. He nodded thoughtfully then began to tell me about the fish in the creek and the wildlife that roamed abroad. I was surprised and delighted with his knowledge which would have come from Brett, I surmised.

Kao had his arm around my shoulders when he suddenly turned to me saying, "Caroline, I hope you don't mind, and I apologize for not discussing this with you previously, but it only occurred to me yesterday. I told Barbara and Brett that they could use the Mercedes when I wasn't here, is that OK with you?" I thought that was a good idea, as they appeared to own only the one vehicle, a 5 year old Holden utility, and said so adding "After all Kao, it is a Company car". We wandered over the creek into the bush which was fairly sparse before retracing our steps across the wonky old bridge and then back to the house. It was from here that the Torii could be clearly seen. It was relatively small, painted red and black, spanning the pathway into the Shinto garden

Kao stopped walking and took my hand. "I almost cried when I discovered this" he said, "I thought what a wonderful addition to our home and how considerate of you to even think of erecting it, leading into the Shinto garden and showing the way to our family shrine. This house is built with love, and it will be filled with love but, dear lady, I cannot but regret that we are too old to bring our children here to this amazing family home. I know you see this differently than I but I cannot but think how it would be with our children around us". He kissed my hand and gently hugged me.

"Kao we can bring our grandchildren here. We can buy some ponies for them to ride. Just think how happy they will be. We shall have lots of children enjoying our home" I replied. Kao laughed and hugged me again. "I cannot have any regrets with you Caroline because you force me to look forward to the future and not back to the past. You are correct and I find it maddening that you always are". We walked through the Torii along the short path into the kitchen.

Exchanging shoes for slippers I quickly made coffee and carried the mugs to the deck as the day was sunny and warm. I had brought a quantity of custard and jam tarts from home, which I made yesterday, and a few slices of fruit cake. I had just placed the mugs of coffee on the table when Kao arrived. His hands were not empty - the famous liqueur! He laughed when he saw the food saying he would have to go on a diet when he returned home. Oh, it was so good to have him back.

CHAPTER 28

LIVING TWO LIVES

A whole month together was great, but time would pass quickly and Kao would leave again to return – well neither one of knew when that would be. We discussed what we wanted to do in the following days and Kao revealed that he would be talking to wagyu breeders and checking on stock agents. He was interested in following up on some land he saw for sale just metres down the road. Only 100 or so acres but enough alternative pasture for young cattle separated from their mothers. I had some community commitments in Ulverstone the following day, a Seniors morning followed by lunch with a couple of friends. All too soon it was time to go but, before I left, I took the lift to our apartment and stripped the bed. I returned to the kitchen showing Kao where the clean sheets were kept after I had put the used sheets in the washing machine. Kao was happy to tidy up after our afternoon tea and remake the bed, as he had nothing much to do today when I left. I kissed him in appreciation as he walked me to the car. We hugged and I settled into the car for the drive home. I waved as I drove away.

It was almost 4 o'clock and Phil would be expecting me. I was looking forward to preparing dinner for us both. I wondered whether I was unusual as I was able to compartmentalize my relationships with both guys. I could turn off one and turn on to the other without any qualms. Perhaps I would feel differently if I had sexual relations with both. I knew in my heart that I loved both of them and I didn't want anything to change but wondered whether it would. I refused to let this line of thought continue any further instead I went through the lamb recipe for tonight's dinner as I drove home. Phil welcomed me with his usual kiss as I walked through the back door and handed me a dram of scotch. We both said Slàinte Mhaith (Gaelic for Good Health) and clinked glasses. I was pleased to see he had set the table for dinner, so I started on the preparations, helped with a swig of whiskey. The lamb was easy, just replacing rosemary with lavender and honey then in the oven. It wasn't long before wonderful smells were emanating from the oven, indicating that the meat was on target for being cooked on time. Phil opened a Peter Lehman full bodied Shiraz and poured two glasses, handing one to me. We drank to our health.

Phil carved the lamb while I made the gravy. Sitting at the table we helped ourselves to the baked vegetables as we discussed our day and our plans for the morrow. Phil thought the meal looked and tasted great and I was pleased that he was always appreciative of everything I did for him. He liked the change to the lavender and honey, which was a relief, for if he had hated it - oh boy, he would just be eating the roast vegetables! There was enough lamb left over for another meal, probably a salad in the next day or so. Phil had a specialist appointment at the Burnie hospital tomorrow morning and was happy to go there on his own. I said I wanted to do some housework and maybe a bit of gardening, so tomorrow planned we enjoyed our food and the wine. Dessert was also pleasant as were the coffees served with a tawny port. After a leisurely meal, the dishes washed, the kitchen tidy, it was time to check the television guide. We found a couple of shows which we liked to watch, *Father Brown* showing on the ABC channel from 7.30 to 8.30 followed by *Mystery Road,* starring Aaron Pederson, on the same channel until 10.00 pm. We settled in the lounge room with a second port to watch our chosen shows.

The days slid by when Kao was busy and we communicated by mobile phone, but at last he had some free time which coincided with mine, so I rushed to Gawler. As I stepped out of the car the cottage door burst open, Kao bounced out enveloping me in is arms and kissed me on the neck. He led me inside and kissed me passionately. "I have so missed you" he whispered in my ear and kissed me again leading me to the lift where we ascended to the first floor and our apartment. He told me that he'd had problems with concentration as when I had visited last a few vestiges of perfume had been left behind which had been everywhere. But now he had renewed the smell as he hugged me.

My heart beat wildly as he led in into the bedroom kissing me and undressing me as we went. We were laughing so much, and hands were getting in the way of hands, until at last we both collapsed on the bed. I said I was too exhausted to do anything but Kao said not to worry as he would do everything that was necessary and we laughed some more. Kao crushed me to him impatient with passion; his hand caressed my body followed by his lips. Every nerve in my body tingled. We eventually made love. As I lifted my hips he entered me and paused. We gazed at each other. I thought, *How wonderful is this? Two oldies having found each other and able to demonstrate the love we feel so completely in all aspect of our lives: love making of course, but just enjoying each other's company so completely – even sharing a simple meal or exploring a new environment.* I wondered what was going through Kao's mind at that moment. We continued gently and lovingly then afterwards we lay quietly in each other's arms savouring this very special moment.

Kao revealed how his heart had ached during the emotional time when we were both ill. Initially, he had believed that I couldn't love him anymore and said he just couldn't have faced life without me. He explained that he felt he had been given a new lease of life – as I had still loved him and, what's more, I had developed a lovely home for us both. He said he would never be able to show his true appreciation. I stopped Kao there and said that we should look forward, never back, and yes, we were entering a new aspect of our lives.

The completion of the cottage had been exciting. I had thoroughly enjoyed furnishing our home, trying to find ancient pottery and other items that would please Kao, hoping the décor would satisfy his tastes. I said I tried to think of everything he may want, finding suppliers with Hiroto's help, and putting in all together. I was pleased that everything had worked out to plan and Kao was happy. He kissed my forehead and said he had a surprise. He climbed out of bed, donned his dressing gown and went into the lounge. In due course I heard the clink of glasses wherein Kao reappeared carrying a bottle of Bollinger champagne and two glasses. He placed these on the bedside table rearranging my pillows so I could sit in comfort. He then revisited the lounge returning with a tray of Japanese delights: pickles, smoked fish, cheese, fingers of savoury bread and two crayfish tails! I must have looked pleased because Kao smiled saying "A meal fit for a princess, my Princess". After positioning the tray on my knees, he removed his dressing gown and slid into bed next to me. I kissed him in thanks. He opened the champagne without spilling a drop and poured me a glass then himself one. We clinked glasses, toasting our happy little home before nibbling our lunch. What a lovely surprise. Every day was filled with happiness when I was with Kao. I felt blessed indeed that our chance encounter had turned into a wonderful relationship. I pondered whether it was by chance or if we had been favoured by the gods or by Kao's ancestors, whatever it was I was fortunate. I was hungrier than I thought and literally devoured everything in sight. Kao said he was pleased he had not been hungry for which he received a clout! We laughed.

The food demolished, the bottle empty, Kao slid out of bed placing the tray on the table before returning. I expressed my appreciation for the lovely surprise. I snuggled up to Kao and he put his arm around me. I was very contented. I could not see Kao the following day and his entreaties were to no avail. Kao decided he would continue with his research, contacting a breeder in the Longford area to discuss the virtue of his bull against AI or embryonic transfers. Kao had obtained loads of information from the internet and planned to meet with Brett in the morning and go through all of this with him. Well, tomorrow was settled for both of us, so all I had to do was go home and back to my life with Phil.

I had enjoyed my time with Kao, but the month was over and now it was time for him to return to Kyoto. I drove him to the Devonport Airport and followed him up the steps into the plane. After he stowed his luggage, my heart ached as we said goodbye. I clung to him as he whispered words of love to me. The engines roared away, the plane anxious to leave. Kao said he must go, and I disengaged myself from our embrace. We held hands and looked at each other. I wanted to remember every detail of him.

"Caroline will you answer me truthfully?" he asked. I nodded. "Will you visit our home while I am away?" I nodded again, tears in my eyes "Of course you know I shall" I answered. "Will you also lie in our bed – as if I were here?" "Yes, I shall" I breathed. He closed his eyes before saying "Oh that is so good. I shall imagine we are both here and, when I return home, there will be the smell of you in our bed, even if you are not there". Kao crushed me to him and kissed me passionately then urged me to go. I sighed and walked down the steps to the tarmac while our hands slowly slipped apart. I turned and waved. Kao waved back, the steps folded, and the door closed. He waved again from the window before the plane turned and taxied down the runway.

I watched it take off until it was no longer visible in the sky and wondered when I would see Kao again however I would keep my promise and visit our cottage as often as I could. A chill wind blew, and I noticed for the first time that the humidity had dissolved so the chillness of the evening was welcome.

I walked to the car and let the tears run freely as I sat in the driver's seat. When I was all cried out, I composed myself and started the car. I powdered my face, replenished my lipstick and quickly brushed my hair. Putting the car in drive I drove slowly back to Gawler. I walked through the house remembering the happy times spent with Kao. I curled up on our bed and visualized him up in the clouds, knowing he was feeling as lost as I was. I left the apartment, locking the door behind me then walked down the stairs. I ensured the lift door was locked as I passed then I locked the front door behind me. I drove across the two cattle grids and onto the highway towards Ulverstone. I had to reset my mind now to my life in Ulverstone and put Kao behind me - until next time.

Gradually, I became used to Kao not being around and looked forward to receiving his e-mails and text messages. It was already late April. I had written to him advising I would be cat sitting at Paradise again in August. He advised he would be in France for two or three weeks in May, then he would be in the New York office for the month of June before flying to Sydney where he would stay for 3 or 4 weeks in July. These dates had yet to be confirmed. Kao was hoping that he would be able to visit Tasmania for a week or two in August. We were both keeping our fingers crossed and hoped Kao's schedule would allow this to happen.

Phil had his health ups and downs, but I tried to keep a positive frame of mind. We enjoyed each other's company and were able to share various household tasks and outside chores. We both enjoyed trying out new recipes and took pleasure in our respected crafts. I am always in awe of Phil's beautiful jewelry designs either in leatherwork or bone carving. It was all Phil could do to keep up with demand. I also sold a few paintings from the various exhibitions and enjoyed completing commissions. We were content with our lives.

CHAPTER 29

CELEBRATIONS

Kao had been gone for a couple of weeks, and I had settled back into my old routine although I missed him terribly. I called into the library to see Connie. It was her birthday tomorrow and I wanted to celebrate with her. I thought she would be pleased with my small contribution for her special day. I was comfortable with her and she knew my innermost secrets and kept them. I was grateful for this as I needed to talk to someone about my time with Kao, together with my thoughts and feelings without thinking my confidant couldn't wait to pass these onto someone else. She appeared happy to be my confidant and never made any judgements, while often giving me another line of thought to consider, which I have always found invaluable. Connie had asked after Phil and I discussed his recent lapse of ill health, which was a worry, but his GP had prescribed a change of medication which appeared to help. Also, Phil was visiting a specialist in Launceston on a regular basis, so his heart was being monitored closely.

I held out a plastic bag to Connie. She took it with a question in her eyes while peeking inside it. I had made Connie a fruit cake, wrapped up Kao's latest book of poems and I had chosen a flowery birthday card for her. She thanked me as she read the card, saying it was lovely then she tore the paper off the gift and discovered the book of poems by Japanese poet Sahashi Kazuyoshi. She flicked through the book and announced she couldn't wait to get it home to read through it. Thanking me profusely, I expressed my pleasure at her joy. We discussed the poet when I divulged to Connie that this poet was none other than Kao. I informed Connie that Kao was launching this book in France the following week and he had wanted me to join him there, but I shrugged and asked,

'"How could I for I'm not a free agent?' Connie nodded then said the cake looked especially appetising, so I couldn't resist and cut ourselves a piece each – most decadent while at work for Connie! I wished Connie a happy birthday and asked what she would be doing tomorrow evening. While munching cake she advised that she was being taken out for dinner by a group of friends. I expressed my pleasure that she wouldn't be on her own.

I was surprised when Connie revealed that Phil had visited the library the other day and, while exchanging books, had shared his concerns with her. I must have looked puzzled, for when she continued, she did so hesitantly. Connie explained that after the usual small talk Phil had suddenly asked, "You talk to Caroline a lot when she comes in, don't you?" Connie said she had nodded, but his next question had left her breathless, "Do you think there is something wrong with her?" and explained further by saying that he had noticed that I had been a little 'different' for some time now and he couldn't put his finger on what was wrong. Connie said she had asked Phil what he meant and how different was I?

Phil had paused before saying, "Well for about a month or so she has seemed distracted. She has been doing everything she usually does cooking, cleaning, washing, gardening, going to Senior's group, running her pastel workshops and curating exhibitions. She still is a good cook and loves trying out new recipes on me and we have a great relationship but sometimes she's a bit distant, as it she was somewhere else".

"My heart went out to him. What could I say?" Connie asked. "We parried a conversation between us that consisted of possible suggestions however, he appeared satisfied when I implied that your level of back and associated pain may be increasing so you may be concentrating on controlling this. I said maybe you hadn't wanted to worry him.

He had nodded thoughtfully saying, "Yes, that could be it." He thanked me and indicated that he would discuss this with you and whether you should increase or change your medication or at least consult your GP. He appeared satisfied as he left the library, but I had some misgivings Caroline. Now I know you love Phil deeply, but I just wonder how you are able to live two lives at the same time. I feel so helpless and wish I could be of more help. I know you often say that destiny lies in the lap of the gods so perhaps this is how you cope. I know you say you are content with your life however painful it may be at times, and I understand you feel blessed by having two wonderful men to care for you and love you, when other women had trouble finding just one man in their lifetime. What amazes me as well, Caroline, is that love in our golden years is just as important and passionate as at any age".

She paused, "I must ask you something Caroline, so please don't be offended". Caroline smiled. "It's about your back problem and whether this is a hindrance when you and Kao make love. I am sorry but I often wondered....."

I trailed off as she laughed and shook her head saying that maybe she wasn't in this world during lovemaking for she hardly felt any pain at all. "No, I am not offended, why should I be? It intrigues me also." We laughed.

I revealed that Phil had indeed suggested a checkup with my GP, after broaching the subject of pain medication, and I had followed his advice and consulted my Doctor. Phil appeared satisfied. I also told Connie that I tried to give Phil some extra attention and had suggested various places we could visit when we were both free at the same time.

Connie nodded saying, "I know you miss Kao, but you cannot neglect your other responsibilities Caroline. You are travelling the path you alone have chosen. Neither Phil nor Kao chose the direction in which your life is going. You need to respect both people or discard one or the other". I was shocked with what she said, but it made me suddenly understand my responsibilities, while accepting that I was in control of my life, and should be, all I needed to show was compassion for both men.

Without saying as much, Connie had pointed to the very heart of the matter (sorry about the pun), that I went through life with very selfish motives. Everything I did was because that was what I wanted to do, sometimes with little regard to how it may affect others. I now had to weigh every decision to ensure that everyone was being treated equally, with love AND, I had to remember to do this until it was second nature to me. Certainly, I'd had flashes of conscience and acknowledged my selfishness, but I had always found reasons to carry on! Yes, I could see this was a basic flaw in my personality – and the reason I found myself in this love triangle. I made my mind up that I would be more considerate towards Phil. He couldn't help the situation we were now in and I alone must take responsibility for this.

Kindness costs nothing, I thought. I may have been deluding myself in my belief that I was treating each guy the same – with love and kindness - but perhaps subconsciously I was blaming Phil for us losing that intimacy we once enjoyed so much. I sighed. I hadn't realised I was such a complex individual. But I guess we all are. We just have to scrape below the surface and look what lies beneath. It may surprise us if we see the ugly side of ourselves, someone we don't want to know – but we must, if we are to live our lives honestly and truthfully. I thanked Connie for her perception and in affording me the opportunity to acknowledge and appreciate my blessings. Connie thanked me again for helping her celebrate her birthday and gave me a big hug. We both waved as I left the library.

***   ***   ***   ***

As I watched Caroline leave, I thought how kind she was to remember my birthday and I appreciated the book of poems and the cake. I suddenly thought of my own situation. I had been on my own for over 10 years and thought well, this is how it is. But perhaps it need not be like this, maybe there was someone out there for me – just waiting for our paths to cross. Caroline always said to expect the unexpected at the most unexpected times. I had always taken this with a pinch of salt but now I was having second thoughts! I examined my lifestyle and wondered how I could possibly meet anyone. I moved within a small circle of friends some single while others were not. I couldn't think that there was anyone amongst these who would fit the bill for a partner. Maybe I should extend my friendships and make new ones. I wondered how possible this was for an almost 60 year old saving for her retirement, to meet someone new. I wasn't attractive. You could hardly call me outgoing, nor did I have independent means. Not much, if anything, in my favour. I was thinking of retirement and wanted to take a cruise then, but should I wait? Perhaps I should take some long service leave and seek out a cruise to faraway places! I shook my head and laughed at myself. What a dreamer! I couldn't hope to replicate Caroline's good fortune. She had found a wonderful partner, a prince, while I would probably discover a frog! I always enjoyed Caroline's visits and I admired how she coped with everything that was thrown at her. She was immensely strong and fair minded. I couldn't hope to emulate her.

I had gleaned from my conversation with Caroline that Phil's next visit to his specialist was due the following week and she had suggested a couple of days away from home. I agreed this would be a lovely break for them both. Phil had apparently scanned the internet to check accommodation availability, deciding on a B & B for 2 nights close to where his specialist was situated. They were apparently booked into

Wombat's restaurant for the first night and they were also catching a live show the following night. Phil had chosen *Mamma Mia,* a live musical at the Princess Theatre, with a pre-show dinner at the Grand Chancellor hotel, both within walking distance from where they were staying. It all sounded delightful, and I was sure both Caroline and Phil would enjoy the time away to recharge their batteries – and for Caroline to get her priorities straight.

***   ***   ***   ***

It was windy the day when we began our trip to Launceston but the sun was shining and the long range forecast was for continuing fine weather. I loved seeing the changing seasons in the landscape and the views were always amazing. We found our accommodation, enjoyed a relaxing meal at Wombat's with good food served by pleasant staff, and returned to our unit around 11.30 pm. We found it was very quiet so had no trouble falling asleep. The next morning we took in the local sights, had a coffee at a local café, checked out a shop selling arts and crafts and looked around an Op Shop. We also visited a museum, an aquarium and the local bakery where we bought a pie each for lunch. These we took back to our room and ate them with cups of green tea. I was happy to have an afternoon snooze after which we both awoke refreshed and looking forward to the evening's entertainment.

The following evening the meal at the Grand Chancellor was also most enjoyable so we entered the Princess Theatre looking forward to the show. It was very entertaining with lots of singing and dancing – and it was real singing, not the screaming that seems to be prevalent nowadays. The story was good with the all the cast having good diction so those of us with hearing problems could hear and understand every word. We left the theatre feeling elevated and in good spirits.

Reaching our room we were surprised the time was close to midnight. Time flies when you are enjoying yourselves!

After breakfast the next morning we checked out and drove to the specialist's just a block away. Phil's Doctor saying all was well and the new medication was doing its job, as he handed Phil a further prescription. We drove home with the conversation covering the dinner, the show, the accommodation and the specialist. We were glad the wind had dropped so it was a pleasant drive. We both agreed that we had enjoyed the break and should do it again in a couple of months. Together with community commitments, I made sure I spent most of my spare time with Phil. It was not forced enjoyment however, as I really did enjoy his company. We had much in common, many similar tastes in all things: humour, food, wine, activities etc. so it was always a joy spending time with him then discussing our experiences together afterwards. Both Phil and I were preparing for our joint exhibition later in the year. I had completed the required amount of new paintings while Phil was happy making jewelry in his.

Kao and I kept in touch via e-mails and monthly telephone calls. He could not give me a concrete date when he would be over in August, so I just had to patient. Meanwhile life passed quietly in Ulverstone. Soon the date had arrived to take the paintings to the gallery. The opening went well with both Phil and I renewing old acquaintances, and selling several of our works. After the exhibition both Phil and I were fortunate enough to have attracted commissions which kept us busy for a while. These completed and delivered I turned my attention to the studio because it looked like a bomb had exploded in it. There were paintings everywhere.. I sorted through them and Phil helped me hang the ones I wanted while I stacked the remaining artworks neatly against the walls. At least those painted over the last few years were now clearly visible and the studio had regained a professional air.

I finally received word from Kao that he would be coming to Tasmania on 8 August. At last I could make plans. I would be cat sitting at Paradise for most of August which would make it much easier for Kao and I to be together. I was excited to be able to see him again. Kao thought he would be able to stay for about 6 weeks, so the balance of his stay would be at Gawler. Brett and family had journeyed to Japan over the Christmas break to visit wagyu breeders and study the artificial insemination breeding programs. Brett had also been able to join a short training program in New South Wales from which Kao required feedback. My absence would allow Kao to do this without distraction.

I began a list of everything I had to complete prior to Kao's arrival but first I had an exhibition to organise. I did the usual: flyers and e-mails to those on my mailing list, then concentrated on compiling the Catalogue, making sure all the paintings had their prices listed. Finally, I stacked the paintings close to the door of my studio, ready to be transported to the exhibition venue. The Art Exhibition opening was well attended and received, and I was pleased selling seven paintings while taking five commissions to paint family portraits and pets. Phil was also happy as he sold a number of leather goods as well as carved bone pendants.

On days when Phil was busy I returned to my list of things required for my Paradise sojourn. I knew I couldn't forget a lamb roast for Kao, as well as the usual vegetables and fruit. I packed my favourite recipe books together with a selection of underwear and day wear. I never left home without my pocket dairy and that was already stashed in my handbag, to which I added my camera. I was ready to go and couldn't wait to see Kao but, I had to remain calm for a few days yet and managed to do so. I was packed and ready for my trip to Gawler. I had spoken to my friend Sonya by phone to confirm previous arrangements. They were expecting me on 6

August and they would return on 29 August. Kao would be with me at Paradise until 28 August then staying at our cottage in Gawler for just over 3 weeks so, additionally, I had made sure that the Gawler home was well stocked. I tingled all over when I thought of being with Kao again and hoped that he had been keeping well. In his e-mails he always told me he was, but one tends to exaggerate good health and minimize poor so I was eager to see him with my own eyes.

At last 5 August arrived and I was on my way to Paradise. Sonya and George would leave early the next morning, leaving Tomtom and I to our own devices until Kao arrived. Kao was flying from Sydney with Hiroto in the Mitsubishi aircraft, landing at Devonport Airport on 8 August before driving to Sheffield where Hiroto would check into the Motor Inn. I would meet the boys there and transport Kao to Paradise, leaving the car with Hiroto. I was planning to cook Prawn Laksa with strawberries and cream for dessert – nice and easy – for the evening meal. I was hoping Hiroto would join us for lunch or dinner the following. While my friends went through the visual checks making sure that I knew how to work everything. I was also made aware of Tomtom's latest likes and dislikes, Tomtom mooched around vying for attention from all of us in turn. Sonya cooked a lovely dinner: Chicken Tagine followed by a berry pie and icecream, while George materialised a delightful bottle of chardonnay which we demolished! After chatting over coffee for a while we had an early night as Sonya and George would be up before dawn to catch their early morning flight from Devonport.

I woke early enough to bid my friends a groggy goodbye then returned to bed. Tomtom blinked and stretched before settling down again. We both slept until the sun was shining through the window. I was reluctant to rise and lay there enjoying not having anything special to do. Tomtom was awake and didn't seem in a hurry to get up also, so we just lay there enjoying the ambiance of the morning and each other's company. I stroked Tomtom and he purred with delight and contentment - all was well with the world! I must have fallen asleep when I became aware that something soft was preventing me from breathing - it was Tomtom who had snuggled up to my face burying my nose in his fur. I pulled back my head but he put out a claw to stop me from moving, he was comfortable, I stroked his head and chin which he liked, so he withdrew his paw. A peace pack negotiated! I lay there for a moment enjoying the warmth and comfort of Tomtom, but I was never one who could lay in bed awake for any length of time, so I gently moved away from the cat and climbed out of bed.

Despite the sun's warmth through the window it was a cold day. Frost was glinting on the lawn and it looked as if someone had spilt a million diamonds. Struggling into my dressing gown I made my way to the kitchen and switched on the electric jug. I placed a couple of eggs in water on the stove to cook while I had my tea and cereal for breakfast. I quickly washed everything and tidied the kitchen. Tomtom was wanting his breakfast too so when this task was completed I showered and dressed – warm slacks and jumper. Tomtom was looking at me expectantly so I said, "Where's that cat?" which saw him tear around the house playing hide and seek with me chasing him. At last he'd had enough and he went onto the bathroom windowsill where he could look out onto the back garden to check out which birds were visiting. While Tomtom was checking the rear of the house I slipped on my coat, grabbed keys and let myself out of the front door, determined to have a walk in the crisp clean air on this bright sunny morning. While chilly it was a lovely fresh day with blue sky and sunshine.

The house was situated in the midst of a farming community so there were plenty of smells permeating the air.

Some people may have found this offensive, but I love the smell of farms so relished in the various odors emanating from the land. I could hear cows mooing and the bark of dogs as well as the chug and clatter of tractors. The landscape was so lovely, rolling hills, copses of trees and green, green paddocks with cows in some and young bulls in others. Oh, I loved being in the country. Everything sparkled with the remnants of frost lying in the hollows. It felt good to be alive in such a great environment. I guess I walked for about an hour before I returned to the house. I had become quite warm during my walk and was glad to remove my coat in the hallway. Tomtom was curled up in his favourate chair and dozily raised his head as I entered. I tried not to disturb him as I unpacked the cooler bag from the car, placing the relevant items in the refrigerator and pantry. This task soon finished, I made a coffee and curled up on the couch with my book.

The house was warm and the sun still shone brightly. It was going to be a lovely day. The mobile phone disturbed me and I was pleased to find it was Phil requiring an update. I discussed the events of last evening and this morning, especially relating to the antics of Tomtom. We both had a laugh. When we disconnected I discovered a text message from Kao, which informed me he was excited to be soon with me again and that he and Hiroto would be arriving in Sheffield around 6.00 pm. He asked if I could pick him up. Kao explained that they would be calling into Gawler to pick up the Mercedes which he would then leave with Hiroto, who would be staying at the Sheffield Motor Inn. I texted back that I would meet him at the Motor Inn at the appointed time. I was really looking forward to seeing him again. I checked the time – 11.55 – plenty of time to prepare however, I put down my book, as I needed to do some baking for the following week, but first I made a coffee and ate the egg sandwiches I had made that morning.

I filled the cake tins with a fruit cake and a gingerbread cake I baked then Tomtom appeared wanting to know what had been happening while he slept. He walked around and inspected every facet of the kitchen and dining room. We played *Chase* for 20 minutes or so and when he had tired of this and settled into his favourite chair, I let myself out of the sliding kitchen door to pick flowers for the house. I gathered a large bunch of roses, calendulas, Sweet Alice and iris' together with some fern-like grass. Retracing my steps, I found several vases for the flowers. I had chosen a crisp white damask tablecloth for the dining table so placed the vase of red and pink roses in its center. The perfume of the flowers was delicate yet permeated the house.

I was sure that Kao would enjoy the prawn Laksa I was making for dinner. It was one of my favourite meals and I knew that Kao loved seafood so I hoped that I couldn't go wrong. Tomtom was meowing for attention so we played *Chases* again but when Tomtom disappeared into my friends' bathroom I knew he had tired of the game, so ran hot water in the spar bath with some bubble bath salts. It smelt and looked great, and it felt good too as I slithered into the water. Tomtom jumped up and sat on the corner of the bath but wasn't impressed. He soon became tired of watching nothing happen and, voicing his disapproval, he abandoned me for better pastures so I settled down and returned to my book to enjoy a relaxing hour or so.

I sipped and read until I decided my soak was over. Reluctantly I dragged myself upright and exited the tub, pulling out the plug as I went. I briskly rubbed myself dry. My skin tingled. I used body lotion lavishly then brushed my hair. Tomtom reappeared and sat on the mat at my feet watching my every move with great interest. I sprayed perfume over my body while Tomtom looked on disapprovingly. I applied light makeup and checked the time – 4.05 pm. Still plenty of time before Kao was due. What to wear? I really wanted to wear something extra special for Kao, but what?

A dress. Decision made but which one? Kao likes red but I have worn the two red dresses I had brought with me many times previously. I looked through my wardrobe and sighed. So – no dress. What did that leave me with? Well, I had a new pair of black faux leather pants, which Kao hadn't seen. I could pair these with a black top which had red shiny beads embroidered randomly on it and on its long sleeves. It was a vee necked top so I could wear the ruby choker and pendant earrings. Decision made, I dressed and viewed myself in the bedroom cheval mirror. *This is as good as it gets at your age,* I thought. I glanced over the table, checked my makeup and attire and deemed all was well and that everything was ready for Kao. It was time for me the meet the boys.

I arrived early. There was no sign of the red Mercedes at the Motor Inn. I parked the car and waited. Kao and Hiroto arrived as I turned off the engine. Kao jumped out of the car as I was alighting from mine and we hugged and kissed. I gave Hiroto a quick hug too then he went into the motel to register. Kao grabbed two suitcases from his car and put them into mine. Hiroto reappeared stating all was well. I asked Hiroto if he would join us for meal tomorrow and Kao suggested that perhaps dinner would be best around 6 o'clock. After checking with Hiroto that he remembered the route to the Paradise house, Kao and I climbed into my car and, with a wave to Hiroto, we drove off to Paradise.

We talked non-stop about being together again and how much we had missed each other. Kao advised me of his plans while in Tassie and appeared keen to get started on purchasing animals and getting the breeding program organised. He advised that he had secured a market for the meat in Japan and was working with the Australian Wagyu Breeders Association and the Australian Government to formulate a proposal that would suit the Australian market for the beef. Kao also informed me that Brett had just returned from meeting with Australian breeders on their properties in South Australia and New South Wales, so he was keen to discover what other information Brett had uncovered. He was particularly interested in the cross breeding of Wagyu with Angus and Holstein breeds.

I was so happy for him. Even though the breeding program would take several years I was pleased that Kao possessed so much optimism for this project. His head seemed to be full of the plans he had been making and the direction he wanted his breeding program to go. He couldn't stop talking. Eventually we unpacked the car and deposited Kao's suitcases in our bedroom. I helped Kao off with his coat and poured whiskey. We clinked glasses and we kissed. Eventually I dragged myself away to finalize dinner.

Kao followed me and put his arms around my shoulders. "It looks wonderful" he said. "It's Laksa" I smiled up at him. He looked relaxed and happy and I reiterated how pleased I was that he was here with me. He squeezed my shoulder. The dish was now hot enough to add the bok choy and the prawns. I reduced the heat and turned to Kao. We kissed and cuddled then I pushed Kao away announcing dinner was ready and declared that he hadn't even poured the wine! Kao saluted me and asked which wine we were having. I motioned to the bottle on the table, a sauvignon blanc, which he duly opened and poured into our glasses on the table. He sat as I placed a bowl of laksa in front of him then I placed my bowl on the table. Kao attacked his meal with enthusiasm stating he was very hungry and was soon asking for seconds. I placed my bowl in the sink and gave Kao more. He announced my laksa was the best in the world! I laughed and thanked him. After dessert and coffee was poured – you guessed it – out came that lovely Japanese liqueur. We sat on the couch and discussed plans for the morrow. Kao was keen to have some relaxing time and called the next two weeks his holiday however, his routine was familiar – gym, shower, breakfast, office then free after 11 am. I didn't mind as this gave me time to sort out Tomtom and the kitchen.

Hiroto was coming for dinner tomorrow and I would get Kao to help me prepare this. I was looking forward to seeing Hiroto as he was a lovely young man who appeared to have his mother's temperament. Takahiro, Kao's eldest son, was very much his father's son. Not only did he physically resemble Kao but he emulated his father in mannerisms and ways of thinking, yet he was very much of the modern age. Hiroto was respectful of his father but I could see he had a much different way of thinking about the Company business than his father. Hiroto would question almost every decision in regard to the business expenditure, although I found him exceptionally helpful in the building of our Gawler home and in accessing artifacts for our apartment.

Kao's youngest son, Haruki on the other hand was different again. He always wore his hair Samurai style and tried to live his life by the Samurai code of Bushido, meaning the Way of the Warrior, which was encapsulated in:

Integrity	To do the right thing by yourself
Bravery and courage	Honesty
Kindness and compassion	Politeness
Enjoy the honour	Of being Samurai
Loyalty to those you serve	And to the Code.

Haruki even had a considerable collection of Samurai object d'art: arrows, spears and guns, and their main weapon and symbol, the sword. Also, suits of armour from various periods of Japanese history. All of this I learnt from Haruki on my last visit to Kyoto. He is a young man with definite ideas about where his direction in life is going, firm in his beliefs and respecting different points of view from his own. I would like to know him more.

Kao was talking, deliberating on the various ways the breeding program may take: buying a bull from Japan, artificial insemination or embryonic transfer were those he enthused about. He asked what I thought. Well, I knew nothing about breeding cattle although many years ago I had friends who owned a dairy farm and they used AI to fertilize their cows. I relayed this to Kao by saying I wouldn't have a clue which path he should or should not take. He nodded thoughtfully obviously still pondering on the options. "According to Osawa Kinio, founder of Osawa Enterprises one of the top breeding enterprises in Australia, over 95% of Australian Wagyu are crossbred with other breeds such as Angus and Holstein" Kao announced. He also stated that good pasture was a pivotal part of producing good cattle. Kao looked across at me and must have seen the glazed look in my eyes.

He laughed and apologised saying "Oh, my dear lady I am so sorry, but I am so excited about getting this program off the ground, but no more talk of bulls, breeding or pasture. I smiled then Kao suggested we retire for the night. I commented that this was the best idea he'd had since he arrived. He gave me his hand and helped me stand, putting his arm around me as we walked into the bedroom. Here Kao kissed me gently before removing my top and pants then my underwear. I slipped into bed. He quickly undressed and followed me. We lay in each other's arms telling each other how deeply we felt, then we made love. Kao possessed me completely. I melted into him. There is no other experience like this. It is so satisfying.

Kao smiled, describing how I looked at this moment and how this affected him. "You make me so proud that I can make you look so happy. When we are apart, I often think of how you are looking now. It always makes me feel good that I can please you so much". I told him that he felt wonderful and, when we moved in unison, it was the most exciting feeling ever. I expressed my incredibility that we fitted so well together and that I had always marveled at this fact. He agreed saying he thought as I did. I settled against his shoulder, his arm around me then he kissed my hair. I couldn't have been happier. I vaguely heard Kao wish me goodnight then I was lost to sleep.

CHAPTER 30

THE PENDULUM SWINGS

Morning clouds were low and visibility poor. In place of the lovely view of the mountain, misty clouds swirled to ground level like a pale grey cloak, so not much to see. It had started out as a dark, wet day and I didn't believe it would improve much, if at all, over the next 24 hours. I was cold but Tomtom demanded his breakfast. Having satisfied him I made a pot of tea and took it through to the bedroom. Kao was just stirring. I poured Kao a cup and placed it on his bedside table. I loved to watch Kao wake up, rubbing sleep from his eyes with his hair all disheveled. I put my pillow behind him so he could sit and enjoy his tea. He smiled and wished me good morning which I returned. We discussed the happenings today and both agreed it should be a relaxing day. Kao was happy to help with dinner tonight. He said, with a grin, that he would be happy to forego today's session in the gym if I could offer him something more stimulating. We both placed our cups down and I returned to bed.

Sometime later we showered, dressed and had breakfast. By this time Tomtom was ready to play but now there were two people chasing him, which surprised him. When Tomtom went into the bathroom to view the back garden Kao and I thankfully took our rest also, enjoying a coffee. Afterwards Kao said he needed to call Sydney and retired to the office while I looked for another book to read, as I had finished mine. I choose *The Cat Who Loved Chocolate* by Maurice Williams, an author I was unfamiliar with, but the book engaged me from the first page – always a good sign. I read for about an hour before Kao rejoined me and suggested a walk. The day was still overcast but the clouds had moved up the mountain so, at least, the lower slopes were visible.

Tomtom, apparently content with his perch at the bathroom window ignored us as we put on coats and boots and, grabbing the house keys, began our walk. The air was fresh after last night's rain and while it was cool it was invigorating, heightening the senses. I put my arm through Kao's as we walked along. Kao enjoyed the pastoral scenery, pointing out the wagyu cattle which I had assumed were Black Angus. We breathed in the farming smells and I commented on how much I enjoyed these. Kao laughed and said he did too and that he loved all the smells of the countryside. It was a lovely walk. I forget all that we discussed but I am sure we solved all the world's problems! Kao talked a bit about the Company and how Takahiro was moving it in a new direction. Takahiro was also interested in dropping some of his Directorships thus giving him more time and energy to devote to examining possible new markets as well as investments for the Company. Kao stated that he was looking forward to his retirement at the end of the year although, he added, he would then become Consultant. I queried his decision and suggested that perhaps he would be working just as hard, but he shook his head and said I didn't know Takahiro. "He has offered me this role to ensure I don't interfere with his plans for the Company, and I shall not for I like the way he works although I would never tell him that. I just frown now and again – it keeps him on his toes". He laughed and I thought how canny Kao was and I understood a little more of how he had successfully run the Company for so long.

We found our footsteps taking us towards the house just as the rain began to fall, gently as first but the drizzle turned to a downpour by the time we were taking off our coats in the hall. Kao poured a glass of white wine and I put together a platter of cheeses, cold meats and pickles. Kao had also put on the heater, as it had become quite cold, and the television informing me that his favourite movie was showing on Netflix

"Shenandoah" starring James Stewart. It is set in the American the Civil War, with a Virginia farmer and his family remaining neutral, until one of the sons is captured by Union soldiers, sending the farmer to his rescue. It was interesting on many levels and I could see why Kao liked it. It covered the futility of war, the importance of loyalty, family values and love. The acting was very good and the scenery breathtaking. I also loved James Stewart so we both enjoyed a few hours of escapism. I guess some people may have judged the movie to be a bit of sentimental nonsense, but I believe the message this movie projected is just as true in today's world, but sadly is often forgotten. We discussed segments of the movie that had impressed us while we cleared away our luncheon dishes, although Kao poured us the last of the wine before throwing the bottle in the recycle bin.

Tomtom announced his presence by jumping on the couch and walking across our knees before jumping back on the floor. He wanted attention, so I filled Tomtom's food bowl and topped up his water. He ate a bit then looked at me expectantly. I said, "Where's that cat" and he was off like a shot with me close behind him. He liked to hide under an antique chair in the lounge but unbeknownst to him his tail would be visible as it swished back and forth, so it was easy to see where he was although I pretended I couldn't see it. The game went on longer than usual and Kao was most amused to see us run from room to room until, at last, Tomtom had enough and settled in his favourite chair for a snooze. I sank down next to Kao with a sigh. Kao commented now he knew how I kept so fit, and we both laughed. Yes, Tomtom was demanding but still very independent. I was sorry he could not enjoy the outside world, but a local farmer was apparently gun happy with everything that moved so both Sonya and George believed Tomtom would not last long if allowed outside, notwithstanding, Tomtom appeared happy enough and I enjoyed our chases.

I curled up to Kao with his arm around me and we both read for a while, then it was time to think about the meal for tonight. Kao prepared the vegetables and I the lamb. It was a large roast and I estimated it would take at least two and a half hours to cook, so I placed the meat into a hot oven. The vegetables I would add in an hour's time. Kao checked out the wine I had brought from Gawler, choosing a 2014 Peter Lehman shiraz. Together we set the table for three, as Hiroto would be joining us. I was looking forward to seeing Hiroto, getting to know him more as I liked all of Kao's sons and the way they addressed me as 'Madam'. Initially, I was a bit put off as this term I related to brothels, but they obviously saw no connection and meant it as a term of respect, which I appreciated. The smell of cooking was filling the house and I could see that Kao was looking forward to the meal – he loved roast lamb.

Hiroto's car announced his arrival by the crunch of gravel under its wheels. Kao opened the front door and Tomtom joined him to say hello. Kao poured scotch for us and we clinked our glasses together saying 'Slàinte Mhath'. Settled on the couch Kao began to catch up on Hiroto's day and how the markets were reacting to the various currency news around the world. Kao then related our news, such as it was, but Hiroto enjoyed hearing the antics of Tomtom. Both had been in touch with Sydney so discussed what was happening there. I pottered about the kitchen and let them discuss their Company business. I enjoyed seeing Kao and Hiroto together, even if it was discussing Company business as it was at the moment. They obviously had a lot of respect and affection for each other. I thought how different they were.

Takahiro could have been Kao's twin if younger, and Haruki resembled his mother but Hiroto, while seemingly had his mother's temperament, was the tallest in the family and resembled neither parent in looks, but they were an interesting family with very separate skills and abilities. I was both pleased and proud to be part of it. I saw that both men were laughing. I smiled to myself. Obviously, business had given away to more pleasurable topics. I announced dinner and indicated where each would sit. Kao poured the wine and I served dinner with the gravy in a gravy boat so they could help themselves. I had also heated some dinner rolls which I placed on the table. The food and the wine were appreciated and soon vanished. I then served dessert with was also appreciated, especially as I served it with a bottle of Kopke Reserve Tawny Port NV. Colheita is extracted from a single year's harvest then aged for over seven years before bottling. Unlike any other Tawny port, it is one of the softest, smoothest and fruitiest and it was absolutely delicious. We all had second cups of coffee so we could have another Port which we lingered over. Kao had helped clear the table between courses so the next toast was from Hiroto to "the domesticity of my Father" which made Kao growl light heartedly with Hiroto and me laughing. It was a lovely relaxed, fun filled evening.

I offered Hiroto a bed for the night and Kao promised to gag me so I wouldn't keep him awake. Hiroto blushed, declining my invitation saying it would not be necessary. We all laughed. I poured more coffee and more port but Hiroto put his hand over his glass explaining he'd had more than enough and anyway it was time he made his way back to the motel. I was aware that the road was pretty curly but Hiroto was confident he could return without incident. We said our goodbyes and watched as Hiroto reversed then drove out onto the gravel road. With a toot of the horn, he was gone. We were met by Tomtom who needed some attention before returning to his chair, which he received. I was now free to go to bed. I switched off the lights and entered the bedroom. A slight snoring came from the mound under the blankets. Kao would sleep well tonight I thought, but tomorrow we would have a day free of anything alcoholic. I fell into bed beside Kao, cuddling up and slipping into sleep.

The sun awakened me much too early. Kao was still softly snoring and Tomtom was sleep at my feet. I lay there enjoying the ambiance of the bright sunshine, a warm bed and two bodies sound asleep. Tentatively I got out of bed and had a shower. The water was lovely and hot and invigorating. I dried myself smeared on body lotion and brushed my hair. I quickly dressed. Tomtom was awake but wasn't moving. He was much too comfortable. Kao had moved but was not awake. *What a pair* I thought as I left the room to make breakfast. I put together a light Japanese breakfast as I thought this might suit Kao after the rich dinner last night. I wondered how Hiroto's journey had gone and thought if he's had problems he would have rung, but all the same, I would ring him after breakfast to see how he was.

By the time breakfast was organised Kao was awake (well almost). There had been a frost last night, hence no one wanted to get up. Kao turned to cuddle me and found Tomtom staring at him. He said I hadn't looked this bad in a morning before, and I said it must have been the Port! Tomtom went into the kitchen for breakfast while I helped Kao sit and made him comfortable. I told Kao he had surprised me last light during our lovemaking. "You were so wild" I said, "and left me wanting more this morning". I smiled, lecherously I hoped. Kao looked astonished. Of course he had no recollection of anything after he got into bed – and there had been no lovemaking. I laughed hard and it was some time before Kao realised I was just joking. "Well Madam just give me a few minutes and you shall see me very wild" and he made a grab for me almost upsetting his breakfast tray. We laughed together, but he raised an eyebrow quizzically and I shook my head. He sighed and went back to his breakfast.

Between mouthfuls we planned our day. First, Kao said was a trip to the gym. Then he suggested a drive then find somewhere to have lunch. I admired Kao's fortitude as I couldn't have gone to the gym after the previous evening, but having lunch out meant I didn't have to think about dinner tonight. Nevertheless, as Kao made his way to the gym, I became caught up in domestic duties, tidying up after breakfast and putting everything away. When Kao returned he showered then Tomtom came up to see why I wasn't giving him his due attention, so we played *Chase* for a while until he grew tired. He then retired to check out the back garden from the bathroom. I had just switched on the electric jug when Kao came out of the office saying all was well for another day. We enjoyed our coffee and discussed options for lunch. We eventually decided to drive to Latrobe and find somewhere there.

It was a pleasant drive. The various colours of the paddocks according to the crop growing, the tall trees, the intermittent views of the river, the farmhouses and buildings, and the grazing cattle and sheep like us, enjoying the ambience of the day – the warm sun, the pleasant breeze and the glorious blue sky. We choose the local Latrobe pub for lunch and we weren't disappointed. We returned home around 4. 00 pm and agreed that it had been an enjoyable day. I had found a game of Monopoly earlier in the week so I challenged Kao to a game or two. Kao had no knowledge of this game but there was much contention caused by Kao's misinterpretation of the rules that I just gave up – he was such a terrible cheat! We sipped wine and nibbled on cheese, cabana and wedges of tomato with savory biscuits while we played – and laughed. I accepted that Kao won all the games due to default. When we curled up together in bed that night Kao kissed me and said some lovely, sweet words before pausing and enlightening me thus, "Caroline you always smell so lovely. Sometimes like frangipani, or oranges, or apples, or pears. You know it is just like sleeping in a fruit market!" I gave him a thump on the arm as we both laughed then I tickled him until he begged me to stop. We kissed goodnight and I went to sleep with a smile on my lips.

Life continued pleasantly until it was time for me to return to Ulverstone and for Kao and Hiroto to move on to Gawler. We would only be separated for a few days we reminded each other as we kissed goodbye. I had enjoyed Kao's company but now I had to get the house ready for the return of my friends tomorrow, and I had to get my head into Ulverstone mode. I soon had the house in order: washing sheets, remaking the bed, vacuuming and dusting. Once the house was organised I took time to relax with a glass of wine and my book. Tomtom sat on my knee and snoozed until I heard the crunch of car tyres on the gravel driveway. George and Sonya were home. I greeted them at the door and we hugged and kissed. They were full of their holiday and it was great hearing of their exploits. Tomtom relished their attention and was obviously pleased with their return. Earlier I had packed the car, so I just pointed out the food I had left them for a meal and said my goodbyes and drove away towards Ulverstone. I drove slowly and enjoyed the smell and sight of the countryside. It was a lovely sunny day and I was relaxcd and content.

I arrived home and Phil was pleased to see me, of course. We discussed the trip George and Sonya had taken and some of their funnier moments over a glass of wine. Phil had plans for dinner but had not started preparations so I suggested we eat out. Phil agreed and we had a lovely meal at our favourite Chinese restaurant: *Wonton Soup* (pork loin, shrimp, rice wine, light soy sauce, green onion, fresh ginger & sugar, mixed and stuffed into wonton wrappers cooked in chicken stock), followed by *Hongshaorou* (red fried pork or pork belly seasoned with star anise, sichuan peppercorn, fresh ginger, soy sauce & sugar). We decided against dessert but washed the meal down with Oyster Bay sauvignon blanc. It was a most enjoyable meal.

Later that evening Phil complained of not feeling well and suggested an early night. He assured me that his condition had nothing to do with the lovely meal, but he was feeling short of breath. I wanted to call his GP or an ambulance, but Phil waved this aside saying no, he was not that sick and would be OK after a rest. He took an extra pain killer and retired. I cleaned up the kitchen then joined him in bed. We watched television for a while but Phil fell asleep around 8 o'clock. The program I was watching finished so I switched off the TV. Later I was vaguely aware of Phil going to the bathroom and when I asked how he was he said 'better'. He was soon asleep and breathing regularly. Reassured I went back to sleep.

CHAPTER 31

TRADEGY - THE FINAL GOODBYE

I awoke early and carefully got out of bed so I wouldn't wake Phil. I boiled the electric jug and made green tea for us both. Phil usually liked cereal so I prepared a bowl for each of us with banana slices on top. The sun was coming in through the bedroom window so I opened the venetian blinds calling "Wakey, wakey" as I placed the tray on his bedside table. Phil didn't stir so assumed he was still asleep. I left his food and climbed into bed and began eating my cereal. As I turned on the television to catch the early morning ABC news I placed my hand on Phil's shoulder and was surprised to feel how cold it was. I shook him, but there was no response. I shook him again and called his name, but again no response. I put aside my half eaten cereal and watched him, but there was no rise and fall of the bedclothes. I realised that Phil was not breathing. I thought my heart had stopped. I froze. I couldn't believe what this meant. I got out of bed and went around to Phil and looked at him. He was cold. He was pale. I had to understand what this meant, but my brain refused to comprehend. I sat on the carpet next to him and stroked his face. There was no movement. I expected him to open his eyes and say something like "There, I fooled you" but this didn't happen. I didn't know what to do. I didn't want to believe what I was confronted with. I don't know how long I sat there, but eventually it sank in that Phil was not going to wake up.

I walked into the kitchen and picked up my mobile phone. I rang 000 and said I didn't know who to talk to but I thought my husband was dead. I had articulated my fears and the operator asked me questions which I tried to answer. I don't know what I said. The ambulance arrived and confirmed my worst fears. The attendants placed Phil on their stretcher which they conveyed to their vehicle. I gave the paramedics Phil's history of heart problems and advised them of his GP. Two police officers were waiting at the door as the ambulance drove away. They also asked questions which I answered somehow. They asked if I had anyone who could stay with me, but I just shook my head. I still couldn't believe Phil was gone. I asked when he would be coming home, but the police officers just looked at each other and said the hospital would be in touch. When they left I didn't know what to do. How would I cope without Phil? I suddenly was very cold. I thought I must be having a bad dream and if I went back to sleep when I awoke all would be well, and Phil and I could have a good laugh about this in the morning. I walked to the bedroom door, but I knew I couldn't go back to our bed. I walked to the front bedroom and climbed into the spare bed and eventually went to sleep. I awoke and reached for Phil, but the bed was empty and cold. For a moment I wondered where I was and thought Phil must be getting breakfast for us until I remembered what had happened – but I found it hard to believe. The clock told me it was 10 past 10 and the whole day stretched before me. I was lost. What do I do now? I got out bed and had a hot shower. I dried my hair and dressed. But everything was still the same, wasn't it?

I rang my friend Esther and asked if she could come over sometime today as I had something important to tell her. She asked if it was urgent and I said it was. She said she would see me soon. While I waited I stripped our bed and washed the sheets etc. The washing machine had just finished its cycle when Esther, as good as her word, arrived. She took one look at me and asked what had happened. I broke down and started crying but managed to explain what had happened and how I felt and that I didn't know what to do next. Esther took my hand. She related when her husband died and how she had felt, which was similar to how I was feeling. She talked for a while and I was aware only of some of what she was saying, but it helped to have someone who understood. Esther made us both a cup of coffee and said she had rung and made an appointment for me to see my Doctor tomorrow, and that she would pick me up and take me. I thanked her, but I was still in a daze. She offered to have me stay with her for a few days if I wanted this, but I didn't know what I wanted. I shook my head and thanked her for her kindness. I said I was feeling better and explained that I had to get used to doing my own thing and coping on my own. She reminded me that I had friends who would help me through the next few weeks and months, if I would let them. I nodded, but life looked bleak without Phil. I suddenly felt tired again. I could hardly keep my eyes open which Esther noticed. She suggested that I lie down and said I should be expected to feel tired as this had been a big shock. She walked me to the front bedroom and helped me into bed.

Closing the venetians Esther said she would take the back door key with her and would see me in the morning, but to ring her if I wanted anything or for her to come over. "I could come for a few days if you would like Caroline" Esther offered. I thanked her but declined her kind offer. I said I would be OK once I had some sleep. Esther said goodbye and left. I must have fallen asleep immediately.

Esther was wonderful. I couldn't have managed those first few days without her. I rang Connie to let her know my 'news'. She also was very supportive in the ensuing weeks, so I survived. I had to tell Kao, but I delayed doing this as I knew he would want to come over and help me through all this, but I didn't want to see him, I felt that my grief was mine alone to deal with. My GP gave me a mild sedative to help me sleep and I had two dear friends to help me. I just felt it inappropriate for Kao to be here. I didn't even know whether I still loved him or not. I felt numb and empty of all emotion -

except great sadness. Every day was a black day to get through somehow, and I was exhausted when I climbed into bed at night. Sleep was difficult though the sedatives helped.

I did eventually send an e-mail to Kao. I tried to be kind, but I had to tell him that I didn't want to see him. I had to get through the grieving process on my own, at my own pace. I told him that I couldn't estimate how long this would take – maybe weeks, months or even years. I promised to contact him when I was able to think straight and to feel emotions again. Kao's reply was instant. I was pleased that it wasn't full of lovey dovey stuff, but restrained and imparting words of comfort. He offered a friendly ear when I was ready and wanted me to know that all our family in Kyoto would be thinking and praying for me. Kao added that he would be in Tassie from time to time organizing the breeding program and he would let me know the dates he would be over however, I was not to presume that he expected anything from me. He would be letting me know so that I could see him if I wanted to talk to a friend and I only had to ring him. I replied thanking Kao for his understanding and in giving me the space I desperately needed at this time.

The weeks passed, encompassing the funeral which was lovely. I hadn't realized how many people knew Phil and respected him, so I was overwhelmed with the support I received. I slowly started to pick up the threads of my life and began painting again. After several months I was beginning to feel that I was getting some control over my day-to-day life. There was a time when I had felt guilty about Phil's death and it crossed my mind that maybe his death was a sort of punishment for me due to my involvement with Kao. I had always thought of God as a merciful God, a benevolent God so why would he punish me thus?

Kao had visited Tasmania many times since my last e-mail and had kept his word by not contacting me. Eventually,] an e-mail arrived containing a really tender poem,

The sun no longer shines.
I am in a dark place, surrounded by sadness.
I no longer hear your voice or feel you close.
You are lost to me.

My heart aches for your heart.
My eyes shed tears with your eyes.
You are my love, my life, my hope.
I grieve with you.

You have filled my heart with happiness,
Given me a reason for living,
So when your grieving is over, return to me.
I am patient. I can wait.

If I were to die before you return,
I shall wait in the afterlife for you to join me
And we shall be together
For Eternity.

I felt no emotion, but it was a beautiful poem and I thanked Kao in an e-mail. I also thanked Chieko for her e-mail offering me the family's condolences, and a place to grieve. It had been eight months since Phil left me and I felt guilty that I was treating the Sahashi family so. I thought that maybe the time was drawing near when I should see Kao again, test the water – see how I felt about him. His latest email advised that he would be in Tassie in 3 weeks and perhaps I would have time for a coffee. I contemplated contacting him, agreeing to a short meeting when we could talk.

I ruminated on this for several days before composing a polite e-mail asking Kao to give me some dates when he would be able to see me for about an hour. Kao's reply was swift. He gave me several dates and times, with alternatives. I checked my diary and chose a suitable date and time when I was free. I sent the e-mail with my heart racing. Kao replied,

"Caroline, thank you for agreeing to meet me for coffee. It is fortunate that I have found a day suitable to both our schedules. I shall look forward to the honour of your company".

A very formal reply, I thought, but what else could I expect after so long. He had probably found someone in Japan and is very happy. I then questioned whether I should see him at all? The next few weeks were filled with the usual: church, Senior's, coffee with Esther or Connie, gardening and painting. I even managed to sort out some of Phil's clothes which I dropped off at the Op Shop. I knew I had to do more but I accomplished all that I was able to do at that moment.

I called in on Connie at the library. She was showing a man how to use the computer, but when she was free she gave me a big hug and said how happy she was to see me out and about and didn't I look nice. Connie is a lovely woman and I had appreciated her support. I suggested she came to dinner one night, suggesting a Friday when she could stay the night if she didn't want to drive back to Forth in the dark. She was delighted to accept so we made a date for the following Friday. Connie promised to bring a good bottle of red wine. We laughed and I left. I was looking forward to Connie's visit as I had found her to be good company over the last few months. I caught up with Esther and invited her to lunch in a couple of weeks. She accepted without thinking and, when I said I would be cooking a roast but it probably wouldn't be as good as Phil's, she chastised me gently saying she thought it would equal his roasts.

I felt there was a glimmer of light entering into my dark

world and I was looking forward to cooking for other people again. Oh, I had cooked for myself and both women had invited me to their homes for meals and I had eaten out - countless times – but I was going to enjoy cooking a decent meal for each of my friends. I knew Connie was a vegetarian so planned to cook asparagus with cream cheese, cauliflower and mashed pumpkin with individual trifle for dessert. For Esther I would treat her to roast beef with Yorkshire pudding plus all the vegetables and dessert would be individual trifle. With both friends I talked for several hours and was able to discuss Phil without tears so I was on my way I thought to becoming sane again. It was nice to have Connie staying over – good to have some else in the house – and she accompanied me to church on Sunday before returning home to Forth. I felt confident and able to make some serious decisions about where I might be going. I just didn't know which direction this would be but I was on the right track. I just had to wait and see what the future held for me.

Today I was meeting Kao. I was nervous. I had agreed to meet him at Gawler and I wasn't sure how I would cope seeing him again - at the cottage, but I took care with my makeup and my choice of clothing. I chose a cream blouse, brown pants and boots, and I had recently bought myself a leather, waist length brindle (mustard and pale brown) jacket which I slipped on. I drove to Gawler with trepidation rising. I tried to calm myself by admiring the scenery but my heart refused to slow down.

I arrived at the prescribed time of 2 o'clock and found Kao waiting on the veranda. He smiled a welcome as I alighted from the car and ushered me inside where he led me to the kitchen. He pulled out a chair for me at the table and when I sat Kao sat opposite me. I saw he had made filtered coffee which stood on the table. Silently, he poured coffee for us both. I thanked him and he proffered a sticky rice cake which I took. I was a bit embarrassed as I did not know what to say and wondered whether Kao was waiting for me to break the silence. Kao smiled again and cleared his throat, saying that I looked well. I also smiled and thanked him saying I was feeling better and, although I still had a long way to go, I felt I was moving forward. To his inquiry, I related how I was gradually picking up my old life but I still feeling numb and empty however, I said day by day life was getting easier. He said this was good and reached over placing a package in my hand, explaining it was a copy of his new book of poems. I was delighted and thanked him. We were being very polite, and I began to think the visit was a mistake, that I shouldn't have come. While we spoke I saw a gleam of hope in Kao's eyes, but I was unable to offer him any. I sipped my coffee and felt I was in an alien environment.

 We were strangers. There was nothing for me here. Kao had always been receptive to my feelings and now he reached over and touched my hand, saying he knew how difficult this must be for me. I stood saying that I shouldn't have come. The words sounder harsher than I meant them to be and I saw hope slide from his eyes replaced by disappointment. I tried to soften my words by explaining I still had a long way to go and perhaps my visit had been premature. Kao smiled but his eyes had lost their crinkle. I was saddened that I had nothing to offer Kao and made to leave the table.

 Kao also stood, his eyes meeting mine, "Well Caroline, you have graced this home with your presence, and you will always be welcome in it whenever you wish to return. It was good to see you again" he said quietly as he walked behind me to the front door. Kao opened the door for me as I turned to say goodbye. Our eyes locked. I saw the despair in them and breathed, "Oh Kao, I am so sorry that I can't give you any definite hope. I just don't know how long this is going to take. I am devoid of all feeling. I just don't know whether I will ever love you again. You deserve better. I even thought that perhaps you had found someone you could love in Japan and I would have been very happy for you, but I feel this didn't happen".

Kao cast his eyes over me, taking in every part of me as if for the last time, then he spoke, "My dear Caroline, long ago I discovered I was a one-woman man. I was fortunate to marry that woman and I have never stopped loving her. Her presence fills this home, memories of her are everywhere, everything she touched is here. She brought much happiness into my life. I await her return as this home awaits her. I am a patient man". He smiled tightly as he said this, "I shall remain in anticipation no matter how long it takes". He gently placed his hands on my shoulders and pulled me close to him in a gentle and tender embrace. I lay my head on his shoulder as he wrapped his arms around me. I closed my eyes. My heart quickened its pace. It was a long time since I had felt the warmth of a man's body and Kao's body felt warm and his arms strong. He kissed the top of my head. I slowly pulled away from him. I thanked Kao and was gratified to see a glimmer of hope return to his eyes. I repeated that I could promise him nothing and he nodded. We said goodbye and Kao made me promise to be in touch when I was ready to see him again.

As I went to the front door I dived into my purse then turned to him. "Kao would you please do something for me?" he nodded so I pressed a $50 note into his hand. "When you visit our shrine again would you please make this offering to the Kami and ask them if they will please smile on us as they once did?" Kao's eyes were bright. He swallowed and nodded saying he would duplicate this and add his own prayer to mine. I held his hand and he squeezed it. "Kao you are a kind and generous soul and I am pleased to see you today". He smiled wanly. The picture of Kao framed in the doorway stayed in my mind. Kao had looked so forlorn, and I wondered what the future had in store for us. I was surprised with the fluttering of my heart when he had held me and thought maybe this was the beginning of the thawing of my emotions.

I stopped the car and opened the package Kao had given me. I flicked through the poems and was keen to get home so I could read them at my leisure. I stopped at the last page which held the last poem – a lovely poignant poem – its title,

Eternally Yours:

The first time I saw you – my heart stopped.
I did not understand, I lacked knowledge,
But I knew you would be
Significant to me.

Before you, I was a child. You taught me to live,
To laugh – to love. I learnt to feel with my heart,
And with my soul.
I learnt to cry with joy.

You filled my days and my nights
You were everything to me.
Our hearts and our souls
Spoke together.

We were one with the Universe,
From different cultures, different lands
Yet our ancestors smiled on us,
And blessed our union.

I long for the sight of you,
The smell of you,
The feel of you.
You are my life.   Eternally Yours.

As I closed the book I saw its title was *Eternally Yours* - a lovely message from a lovely man. I sighed and sat quietly for a while with the book pressed against my heart, holding back the tears. I realised that this was the first time in many months that I had shed tears for someone other than Phil.

Only time would heal my heartache, and I knew that Phil wouldn't want me to grieve forever. Time would tell what the outcome was to be for Kao and me. Would I be able to love him again? That, I couldn't predict.

Whether it be the Christian God or the Shinto Gods or Kao's ancestors, our destinies lay in their hands:

> *Yearning will not change destiny.*
> *Only patience and a pure heart*
>   *Can change dreams into realities.*

www.ingramcontent.com/pod-product-compliance
Lightning Source LLC
Chambersburg PA
CBHW070541120726
47909CB00007B/2199